Lucena in the House of Madgrin.

Also by Goldeen Ogawa

PROFESSOR ODD
The Complete Season One (Episodes 1–6)
Episode 7: The Dogs of Canary Island
Episode 8: Chronostrophe
Episode 9: Star Walkers
Episode 10: The Thousand Songs
Episode 11: Davebot
Episode 12: Cerberus Retired

DRIVING ARCANA
By Moon & Star (Wheel 1)
Paving the Road to Hell (Wheel 2)

THE ADVENTURES OF BOURAGNER FELPZ
Volume I: A Study of Magic
Volume II: Anatomy of a Magician
Volume III: The Aubergine Spellbook

LUCENA
in the
HOUSE of MADGRIN

by
GOLDEEN OGAWA
illustrated by the author

a Heliopause Production
heliopauseweb.com

Dedication

For Marian
Like the librarian

Lucena in the House of Madgrin

Copyright © 2020 by Goldeen Ogawa
Illustrations copyright © 2020 by Goldeen Ogawa
Cover illustration and design copyright © 2020 by Goldeen Ogawa

All rights reserved. No part of this book may be reproduced or distributed without permission from the author, except in the form of personal sharing and brief quotations within critical reviews or essays. For information contact Heliopause Productions at *www.heliopauseweb.com.*

All characters in this book are fictitious. Any resemblance to real persons, living or dead, is entirely coincidental.

FICTION/Fantasy, Historical
FICTION/Fantasy, General

First Edition 2020

ISBN: 978-1-945781-14-8

Contents

1	At the Munsmire School for Girls	1
2	The Maker	12
3	In the House of Madgrin	22
4	The Groundsguard	36
5	Beruse and Willic Decide to Throw a Party	57
6	Orrus and Abneialaemh	73
7	Keelback	86
8	Going Hunting	98
9	A Parliament of Vampires	113
10	Midsummer Night	132
11	Somna Ebulis	153
12	Mirror, Candle and Book	164
13	Undergate	184
14	Amstrass	198
15	The Two Vampires	214
16	Beyond the Teeth of Dream	237
17	Through the Sea of Stories	244
18	Grimbald	260
19	Madgrin	270
20	Dawn	283
21	Badgrave	297

Foreword

I, who was once Lucena Clarian Ashmoor, now Badgrave, the Mistress of Monsters, will attempt with this narrative to tell the story of my short life, its untimely end, my second death, and all the things that happened in between.

I got that far in this manuscript and then could not continue for a very long time. It was not that I had nothing to tell, but that the telling of it felt awkward. Dictatorial. All straight lines and orderly progression from one point to the next. Not at all like the graceful stories I enjoy and which have so benefited me in the past.

"Have you tried telling it from the third-person perspective?" my librarian suggested when I confided in her my problems. "It is Lucena's story, after all, and she was in many ways a different person from who you are now. Perhaps it will help you to see yourself as a character rather than just a narrator, and that will allow the story to flow."

I have a wise and insightful librarian. But even with this change I found the physical writing to be nearly impossible. I became mired in memory and would spend hours poised over my desk, quill in hand, while the ink it dripped blotted out what precious words I had managed to write.

Again my librarian came to my aid. She had been a writer herself, before she came to my house, and though she professes to be done telling her stories, she generously condescended to take dictation of mine. This is my story, but it exists by the grace of her hand, and I cannot express gratitude enough for it. And, since the reader will not meet her in the course of this narrative (she and I met long after its conclusion), I wanted to take a page (or two) here at the beginning, to acknowledge her contribution, and to thank her for it.

This narrative would not have come to be without the generous contribution of time, energy and skill by Corianne Birch, late of Staunton Leaning, Kyreland. Thank you. May your stories become mountains and travel beyond the bounds of this universe.

—*Badgrave*
House of Badgrave
Outer Dreaming

CHAPTER 1:

At the Munsmire School for Girls

THE YEAR OF 1943, by the Kyrish calendar, was a tumultuous one for that country. It saw the death of Queen Genoa II, the reign and death of Prince Lames, and finally the ascension of Mordigan VI as sole monarch of Greater Kyreland. At this time well-to-do families were expected to subject their daughters to five years of mandatory schooling in language, poetry, grammar, dance, song and art. This was an opportunity for young girls to develop the sharp and educated minds that Mordiganian Kyreland was so famed for, so most girls considered it a great honor and looked forward to their tenure at school.

Lucena Clarian Ashmoor loathed it. She was an orphan whose adoptive family sent her away to school out of spite rather than pride. They picked the rankest, cheapest, most poisonous school in the country, and required her to stay there permanently until graduation, at which point she was to marry an equally repugnant youth whose favorite hobby was killing rabbits.

The institution was the Munsmire School for Girls, and it lived up to its name. It was mundane, brown, and drab, and constantly stank, being built on the edge of a great mire. The desks were of unfinished wood that gave one splinters, and the rooms smelled of dead spiders and rat droppings. Except the lavatory, which smelled of something worse. This alone was enough to warrant a strong aversion to the place, but Lucena had further reasons. The teachers were emotionless and strict, but easily blinded by supplicant behavior: you could get away with murder if only you knew how to properly smile and flatter. And—this was what fully sealed Lucena's misery—some students very nearly did.

On her first day, at the age of eleven, she had been dragged blindfolded by a gang out onto the mire and left to find her way back alone. It was a terrifying journey, for the mire hid deadly sink traps under seemingly solid ground, and there were things that lived in the mire: old things, magic things, things that did not appreciate being disturbed. Lucena returned unhurt, but very late, and she was punished. But she recognized her luck when, the very next year, a new student was dragged onto the mire and did not return.

There was an investigation about that. Serious men came to the school to search the mire. They found the body, torturously near the edge, but no one was blamed. No one, because the teachers couldn't fathom why any student would do such a thing, and no student was stupid (or brave) enough to expose the offenders. But it did scare them, and for a few months things were more tolerable.

More tolerable for some, but not for Lucena. For she was a slow-speaking, round-faced, chubby girl. Short for her age, with acne and dirty-water blond hair, she was a prime target for bullies of any sort, and all sorts were bred at Munsmire. She developed a permanent scowl, and seldom spoke to anyone, thus alienating even the least antagonistic of the students. The teachers thought her stupid and said so when they thought she couldn't hear. The other girls thought her an idiot, and said so to her face. She was always the last person to rise in the morning; if she didn't wait until everyone was gone someone would knock her down again. She rarely had enough to eat; there was always someone waiting to steal her bowl before she was done, and after a time she started giving it away before they could snatch it. Yet somehow she managed to retain her overly plump figure, and this was a source of great derision from the girls. Not that these were beauties, even by comparison. They were a stringy, grey lot, as unhappy as Lucena in their way, but who gave themselves airs for how mean they could be and how much they could get away with and so quite overturned any sympathy she could have held for them.

In that miserable place Lucena grew to believe she was an idiot, that she was ugly and worthless. Her only thoughts were of survival and of her fifteenth birthday, which would herald her final year at Munsmire. She tried hard not to be cruel or to bully the girls who were smaller or younger than her, but all this did was send her to the bottom of the pecking order. And there she stayed, believing herself fat, ugly and stupid so strongly that perhaps she did become fat, ugly and stupid; her appearance gradually deteriorated, her hair went from dirty blond to dirty grey, and she kept it pulled back in a tight bun to hide it. In this style the girls said she looked like an old hag, and told her so many times. She stopped paying much attention in class, and barely earned the grades to continue (her only motivation being fear of the wrath of her foster parents were she to be expelled), and finally with the onset of puberty she became a lumbering mass of sullen, sulking gloom.

Despite all this she retained a streak of gallant bravery. One autumn day, just weeks before she turned fifteen, one of the first-years had been tied to the spire above the astronomy lab. The little girl hung there, helplessly buffeted by the wind, and scared stiff by the terrible fall below her. Lucena had seen the perpetrators, one of them a witch, fly the girl up there and lash her loosely to the spire, while the others cruelly laughed. As soon as they were gone Lucena ran up to the attic and climbed out through the trapdoor. She scaled the narrow, slanting roof, and freed the little girl, using the rope that had bound her as a lifeline to guide them back to safety. She received no heroic praise for this, and soon the little girl had been turned into another snide and sneering grey-brown fiend. The gloom pressed down harder than ever.

But somewhere, deep in that gloom, a small fire still flickered. It was slender and delicate, but it burned fiercer and brighter the more the gloom clamped down. Lucena nurtured that fire, deep in the cold winter nights in the dormitory, feeding it stories and tales, and it repaid her in full with hope for a better future. But that future turned out to be something very different from what she had imagined.

It came in spring, on the seventeenth of April.

Lucena had had bad dreams the night before, and the worst part was she couldn't fully remember them. There had been a man. An impossibly tall man with hair like night and glowing eyes, and she had run from him. He was chasing

CHAPTER 1: *At the Munsmire School for Girls*

her, she somehow knew, and chasing her towards something even more terrible, so she had stopped. Then he stopped too. He said, "Splintered wood will kill the dead," and then something truly horrible had happened, which she couldn't remember.

The day was bright, the blue sky streaked with thin white clouds, and the mire was abloom with pungent smelling flowers. On her way from the dormitories to the mess hall Lucena stopped to look out across the mire. If she held her nose and breath, it looked almost beautiful.

Yet there was something wrong. The air was too quiet, and it felt like something filthy had settled behind the pretty scene.

They had a new teacher that day. Her name was Miss Smael and she came bumbling into the classroom wrapped head to toe in a cloak with a hat perched on top. The first thing she did was close all the blinds and light the lamps, saying they needed no distraction from the outside world. Only then did she unwrap herself, and Lucena was struck by the sight of perhaps the most beautiful woman she had ever seen. She was slender and tall, with pale skin, luxuriant auburn hair, and a glittering pair of bright hazel eyes. Lucena was entranced, along with the rest of the class, and they listened in rapture to her lesson, although later Lucena could not remember a word of it.

As class was being dismissed, Miss Smael asked that three of the girls stay behind to help her prepare her next lesson. She then went through and picked three of the prettiest girls, shutting the door behind the rest of the class with a snap. Lucena saw nothing of those three girls for the rest of the day. They only showed up just in time for roll call that evening, and then Lucena thought they looked even more nasty. But it was hard to say, they were always so cruel anyway.

They refused to answer any questions, only snickering among themselves. Lucena, who was used to the way girls would clot together in cliques, decided to keep her distance. She lay awake in bed that night, listening to the three girls bully and tease a fourth year, going at the poor girl like cats torturing a living mouse.

Then came cries, not just of anguish and humiliation, but of real pain. This roused Lucena; she rolled out of bed and lumbered down the dormitory to see what could be done.

To her shock and horror she found all three of the girls with their teeth buried up to the gums in their unfortunate victim, who was still struggling weakly. Lucena, who could be strong when she wanted, grabbed two by the collar and yanked them off, giving the third a good kick in the side. The unfortunate victim fell to the floor, blood oozing from her arms and fairly gushing out of her neck. There was nothing Lucena could do. She watched as the girl's color drained away, and in less than a minute she was dead.

By that time Lucena was no longer paying attention to her. One of the girls whose collar she was holding twisted around like a crazed animal and tried to bite her as well. Lucena threw them both against the wall, from which they sprang up with inhuman speed. Only then did she see their elongated fangs, their dead, shimmering eyes, and the strange paperlike smoothness of their skin.

"Good Lady Chandara," Lucena gasped, backing away. "Vampires!" And then louder so the whole dormitory could hear: "*Vampires!*"

It was not necessary for her to shout; those who had not been kept awake by the dead girl's torture had already been roused by the commotion Lucena had made. Most of the girls only lay in bed, paralyzed with fear, and the ones who sprang up were immediately attacked by the vampires. Lucena grabbed the hand of the one nearest to her and pulled her bodily towards the door. The other girl tripped, and in that moment one of the vampires noticed their escape and lunged at them. It got hold of the other girl, and Lucena felt her grip fail as she scrambled through the door. Looking back she saw the vampire lunging at her, teeth bared, before she had the presence of mind to slam the door in its face. She heard a satisfying crunch from the other side, but there was no bolt to secure the door, so she turned tail and fled.

All along the corridor, doors were bursting open and frightened faces were poking out into the hall.

"Go back inside!" Lucena shouted as she ran past. "Lock your doors! Vampires!"

A few of the girls heeded her warning, but many of the older ones scoffed and came out into the hall. Lucena shoved her way through them and hurtled down the stairs to the common room. She heard a crash as her dormitory door came open, and the sniggering from the other girls turned first to shouts of dismay, then fear, and finally panic.

Lucena ran on. She thought perhaps if she got outside she could run to the nearest town, not half a mile away. But she was stopped in her tracks at the front door, which had had all the furniture from the nearby classrooms piled in a heap in front of it. Beginning to feel panicked herself, Lucena turned around and ran first for the back door, and then the kitchen and postern, only to find them similarly blocked. She was just considering climbing out a ground-floor window (even though it would be a tight squeeze), when the door to the teacher's study was ripped off its hinges by a body being flung against the far wall. Lucena recoiled in horror at the sight of the deputy headmistress, her neck arched in a very bad way, lying in a pale bloody heap against the wall.

But that's wrong, Lucena thought dumbly as she watched the body crumple to the ground. All the vampires are upstairs . . .

Then her senses returned, and she realized what an idiot she had been. The vampires upstairs were nothing—mere fledglings—the original vampire had been Miss Smael. And Miss Smael was . . .

Miss Smael was just coming out of the teacher's lounge, her hair a little out of place and a long red smear down her neck.

Lucena nearly tripped over her own pudgy feet as she turned tail and sprinted away. Miss Smael's laughter echoed down the hallway after her, and it was a long time before the pounding in Lucena's ears subsided enough for her to think. She collapsed in a corner, panting and shaking with a stitch in her side, as she listened to the distant screaming from upstairs.

It was then the strange dream came back to her. *Splintered wood will kill the dead*, the man had told her.

CHAPTER 1: *At the Munsmire School for Girls*

Slowly Lucena got up and walked unsteadily down the hall to the linen cupboard, where the cleaning supplies were kept. She opened the door, intending to find herself a broom or some other wooden weapon, but instead found herself looking down on three first-year girls crouched over the deceased heap of what had once been their music teacher. Three pairs of blank white eyes looked up at her, and Lucena didn't even have time to slam the door before they leapt on her.

Lucena, her blood raging in her ears, caught one by the shirt front and hurled it to the ground, kicked another in the groin, and grabbed the third by the hair and swung it around in a full circle before letting it fly off down the hall. Then she dove into the linen closet, stepping over the body, and grabbed the nearest broom. She had no idea what to do with it; supposedly you drove a wooden stake through a vampire's heart, but the tip of the broom handle was far from sharp, and she wasn't sure if she could even find the heart at all. Still, it felt good to have a weapon in her hands as she ran out from the closet, leaving the three first-years to gather themselves.

Lucena's next thought was the kitchen; there would be knives there and perhaps she could whittle the tip of the broom away into a spike. But first she had to get there, and now it seemed the school was overrun with vampires. Lucena beat her way through them, pulling hair, shouting, and whacking with all her might.

Bodies lined the hallways, teachers and students alike, and blood pooled on the floor. Lucena tried her best to look straight ahead, and as a result nearly slipped in a particularly large puddle.

But she made it to the kitchen with only a few scratches, and by some miracle the vampires had not occupied it, although there was a gruesome pile of bodies in the corner. Trying to ignore them Lucena bolted the door behind her, and stood panting for a few minutes while she waited for her heart to stop pounding. The outside door here had been similarly blockaded, and even the windows barred, and for several moments she was nearly blinded by panic and despair.

When again she could think clearly, she made her way to the chopping block and found a good-sized knife used for cutting vegetables. She set the broom across her knee, and with shaking hands began to whittle away at the end.

It took a while, and before she had anything like a reasonably sharp point the door was being rattled and banged so it seemed like it would come off its hinges at any moment. Lucena said a prayer to her god under her breath as she worked, and the door held. It held long enough for Lucena to finish turning her broom into a lethal weapon and thoughtfully hide all the knives. Then it burst from its hinges, and the vampires swarmed inside.

They were a disorganized bunch, and did not all go for Lucena at once. This proved to be her salvation, for she was stricken with fear for a moment at the sight, and only raised her weapon just in time. Then it was furious action. Lucena stabbed at the mob wildly, and although she killed none, she found they recoiled from getting stabbed with a sharp stick as much as anyone.

Then one of them made a grab at her elbow, and Lucena was jerked around to find herself face to face with one of her late tormentors. The girl stared at her out of blind white eyes, her mouth hanging to open show two lines of broken-looking sharp teeth. There was blood around her mouth too.

5

Without pausing to think Lucena promptly drove the stake end of her broom into the creature's eye with all the force she could muster, yanked it out again, and turned to fend off another wave of vampires. One of these lunged at her, and Lucena held out the broom like a lance and skewered it neatly on the end. It hung there, howling, until she had the presence of mind to tug the broom out and stab it again, this time in its chest. The vampire let out one last pitiful gasp, and moved no more. Lucena didn't wait to see if it turned to dust like the stories said, she was too busy fighting for her life.

The vampires changed tactics then; instead of coming at her in a mob, they began to herd her slowly out of the kitchen. Lucena fought them all the way, and even killed two more, before she was out in the hall. They were stupid, slow creatures, she realized, and moved in forced jerks as if they themselves were not in control of their bodies. Once she noticed this she found she could anticipate their moves, and like that was able to hold her ground in the hall, beating them off, as they came at her.

Lucena's mind was a whirl; she thought only of second-to-second survival, and never had the time to consider escape nor, thankfully, the prospect of dying. All she thought about was fighting, of dodging and stabbing and ducking.

So she was surprised and alarmed when suddenly all the vampires drew back, retreating down the hall. Then from the direction of the teacher's lounge there was movement as the vampires flattened themselves against the wall to let Miss Smael through.

Miss Smael had cleaned herself up, tidying away her hair and wiping the blood smear from her neck. She looked perfectly composed and relaxed as she walked down the hall and, Lucena noted with bitterness, still stunningly beautiful.

Watching her, Lucena felt a strange compulsion to lay down her weapon and give up. It was so strong and came on so suddenly she nearly capitulated, but caught herself at the last moment. She tightened her grip on her broom and held it point out towards her enemy, planting her feet apart and squaring her shoulders.

Miss Smael came closer, and now she looked a little annoyed, but she laughed when she saw Lucena's makeshift weapon.

"Silly little girl," she said. "You shouldn't play with dangerous toys." She wagged one of her long, elegant fingers.

Again the compulsion hit Lucena, but she gritted her teeth and held fast. That made Miss Smael really annoyed.

"You are a stubborn one," she said, coming right up to the broom as if it could do no more damage to her than a sewing needle. She put her hands on her hips and looked down at Lucena contemptuously. "Such a nice spirit, but so ugly. You probably taste of mold and disappointment, don't you? Just a worthless, fat little brat."

Despite her best efforts Lucena's hands were beginning to shake. She was terrified, absolutely terrified, but she made herself stand rather than run.

CHAPTER 1: *At the Munsmire School for Girls*

Miss Smael regarded her for a moment, then moved so swiftly Lucena didn't know what had happened until she saw the broom point plunging into her own belly.

She stared first at the protruding piece of wood, then at Miss Smael, who had somehow yanked the broom out of her hands and then stabbed her with it. The shock was so great that for a moment Lucena felt nothing at all. But she knew it would hurt soon, and it did. She almost fainted when Miss Smael roughly jerked the broom out, and keeled over backwards, hitting the ground with a thump.

Lucena lay on the floor, very still, watching the ceiling wheel above her. The pain was overwhelming, and it was spreading too, so that she felt it all the way out in her fingertips. Then the ceiling solidified, and she took a breath. This brought on a coughing fit that, when it subsided, left blood on the hand she raised to cover her mouth.

Through all this Lucena was vaguely aware of Miss Smael, first coming towards her with the broom in hand, perhaps to deliver the final blow, and then pausing, as if she had heard something that disturbed her. A minute later Lucena's pain-wracked brain registered it too.

It was a humming, low and melodic, and it vibrated in her bones. From somewhere deep in the back of Lucena's mind, she felt something go bump. Miss Smael felt that too, and jerked visibly.

Muffled screaming drifted up from the direction of the front door, then was suddenly cut off.

Silence. The vampires all around them were slowly retreating further and further up the hall, towards the dormitories. Lucena couldn't see Miss Smael's face, but the vampire's posture had changed. Where before it had been proud and fearless, now her shoulders were hunched and her neck thrust forward, like some cornered prey animal about to make its last stand.

Something was coming up the hallway. Something that walked with an even step and brought darkness rolling with it like a cloud. The lamps went out, one by one, until the only illumination was filtered moonlight drifting in from a distant window.

Oddly enough, when all the light had been put out, a strange new light filled the hall. It was pale, like moonlight, but soft and dim, and crept into every corner. It filled the hall like smoke, making it difficult to see whatever was approaching.

Then through the smokey light a man appeared, walking steadily down the hall. He was by far the tallest man Lucena had ever seen, although perhaps that was because of the strange hanging robe he wore. It was black, and fell in a straight line from his shoulders to his feet, making his body look like one long shadow. His hair too was black and straight, and long enough to frame his face, which was ghostly white. From a distance it looked almost skull-like, for he had dark shadows around his eyes, which were also dark until they caught the light. Then they gleamed like a cat's.

The man came to a stop when he was within ten feet of Miss Smael, and smiled. He had thin, dark blue lips, and his teeth shone as bright as his eyes. Something in the way he smiled, in the way he looked, made Lucena very glad that she was not Miss Smael.

"Well?" the man said in a voice that sounded like velvet.

It was Miss Smael's turn to hold out the fateful broom like a spear. The man looked at it with obvious amusement, though he frowned when he saw the blood.

"You can run, if you wish," he said. "Or you may fight. The end will be the same."

With a snarl Miss Smael lunged at him. It seemed to Lucena that she grew wings, huge talons burst from her fingers, and her whole body enlarged. Lost in her shadow, the man's disembodied pale face smiled up at his attacker, and he held up an equally white, disembodied hand.

There was a clap, like someone slamming a door very hard, then a rush of stale air, and then a burst of flame. And then the man was calmly dusting off his hands, and shaking the ash out of his robe. There was no sign of Miss Smael. He picked up the bloodied broom from the floor, and came over to where Lucena was lying. He knelt down before her, and she caught a whiff of something that smelled like the night sky.

"This is yours," the man said, and he smiled again. A kind smile this time, with no teeth. He gently placed the broom in her hand and closed her fingers around it.

"Warriors should keep their weapons," he said, standing. Then he swept past her into the darkness.

How long Lucena lay in that hall she didn't know. Every time she moved, the pain redoubled, so she lay as still as possible. The light faded once the man was gone, and Lucena thought perhaps she fainted. In the distance she heard muffled screams again, quickly cut off. Then slowly she became aware of the smell of smoke creeping down from the dormitories, and then the light began to grow again.

It was him, coming down the hall. He passed her and went into the teacher's lounge, but was only there for a moment. He reappeared, closing the door behind him, and came back to kneel before her. Gently he placed one hand behind her shoulders and one under her knees and lifted her up.

Lucena cried out in pain at being moved, but she didn't struggle. Dimly she caught glimpses of the school hallways and corridors drifting past, all strangely empty. The place was silent too, except for the muffled crackling of fire.

They came to the front door, now cleared of rubble and wide open. Lucena felt the cool night air brush her face, and began to shiver. She had broken out in a cold sweat, and her grip on the broom was loosening.

Warriors should keep their weapons, the man had said. He had also said something else, to her. *Splintered wood will kill the dead.* It was him. The man from her dream. Lucena wondered if she should be afraid.

The man carried her out of the school and away from that terrible place. Once they were clear of the grounds he stopped and turned around, and Lucena saw that all the buildings were ablaze, the flames leaping high into the night like voracious demons.

The man set her down in the grass by the side of the road. This made her cry again, but he passed a hand over her brow, and the pain lessened.

CHAPTER 1: *At the Munsmire School for Girls*

Lucena lay in the grass, staring blankly at the heavens. The stars were mere smudges of white on the dark sky, her vision had become so weak, and although the pain in her abdomen was slowly receding, she was having difficulty breathing. Her vision wavered. Every time she blinked it was harder and harder to open her eyes again.

"Am I dying?" she asked the dark shadow which was all she could see of the strange man.

"Yes," he answered.

"I don't want to..."

"I am sorry, but there is nothing I can do to stop that."

The shadow moved out of her field of vision, and she felt herself alone. Lying there, dying alone in the dark at the edge of the mire, she wept. It seemed that all her life had been spent waiting for something wonderful, and now all she could do was lie and wait for death. Such a terrible waste. And all those girls in the school too, and all the teachers and the staff. Lucena had no love for them, but she did not wish them to die in such a terrible place or in such a terrible way.

The shadow reappeared, and this time it was his face, close enough so that she could make out the glowing eyes.

"If you wish," he said softly, "there is something I can do. I can't stop you dying, but..." he trailed off. His eyes grew dim, so they were only black holes in his face. Then she saw them glimmer again, and he went on. "I can give you a second chance. I can't promise you will get what you want out of it. What you do with it is up to you. Do you understand?"

Lucena tried to consider what he was saying carefully, but it was difficult because her brain was not working very well. Still, on some level she knew exactly what he was talking about. It was a door, and in dying desperation, she leapt for it.

"Yes," she said. The word came out in a long, thin wheeze, but he knew what she meant.

He knelt by her side, gently brushing a stray hair out of her eye. "You wish to continue, then?" he said. "It is a strange journey beyond the stony wall, to the other side of the shadows, but I can lead you."

There was no answer; Lucena could no longer speak. He put a hand beneath her chin and lifted her face to his. "Answer me, Lucena Clarian Ashmoor. Will you follow me?"

She wanted to say yes. Anything but to die here. She would follow the pale man anywhere. Finally she was able to force out one word:

"Follow..."

A lot of blood came out with it, and then her vision blacked out entirely. She felt hair, smooth and soft as warm water, brush her face. There was a smell of wet grass and old, unopened books, a sensation of falling, and then nothing.

Lucena walked in the darkness, but she was not afraid. After a time a wall appeared out of the blackness before her. It was a low wall, made of rough stones piled together, and beyond it was a dark land filled with rolling shadows. A pale path ran beside the wall, and without thinking Lucena began to walk along it.

A voice like velvet called her name from beyond the wall, and she turned to look. Strangely, she saw herself: a pale, faint version of the young chubby girl with ashen hair who stood across the wall from her. Then the vision was consumed by the rolling shadows and he appeared. He held out a long white hand, thin as bone and tinged blue, offering it to her.

Reaching over the stony wall Lucena took it, and he helped her scramble across.

"Come along then," he said, and led her away into the all-consuming shadow.

It was Miss Smael's turn to hold out the fateful broom like a spear.

CHAPTER 2:

The Maker

LUCENA WOKE FEELING DESPERATELY THIRSTY. It was that terrible, debilitating thirst one has after a long day in the sun. Her mouth was dry as paper, and her whole body cried out for something—anything—to drink. She rolled out of bed, which took longer than she expected, as her bed had somehow become much bigger. But there was an open wine bottle on the bedside table, and this she grasped, ignoring the glass beside it, and drank nearly all of it down before she realized what it was.

When she did she choked and hurled the bottle across the room, where it smashed on the stone floor. Blood splashed everywhere, sending spatters up the wall and onto the fringes of Lucena's nightgown. She backed herself against the bed, nauseated and dizzy, but when her head cleared, her thirst was gone, and her wits returned sufficiently for her to take in her surroundings.

She was not, as she had first assumed, in her cot in the dormitory of the school at Munsmire, but in a long square room with a stone-flagged floor and walls. The ceiling was stone too, and from it hung an ornate closed lantern, which was the only source of light. Brightly colored banners hung on the walls, all of them bearing heraldic emblems; a red lion and a white horse faced off on a gold and orange one; twin white snakes entwined themselves on one of deep navy; and the one directly across from the bed was black with white stars, with a great white stylized G in the center.

There was a mottled green carpet covering most of the floor, the kind with a fringe. One end of the room held the bed that Lucena had just vacated, a great four-poster complete with drapes and a nightstand (which had until recently held the bottle of blood). Along the wall next to the bed was a bureau with a looking glass, a washbasin, some linens, and an assortment of hair brushes set on top. Across from this there were a bookshelf, a book table with a candelabra on it, and a very comfortable looking armchair. In the middle of the room, facing away from the bed, was a writing desk and a chair, and in the opposite wall was a single square door.

There were no windows.

Lucena barely had time to register all this before the door sprang open and in came the most astonishing creature she had ever seen. She (for the creature was female) was a little shorter than Lucena, but appeared much smaller because she was so scrawny. She had strange, bent-backwards knees and large furry feet with long toes. She was wearing a loose garment the same color as her skin (a creamy light brown) belted around the waist with a leather strap, from which hung a set of keys, a pair of gloves, a folding knife, a small broom and dustpan, and a bell with a stopper in it. She had slick black hair that had been pulled back into a bun even more severe than the one Lucena usually wore, and long black

CHAPTER 2: *The Maker*

eyebrows that swooped up on either side of her face. She also had extremely long and pointed ears, with tufts of fur on the end, and large golden eyes. These narrowed sharply when she saw the smashed bottle and splattered blood.

"Hopeless," she muttered grimly, coming further into the room. She had an odd, catlike walk because of her backwards knees. She looked from the smashed bottle to Lucena backed against the bed, and fairly glared. "*Completely* hopeless." She unhooked the broom and dustpan from her belt and began sweeping up the broken glass. As she worked she continued talking, mostly in jerks and incomplete sentences, as if speaking to herself. "Don't know what Himself was thinking . . . we're here to clean up his mess, not spread it! Stupid thing doesn't even know what it is . . . One of my favorite bottles, too. No chance Cobbin will mend it. Bugger and blast them both."

As the strange creature worked, Lucena slowly got over her shock. She was beginning to feel better too; the heaviness of sleep was lifting from her head, and slowly her mind began to remember the events from the immediate past.

The school. The vampires. Miss Smael. Miss Smael had been a vampire all along. The strange man. The fire.

She was forgetting something, Lucena knew. Something about a wall, and she had been stabbed, hadn't she? Quickly she checked herself, but she had no wounds that she could see or feel. That brought back more memories; the sight of herself across the stony wall, the strange man offering her his hand.

"What in the Name of Heaven has happened?" Lucena said aloud.

"Completely and *utterly* hopeless!" exclaimed the strange creature. She had swept the broken fragments of glass into a cloth and was now mopping up the spilled blood. Angrily she finished her work and stomped out of the room, muttering under her breath, "'She's a sharp one,' Himself says. 'She'll do well,' he says. Pa! Silly little vampire doesn't even know what it is!"

Lucena sat frozen on her bed, the word ringing in her ears.

"Vampire?"

There was one way to find out. She had heard that vampires had no reflection, so she went over to the bureau, turning the glass to face her. What she saw made her recoil in horror. She did have a reflection, but it was misty-white and transparent. She looked like a spotty ghost with messy hair. The sight was enough to send her scrambling back to bed, where she cowered against the pillows, trying not to weep.

How long Lucena lay there she did not know, but she must have fallen asleep again, for she woke with a start to the sound of someone speaking her name.

Lucena?

Whoever they were they sounded like they were standing right behind her, so she sat up and looked around.

She was alone.

Lucena, come to me. It is time we spoke, face to face.

The voice, she realized with a shiver, was coming from the back of her own mind. But it was a pleasant voice, soft as velvet and gentle as a tranquil pool, and she knew who it belonged to.

"How do I find you?" she asked, her own voice hoarse and shaky.

Get out of bed. Go out the door. You may want to put on some slippers, for the floor is cold.

"Slippers?"

There is a pair in the bottom drawer of your bureau.

Obediently Lucena got out of bed and went over to her bureau. Careful not to look in the mirror she stooped and opened the lowest drawer. There, sure enough, were some lovely silk slippers, along with an extra nightgown and some linens. She removed the slippers, looking them over in awe and feeling the soft texture of the cloth before putting them on. Then she went to the door and opened it.

Poking her head outside she saw a long hallway, lit with small orb-shaped lanterns hung from the ceiling. Although the stone walls were bare, the floor was covered by a frayed red carpet, which stretched away into the distance before being swallowed by the shadows. Lucena could see no other doors or windows.

"Which way do I go?" she asked.

Can you hear the music?

Now that the voice mentioned it, Lucena could hear some distant notes, too faint to make a proper tune, but they sounded as though they were being played on a spinet.

"Yes, yes I can hear it," she said.

Follow the music, the voice said, so she did.

It was a strange journey. At first the hall appeared empty, with no doors or windows, but after a time Lucena began to notice how things would appear on the edge of her vision when she was not looking straight at them. In this way she saw that there were many doors leading off from the hall, and even a few passages and stairways. There was also a long window once, but of course when she turned her head to see out all she saw was solid stone. This was frustrating, but Lucena didn't have any real problems until she passed one of the stairways and heard the music she was following become much louder.

The voice had said follow the music, but of course when Lucena turned to climb the stairs she was faced with a solid wall. So she stood, undecided, keeping the stairway in view out of the corner of her eye. Eventually she managed, by walking sideways and keeping her head turned away, to make it onto the stairs. Only when she was standing firmly on the first step did she dare look ahead, and there were the rest of the stairs, solid as could be, leading up to a lighted corridor. But when she turned around to look back into the hall, all she saw were even more stairs, leading down into the darkness.

Confused, Lucena walked back a few paces, keeping the corner of her eye peeled, as it were, and sure enough there was a doorway into the hall. Satisfied with this discovery, she marched up the stairs with more confidence, following the sound of the music.

She ultimately made several more turns in the same manner, and so managed, at last, to come to a wide-open hall with a vaulted ceiling and marble floor. Here she could tell the music was only a little ways further, through a small door at the end, but her first attention was to the opposite wall, which had a string of long windows in it. These were proper windows, which stayed put when she

CHAPTER 2: *The Maker*

looked at them, and they were enormous. The hall's ceiling must have been easily fifty feet high, and the windows fell only a little short of that. Although this made them look narrow, when Lucena went over to one she found it so wide she could not touch both sides with her outstretched arms. But at first all her interest was held by what she could see beyond them.

It was night, with a brilliant full moon hanging low on the horizon. Lucena could see a maze-like garden covering the ground below, with tall cypress trees and a bubbling fountain. In the distance was wide-open parkland, with a few dark buildings dotted here and there.

"Do you like the view?" a voice asked. It was not *the* voice, the one that spoke in the back of her head. This one came from a real person, and echoed a little in the huge hall. Lucena looked around with a start, and saw a tall man standing beside the window. He had a somber face with a sloping brow and short dark hair, and wore a sort of pleated robe that covered all of his body, except his feet, which were bare. Lucena thought she was frightened of him at first, but on second thought decided not to be.

"Yes indeed," she answered. "It's very beautiful."

"I have some others," the man said humbly. He seemed to concentrate for a moment, then relaxed. "There," he said, gesturing at the window.

Lucena looked, and gasped, for the view had completely changed: now it was a deep moonless night over what appeared to be mountains with snowcapped peaks. Bright stars twinkled in the sky, and Lucena thought a few of them moved.

"It's lovely," she said, but she felt confused. "How did you do that?"

The man shrugged. "It's something I can do. It's not much. I can also make music and light, but not as bright as Ballroom, and Maker likes to play his own music. Mostly, I do the views."

"The ballroom?" Lucena asked.

"Just Ballroom," the man said. "You'll find her through there." He pointed across the room to a grand double door with statues on either side. "And there"—he pointed back up the hall from where Lucena had come to a small door in the shadows—"is West Antechamber. He serves coffee and desserts when Maker has a ball, and has very comfortable chairs. There"—he pointed down the hall to the door from which the music came—"is East Antechamber. Maker has his piano there, as you can probably tell. East Antechamber is good at sound projection, which is probably why he chose her."

Lucena took all this in with amazement; it sounded insane, the way he talked of the rooms as if they were people, but he did it in such a calm manner she couldn't help believing it.

"Who are you then?" she asked, genuinely curious.

"Me?" the man said. "Why, my little 'pire, you're *in* me. I'm North Hall." He bowed low. When he rose again, he was smiling. It made his somber face much more handsome. "I'm glad you liked my views, but I'm afraid I'm keeping you. Maker wants to see you, and I believe he has nearly finished playing."

The music indeed seemed to be coming to an end, so Lucena thanked North Hall, dropped a curtsey, and hurried towards the door.

"One little tip," North Hall called after her. "East Antechamber prefers it if you knock first."

Lucena nodded to him, and when she arrived at the door, knocked gently on the wood.

The door swung open of its own accord, and the voice, instantly recognizable even if it was no longer inside her head, said, *"Come in."*

The east antechamber—the room itself—was dark, lit only by a single candelabra which stood on a little table beside the largest, darkest, glossiest piano Lucena had ever seen, but all she could do was stare raptly at the person sitting on the bench behind it, moving his hands fluidly up and down the keys.

It was the mysterious man from before, although now he was wearing a pale grey-blue robe like those worn by royal wizards, and so looked more like a person and less like a living shadow. But he was still a strange sight: his hair, which was just long enough to brush his shoulders, was so black it did not reflect the candlelight, and gave his face a strange disembodied look. This face, now Lucena got a chance to look at it again, was not skull-like at all, but smooth, like an upside-down teardrop, if a little on the narrow side. He had an elegant pointed nose, a perfectly formed chin, and his eyes were neither too big nor too small, although when they caught the light they sparkled like diamonds. This effect was made even stronger by the dark shadows around them, which, Lucena saw now she drew closer, were an actual discoloration of the skin. It had been this that gave her the impression of a skull face; that and his pale color everywhere else, which even in the warm candlelight was still bone white.

Lucena was so intrigued by him that she walked right up to his side, where she stood and gazed at him, and all the while the man continued playing, his hands deftly dancing up and down the keys and his head bent forwards.

The finale of the piece was a rolling wave of notes that sent both hands flittering over the keys like agitated butterflies. He finished with a resounding chord that echoed down the whole room, and sat back to let the sound die away. But before it was gone, almost as an afterthought, he darted out his right hand once more and hit a single note as a sort of final stop.

It made Lucena laugh, although she quickly stifled it. But when the man turned to look at her his eyes were twinkling like stars and he was smiling.

"You like it?" he asked. His voice was still as soft as velvet. No matter how many times Lucena heard it, she would never get used to how soft it was, and in that moment it threw her off completely.

"Oh yes, yes sir," she stammered.

The man reached out and lazily played a few notes with his left hand. "Do you play at all?"

"A little," Lucena admitted. "But I'm not very good."

"That is no reason not to play, if it brings you joy," the man said. "I would like to hear you."

He said it so earnestly and sincerely, and it was so completely different (not to mention kinder) than anything Lucena's teachers had ever said to her, that combined with the trauma and excitement she had recently experienced, it all became too much and, to her utter shame, she burst into tears.

CHAPTER 2: *The Maker*

The man neither sneered nor regarded her with pity. He just looked expectantly at the darkness behind her head, which solidified into the shadowy figure of a woman. This figure pushed forward an armchair, which Lucena gratefully sat down in, and offered her a handkerchief, which she took.

The man slid to the end of the piano bench, and sat with his legs hanging off the side while he waited for Lucena to regain control of herself. But Lucena found once she started crying it was quite impossible to stop; when she felt the tears abate she thought of the bottle of blood again and burst into a fresh bout of sobbing.

"Come, come," the man said, after this had been going on for about five minutes. "Tell me what is troubling you." He sounded genuinely concerned, another thing Lucena was not used to, and so it was another five minutes before she could even begin to speak. Even then every other word was punctured by a hiccuping sob. Eventually, and with a great effort, she regained control of her voice.

"T-the bottle," she said, still stammering slightly.

"Yes?"

"There was blood in it..."

"Yes."

"I drank it..."

"A good thing too; you would not have lasted long had you not."

Lucena stared at him. The man was looking at her a little sadly, his head on one side.

"But it wasn't... I didn't... it's not..." Lucena trailed off, unable to complete the question. But the man knew what she meant.

"I'm not *certain* of the particulars," he said. "But I believe it came from some poor fowl whose time in this world was at an end."

That was a relief. But it did not make the fact that she had drunk raw blood much less disgusting, and it opened up a new venue for her concerns.

"But I'm a vampire now," Lucena said.

"Yes."

Dejected, she collapsed back into her chair, idly toying with her handkerchief. But she no longer felt like crying. Then the full implication of the situation hit her, and she recoiled, curling up in the chair into a defensive ball.

"*You* made me like this!" she cried.

The man nodded, gazing at her with sad, starry eyes.

"That means *you* are a vampire!"

The starry eyes blinked, and the man looked away. He seemed embarrassed. "Not exactly," he said. "Not at all, in fact. As it happens I'm something quite a bit different."

"You *look* like a vampire," Lucena said accusingly.

"So I have been told," the man said good-naturedly. "I have also been told I look like an elf, an incubus, a wizard-king, and the old Cairdrian night goddess." His eyes twinkled merrily at Lucena's shocked expression. "I have only been mistaken for the goddess once," he added, a lopsided grin pulling at his thin, blue lips.

Lucena's feelings of horror were not assuaged. She slumped in her chair and glowered at him. She had a good, jowly glower; she knew from practicing in the mirror at school. But thinking of mirrors made her think of her last encounter with one, which made her even sadder.

"Lucena?" the man said. "Tell me what is wrong."

"You turned me into a monster," she said quietly.

"You say that as though being a monster is a bad thing."

"Isn't it? Aren't monsters evil?" Lucena had meant it as sarcasm, but she was not good with sarcasm, and the man took it literally.

"Not entirely," he said placidly. "In my experience they are just like humans: some are good, some are bad, but mostly they are misunderstood."

"Misunderstood?"

"Misunderstanding breeds hatred, which in turn is often mistaken for evil."

Lucena sat and thought about this for a while.

"Why me?" she asked.

The man leaned forward and rested his elbows on his knees. Bent double like that, his face was at the same height as hers. The edges of the shadows around his eyes were vivid blue, she saw, almost the same as his lips.

"Many reasons contributed," he said. "Mostly, it was because you seemed to want to follow me."

"I didn't want *this*," Lucena said mulishly. Only . . . only she *had*, hadn't she? When she'd been dying and there seemed no other option. She would have grasped at anything, any chance. Now she had one, she wasn't sure she wanted it after all.

The man shifted in front of her, a hand emerging from the sleeve of his robe to hover over her knee. After a moment, however, he withdrew it again, and sighed a little. Like a breath of wind through an open window at night.

"Lucena," he said softly, "did you ever feel like the world was bigger than what you could see of it? That there was a wider realm, waiting just beyond the edge of your awareness?"

Lucena had to think about this for a while as well, although what he said described exactly how she had felt at school.

"I felt like I was waiting for something," she admitted. "Like there was some big, magical world just around the bend, or something, but I didn't know how to get there."

The man smiled, widely, and his starry eyes fairly sparkled. "Well," he said. "You are *in* that magical world now. And here, you'll find, things are a little different. What worked one way in your old world works two, or three, or four ways here. You cannot judge people for how they look or even what they are. Here the rules are different. You must forget what you *thought* was evil, and what you *knew* was good. What hunted you, now you may hunt. What is darkness, now you can see in it? What opportunities open in the night like doorways at the edge of your vision?"

Lucena remembered the hidden passages she had seen on her journey, and thought she felt a hint of understanding. And, for the first time, she felt a little

CHAPTER 2: *The Maker*

flutter of excitement; a hope that, against all odds and contrary to appearances, something *good* was about to happen.

"A very astute human once put it this way," the man said, his voice hardly above a whisper. "*Not all darkness is evil, not all light will be safe. Saints have been saved by the devil; many fates come out of faith.* It has often been misinterpreted, but it deserves remembering, if only because of its relevance to our kind."

"Our kind?" Lucena repeated, also whispering. She had leaned forward to catch the man's words, and now they sat, face to face, so close Lucena could almost pick out the individual stars in his dark eyes.

"We who live in shadows and in mystery," the man replied. "Who set ourselves to find the truth in illusions and in lies. Are you certain you would not like to have a turn at playing?" He sat up and gestured towards the row of keys.

"I, well, I don't know . . ." Lucena blustered, feeling off balance and uncertain.

"Please do," the man said. "It is a good way to unburden oneself, I find."

"I, oh . . . oh all right, I suppose . . ." Lucena got up, and the man slid down the bench to make room for her. As she sat down beside him Lucena realized she had forgotten to ask the most obvious question of all.

"Who are you?"

The man folded his hands in his lap. "My name is Madgrin," he said modestly. "It is a good name, though my staff call me lord or my lord or whatever honorific takes their fancy. But the parts of my house that are inclined to speak call me Maker, as I am the maker of this house. You may call me Maker too, if it suits you."

"Maker . . ." Lucena repeated. It was an easy word to say, unlike Madgrin, which was a strange and frightening name. She set her fingers to the keys and began to play.

Once again music filled the east antechamber, faltering at first, with a few flubs and jerking repetitions, but slowly it smoothed out as Lucena remembered the joy of playing at random.

North Hall leaned against one of his pillars and smiled as he gently nodded his head in time to the music.

Slowly the sweet sound spread, filtering down into every corner of the strange place. Things that were awake and at work paused to listen, and those sound asleep turned over in their slumber as they dreamed of dancing notes.

And all the while Lucena played, Madgrin sat beside her, watching her fingers dance up and down the keys, as though there was nothing in the world more fascinating. When she finished he took her by the hand and led her back along the hidden passages and stairs. Lucena followed like one in a dream, never speaking, only watching, until at last they reached her door. She could tell it was her door because it was the only door she could look straight at and still see.

Madgrin turned to her then. He had to bend almost double in order to be face to face with her.

"I have business that requires my presence elsewhere now," he said. "But should you have a question, or need any help, you only have to ask. Think of me, and I will hear you. Wherever I am."

Uncertain of her voice, Lucena nodded. Madgrin smiled, bowed, and faded away. At first Lucena thought he had just gone invisible, but when she reached a hand out to feel the place where he had been, all she found was air. Standing in the hall, Lucena suddenly felt lonely. With a sigh she opened the door and went inside.

And discovered she was not alone at all. There was someone sleeping, curled up in the middle of her bed. On closer inspection she found them to be a small, young man in simple but well-made clothes. He had a heart-shaped face and a mop of grey-brown hair. It was a very messy mop, falling all which ways, so Lucena didn't see that he had cat's ears until she was practically standing right over him. Then she also saw that he had a cat's tail, which was wound around his feet.

Despite her astonishment, Lucena's first thought was "My, what an adorable person!" Indeed he looked so soft and sweet all she really wanted to do was pick him up and hug him like you would a real cat, but she felt that would not be a good idea.

Then his tail twitched slightly, which made Lucena gasp.

The sound woke the strange youth, and he opened one brilliant gold eye sleepily. When he saw Lucena he shut it again, stretched luxuriously, just like a cat, and sat up blinking. He yawned, revealing a red mouth with very white, sharp teeth.

"Hullo there," he said, his voice a pleasant purr. "You must be Lucena."

"Yes, yes I am," Lucena said, guiltily hiding her hands behind her back. "Who are you?" She nearly added, "And what are you doing in my bed?" but decided not to.

"Oh, me? I'm Willic," the cat-man said. "I'm sorry I wasn't here to meet you earlier. I'm the Housekeeper, you see. But welcome all the same."

"Welcome?" Lucena asked.

"Welcome," Willic said, sliding off her bed and standing up. He made a formal bow. "Welcome to the House of Madgrin. Allow me to show you around."

. . . all she could do was stare raptly at the person sitting on the bench behind it, moving his hands fluidly up and down the keys.

CHAPTER 3:

In the House of Madgrin

WILLIC LED LUCENA OUT OF HER ROOM and down the hall. Lucena hurried after him, careful to keep close to his waving, tabby tail, yet even so nearly lost him at once when he turned sharply right and plunged through a hidden doorway. Hastily she turned herself sideways and sidled after, coming through onto a narrow flight of bare stone stairs to hear him say: "We'll start with the *cellars* and work our way *up*. That's the best way to meet the House. Bottom-to-top; the way it was built. Cellars may not be the most exciting place, but they are very important, you'll see!"

The cellars turned out to be a labyrinthine maze of rooms and doors that were always changing. They were packed with crates, boxes and bags, and everywhere it was so dark, and so full of strange, unpredictable things, that Lucena felt she was inside a huge cave rather than the basement of a house. As her eyes adjusted to the gloom she thought she saw writing on the walls, windows painted on the stone, and in one spot she nearly tripped over a giant, stone gear that protruded from the middle of the floor. In some areas it was dead quiet, but other times she thought she could hear a distant roaring sound, like the sea; and once she thought she heard, muted in the distance, the sound of someone laughing.

"Think of the cellars as *roots*," Willic explained. "They stretch out around the House, and far off into distant places. It *can* be easy to lose your way," he added, catching Lucena's skirts to keep her from wandering off in the wrong direction. "*But*, if you can imagine very clearly where you want to go, and keep walking, eventually you'll get there. This is the same wherever you go in the House. It's nice that way."

"What if I can't clearly imagine where I'm going?" Lucena asked.

"That's why I'm showing you *all* of the House," Willic said, giving her a whiskery grin. "So you'll have some places *to* imagine. For example, I'm imagining kitchens, so walk this way...."

And he led her through the shadowy maze, and as they walked Lucena found her eyes adjusting further to the dark, such that she could eventually see as well as in daylight.

So when they rounded a corner into another room and were met by the blaze of a torch, she stumbled backwards and threw up her arms with a cry of pain.

"Oh, *terribly* sorry!" the person holding the torch exclaimed.

"Gydda? What are you doing down here?" Willic asked.

"Looking for some red lentils. I know I saw a sack around here somewhere a few years back, and Grimmach asked if I could manage something Dahlsanese tonight, and I thought a nice curry with, oh say, who's this?"

Lucena was about to echo this last question, for her eyes had adjusted to the light, and she could now see the speaker clearly.

CHAPTER 3: *In the House of Madgrin*

It was a small woman, even shorter and wider than Lucena. She seemed to be the same kind of creature as the disgruntled maid, with her swooping eyebrows and long tufty ears, but where the maid had been rake thin, this one was wide all over. She had a wide smiling face, round, twinkling black eyes, a great wide bosom and even wider hips. Lucena could see her feet were nearly as wide as they were long and very furry indeed, although since she was wearing a proper dress it was hard to see which way her knees bent. She also had her hair in a bun, but it was a messy one, with many stray hairs fanning out from her head.

Willic was already introducing them: "Gydda, this is Lucena, she's Himself's fledgeling. I'm giving her the tour," he explained. "Lucena, meet Gydda. She cooks good food."

"If you eat food, that is," Gydda said, and giggled nervously. It was not a titter, but a kind of clucking "*Hk, hk, hk,*" like a bird. "For you I just do the blood."

"Oh." Lucena felt her face fall at the thought of the blood, but Gydda was already turning back to her search.

"It was *lovely* meeting you," she said over her shoulder. "But if you'll excuse me, the cellars can be difficult when you're trying to find a specific thing. Bring her by the kitchens Willic, if she gets hungry."

"That was Gydda," Willic said unnecessarily, when the flare of the torch had dimmed as it moved off down a passage.

"Yes," Lucena said quietly. She was thinking about Gydda and the maid, and how she had never read of any creature quite like them.

"I met someone else like her, earlier today," she said eventually.

"Tonight," Willic corrected her amiably. "That was probably our maid, Rhyse."

"Oh yes," Lucena said. "But what *are* they?"

"Why, they're *hoblins*, of course. Not hob*goblins*, mind you, those eat children."

"Then what are *hoblins?*"

"You could think of them as grumpy, furry elves," Willic said, grinning. "But don't tell *them* that. Really, they're not elves. Nor fairies either. Older than both. *Hoblins*. And not many of them left."

Despite this somewhat dire pronouncement there were no less than four hoblins employed in the House of Madgrin, and Lucena was introduced to all of them that first night. After wandering the cellars for a while longer, during which Willic let Lucena lead, and Lucena contrived to get them spectacularly lost, they came up through what appeared to be a kitchen. That was a wonderful place, full of steam and light and warmth and the sound of frying, although Lucena found with disappointment that the smell of cooking food was no longer attractive to her. But she had little time to think of that, for the kitchen was also full of bustling Gydda, who had found her lentils and was cooking up a frenzy. Willic rushed her through with only a quick "hullo!"

Lucena would have liked to stay and look at all the interesting herbs and vegetables hanging from the ceiling, and also to see what Gydda was cooking, but Willic explained that she was liable to make them help wash up if they stayed to chat.

Hurrying out of the kitchen they crashed headlong into the third hoblin. He was on his way in, carrying a precarious stack of potatoes in his arms. These went flying when Willic and Lucena barreled into him, and for a moment it looked like they would be scattered everywhere. Then Willic put on a burst of catlike speed and snatched them out of the air, and before Lucena could say "Terribly sorry!" he was carefully carrying them in the crook of one arm, while offering the other to the hoblin, who had been knocked off his feet.

"Fleeing the long arm of the cook, Willic?" the hoblin said, taking the offered hand and pulling himself up. Unlike the other hoblins he was tall, and wore a dark squire's outfit that contrasted harshly with his bare feet, which were very long and furry and seemed mostly made of toe. He had a long, serious face, and his slanting eyebrows drooped a little at the ends. He had shoulder-length black hair, slicked down with grease, although a few strands had come loose in his fall. These he pushed back irritably before relieving Willic of the potatoes.

"Nothing of the sort," Willic protested. "I'm giving young *Lucena* here the grand tour."

"Oh, is this the one who sent Rhyse into such a spin?" The hoblin peered down at Lucena curiously.

"Yes, this is Lucena. Lucena, meet our footman, Cobbin."

Lucena bobbed a curtsey and Cobbin bowed, no easy task when you are carrying an armful of potatoes. He smiled, showing a lot of yellow, crooked teeth. "Well, take care you don't run into Grimmach like that," he warned. "Rhyse put honey-whisky in his tea again, so he's moving a bit slow."

"Who is Grimmach?" Lucena asked once they had left Cobbin behind and were on their way up one of the endless stairs.

"He's our steward," Willic said. "And if Rhyse spiked his tea like normal, it probably means he's sleeping it off in the library."

"Library?" Lucena said, perking up at the thought. "You have a library?"

"Oh yes," Willic said. "Do you like libraries?"

"I like books," Lucena said.

"Well, we do have an *awful* lot of books," Willic said, a smile spreading across his face. "Along with some other things. Would you like to see the library next?"

"Oh yes," Lucena said. "Yes please!"

So they went and saw the library. It was across the house from the kitchen, and up and down more hallways than Lucena cared to count. As always in the house it was difficult to keep one's bearings, for on the one hand it felt like they had hardly gone anywhere, while on the other that they had been walking the quiet, carpeted passages for miles before they finally came to a huge set of double doors carved all over with books. Books lined the edges and flapped across the middle, even the handles were in the form of books.

Inside was a large, circular room built in many layers, all rising up from the center like a silent coliseum with books in place of spectators, and armchairs and reading tables in place of combatants. Each level had books in the walls, and doors leading in and out, and ladders for getting up and down, so once you were in it the whole place was like a great three-dimensional maze. Everything

CHAPTER 3: *In the House of Madgrin*

in the library smelled of old paper and dust, though sometimes Lucena caught a whiff of dried roses.

There were no card indexes, and no way of telling which books were where. Willic explained that this was just like the rest of the house; all you had to do was think of the book you wanted, or kind of book you wanted, and start walking. But the library could also be playful, and keep the book you really wanted just out of reach for hours on end.

"When that happens," Willic said, "the best thing to do is go ask *Orrus* for help."

"Orrus?"

"Our librarian. Not a room spirit; a proper person. Madgrin found him and brought him back a while ago. He's around here somewhere..."

But no matter how they looked they could not find Orrus, though they wandered among the walls of books and trapdoors for so long that eventually Lucena became brave enough to do some searching on her own. She found many niches in the walls for chairs and lamps, as well as some dangerously placed trapdoors. She concentrated so on where she was going, and not putting her foot through a hole, that for a while she had no attention to spare for the books themselves. When she did begin looking at their titles and taking them down, to her dismay they were all written in foreign runes, and some of them made screaming sounds or bled from the binding when they were opened. These she shut carefully and put back on the shelves, where the other books crowded around protectively.

"You have to be gentle with those," someone said behind her after she had just shut a particularly anguished tome.

Lucena whirled around and found herself face to face with a middle-aged, slender man with light auburn hair and round spectacles. He was wearing the same sort of loose-fitting, hanging robe that North Hall had worn, although his was dark grey, and he seemed as a whole more solid. There were ink stains on his right hand, and he carried a number of books under one arm.

"I'm so sorry," Lucena said, feeling embarrassed. This man had such a quiet, modest nature that she suddenly felt it was very important not to offend him. "Are you Orrus?"

"Indeed so," the man said. He came over and pulled the book that had screamed off the shelf again. Gently but firmly he smoothed its cover, and then slowly peeled it open. Lucena noticed he was careful not to open it all the way, and so not over-flex the binding. He held out the open book to her. "There," he said. "These ones are just a little sensitive."

"Why?" asked Lucena, taking the book with utmost delicacy.

Orrus looked sadly at the shelf, where the remaining books had crowded forward to peer concernedly down at their fellow. A few of them flapped their covers nervously.

"Many reasons," he said. "Some were read too much, some left on the floor to be stepped on. Some were not read enough, and left on shelves and forgotten. We have a lot of those here; this library is where all forgotten or lost books come, eventually."

Lucena looked up wonderingly at the shelves; there were certainly a lot of books, and some of them looked extremely old. She could feel the book she was holding trembling gently in her hands, like a frightened animal.

"Perhaps I should put it back?" she suggested.

"Put it back?" said Orrus. "Of course *not*. Books were meant to be read, you know. If no one reads them they start thinking ill of themselves and turn into grimoires, and that is something we do not need any more of. So come, let us bring"—he paused to look at the title of Lucena's book—"*The Compendium of Secrets* down to Library and see what she has to say. By the way, who are you?"

"I'm Lucena," said Lucena. "Er, I think I'm Madgrin's fledgeling..."

"Oh, of course," Orrus said, adjusting his monocle. "Well, then you'll also want this one." He shot out a hand for a book. When he offered it to Lucena she saw that it was *Vampires: A History* and had what looked like a blood smear down the front.

"Oh. I'm not sure I want to read that," Lucena said, taking an inadvertent step away.

"Really? It's quite good: very thorough and informative. And sympathetic, it was written by a vampire, you know."

Given such an argument Lucena had to accept the second book, and she carefully closed *The Compendium of Secrets* so she could carry them down to the main reading area.

This was the lowest part of the library; the round arena of the coliseum; and although it had no trapdoors or shelves to make things difficult, it was so crowded with chairs and tables and sofas that it was still problematic to navigate. Willic was there, taking up an entire sofa while he looked through an enormous picture book, and on the chair beside him slumped the recumbent form of what Lucena assumed was Grimmach. He was portly, like Gydda, but with a narrow, harsh face like Rhyse, and dressed in the manner of Cobbin. He was sleeping with his head turned into a cushion, snoring gently.

Orrus led her to the very center of the room, where there was a wide, square table with books stacked high on either side. Behind the table sat a small woman with messy pale hair and huge thick glasses. She was also wearing the same shapeless robes as North Hall and Orrus, but unlike theirs, hers were a dusty white. She was writing away industriously in a notebook as they approached, but looked up when Lucena set her books down on the table. Orrus didn't say anything, but Lucena was sure this was Library herself.

"Did you find everything all right?" Library asked, her spectacles glinting mischievously.

"Oh yes," Lucena mumbled, feeling a little shy. Library smiled at her and flipped open the books (the *Compendium* gave a sharp "Eep!") to check their contents. She made a little note in her ledger, and handed them back to Lucena. Then Orrus took her by the elbow and led her over to a table near Willic and Grimmach.

Orrus did not sit down. He made a low bow and said, "I will see you next time," before wandering off back into the maze of walls and ladders and books.

CHAPTER 3: *In the House of Madgrin*

Willic had also gone to sleep, so Lucena turned to her books. Still a little nervous about opening the *Compendium* she decided to start with *Vampires: A History* since she thought it wouldn't hurt to be well informed.

The book was informative, but it was written in such an archaic way that Lucena had to think very, very hard about each sentence to figure out what it meant. If she hadn't been such an avid reader, she probably would have given up in frustration. But she kept at it, until outside the House the sun crept up and brought dawn into the world. Then Lucena's eyes closed of their own accord and her own world turned to darkness and nothing, as the first night of her new existence came to an end.

Lucena woke, as she had done the night before, in her bed in the room with no windows. She also found she had a rather painful bruise on her head. That reminded her of the previous night: Willic, the Library, Orrus, and the books. The books, she soon discovered, had been set neatly on her bedside table, along with a tall bottle of blood. Suppressing a shudder at the sight, Lucena sat up and asked Madgrin what had happened.

He didn't answer at once, and for a moment Lucena felt a proper fool, but then his voice sounded in her head, as close and clear as ever.

Sunlight is one of the few things that can kill a vampire, he explained. *You have me to blame for that, I'm afraid, but the only thing to do is not get about during the day.*

"You mean all vampires do this? Go to sleep every day?" she asked.

Some of them.

"Oh." Lucena lay back in her bed.

You may also blame me for that, Madgrin said, his voice apologetic.

"Why?"

It is a compulsion. Not something I am glad of, but necessary, and it will wear off as you grow stronger.

"Stronger," Lucena said dubiously. "Will I still continue to grow, even now that I am like a corpse, in a body whose heart does not beat and which need not even breathe?"

There was a silence in the back of her mind, as though Madgrin were trying not to laugh.

Oh yes, La Flein, oh yes.

La Flein, Lucena would learn, was how Madgrin liked to address her. She thought it sounded Fortaun, but she didn't feel comfortable asking him about it. So she asked Willic.

"It's not strictly Fortaun," Willic allowed. "It's from the language that *became* Fortaun, and Purainish and Milanian Duscan. It means, 'little bird who is weak now but will one day grow big and strong.'"

"Oh," said Lucena. She felt a little embarrassed at being compared to a little weak bird, for she certainly did not resemble one.

"You would say 'fledgeling,'" Willic added.

"Oh," said Lucena.

Willic looked at her with big saucer cat eyes. "Did Himself really call you that?" he asked, and when Lucena nodded his heart-shaped face broke into a great smile.

Everybody in the House called Madgrin by name, though they sometimes didn't even bother with that: a simple "Him" or "Himself" or "He" was enough to indicate who they were referring to. Everybody, that was, except those persons who were part of the House itself. To the rooms and the halls, the vestibules and the foyers, he was always "Maker." And though she sometimes thought it an odd thing to call someone, she soon discovered she could not address him as anything else; the name "Madgrin" died in her throat and "Maker" came out instead. It annoyed her at first, but secretly she still felt that "Madgrin" was a strange and frightening name, and she didn't like to say it even when she could, as when referring to him in the third person.

"Maker?" she would say upon waking, trying to get her bearings. She always felt disoriented and lost when she first woke, and it was comforting to hear his voice.

Yes? he would answer, in the back of her mind.

"Where are you?" she would ask. And he would answer; sometimes he was in his study, sometimes the library, sometimes he was not in the house at all, and sometimes he was very far away indeed. But his voice always sounded like he was standing right behind her.

Then he would ask if she had drunk yet, and that would make Lucena grumpy. She hated drinking blood; it tasted sour and metallic, and made her feel like vomiting. But if she didn't drink it she grew dizzy, and sometimes her body would refuse to move, as if the joints had frozen up. But she had a hard time bringing herself to drink, and never managed to finish the bottle that was set out for her.

Madgrin was sympathetic. *I too have been obliged to drink unpleasant things. Perhaps if you didn't think of it so much as food, but as a sort of nasty medicine?*

"Yes, nasty medicine I'll have to take forever and ever and ever!" Lucena wailed.

Madgrin was silent at this, as though there were something he were going to say but didn't. But it did help to think of the blood as medicine; certainly it tasted less awful than the stuff she had been given for fever back at school.

But it never failed to put her in a bad mood, and she would dress quickly before tearing off down the halls to find Willic, because Willic was always more than eager to show her new parts of the house, and that was a welcome distraction.

They visited the main hall next, which had the front door and was the only place in the whole house whose windows revealed what was really outside. Lucena spent a long time peering through these into the dark, but all she could discern was an expanse of grassy lawn with shaggy trees in the distance and pale paths pricked out against the night. Gazing out through the windows, Lucena was seized with the desire to get out and explore.

"All in good time," Willic said. "But you'll have to wait until Harga gets back; he's the Groundsguard, and *he'll* show you the outside."

CHAPTER 3: *In the House of Madgrin*

So they left the main hall for the time being. They visited the great hall, where Madgrin entertained important guests, and the ballroom, the west antechamber and the south hall, as well as revisiting the north hall and the east antechamber. That was a gloomy, silent place without Madgrin's music, and they didn't stay long.

"Come on, I'll show you the observatory," Willic said. "You'll like her!"

Lucena did like the observatory—both the room and its spirit. She was a comfortable, plump woman with frizzy yellow hair, and was more than pleased to show off her great domed room with star charts plastered all over the walls, and the magnificent gold telescope that sat on a rotating platform in the center. The ceiling could be rolled back by a series of cranks and levers, revealing a great swath of night sky. Even better, there was a ladder that led you up outside the domed ceiling, and if you had a good head for heights you could sit out there and stargaze. Lucena found herself very comfortable up on the dome, and it was a wonderful experience to be out in the fresh air again. Furthermore, it was a new moon, so the stars shone particularly brightly, and Willic could point out all the good constellations. He had different names for many of them, and would say things like: "There is Elrud in his Ship, which you call the Great Cauldron, but it used to be the Staff of Thash back when Vidun—that's the bright red star—was farther north and the stars made more of a straight line . . ."

"I didn't know the stars moved . . ." Lucena marveled. "I thought only the planets did that."

"Oh, they move," said Willic. "We *all* do."

Lucena gazed up at the stars in amazement, and tried to catch them moving. Like that, she was able to track their slow, stately progress across the sky—but no movement in relation to each other. The only stars that moved like that were the shooting ones, which flared in bright, brief streaks, before disappearing into the dark. Lucena counted five of them before Willic grew tired of staring at the sky and took her off across the roof, where she could look out and see the dark, rolling woodland of the grounds, and through a small door into what turned out to be the laboratory.

The laboratory was dark and dusty and very cluttered. Willic explained that a magician had once come to live with them, and Madgrin had set up this room to be his study. But he had left many years ago, so now the room was rarely visited.

Lucena found it a little creepy; there was a large work table with many strange-looking implements on it, and crude, wooden cages stacked all along one wall. A huge cauldron stood in the center of the room, and when she peered inside she found, to her disgust, a shallow puddle of rancid black sludge at the bottom. And in one corner there was something that gathered darkness around it like a shroud. So thick, Lucena could almost see it, like a floating mass of vaporous snakes twining through the air.

Willic told her that magician had left it behind when he went away, and Madgrin had decided to keep it. No one knew what it was.

"Why ever did he do that?" Lucena asked, shivering. The whole atmosphere of the room was putting her out of temper.

"I'm not sure," Willic admitted, rubbing his chin. "but I think he's curious. Anyway, it's not evil, if that's what you're worried about."

"How can you tell?"

Willic gave her a quizzical look, then went over and stuck his paw-like hand into the center of the darkness. It recoiled from him at first, but slowly eased back, covering his arm up to the elbow in swirling misty blackness. "Just because something's dark doesn't make it evil," he said solemnly.

On the way down from the laboratory they passed through a door much smaller than the others, which Lucena had to squeeze through on her hands and knees. Crawling along a tunnel, they eventually emerged into a cozy chamber which turned out to be Willic's very own room.

It was full of curiosities, from the round, gilt bed and the draperies, to the thick rug on the floor and the velvet banner that stretched across half the wall with an ornate M and G on it. But his real treasures were a ball of twine, a silver bell, three tiny gold apples, and a battered old cap. This last looked like it had once been very fine indeed—made of plum colored velvet, now faded and worn, with a royal blue feather stuck in the band, which was similarly tattered. Willic handled it with reverence and respect, telling Lucena it had been a gift from Tobius Leander.

"Who is that?" Lucena asked.

"Tobius Leander?" Willic said, gently replacing the hat next to the gold apples. "I'm surprised you haven't heard of him. He's a little shorter than you, and looks like something between a rabbit and a cat; he has golden fur and wears a monocle, and he does impossible things."

"What kind of things?" Lucena asked, curious.

"All sorts: getting blood out of a stone, making boneless creatures made of bone; running circles 'round the moon, and turning midnight into noon... that sort of thing."

"I remember reading stories about someone doing those things," Lucena said. "Only it was a magical rabbit and his name was Tobilly."

"That's him," Willic said, yawning. "Some details get muddled in the telling."

It was very warm and cozy in his room, full of comfy armchairs and pillows heaped this way and that. There was also a wide window (curtains drawn) with a window seat.

"I thought they were just stories... for children, like." Lucena said.

Willic laughed. "You'll discover, Lucena, that a lot of those stories exist because they really happened, in one way or another."

This prospect struck Lucena still with awe. The thought that all the stories that she had clung to in school could actually be real, that the heroes she had read about had actually existed, was enough to lift the morbid feeling left over from the laboratory and cause a great bubble of joy to rise in her chest.

Willic didn't notice. He curled up on some cushions and went to sleep in a very catlike fashion. Lucena was too full of her joy bubble to sit still and wait for him to wake, so she decided to do some exploring on her own. After all, to get back all she had to do was think of his room.

CHAPTER 3: *In the House of Madgrin*

The hallways were just as dark and mysterious as ever, but Lucena noticed that they changed as she went along: some of them were bare stone, others had rich carpeting, and still others had wood paneling with polished, gleaming floors. It was as if they all belonged to different houses or castles. But everywhere she went the light came from the same candle lanterns hanging from the ceiling, and these cast rings of light onto the floor leaving dark patches in between and right beneath.

By now Lucena had got the hang of looking at things sideways so they didn't slither out of sight, and so was able to wander freely up and down the corridors. She also tried several doors, but found many of them locked; and those that were not led only into more uninteresting hallways. One of these dead ended in a door that was strangely more solid than any of the others. Hoping that a door that was solid might lead somewhere more interesting, Lucena tried the handle eagerly.

The door swung open easy enough, but as soon as she put a foot over the threshold the air erupted with the sound of tortured screaming. It poured out of the room in waves, so loud Lucena put up both her arms over her face to shield herself. She stumbled back from the door and fell into someone standing in the hall behind her. Fearfully she looked up and found Madgrin's pale face looking down at her out of the darkness. He was wearing black again. Calmly he reached around her with a shadowy arm and pulled the door shut. Slowly the screaming died away, breaking off into choked sobbing before fading out entirely.

"That's better," Madgrin said, helping Lucena to her feet.

"Maker, I'm sorry—I didn't know it was forbidden," she said, terrified that she'd done something wrong and would be punished for it.

"It's perfectly all right," Madgrin said. "Nothing in my house is truly forbidden. Except Rhyse's medicine cabinet, but that is another matter."

"But, but the screaming? I thought..."

"Oh yes," he looked at the door sadly. "Some rooms don't like being entered. That one had some very nasty things happen inside it. I made it a part of the house in order for it to recover, but it has been slow going."

Lucena looked back at the door solemnly. Part of her wanted to ask what the nasty things were, and part of her didn't want to know. Madgrin settled the matter by changing the subject:

"Has Willic shown you to my study yet?"

"No, not yet," Lucena said.

"Would you like to see it now?" he asked.

"Er," Lucena said, taken aback. "Yes, yes please."

Madgrin smiled a wide, blue-lipped smile, and offered Lucena his hand. She took it, and found herself immediately whisked off her feet.

Madgrin did not walk through his house; he flew. Through corridors and up stairs he went, swift as a dark wind. Lucena trailed behind, hanging onto his hand for dear life. She gasped every time he dove for doors she didn't see until the last moment, and very nearly fainted when they whirled up a spiral staircase at top speed. When her head stopped spinning she found they were floating sedately through a room filled with doors. Not just doors in the walls, but doors floating in midair, drifting lazily across the room. Madgrin made for one in particular; a wide one of carved dark wood. He reached out a hand and pulled the door open by the gold ring fastened in place of a doorknob, ushering Lucena inside.

She stumbled into a long oval room with a wide oak desk at the far end. This was intricately carved with decorations and legs like dragon feet, and an equally carved lamp sat on top of it; behind it was a very grand chair draped in blue velvet with silver edging. Beside the great desk was a smaller writing desk, and here a thin woman sat in a plain chair working with a stack of parchment and books. She was scratching busily away at a long roll of parchment, and didn't even look up as Lucena took a shaky step forward.

Behind the desks the room rose up in three tiers, each tier holding shelves of books, like a miniature of the library, curving around the two desks. Through these she saw a triptych of stained-glass windows: a horse on the left and a bird on the right, and something that looked like a winged lion with horns in the center. There were also some nice armchairs placed here and there among the shelves, so if you found a book you liked you could sit down without going far.

The floor of the room between herself and the desk was covered by a carpet. At first Lucena thought it was just random blotches of green and brown and blue with white streaks, but as she drew closer she saw it was in fact a map of the continents of the world. And it was different from the ones she had studied in school: Adamanta was a lot smaller, and the Beranicas were bigger. There was also a lot of white ice around the south edge that had not been on the maps at all.

It was a magical carpet, Lucena soon discovered; the more she stared at a certain place, the more it enlarged. At first this was nice, for she could see the details of mountains and rivers and forests and cities, but as they grew larger they also grew more real, until she could see every blade of grass and feel the wind on her face. Almost like she was really there.

Madgrin came over and touched her gently on the arm. She came back to herself with a gasp to find him twinkling an amused smile at her.

"Careful now," he said. "Wouldn't want you to slip away as soon as you arrived."

Avoiding the carpet, Lucena cast her gaze elsewhere and arrived at the fireplace set into the wall to her left. This was currently holding a drowsy fire that cast more warmth than light, and seemed to glow faintly from within, though it was made of grey stone. This was carved in the shape of a yawning dragon, whose lower teeth made a sort of grill to keep the fire from spilling out into the room, and whose tongue held the logs. Its horns and the fringes on its cheeks twisted out from the wall to make hangers for drying coats or hats and for holding pokers and dustpans. Surrounding the lower jaw of the dragon were nine tiles of polished marble, each one carved with a different design: Lucena made out a ring surrounded by flames in one, a roaring lion on another. There was also a pure white one with a black bird in flight upon it, and one with a curious silver person in a bright green wood. But considering what had happened with the carpet she didn't look any closer.

CHAPTER 3: *In the House of Madgrin*

There were four banners hanging to each side of the hearth, each holding a different animal: a raven, a wyvern, a dog and a snake to the left of the hearth, and a cat, a bear, a dragon-horse, and an owl on the right. Lucena fancied the cat looked a little like Willic, with its mushroom-brown hair, and comparing the woman working behind the desk to the banner with the snake, Lucena thought she saw a distinct resemblance.

Turning around to look more closely at this woman, Lucena noticed the wall opposite the hearth. This was wood paneling, and hung all over with pictures. Again wary of looking too closely, Lucena only glanced at these. She saw a mountain, a ship with a purple sail, a craggy rock with a dragon perched on it, a city overshadowed by a truly gigantic tree, a lonely spire rising from the sea, and a few other landscapes so strange and bizarre that she couldn't make sense of them. The only piece of furniture on this side of the room was a wardrobe: a tall one with an intricate filigree of oak leaves carved on the front. For a moment she felt a sudden, unexplained urge to open it and look inside, but here she was distracted by the most wondrous thing in the whole room: the ceiling.

This was covered with tree branches, so looking up at it was rather like looking up at the canopy of a forest. Except these trees were carved from the wood of the ceiling, and their leaves seemed to be made of dark green crystal. These were packed together so closely that in places it was like a spiky green bush growing from the ceiling. And in amongst the leaves and the branches were clusters of twinkling lights. These brightened and dimmed, so that first one patch of leafy ceiling would glow, and then another, their light reflecting off the crystal leaves so they glittered and sparkled.

Lucena stood in the center of the room, her neck arched back, and stared at the ceiling in wonder. She imagined, or perhaps thought she imagined, that the lights were in fact tiny fairies, darting about among the crystal leaves.

"Do you like it?" Madgrin asked.

Lucena jumped, and found that Madgrin was looking at her expectantly—almost *nervously*—as though Lucena's opinion meant a great deal to him.

"Oh, yes," she said, smiling widely. "It's *beautiful.*"

"The inconsistent lighting is not the best for writing," said the woman behind the desk. She had a neat, clipped voice, and spoke with cold precision.

"Soloma is entitled to be critical," Madgrin said. He leaned towards Lucena, and added, "She's really a snake, you see, and is always grumpy from having to use her arms. But she does need them; she's the Secretary."

"I managed quite well without them for several hundred years," Soloma said, angrily writing away. "Who is this? I don't recall you hiring help."

"This is Lucena," Madgrin said, putting a hand on her shoulder. "She's my fledgeling, remember?"

Soloma's head went up at that, and Lucena found herself looking into a pair of flaming red eyes with slits for pupils. She swallowed hard. Soloma snorted and flicked her tongue out. It was long, thin and forked, and made Lucena shiver.

Madgrin sighed and wandered over to look down at Soloma's papers.

"Still working on the Baronian problem?" he asked.

"No," Soloma said, shuffling through the papers. "I'm on to the Cairdrians, and they're even worse."

They fell to talk of business, and not wanting to disturb them Lucena edged her way around the great desk and up into the shelves of books. If the books in the library were anything to go by, she figured these were probably even more touchy. But to her pleasant surprise none of them screamed or bled from the pages or tried to bite her, and she spent an enjoyable half hour reading a collection of Urvian folktales.

She was pulled from her fantasies by a new voice down in the study. Curious, she closed her book around her index finger and went to investigate.

Madgrin was standing by the hearth, talking earnestly to one of the banners. It was the dark blue and silver one with an owl, only now the owl was somehow alive and talking back.

"And you are absolutely certain they were vampires?" he was asking gravely.

"No doubt, my lord," the owl replied. It had a melodious, feminine voice, and gave a little hoot after every sentence.

"Thank you, Halfain, I will see to it." Madgrin turned away from the banner, which was just a banner now and not alive at all, and saw Lucena. "I'm afraid duty is calling me elsewhere," he said. "But if you are enjoying that book feel free to keep it." He moved on down the line of banners to the cat, and said, "Willic, would you be kind enough to come to my study?" And, while the cat was still yawning and saying in what was unmistakably Willic's voice, "Yes m'lord, on my way," Madgrin turned to the banner next to him, the bear, and pulled it smartly by its fringe. "Beruse," he said. The bear grumbled and turned its great shaggy head to him. "We have a hunt this morning." At that the bear smiled a wide, bestial smile, and said in a rumbling voice, "Good. My bones were growing cold."

Lucena watched this with fascination, and was so enchanted by the living banners that when Soloma reached up to check the title of the book Lucena was holding she flinched. Soloma made a "*Tss, tss*," sound, flicking out her tongue. Having satisfied herself as to the book she retreated back to her desk, where she put away her quills and papers and got out a shawl.

Lucena was about to ask where they were going and what was going on, but then a familiar dizziness began addling her mind, and a grey mist spread before her eyes.

"Oh, oh bother!" she cried, feeling her legs give way. The last thing she saw was Madgrin swooping towards her. Lucena did not remain conscious long enough to know whether he caught her, but she had no bruises when she woke the next evening.

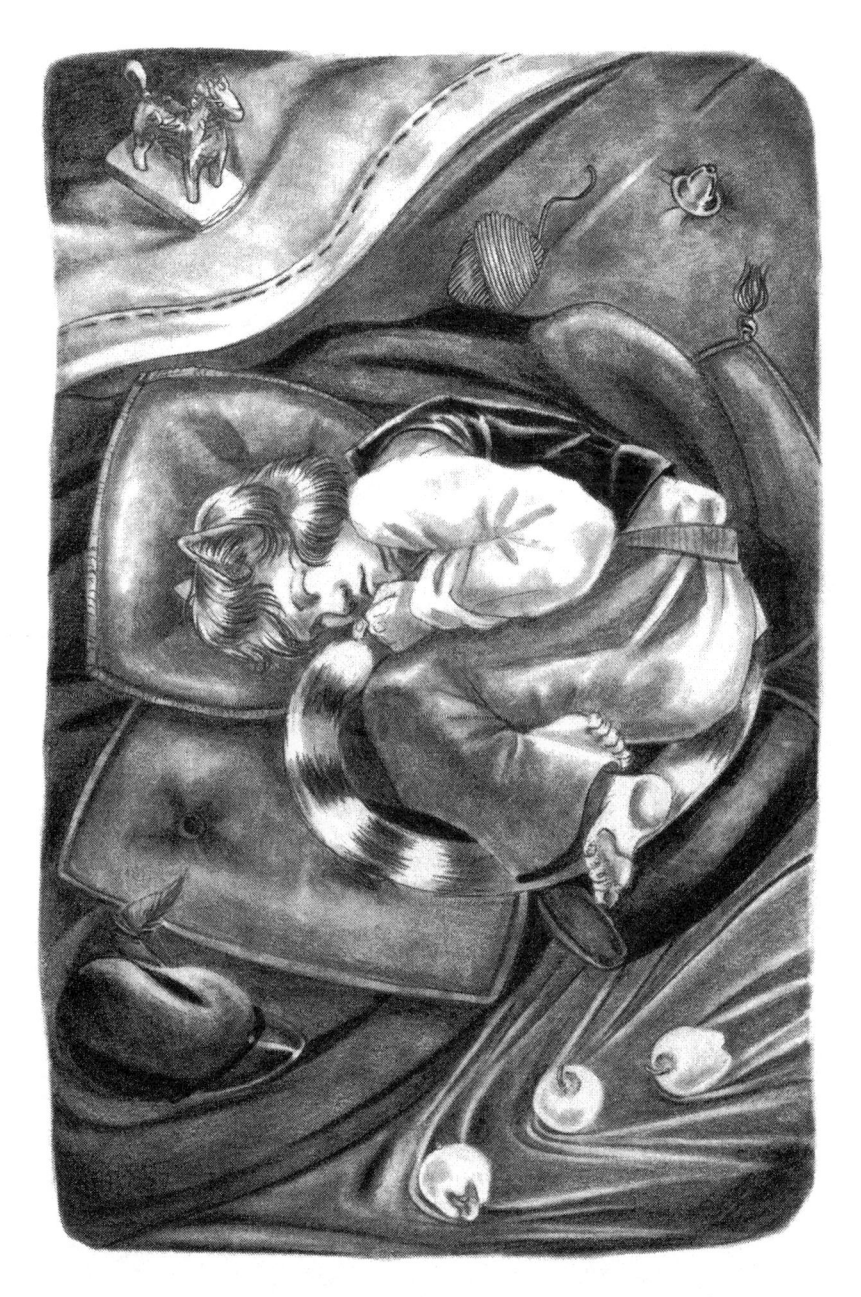

He curled up on some cushions and went to sleep in a very catlike fashion.

CHAPTER 4:

The Groundsguard,

LUCENA HAD JUST CHOKED DOWN most of her bottle of blood (she still couldn't bear to drink it from a glass), when Rhyse stormed into the room. She was carrying a worn dress with patches in the skirt and a heavy apron, which she threw on Lucena's bed.

"You'll want to wear that tonight," she said, her voice grating with displeasure.

Lucena couldn't tell whether the displeasure was directed at her or if it was a symptom of Rhyse's generally bad temper, so she only nodded meekly. But Rhyse didn't go away. She rambled around the room dusting the already dustless bureau and polishing the unused mirror, grumbling under her breath the whole time.

"Er, is something wrong?" Lucena asked timidly.

Rhyse froze. Her whole posture tense, she looked ready to lunge for Lucena's throat.

I'm a vampire, Lucena reminded herself. *She can't kill me unless she stabs me with her broom handle.*

But all Rhyse did was scowl and storm out of the room.

Feeling bewildered, Lucena dressed herself in the shabby clothes that had been laid out and went to find Willic. Instead, along a particularly dark corridor, she ran into the back of a large someone who was struggling along under a load of cloth-wrapped parcels.

The parcels came down in a thudding crash, one of them nearly squashing Lucena against the wall. The person said, "Oh bother and butcher this!" as the last parcel slipped out of her grasp and fell on what must have been her toe. She cursed, deeply, in a language Lucena did not know, and hopped about on one foot. In the dim light Lucena hadn't been able to make her out under the parcels, which had been wrapped in dark cloth, but now she had dropped them Lucena saw her clearly.

She appeared to be a woman, even though she was wearing baggy trousers and the kind of men's boots that came up nearly to one's knees. She wore a leather vest tied up the front with string, and a necklace made of large, round pendants. She was a good deal taller than Lucena, but didn't look it because she was so wide. She had thick, wide shoulders, massive arm muscles, and short, strong legs. She had a round, dark face, which was made even darker by her flush, surrounded by a thick mane of golden-brown hair. Her hair was so thick, and fell about her shoulders in such a shaggy heap, that Lucena was immediately put in mind of a lion. She even had small, rounded furry ears growing out the top of it, rather like Willic's. But something about her massive frame, and the way she loomed

CHAPTER 4: *The Groundsguard*

over Lucena, blinking down at her with bright, black eyes, made Lucena revise her opinion.

Not a lion, she thought. A *bear*.

"Oh, I'm terribly sorry!" she gasped, backing herself further against the wall, wishing to heaven a door was there.

The bear-woman gave her a dim, slow look. She scratched herself behind her neck, making her mane of hair even bushier. She looked from Lucena to the spilled parcels, put her hands on her hips, and heaved a great sigh.

"Don't apologize," she said. "No harm done. Probably. Harga will understand."

"I'm sorry all the same," Lucena said. "Here, let me help you carry them," she added, moving to pick one up.

"I don't think so," the bear-woman said. "They're too heav—" She broke off as Lucena wrapped her arms around one and lifted it into the air. It was heavy, but Lucena fancied she had gotten stronger from being a vampire, and she could carry it with little difficulty.

The bear-woman stared at her in amazement. Then something occurred to her and she dashed round to Lucena, grabbing her by the hair and pulling up her lip to get a look at her teeth.

"Argh, *hey!*" Lucena said, which was all she could manage. The bear-woman gave a satisfied grunt and let her go. She was beaming.

"I thought so!" she said. "You're Himself's fledgeling, aren't you? He was telling me all about you just this morning."

"I'm Lucena," Lucena said, tenderly feeling the inside of her lip with her tongue.

"You can call me Beruse," the bear-woman said. She picked up the three remaining parcels, one in each hand and the other in her arms. "I'm the Porter."

Of course, Beruse was the name of the bear on the banner in Madgrin's study. The one he called to help him fight vampires.

Lucena eyed her new acquaintance warily, searching for signs of aggression, but found none; Beruse only looked at her expectantly, which made Lucena remember her manners.

"I'm very pleased to meet you. Where are we taking these?"

"Down to the postern door," Beruse said, walking sideways so she could see Lucena. "And then out to Harga's den. Have you been outside yet?"

"No, not yet."

"Hmph. That's our Willic for you. A good cat, but he's completely housebound. If you ask me, I think he's *scared* of the outdoors, but don't tell him I said so. He's a dear, really, and brave on his own terms."

Beruse talked cheerfully in this way all the way down to the postern door, which was through a small entry hall decorated with suits of armor not far from the kitchen.

There was a man waiting for them there. He stood beside the door, looking hunched and uncomfortable. He was wearing a rain-speckled overcoat and gloves with holes in the fingers, shabby mismatched boots, and an extraordinary hat that looked like a frilly mushroom someone had stepped on. This he took off guiltily when he saw them coming, and Lucena saw he had a mane of messy hair similar to Beruse, only his was shorter, less bushy, and black with white flecks. He also had floppy dog ears, which perked up when he saw the parcels. He had a weathered face with a heavy brow, soft brown eyes and about a week's worth of stubble on his chin. Lucena found herself liking him at once.

"Ah," he said in a hoarse voice as Beruse plodded down the hall to him. "They came?"

"Yes indeed," Beruse said proudly. She held out the parcels to the man, who must have been none other than Harga. He reached for them gladly, realized he was still holding his hat, slapped it back on his head, and took them into his arms. He counted them.

"There's only three," he said, looking dismayed.

"Please sir, I've got your fourth," Lucena said, trotting up as fast as she could. Harga looked around his parcels at her, surprised. Then his eyes crinkled up around the corners, and he smiled. It was a wrinkly smile full of yellow teeth, but so kind and genuine that it made Lucena feel warm all over. "I can help you carry them," she offered. Harga, she decided, was very much like Willic; he was one of those people that made you happy just by being present.

"Thank you very much," Harga said, bobbing his head. "You must be Lucena."

Lucena nodded vigorously.

"She hasn't been *outside* yet," Beruse added, rolling her little black eyes.

"Well, we can change that. Come along then," Harga said, his eyes twinkling. He went over to the door and tapped it gently with his foot. "Frayne, let us out if you please."

For a moment Lucena wondered who he could be talking to, but then the postern door swung open, as if of its own accord, and Harga stepped through it. Lucena stared at the blackness that was all she could see of the outdoors. She felt the cold night air on her face and was struck by the smells from outside: wet grass and earth, with a hint of rosemary from the kitchen garden.

"Off you go," Beruse said, giving her a small push. Lucena jerked back to herself, squared her shoulders, and followed Harga outside.

They emerged from the confines of the House into a world of silver and blue, lit by an army of stars (the sliver of the waxing moon already setting low in the west). This light was reflected back by a wide expanse of closely cropped lawn, covered in dew, which stretched out like a glittering green sea around the House. A cold wind blew up to them across the lawn, bringing with it the smell of wet grass. Lucena shivered at its touch, but only out of habit; she found in her new state that she no longer felt the cold as any form of discomfort, though Harga was pulling at the collar of his coat.

A dark path cut across the lawn, leading away from the House, and Harga took this. It led them over a gentle swell of lawn, past some odd-looking trees (one had grown itself into the shape of a heart), and a fountain that bubbled and gurgled with frigid, crystal water. Lucena paused to admire this, and when she glanced back the way they had come, she saw the House looming at the other end of the path. The House, she discovered, was difficult to look at; it never set-

CHAPTER 4: *The Groundsguard*

tled on one shape, but shifted forms from moment to moment: once it seemed a great square manse, then a castle, and then a strange cross between a palace with turrets at the front and a tumbledown barn at the back. A few golden lights twinkled in its upstairs windows, but for the most part it was dark, and Lucena saw it as a black silhouette against the star-filled sky.

Turning her back on the puzzling sight, she found that Harga had drawn ahead of her. He had reached the shadows of an orderly row of trees that lined the path about fifty yards ahead, but Lucena could still see him clearly. She felt startled; truly her vision had improved, for not only could she clearly see Harga's figure in the shadows of the tree, but she realized she had also been seeing in full color—not in the greyish tones she remembered from working in dim light.

The night spread out around her, and though it was dark it was also full of color. The green of the grass, the deep brown bark of the trees, even the velvety blue of the sky—and the stars twinkling in its depths burned with gold and green and red and flame-blue. There were even patches of the sky that seemed flushed with color, like clouds at sunset.

It was wonderful: Lucena kept finding herself seeing things that would have ordinarily been covered in shadow, and seeing them clearer than ever before. She got so distracted with seeing things that she didn't notice when the trees lining the path spread out and became a proper wild wood. But she noticed when the path became a mere trail, and she had to pick her way over roots and rocks.

Here it was even darker, but Lucena found that all she had to do was look hard at something and it would come into focus. Like that, she was able to see the little gnomish people crouching by the side of the trail, looking up at her with wide black eyes. She also noticed how some of the trees had faces on their bark, and how a few things that she might have mistaken for large rocks were actually small dragons, curled up and asleep. Lucena was so fascinated with seeing what was all around her that she nearly ran right into Harga's back when he stopped to open the door of his den.

This was difficult to make out, even when she looked at it properly. It appeared to her like a pile of rocks by the side of the trail, with a rowan tree growing out the top, its roots trailing down and twining around the boulders like a net. There were no lights, no outward sign of shelter, and no windows that she could see. It looked like more forest. But then Harga gave the nearest rock a smart kick, and it rolled away inwards revealing a yawning black hole. Lucena saw it yawn farther as Harga edged inside with his cargo. The blackness seemed to swallow him like a liquid, no matter how Lucena stared.

His voice drifted back to her from inside, "Are you coming?"

Lucena shook herself and stepped into the dark.

The dark only lasted one pace. After that a warm orange light, like a low fire, began to spread up the corridor. For corridor it was, made of rocks and packed earth, but lined with dead moss and bracken so it steadily became more cosy. At last Lucena emerged into the main den: one large round room with a domed ceiling. The ceiling was bare, made of closely packed rocks, but the sides were covered with mismatched panels of wood that looked like they had been scavenged from many different places. There was a little hearth in one wall, and this was the only source of light. Harga was just standing up from lighting it, warming his gnarled hands over the flickering embers.

One half of the room was filled by a wicker basket the size of a dining table, which in turn was filled with an assortment of patchwork quilts and pillows in tattered cases. Beside it stood a small cupboard on which sat a stub of a candle, some books, a battered mug, and a pair of reading glasses. From this Lucena deduced that the basket affair must be the bed—not unlike Willic's. There was also a proper eating table; bare and unvarnished with many chips and stains, and a water pump to one side with a bucket. The floor was covered with a soft mottled carpet that she found on closer inspection to be a patchwork of different animal hides, and more hides hung on the walls. All around the edge of the room were piles of pillows, substituting for proper chairs. Finally, on the wall next to the hearth was a banner similar to the banner in Willic's room. But where Willic's had been made of fine velvet, this appeared to be old wool, and the M and G were not so fancy, and seemed to have been done in needlepoint rather than embroidery. Lucena frowned, remembering the banners that hung in Madgrin's study. The cat had been Willic, and Soloma was certainly a snake, and the bear was Beruse. Would that make Harga . . .

"Say," Lucena said, before she had quite finished thinking. "Are you really a dog?"

Harga gave her a big-eyed, soft look. But she didn't seem to have hurt his feelings at all. "I prefer to think of myself as really a person," he said. "But originally yes, I was—and still am—a dog."

"I suppose Willic is a cat," Lucena said, following Harga to the table where he set his load of parcels down. She did the same with hers. "Soloma is a snake, Beruse a bear." She frowned.

"You have it right," Harga assured her. "Indeed, we do not try to hide the fact. It is only that these human forms grant us certain advantages in the performance of our duties." He lifted his hands, fingers spread wide, and wiggled his thumbs.

Lucena shook her head. "No, no, it's not that. It's only . . . there were *eight* banners in Maker's study. Eight banners with a different animal on each. I've only met four of you."

Harga was nodding, and beginning to unwrap the first parcel. "You have met the Staff, which to be fair also includes our hoblin friends. The others are the Keepers, one for the doors of the House, one for the gates of the grounds. And there is the Watch for day and night."

The images of a horse and a wyvern, followed by a raven and an owl, flashed through Lucena's mind as Harga spoke. It gave her a thrill of excitement, and she caught her breath. Harga looked at her with a crinkling smile that reduced his eyes to twinkling cracks.

"You have already met Frayne, the Doorkeeper," he remarked. "Though perhaps you did not see her. She's the horse."

Lucena opened her mouth to ask about this, but at that moment the last of the wrappings fell away from the parcel Harga had been working at, and the words died in her throat as she stared in amazement.

CHAPTER 4: *The Groundsguard*

It was a large egg-shaped stone, with a flat side on its bottom so that when Harga stood it on end it balanced there. Its color was blue-black and glossy, and for a moment Lucena thought it was speckled with white. But as she looked she saw that these were in fact tiny spots of light drifting about *within* the stone. Leaning closer she saw some of them dart about, almost like little fishes.

Harga grunted in satisfaction, pushed the amazing thing aside, and began unwrapping the next package. This time, Lucena watched with rapt attention.

The second one turned out to be a giant stone rose, with delicately carved petals as cool and smooth as marble, but it was hard and grey, even in the warm firelight. Harga set it gently aside and pulled the next one closer.

When unwrapped it was revealed to be a stone the size of a large, round dinner plate; thick and fat, with an odd, loopy sort of spiral carved on one side. This spiral troubled Lucena, for she could not follow the pattern at all; it changed right before her eyes. But Harga seemed pleased, and reached for the final package.

The fourth stone, when it was revealed, looked like nothing so much as a turtle with its head and legs drawn up into its shell. But there was moss growing in the crevices where its limbs ought to have been, and a battered flower in place of its head.

"Oh my," Lucena whispered. "They are beautiful."

Harga put his head on one side and looked at the four strange and lovely objects lined up on the table. "They are a fair sight," he conceded. "But that's not what they're for. They're binding stones, see? Very important."

"What are binding stones?" Lucena asked.

Harga scratched at one ear. "Think of them like anchors. Where we are is floating between two worlds, see? Most of this place wants to slide back into the world it came from, so we have to throw bits of it back into your world to keep us here."

"My world?" Lucena echoed.

"I suppose you would still think of it as the *real* world," Harga said, smiling sympathetically.

This made Lucena frown. She had been taught there were three worlds, Heaven, Earth and Hell, and having been educated by an Etherealist school she knew that all three were equally real. And this made her pause; if the House of Madgrin was from a different world, which one was it? Could it be Heaven? Could Madgrin and the rest be exiled angels? Then Lucena remembered what she was, and realized that an angel would surely never harbor a vampire, much less *create* one.

So she asked, "Which world are you from? Heaven or Hell?"

Harga put his head on one side. He seemed surprised. "Neither," he said. Then, seeing the troubled look on Lucena's face, "I'm afraid things are a little more complicated than what you've been taught. Would you like to help me place these binding stones?"

Glad of a distraction, Lucena agreed whole-heartedly. She helped Harga load the stones into a large, leather sack, and together they set off into the forest.

Harga led her back up the way they had come, stopping only once to kneel by the side of the path. There he lifted a large leaf off what Lucena had thought was a rock. But as soon as Harga removed its cover it came alive, blinking beady, stone eyes and yawning a mouth full of teeth.

"Sorry for disturbing you," Harga said, giving the stone head a soft pat. "We're replacing the binding stones tonight. Hold steady." He replaced the leaf and moved on. The stone head made a grumbling noise and chomped its jaws after him.

Lucena was tempted to lift the leaf again to get a closer look at it, but those jaws had looked strong, and she did not want to annoy it.

Soon she noticed the trees becoming thinner, less wild, and more and more starlight filtering in through the branches. The path became mottled with light and dark patches, and then they were walking down an avenue of orderly trees, and Lucena could just see the dark shape of the House across a swell of bright green lawn. When they had come out of the trees completely Lucena looked back at the forest out of which they had come, and gasped.

There was no forest. Behind her was only the path, with the orderly row of trees, and these lasted for maybe fifty yards before they stopped, and the path stopped too; dead ending in a garden bench that looked out over rolling hills of perfectly manicured parkland.

When she exclaimed at this, Harga smiled and patted her kindly on the shoulder.

"Distance is flexible here," he explained. "You can get to the forest simply by going into any group of trees."

"Then how do you get over there?" Lucena asked, pointing beyond the trees to the rolling hills.

"You go around them, don't you?" Harga replied. "Here, I'll show you." And he left the path and stepped off over the grass, leaving dark footprints in his wake.

Lucena followed him, back down and around the orderly row of trees, until they came to the garden bench. Here Lucena could see more of the parkland; it fell away from the bench in a gentle curve down to where a slow river wound its way through the grounds. Between the bench and the river it was covered in a mass of hedges, and these she saw were cut into the shape of a great maze.

"That is the Labyrinth," Harga said, gesturing at it. "Like the trees, it also leads to broader places. We'll be stepping just inside to replace its binding stone, but don't enter it otherwise unless you have either myself or your Maker with you."

Lucena nodded gravely and followed as Harga ambled down the gentle slope to where the hedges began. Up close they were much taller than she had thought before, thick and prickly, with leaves so dark that even with her excellent night vision they appeared black. There was a gap in the hedge just wide enough for one person to pass, and here was a path laid with pale stones that shone brightly in the starlight. Harga stepped through the opening, looking neither left nor right, and Lucena instinctively did the same. So she did not see much of the inside of the Labyrinth, though she got the impression of high, dark hedges on either side, with twiggy branches that reached out and plucked at her sleeves.

A few paces into the maze Harga stopped. Here the path was wider, though paved with the same pale stones, and at his invitation Lucena came around and

CHAPTER 4: *The Groundsguard*

saw why he halted: there in the path before his feet was one stone that did not reflect the starlight. It was dull and grey and so cracked and crumbled it had nearly turned to earth, but Lucena thought she could just make out the remnants of what might have once been a spiral groove carved into its face.

"He left this one rather late," Harga grumbled, putting down the sack that held the replacement stones. "Here, help me clear away what's left of it. Then we'll set its successor in place."

This they did, and when all the fragments of the old stone had been removed, Harga took the new one from his sack, and Lucena helped him fit it into the neat hole they had created.

The moment the stone slid home there was a snap, and all the shadows suddenly became darker, deeper, and the stones glowed more brightly than before. There was a rustling in the hedges, and when Lucena looked up she saw they were no longer on a path, but in a small square with only one path leading away through the hedges. She gasped in surprise, but Harga just gave a satisfied sigh.

"It's working already. See? The Labyrinth is showing us the way out." He hefted the sack over his shoulder and walked confidently out through the hedges. Lucena followed, suddenly less sure of the place. But the path ran straight and true, and soon they emerged from the bushes.

"One done, three to go," Harga announced, and set off across the lawn. Lucena kept close behind him, darting glances over her shoulder at the dark twisting mass that was all she could see of the maze.

At first the grounds stumped Lucena as much as the house had, and unnerved her almost as much as the Labyrinth. As Harga had said, distance was flexible. It was so flexible Lucena had to think of the whole place as having different levels. There was the flat, real level with the house and the main roads and paths, the lawns, the maze, the river and the row of trees. But if you went into the trees, you left that level and entered another one (Lucena thought of it as going upstairs), which was the real forest. Similarly, once they left the path and proceeded across the wide, stretching lawn, she found the grass much taller, with patches of heather growing here and there, and gorse bushes and small trees in place of statues. There was no sign of the house, or the trees, or the maze. There was a great dark outcropping in place of the house, but as they drew nearer Lucena saw it was the outline of a person, sitting with their legs crossed and their head sunk upon their chest in sleep. Harga took no notice of the giant, pausing just beneath its elbow. Here he knelt and poked at something, before giving a satisfied grunt and wandering off among the high grass. Soon they came to a rough trail, which gradually become clearer and clearer, until Lucena found they were walking along a gravel path beside one of the sloping lawns.

"Where was that?" she asked Harga.

"The moor," Harga replied. "It's one of the anchors where the binding stones lie. That one's still fresh, so we needn't bother with it. We already took care of the Labyrinth, but there's still the Wood, the River, and the Sea. We always have Wood, River, Sea and Labyrinth, and Land—but that changes whenever we move. These days it's a moor, but a long time ago it was a desert. That was when we lived near Tokmuk."

"Tokmuk?" Lucena echoed, turning the word over in her mind. That was on the other side of the Dragonridge Mountains, and far to the south. She had read that the people there were dark savages who had rejected God, and so they were not made to read very much about it. It had always felt like the other side of the world to her, and then she realized she was not sure she was even in that world anymore. It made her feel lost.

"Just where are we? I mean, where is the House of Madgrin?" she asked.

"Between dream and day and night and fear," Harga recited. "But geographically? We're closest to Kyreland, although he moves it about from time to time."

That was some comfort, Lucena supposed. But she was still feeling slightly lost as they came over a rise in the lawn and stood looking down at a small pond. It had rushes growing all around its banks, and the place rang with the croaking of frogs. There was a tiny island at its center; hardly more than a jumble of wet, mossy rocks, it was connected to the shore by a high, arched bridge.

"This is the Sea anchor," Harga explained. "It's one of the oldest. Perhaps you would like to replace its stone? You've seen, it's not so difficult."

Lucena was not at all sure about this, but Harga seemed so earnest and sincere that she hated to disappoint him. So she agreed, and he reached into his sack to give her the stone. It turned out to be the blue, egg-shaped one with specks of light floating inside. She took it reverently and began to make her way down to the pond. Halfway there she paused and called back, "How will I find the old one?"

"You'll find it in its own house," Harga answered, "but you must cross the bridge to see it."

This turned out to be harder than Lucena expected. The bridge was so high she could not see over its top when she stood at the bottom, and so steep that there were planks nailed across it to act as steps. She was forced to clutch the egg-stone to her chest with one arm and pull herself up by the railing with the other. Once or twice her foot slipped, and she nearly slid back down again.

As she crested the bridge she found herself blasted by a strong wind. It smelled of salt and seawater, and tugged her hair from its neat bun and blew her skirts every which way. Raising her arm against this assault she looked back and saw the peaceful grounds and rush-lined pond. But ahead . . .

Squinting through the wind, Lucena saw the bridge go down, down, farther than she had climbed, to a small, grassy island with a hut and a rocky knoll and a few twisted trees. And all around the island was a great, grey, crashing sea.

Clutching the egg-stone tightly to her side, Lucena used her other arm to grip the railing, now for support against the wind as well as balance. It seemed a long way down to the island, as though she were coming down from the clouds themselves, and when she stepped at last from the slick, wet wood of the bridge to glorious, solid land her legs were shaking.

Crouching in the relative calm of the knoll she took several deep, calming breaths, even though she didn't need them. The island was all wet rocks and slick grass and dripping, twisted trees. Even the hut seemed to be made from the same gnarled, dark wood. Still, it was bound to be quieter and drier inside,

CHAPTER 4: *The Groundsguard*

and remembering Harga's instructions, Lucena stumbled over to its low door and went in.

She found herself in a small, square room, one wall of which held a complicated mass of knobs, wheels and cranks. The opposite held a bookshelf filled with books, and there was an armchair tucked away in the far corner. In the center of the room was a chest-high table, the sort used for displaying heavy, valuable books, but instead of books it held a chipped, egg-shaped stone the color of a stormy sea.

Found you! Lucena thought with delight, and carefully set the new binding stone down so she could remove the old one. But the moment she touched it it cracked violently and then disintegrated into a thousands shards of sea-colored rock. Outside, the wind howled more fiercely than ever. Moving quickly, Lucena swept away all the shards and then took up the new stone, fitting it carefully into the slight dip in the table left by the old one.

As with the Labyrinth, the moment the new stone slipped into place she felt the world shift around her. The wind ceased, and the sound of the crashing waves became more gentle. Lucena gathered up the remains of the old stone in her apron, and went back outside.

The island was unchanged, but everything else was completely different; now the waves rolled peacefully under a clear, starry sky, with only the softest breath of fresh wind humming through the trees. The bridge too, when Lucena looked at it, seemed somehow sturdier, more solid.

Pleased with her work, she climbed proudly back up the bridge—up, up, up—careful all the time to keep the shards from the old stone safe in the folds of her apron. There was an odd moment at the crest of the bridge, when she could look back down at the island on one side, and to the grounds of the House, much closer, on the other. But then she passed it and was engulfed in the sweet, calm air she was familiar with, and could only see the solid shapes of the hills and trees of the grounds.

Harga was waiting for her on the far side of the pond, rearranging his sack, which by the look of it was much lighter.

He must have gone and replaced a different stone while I was away, Lucena mused. I wonder which one?

"How did it go?" he asked when she arrived, forestalling any questions on her part.

"I did it!" Lucena announced proudly, and offered up the shards in her apron as proof. "But I didn't know what to do with the remains of the old one."

Harga seemed surprised. His eyes went wide and round and his ears perked forward, like a dog that sees a squirrel. Then he smiled and shrugged.

"That don't matter much of anything," he said. "But it was thoughtful of you to bring them back. Here, I'll take them..." and so they transferred the shards to his sack. Lucena was glad; it had been a bother holding her apron up.

They left the pond behind, following a narrow path that cut through the grass and led them into a little wood.

"Wood anchor here," Harga said. "I replaced its stone while you were on the island."

"I see," said Lucena. Then a thought occurred to her: "But what about the other wood, the one where your den is?"

Harga looked over his shoulder and blinked at her. "This *is* that wood," he said, and walked on.

Lucena decided the less she tried to make sense of that the better she would feel. She was the sort of person who liked to have an internal map in her head of the place she was in, but in the House of Madgrin that was impossible.

Then, just as she was beginning to feel truly lost, they stumbled out of the trees and onto a proper road. Dusting leaves and twigs off her dress, Lucena looked around to find they were on a wide, gravel drive with laurel bushes on either side, which ran in a gently curving arc back to the house. She could just make it out, a black silhouette behind a swell of green lawn.

"This is the main drive," Harga explained. "It's the only way to get from the house to the front gate. Since we're here, I can show you. Besides, you should meet the Gatekeeper." So saying Harga turned and crunched off across the gravel, away from the house.

Along a curve of the road, when the house was completely out of sight, the road came to a river, wide and dark, which it crossed with a high stone bridge. There was a dock on the near bank, at the base of the bridge, lit by a lonely yellow lantern. Craning her neck back to see, Lucena wondered at how the dock was empty; not even a raft was tethered there. She asked Harga where the boats were.

"Boats?" he said. "We don't use boats. That's our river, and a boat can't navigate all of it."

"What do you use then?" Lucena asked.

Harga chuckled. "All in good time."

They had crossed the bridge, and now the road was lined with tall oak trees. Lucena wondered if these were another part of the wood, and if the road would become a tiny path once more, but it never did. The road ran, straight and true, all the way to the front gate. This was a massive, wrought-iron contraption set in a wall at least twenty feet high. The wall was made of huge slabs of stone, so old they were chipped and crumbling in many places, covered in swathes of moss and hanging lichen. The gate looked equally ancient, brown with rust and its prongs bent and distorted. Or perhaps it had been made that way. This was the kind of ornate gate Lucena's adoptive family had on their own grounds; the sort that opened in the middle, and was made of twisting bars of metal set under a stone arch. But where that other gate had had designs of flowers and vines woven into the bars, this one had more mysterious patterns. Lucena had difficulty making sense of them, for they seemed to move and wriggle under her gaze, but they put her in mind of spiked, winged serpents. And even though there were plenty of open spaces large enough for Lucena to stick her head through, she could not see anything beyond the gate.

"A-*hem*," said a hoarse voice, from somewhere above them.

Lucena looked skyward, and found herself staring into the glowing red eyes of what she had at first taken to be a statue set at the crest of the stone arch. It still looked a little like a statue, but only because it was the same mottled grey-brown with patches of mossy green as the stones beside it, for it was undoubtably alive.

CHAPTER 4: *The Groundsguard*

"Do you need this gate open, or are you just going to stand there?" the not-statue creature said, its beak-like mouth opening and shutting with a snap. Lucena realized that she was looking at a wyvern, but a much bigger wyvern than any she had seen before. Those had been mere pets, hardly bigger than a cat. This one was the size of a lion. It perched on the arch, its bird feet digging long talons into the stone, its snake tail drooped over one edge, the tip flicking impatiently. The feathers of its wings were tattered and stuck out in a bush near its shoulders; it had a crest of scales along its neck that identified it as male, and two corkscrewing horns grew out of ridges that cast shadows over its intense red eyes. These looked from Harga to Lucena and did not blink.

"Greetings, Kerebryt," Harga said, touching his hat. "We won't be needing your service now. Just wanted to introduce you to young Lucena here. Lucena, meet Kerebryt, our gatekeeper."

"Very pleased to meet you," Lucena said, dropping a curtsey. She had read one should be polite to wyverns, for they were related to dragons and thought highly of themselves.

Kerebryt was amused. He ruffled his wings and craned his long neck down to get a better look at her.

"So *you're* the little thing I saw Madgrin carting back here last week." He chuckled in his throat, not an unpleasant noise. "He's never had a fledgeling before, you know. You're going to have an interesting time of it."

Lucena was not quite sure what to say to this, but Kerebryt apparently didn't expect an answer. He turned around on his perch, his back to them and long snake tail curling around a prong of the gate. Turning his head all the way around to look at them over his folded wings, he added: "Don't worry, little fledgeling. My gates will open for you and close on your enemies." Then he stuck his head under a wing, and went to sleep.

"My, I think he actually *likes* you," Harga said as they walked back along the drive. They crossed the bridge, then turned left to follow a well-worn path down to the dock. Here he paused, hefting the weight of his sack. There was only one binding stone left.

"Where do we go next?" Lucena asked, peering out across the water.

For answer Harga lifted his head and . . . howled. Lucena had read stories which described the sound of a wolf howling, but she had never heard it with her own ears. It was louder than she expected, and stronger; one pure note that held so that it rang out through the night air. It raised the hairs on her neck and sent a shiver down her spine; but stranger still was the incongruous sight of that sound coming from Harga's human mouth.

"What was that for?" Lucena asked when he had finished.

"To get to the last anchor we need a ride," Harga explained. "Look, here he comes now," and he pointed with his free hand out across the water.

Down the river, paddling sedately towards them, was a giant duck. It was unmistakably a duck: a very fine mallard, with a glossy green head and bright white neck band. But he was the size of a draft horse, only wider, and his bill was as long as Lucena's forearm. He paddled up to them and waited by the dock, effortlessly keeping in place against the gentle current.

"Good evening, Tem," Harga said gravely, and bowed. Lucena did likewise.

Tem bobbed his head respectfully to Harga, but he eyed Lucena sharply.

"This is Lucena," Harga explained. "She's Madgrin's fledgeling, and she'll be coming along, if that's all right."

Tem made a hissing snort, and shuddered his head.

"Now, now, Tem," Harga said reprovingly. "There's no need to be difficult; of course she won't bite you."

This mollified the giant fowl, and after some more muttered encouragement from Harga, he allowed her to climb onto his smooth, wide back.

Sitting on a duck the size of a cart horse was a tricky matter. While Harga sat in front, with his legs dangling neatly on either side of Tem's neck, Lucena kept trying to sit sideways on his back, and nearly slid off into the water more than once. At last she settled for sitting with her back against Harga's, and her legs trailing off over Tem's folded wings.

At first this suited her very well; Tem did not pitch up and down like a boat, so holding on was not an issue. He was completely stable in the water, as all ducks are, and only rose and fell with the swell of the small waves. But he moved swiftly, his bright orange feet powering them effortlessly down the river.

Once they were properly on the river, having passed under the bridge of the main drive and coasting along the oak-lined shore, Tem began to relax. He talked to himself in a crooning undertone, which mingled with the rushy sloshing of the river. After a few minutes of this, when she was not unexpectedly ejected from her seat, Lucena began to relax as well. Peering around with her powerful new eyes she saw a lightness up ahead; this turned out to be the oaks giving way to wide grassy shores with weeping willows bending lazily in the breeze. The river itself slowed so much it became almost like a pond, and she could smell the odor of water plants and flowers thick all around her.

Growing braver, Lucena took firm hold of Harga's sleeve and leaned her head out over the dark water. Looking straight down, sometimes she thought she caught glimpses of pale shapes darting about beneath them. But whether they were fish, or something else entirely, she could not be certain.

She had forgotten her vampiric strength. Harga made a keening sound, and she felt his thick fingers gently pry her hand away from where it was clamped on his arm.

"Oh, I *do* apologize!" she said, hastily letting go. She steadied herself by bracing her hands on Tem's smooth back. "But I cannot swim."

Harga laughed, a great, deep, woofing laugh that made Tem ruffle his feathers in irritation. "Ah, don't worrying about falling in, we'll fish you out."

"But, what if I sank?"

"That's what we have poles and fishing lines for, don't we?"

"But I could drown!"

Harga twisted his neck around and gave her a quizzical look, shooting it over his shoulder from under one tufty eyebrow. "Lucena," he said kindly, "you *can't* drown. You don't have to breathe in the first place."

CHAPTER 4: *The Groundsguard*

"Oh," Lucena said in a small voice. She didn't like that idea at all, but she supposed it made sense. Still, she made a conscious effort to keep taking air into her lungs and to force it out again, even though she knew it was pointless.

The river kept drifting, and they drifted swiftly with it—sometimes past open fields with the misty shape of the house in the distance, and sometimes through thick woodland where the trees sent branches so far over the river they dragged in the water. Tem wove his way in and out of these, until at last they emerged onto a wide, placid lake, so huge Lucena could barely glimpse the shores on either side.

Tem put on speed across the lake; it must have been very long, for even going fast enough to leave a wake of turbulent water it felt like they were out in the open for an hour at least. But eventually Lucena could see a current forming in the water again and guessed the river continued on out of the lake. Sure enough, the banks closed in, and with a rush and a whirl they were in swift water again.

They sailed on past a steep, grassy bank dotted with the pale tubes of closed flowers. Beyond that, the ground rose in green swells, and just beyond those she could glimpse the spiky turrets of the house, as well as the dome of the observatory, which glinted darkly in the night.

They passed another dock, simple and wooden, with a well-beaten path leading up to an avenue of trees and from there, through the now familiar, manicured parkland. After that the banks became wilder, with longer and longer grasses leaning over the water, and rushes and cattails growing in it. Every now and then they would pass an oak tree, one of the great, twisted kinds whose branches seemed to make faces at you. Aside from these there were no other trees in sight on the left-hand shore, and it was all strange meadow with long, waving grass. A sweet but heady smell of roses and pollen drifted over the water in waves. This made a stark contrast to the shore on their right, which was covered with forest down to the bank, and smelled of pine and cedar.

The river wound gently through this oddly divided landscape, until it came to a sharp bend that cut off the view of anything further downstream. The turn was so sharp Lucena felt as though they were heading into a dead end. But at the last minute Tem turned almost sideways, and they wheeled around.

Past that turn was a completely different world. The trees on the right gave way to splintered shafts of stone, while the meadows on the left were suddenly barren and rocky.

As they continued, Lucena saw stone formations rising in front of them, always on the right. She thought she could see ruined towers and castles, full of spires and battlements, with dark gaps for windows. There was also one rocky formation which looked the very image of Madgrin's profile; but as they came even Lucena saw it was just many differently shaped slabs of stone lined up side by side.

"This is the home of the fourth anchor," Harga said softly. "We call it the Roc City."

"A fitting name indeed," Lucena said, her voice full of wonder. The rocky towers and castles delighted her, they were so full of mystery.

"Fitting, but perhaps not in the way you think." Harga said. "It's not *rock* like you build walls out of, but a roc, like one of *those*," and he pointed with one thick finger to a nearby outcropping.

Lucena looked, and then had to look again because the outcropping was not stone at all, but a giant, hawklike bird. Its head was sunk on its breast, and it seemed to be fast asleep. Lucena was glad, for it was easily twice as big as Tem, and the one taloned foot she could see looked wicked. But she could understand why at first she had thought it was simply a piece of rock, for the entire bird looked like stone, from its granite beak to its chipped marble tail feathers. The ruffled feathers of its breast were hard and jagged, and its hunched wings rose like crags on either side of its head.

She understood at once. This was *roc* the Titan's bird, the king of eagles. But she had never heard of them being *stone* birds before.

This last thought she wondered aloud. Harga nodded. "Only the older ones. It is from them the phrase 'hard as a rock' comes from. Though in the earliest days the speaker meant the *birds*, not the stones."

"These ones are very old?"

"They are the oldest. They come here to sleep. And they guard an anchor." Harga hefted the bag containing the last binding stone. "We shall have to tread softly here."

Tem was becoming noticeably flustered as they paddled farther into the Roc City; the feathers on the back of his head and neck were raised, and he moved forward in jerks and surges, always looking sharply about him. Harga had to keep a firm hand on his neck and guide him with murmured instructions. Reluctantly he drew nearer the right-hand shore. The outer shore. There was a dark crevice between two pinnacles of rock, which in turn were topped with two actual rocs, asleep with their heads under their wings. Tem made for this crevice in a wide curve that brought him about so he was facing upstream when his side touched the shore. He treaded current while Harga disembarked, then helped Lucena to get down. He stayed on after that, though his wide orange eye rolled upward, peering fearfully at the towering birds above.

Harga muttered further instructions—Lucena caught only the word "*wait*"— and then he was pushing her up the crevice in front of him, away from the water.

There was a path, she discovered, carved at the bottom of the crevice, and made of a stone that mirrored the surrounding starlit cliffs, so even deep in the shadows of the pinnacles it glowed like the moon. Then it rounded a curve and terminated in a small circle of bright sand, in the middle of which she could just make out the remains of a stone that might have once been carved to look like a flower.

"Just in time," Harga muttered, and let his sack slide off his shoulder. Without needing to be told, Lucena hurried forward and cleared away what was left of the old binding stone while Harga got out the new one. Together they carried it forward and placed it in the center of the sandy circle.

By this time Lucena was ready for the click and shift as the stone slid into place. What she did not expect was to suddenly be cast into a deep shadow. Looking up sharply she found she had to crane her neck up, and up again, to see

CHAPTER 4: *The Groundsguard*

that a piece of the surrounding crags had moved and was now perched between them and the moon, staring down at them with glowing green eyes.

Even with her vampiric vision, Lucena found the backlit roc difficult to make out in detail. But she got an impression of sharp, jagged breast feathers and even sharper talons that had gouged streaks in the rock it perched on.

"Look it in the eye, and bow," Harga whispered to her through clenched teeth. "They respect that."

So Lucena dragged her eyes up from those wicked talons to where a sharp beak poked through the feathers of its face and its wide round eyes glowed like twin beacons. Not breaking eye contact, she bowed.

A crag of the roc's shoulder, which she had at first assumed to be part of its wing, swiveled around and Lucena found herself faced with *another* mean beak and *another* pair of glowing green eyes. It took a few moments for her brain to process the fact that she was not seeing two animals, but one with two heads, and when she did she found herself backing slowly away.

Harga seemed to have the same idea. But he had the sense to turn and walk back the way they had come, even stooping to retrieve his now-empty sack. Somehow Lucena forced her legs to reverse their direction and followed him, though she could feel the roc's twin stare boring into her back the entire way down to the river bank.

Miraculously Tem was still there, though the two rocs on the pinnacles had also woken. But these were apparently the sort with only one head each, and so Lucena found them rather more bearable. Still, she breathed a huge (if superfluous) sigh of relief when they had left the eerie city behind and followed the river to greener pastures.

The rocky crags of the city gave way to deep forests once more, and on the inner left-hand banks of the river they passed grass-covered fields and knolls. After a few weaving turns the river spread out to become a narrow lake, and Tem paddled swiftly over to the left shore, where he came to rest against another simple wooden dock. Harga dismounted nimbly, then helped Lucena. They thanked Tem for his help, for which the duck seemed pleased; he bobbed his head and nibbled in a friendly manner at Lucena's hand before swimming away.

Looking about her Lucena discovered some familiar landmarks: downstream, over some rolling and deceptively innocent-looking parkland, she could see the avenue of trees and the dip that held the Labyrinth, and following the path up she saw the house, looking like a castle crossed with a tumbledown barn from this side. Then she looked back at the river, which was flowing towards the front gate. Lucena frowned. There was something wrong with that. They had gotten on the river just next to the bridge of the main drive, and traveled in almost a complete circle.

"Hold on," she said. "Where does the river come from? Where does it go?"

Harga gave her a puzzled look. He made a circular motion with his finger. "Around," he said.

"But rivers don't run in circles," Lucena protested.

Harga smiled. "This one does. It rises from itself and pours into itself. It is the Neverending River, ever flowing, always turning. If it has an ending-beginning, say it is the lake, and call it only a transition."

Lucena could only glance wonderingly at the river before hurrying after Harga, now striding briskly away from the dock and up the path. This led them over the low green hills she had seen from Tem's back, and past the little thatched cottage. The top of one of these hills afforded them an excellent view of the house, rising from a sea of darkness that Harga said was the orchard. But there was another structure in view now: it lay at the base of the hill and commanded all of Lucena's attention.

It was a circular, high wall, easily a hundred feet tall, pierced with arches and tracery, and encasing row upon row of descending steps, that eventually cut off in a final drop, leaving the center a bare ring of sand. Lucena knew it by its shape alone; years ago as part of their studies on the Crowan Empire her class had visited some Important Historical Sites, one of which being the shambling ruins of the Highland Coliseum. Lucena had been awed by the majesty of the ruins then; now she was awed by the sight of that exact coliseum in all its glory. Gripped by the same wonder that she had felt as a small child, she wanted nothing more than to run down the hill and explore this majestic structure. But Harga was already making for the orchard without so much as a glance at the coliseum, and Lucena was forced to follow.

"That was the arena," he said when she drew even with him, now under the protective shadow of the orchard's trees. "Himself uses it when he has to entertain certain ... guests." And something about the hardness of his tone prevented her from asking further questions.

The trees around her had dark glossy leaves, and their branches were filled with pale apples. The tantalizing aroma of ripening fruit wafted down from above, tickling the inside of her nose.

Lucena loved orchards; her aunt, who had been a hateful stick of a woman, had an apple orchard, and Lucena's only happy memories of her time on her relative's estate was when she could flee to the orchard with a good book.

After some time the ambiance of the trees lifted Harga's mood to its natural amiability, and he began to talk again.

"The hoblins keep the orchard, for the most part. But it's my job to guard it; we've had problems with heroes sneaking in and stealing fruit."

Lucena fancied she had heard some of the stories behind these heroes, and couldn't help feeling sympathy for them. She said so.

"Oh, it's not so bad if they ask nicely and only take what they need," Harga admitted. "And you know, we had some tree ladies living with us ... oh, must have been a few millennia ago now, and the heroes never had any problem being polite and respectful to *them*, but when it's me, or Gydda, or Rhyse they run into ... well...." He grinned wryly. "They'd rather grab and run. And that's not only rude, it can be dangerous; every tree has different fruit, and without our help they can't know if they got the right one. But you know, sometimes it's not a hero that comes in over the wall; sometimes it's a villain, and then we best take care."

"What sort of care do you take?"

CHAPTER 4: *The Groundsguard*

"Actually we usually let Beruse take care of them."

Lucena thought of the large bear-woman, with her bushy hair and strong arms, but felt no sympathy for these villains.

"Does this happen often?" she asked, glancing nervously around the trees. But all was silent, dark, and peaceful.

"No, not often," Harga admitted. "But enough that we remain prepared."

They walked in silence for a time on a path between rows and rows of gnarled fruit trees, while the dark shape of the House loomed higher and higher before them. As they drew closer Lucena began to recognize the familiar smells of stonework and old wood; there was also the heady tang of fresh herbs from the kitchen garden, and another scent, behind all of it, that Lucena didn't recognize. It was a delicate, tantalizing odor that wafted through the trees. It put Lucena in mind of crystal-clear water running through dark places where pale flowers glittered like stars. Although it came and went, when she could smell it it seemed to be coming from somewhere across from the kitchen gardens. To her secret delight, Harga veered off the path in this direction, leading her through the orchard until they came to a grove of truly impressive fruit trees. These were so old they were twisted into odd shapes, like whoever had pruned them hadn't done a careful job. Still, their leaves were as bright and glossy as any; their fruit was big and round and glowed faintly. Lucena could smell them, rich and sweet and sharply tangy.

"He planted these for me," he said. "When he first made his House."

"What kind are they?" Lucena asked. Oddly, the fruit was difficult to make out from the ground. It blurred around the edges.

"All sorts," Harga said dreamily. "They change too; golden apples, silver apples, quinces, pears . . . once I had cherries with ruby pits. Here," he reached up into the lower hanging branches of the nearest tree and plucked a fruit. The leaves rustled as he pulled it free, and then snapped back into the air, as if a great weight had been removed. Harga clutched the fruit with both hands and passed it to Lucena.

"There," he said. "Have it as a gift, and tell me what it is."

Lucena turned the heavy fruit over in her hands. It was the size of a grapefruit, with thick fuzz covering the outside. When she rubbed it clean in one spot she found the skin underneath was very smooth and a rich gold. At first she thought it was an apple, but it smelled much too strong for that, and it was lumpier than an apple.

"Quince?" she guessed, hefting it.

"A *gold* quince, by the look of it," Harga said. "That's a good pick. The poets may wax on about golden apples, but in my experience, one golden quince is worth three golden apples."

Flattered, and a little awed by the fuzzy gold orb in her hands, Lucena held it close to her chest as Harga led her back towards the rear door. On their way she caught another whiff of that mysterious tantalizing fragrance, and this time it was so strong and close that Lucena stopped in her tracks and nearly turned to go find it. But Harga caught her by the arm and pulled her back.

"Ah, I'm afraid we can't go there," he said apologetically.

"Where?" Lucena asked.

Harga pointed, and she saw, through the trees, the outline of a high, jagged wall.

"That is Madgrin's private garden," Harga explained. "No one goes there unless he takes them. It can be . . . dangerous."

"It smells wonderful," Lucena said, so entranced by the scent that she barely heard Harga's words.

Harga paused, his hand still on Lucena's arm. Glancing over at him she saw he was gazing wistfully up at the wall.

"It smells of home," he said quietly. He tugged at her arm. "Come, we should get you inside; dawn is coming."

He was right. Lucena could feel it as well: a looming presence that weighed on her mind like a great, grey blanket. With one longing glance back at the wall, she allowed herself to be led up the path, out of the orchard, and to the rear door. This was a modest wooden gate set in a framework of climbing roses, their red flowers singed by the light from a small window made of orange-tinted glass set in the center. Twinkling golden lights hummed about the roses, creating a warm, welcoming vision.

This effect was ruined somewhat by the strange creature standing guard before the door, all four of its hooves planted in an aggressive stance, its horned head lowered, and its spiked tail twitching ominously. It only came up to Lucena's waist and looked like a miniature horse—but with huge, wickedly curved horns growing from its forehead and along its neck. Its eyes were black and stared at them malignantly.

Oblivious to its glare, Harga walked right up to it and bowed. "Good morning, Frayne, would you be so kind as to let Lucena in?"

Frayne shook her head and snorted. "You never introduced us properly, Groundsguard." She had a large, rumbling voice for so small a creature.

Harga was not deterred. He reached into his pocket and pulled out a carrot, which he handed to Lucena with a meaningful look.

"Lucena, this is Frayne. She's our Doorkeeper. Frayne, will you let Lucena in now?"

"Um, I'm very pleased to meet you," Lucena said, offering the carrot on her flat palm.

"Hmm?" Frayne blinked at Lucena, her tufted ears perked forward. She nosed at the carrot in Lucena's palm, nearly rolling it off. Then she lipped it up and devoured it with some alarming crunching noises. "Oh yes, yes, my pleasure and all that," she said with her mouth full. "Well go on in before you fry, and good luck."

The door behind Frayne swung open with a creak, and as it did the little beast faded away into thin air.

Clutching her golden quince, Lucena stepped up to the door, breathing in the intense smell of roses. She turned around before she went inside. Harga was still standing in the dark, his hands in his pockets and his floppy hat askew. He smiled at her.

CHAPTER 4: *The Groundsguard*

"Thank you," Lucena said, holding up the quince. "And thanks for showing me the grounds. They are quite wonderful."

Harga looked pleased. If he had a tail, Lucena thought, he would have been wagging it. He waved at her. "Good luck," he said, and disappeared into the dark.

*She thought she could see ruined towers and castles,
full of spires and battlements, with dark gaps for windows.*

CHAPTER 5:

Beruse and Willic Decide to Throw a Party

THE DEEP SLEEP WHICH TOOK LUCENA during the day continued, as absolute as death but mercifully temporary. Yet in that stone-cold slumber her mind did wander and occasionally found itself in strange places which were dreamlike in their surreality, yet felt much to her like waking life.

It was in one of these not-dreams that she found herself seated across from Madgrin at a small, homely table. There were the remains of dinner on the plates before them, and Lucena had the complacent, contented feeling of one who has just consumed a large meal, but with no recollection of it.

"Is this a dream?" she asked, just to make sure.

Madgrin shrugged. "That depends," he said, "on what you think a dream is."

"A dream," Lucena said, "is something your mind does when you're asleep. To amuse itself, I suppose. But it's just your mind; it's not real."

"Why shouldn't it be real?" Madgrin asked. "Your mind is real, isn't it?"

Lucena frowned.

"You said your mind does this to amuse itself," Madgrin said, sounding a little concerned. "Tell me, La Flein, are you bored?"

Lucena looked around the room. She had to admit there was nothing interesting to do.

"Well then, perhaps you would like to accompany me; I have a task to perform which you may find diverting."

Then they were on the roof of one of the highest towers of the house. The sky was unnervingly bright; especially in the east, where it was almost golden. But Lucena felt none of the anxiety or fatigue that usually accompanied the sunrise.

The roof was shaped like the prow of a boat, and staggered; there was a circular tower with a pointed roof and a door in its side that let out onto the flat bit they were standing on. This started out wide at the tower end before tapering off to a narrow point. A low stone wall ran around the edge, and at the narrow end was an unusual structure—part bush, part wasp's nest—covered with flaking white strips of clay with foliage sprouting out here and there. It reminded Lucena of the fungi she would find growing on old trees, except it also had a small wooden door set in its center, and two round windows of wavy glass.

Madgrin was standing beside the door, and as Lucena got her bearings she saw it open, and an astonishingly untidy man stepped out.

He was tall, though not as tall as Madgrin, with rumpled black hair that stood on end in places. He had a high, arched nose and heavy brows; his eyes were black and so was his skin, and he was clothed in what looked like a cape made of tattered pieces of black cloth.

"Good morning, Rusion," Madgrin said.

The man, Rusion, bowed, and as he did Lucena saw that the fluttering pieces of black cloth on his back were not cloth at all, but a pair of wings, as black and rumpled as his hair. He stretched them out so they were impossibly wide, shrugged, and rubbed his eyes. Blinking the sleep out of them he looked right at Lucena, and frowned, as if he were not certain what he was seeing.

"Rusion, this is Lucena," Madgrin said. Lucena curtseyed. "Rusion is my Day Watch," Madgrin added, for Lucena's benefit.

Rusion peered down at Lucena out of those bright black eyes. He scratched the stubbly bristle on his chin lazily, his head on one side. Without a word he went over to the parapet and crouched there, his shaggy wings half unfolded as he began to preen. In between smoothing his feathers he kept glancing at the sky, as if waiting for something.

Madgrin was doing the same. He stood with catlike stillness, the only movement being the soft dawn wind that plucked at his robes and hair. His head turned, slowly, so that his eyes passed over the entire sky, but Lucena noticed that most of his attention was focused on the southeast, where there was a head of clouds lit pink by the dawn.

She had forgotten how beautiful dawn light was; the way it lit the high clouds like delicate flower petals, and how the distant rolling greens of the grounds were coming into intense color.

They had a spectacular view of these: she could see the parkland, and the odd spiraling maze of the Labyrinth, and the gently winding strip of the main drive. If she turned around she could see the orchard, and beyond that the large green field and the tannish blob of the arena. The river was a dark streak, except where the light touched it; there it sparkled dazzlingly, reflecting the pinks and golds of the brightening sky.

It was all incredibly beautiful, but Lucena could not fully enjoy it, for even as the light grew, so did her feeling of dread. But this was different from the compulsion for sleep that she normally felt; instead of feeling dead tired, she felt more awake than she ever had. Light-headed almost, and her limbs felt like they weighed nothing at all. It was a frightening feeling, as if at any moment she could blow away like a wisp of smoke on the morning breeze.

Madgrin still stood, silent and immovable, until at last Rusion raised a hand and pointed to the southeast, where the clouds were now gold-pink. "There," he croaked in a deep, gargling voice.

Lucena looked, and by straining her eyes to their very limit, she saw a fleck of white that was not cloud. Furthermore, it was coming towards them. Madgrin watched it, a fond smile spreading across his face, and he raised one hand, trailing the fabric of his cloak, in greeting.

As the white speck drew closer, Lucena recognized it as a great pale owl. It was not entirely white; once it was close enough she saw that it had tawny wings and a speckled underbelly.

CHAPTER 5: *Beruse and Willic Decide to Throw a Party*

Lucena kept waiting to hear the beat of its wings, but that never came; it flew up, perfectly silently, and landed gently on Madgrin's outstretched hand. He brought the owl up to eye level and inclined his head, seeming to listen intently, though Lucena heard nothing at all.

When they had finished, Madgrin set the owl on the stone wall, and with a poof of rushing air there was no longer an owl, but a small woman in a frilly lilac dress with messy tawny hair that still held something of the owl about it. She also had soft, white-and-brown wings, which she folded neatly along her back after a good stretch. She seemed not at all perturbed by Lucena, and peered at her curiously out of wide amber eyes.

Madgrin beckoned to Lucena, who had backed herself up against the wall of the tower for protection against the growing light. She walked over, a little shakily, and Madgrin took her hand.

"This is Halfain," he said, "my Night Watch."

Halfain smiled a small, birdlike smile. "Very pleased to meet you," she crooned.

"P-pleased to meet you too," Lucena stammered. Her light-headedness made it difficult to talk.

Madgrin must have noticed; he pulled her in close and wrapped her in a fold of his voluminous cloak, spreading a soothing shadow over her. Turning to him Lucena caught sight of the eastern horizon, and saw with a shock that there was already a thin sliver of bright golden light creeping across it.

Madgrin raised his other hand, the hand that was not already holding Lucena's. "Rusion," he said.

Rusion stood up from the parapet, no longer messy and unkempt. His wings, freshly preened, gleamed in the morning light, and his hair was pushed back into an orderly wave. The fluttering scraps of cloth at the front of his shirt had somehow been made to lie flat, and he looked sleek and majestic.

He took one bounding stride, and in the middle of it transformed into a huge black bird. A raven, Lucena decided, as he flapped up and alighted on Madgrin's wrist. Again they spoke together silently, and in that silence Lucena's ears were gradually filled with a distant roaring sound. She saw Madgrin's lips move, and Rusion's thick beak open and close. The brightness in the east was almost overpowering. Then Madgrin dipped his arm and launched Rusion into the sky.

And then...

Then the world around her shredded away, her last glimpse that of a black shape beating its wings furiously across a bright blue morning sky.

That evening she woke in her bed in the same position in which she had lain down, with all her things in order. But she held a stiff black feather and a soft tawny one clutched in her hand.

Lucena did not see Madgrin again for many nights after the strange dream—which had not, she was inclined to think, been a dream at all. She put the feathers in an empty blood bottle, and put that on her bureau, to remind her of this. But she did not talk to anyone, not even Willic, about it. At first she told herself that it was simply a ludicrous story and she would be laughed at. But in her heart she knew her new friends would not think it so, and the real reason she did not speak was out of fear.

Fear, not of Madgrin, but of what he might be. What he had to be, in order to make a dream so real. Lucena had read of creatures of the night who toyed with and tortured mortals in their dreams; such victims were often driven mad by fear of sleep, and went to great lengths to stay awake, only to succumb at last to fatigue, and die in gruesome, mysterious ways.

She did not want to think of kind, smiling Madgrin as one of them.

Yet it was a nagging thought, as persistent as a fly at a window, and she couldn't stop pondering the idea of Madgrin, and who and what he was.

This condition was only exacerbated by his behavior, for though she spoke to him nearly every evening she rarely saw him in person; he was always away "hunting" according to Willic. And the staff made no secret that his prey was other vampires.

Lucena had been taught that vampires begat vampires and were the enemy of humanity. So what did that make someone who could create a vampire, yet asserted that he himself was *not* one? Well, if he was not a vampire then perhaps it made sense for him to hunt them. And she took comfort in this; for if he hunted vampires then surely he was on the side of good. But the fact remained that he had turned *her* into a vampire, and the only thing Lucena knew that could create a vampire was *another vampire*. The whole string of questions ran itself around in circles so much that it wore tracks in her mind and stuck there, so the next time Madgrin spoke to her she blurted it out without really thinking, before she had time to be afraid.

There was silence, as he considered the question. Finally he answered with a question of his own:

Do you still have the book Orrus gave you?

"The book? You mean *Vampires: A History?*"

Yes.

Lucena swallowed. She had carefully put the book away atop her bureau and not touched it since. The bloodstained cover filled her with dread; she had no desire to read it.

Do not be afraid to seek out knowledge, Madgrin said, seeming to read her thoughts—silly! She corrected herself, *of course* he read my thoughts!

I recommend you try it.

Lucena did not fancy herself the brightest person, but she could take a hint. Yet she was not so masochistic as to read that book on her own; she took it down to the warmth and light of the kitchen, where Willic was napping, and obliged him to read it with her.

It became a part of her night's routine; once she had finished helping Gydda with the evening's chores she, Willic and whoever else cared to join them would gather in the kitchen to hear the book read aloud.

But though Willic was an excellent reader, their progress was slow; he could only read for an hour before growing sleepy. This was just as well, since '*Vampires*'

CHAPTER 5: *Beruse and Willic Decide to Throw a Party*

was a dense Mediaeval tome, and Lucena found she could not take much before she needed a break to digest what it said.

And what it said was often disturbing, especially because, as Lucena was reminded every time she woke up, everything in the book applied to *her*.

Some of the information contained in the introduction Lucena already knew: Vampires were walking dead who rose every night to feed on the blood of the living. They had adverse reactions to sunlight, some being known to burst into flames or turn to ash if they stayed out during daytime. They could be killed by a wooden stake through the heart, fire, coffin nails, and various holy instruments. Listening to all the ways a vampire could be killed, which were far more numerous and simple than Lucena had previously known or imagined, she wondered if she was better off at all for being a vampire, or if it was just as easy to get killed when you were already dead.

Then came a statement that really made her uncomfortable; vampires did not have souls, therefore they had no morality and no conscience, their motivation coming entirely from the primal instincts of the demonic spirits reanimating their dead bodies. Only in rare cases were vampires known to have souls, and these were often fractured, incomplete, or otherwise corrupted.

There were documented cases, the book said, of a breed of vampire which retained their souls during the transition. But these were often driven mad by their predicament, and were now thought extinct. At least, they were thought extinct five hundred years ago, when the book was written. Willic gave her an intense look over the top of the book after he had read that passage, and told her that he had met a few of these "souled vampires."

"Sad people," he said. "Possessed by despair. And the few who weren't were right strange in the head. Don't you let yourself get dragged down like them, Lucena."

"So I'm a souled vampire?" Lucena said, unsure if this was a good thing.

Willic set the book down and surveyed her with one eye shut. He seemed thoughtful. "I . . . don't know," he admitted. "I'm not sure what Himself did, but you've got the spark all right. And room to grow."

That made her feel a little better. But after the dense introduction there came the historical accounts of the earliest known vampires, and Lucena forgot all about her own worries as she was swept away by the horror of it all.

Not so much by the horror of the vampires—no matter the era they all behaved in the same way—but by the reactions of ordinary people: nailing perfectly innocent corpses to their coffins, stuffing thistles in their mouths, or simply heaping them on a huge bonfire. Worse was what they did when they found a real vampire: all the different ways of slaying one which had been covered by the introduction were carried out with a grim enthusiasm that made Lucena shiver.

After hearing about one particular vampire (and to be fair, he had done some nasty things indeed) who had been drawn up on a crucifix, disemboweled, dismembered, and finally (while he was still conscious) laid out in a field to burn in the sun, Lucena had to beg Willic to stop.

"Oh, but that will never happen to you," Gydda assured her. "You're safe here, and besides, there are vampires . . . and there are *vampires*. Each one is a little different."

"Different? How do you mean?"

Gydda smiled a twinkling sort of smile, and tapped her nose. "Well, *you* for example. You've got *opportunities*, haven't you? To do things *your* way, I mean. You don't have to kill anybody, and well . . . Himself hasn't made a vampire in a very, very long time. There are lots of rules and reasons why he couldn't. So I think you are very special indeed."

Lucena had never been told that she was special in all her life before, and had never thought of herself as anything more than a disappointment, no matter what she did, so this statement made her feel awkward. She put her hands behind her back and looked at her feet, which were tucked into the same silk slippers she had worn on her first night.

"I don't feel special," she said.

"People who are rarely do," Gydda told her. "But you'll understand, once you meet some other vampires."

The thought of meeting other vampires was a disturbing one, but Lucena was soothed by Gydda's words, and the readings continued.

One evening, when they were engaged in a particularly gory chapter about the slaughter (by vampires) of a small Hartfordale town, and the subsequent massacre (by humans) of the vampires responsible, Beruse turned up to lean on the door frame and listen appreciatively to all the creative methods the humans had used to destroy their enemies.

Lucena had seen very little of Beruse, for she seemed to mostly get about during the day, and was often away with Madgrin on one of his expeditions. But now here she stood, looming in the doorway with her bushy hair frilled about her face and looking more like a bear than ever, her head cocked to one side and listening intently.

By the time Willic reached a stopping point, Beruse was rocking back and forth on her feet, nodding eagerly, and Lucena was curled up into a ball on her chair. As soon as Willic stopped she strode over and lifted the book out of his hands, flipping through the pages and muttering.

"Have you gotten to the bit with Vlagurd and Morida yet?" she asked. "I loved that bit. Morida was so clever and—"

Here Willic cut her off with a forced cough, and indicated Lucena, who was looking even paler than usual. Beruse gave her a confused look, but she shut the book.

"Eh, what's eating at you?" she asked.

Considering that one of the methods employed by the humans to kill off the vampires was to send maggots to eat away their flesh while they slept, this question made Lucena shudder.

"Maggots!" she whispered, drawing her knees further up into her chest. "I had no idea they went for one's eyes first!"

"Only the magical ones," Willic assured her. "And they have to be enchanted to go after vampires at all. You heard that part, right?"

CHAPTER 5: *Beruse and Willic Decide to Throw a Party*

Lucena had, but it didn't make her feel better.

Beruse, who had been looking from Willic to Lucena and back, finally burst out laughing. This brought reproachful looks from both sides, and from Gydda, who was just bustling over with a mug of warm blood for Lucena.

"I've put some cinnamon—that's one of those Idrian spices—in it. You tell me how it tastes," she said, pushing the mug into Lucena's hand and turning to glare up at Beruse. "What do you think is so funny?" she demanded.

Beruse, still chuckling, dropped the book back into Willic's lap. "Our little fledgeling doesn't get it," she said, rounding on Lucena. "You listen, all right? Just remember: There are vampires, and then there are *vampires*. Just like there's humans and humans. You can't generalize them into just monsters, or just bloodsucking mopers, or just . . . anything. And personally, I don't think maggots are the way to go. That's a cowardly way to fight. That's why I was asking about Vlagurd and Morida; that is a *good* example of how to kill a vampire!"

"Beruse!" Gydda objected, her voice gone shrill. "Have you no tact at all?"

At the same time Willic was saying, obviously trying to be reasonable, "But Beruse, I hardly think that will make her feel any better!"

"Of course I don't," Beruse snapped at Gydda, and then to Willic: "But it made *me* feel better, so!"

"*You're* not a vampire!" Gydda screeched.

Lucena sighed, and sat back to drink her blood. The cinnamon gave it a strange aftertaste, but at least it tasted different, which in itself was a welcome change. She listened to them bicker, and slowly began to relax. It seemed to be something the three had done a lot of, for soon the topic veered off vampires, and Gydda started haranguing Beruse for never properly caring for her weapons, and just leaving them about for herself to clean. At this Beruse looked so harassed that Willic was obliged to drop his side of the argument and go to her rescue, saying that he thought Beruse deserved some slack for all the work she did. This remark made Gydda bristle, and both Willic and Beruse flinched visibly. Gydda said that no one ever cut her slack for all the work she did, and if Beruse had time to come down and sneer at her she had time to wash some dishes! Then she snatched a broom from a nearby corner and, holding it brush end out like a spear, proceeded to chase Willic and Beruse around the room with it.

Willic's response was incredible; in a flash he was gone, replaced by a soft sandy-brown cat, who streaked to the highest shelf and crouched there, tail lashing. Beruse had no such recourse. She was forced to flee, ducking blows from the broom, and several times leapt onto the counters to avoid Gydda's wrath.

It might have been alarming, except Beruse was a very large person and Gydda was not, so the way she pursued her enormous target around the room was nothing less than absurd. Finally, when she had backed Beruse into a corner and was getting ready to give her a good sweeping, Beruse hopped right over her head and fled out the door.

Or she *would* have fled out the door, except she ran headlong into Cobbin, who was just walking in under a pile of books.

There were shrieks of dismay from both parties, books went everywhere, and Willic withdrew further into the shadows up on his shelf. To make matters worse, when Beruse tried to catch the books as they fell she only succeeded in knocking them away, and Cobbin stepped on one that had fallen face down and his feet slipped out from underneath him. Down he went with a plop in a further shower of books, and Beruse, trying to salvage what she could, tripped over his legs and fell flat on her face.

In the wake of the disaster, one lone sheet of paper fluttered to the ground. Lucena picked it up, wondering if it had been torn from one of the books. But it was only a list of all the volumes Orrus wanted cleaned or rebound, with little suggestions written beside each title, and a warning at the end to handle the books with extreme care.

"Oh," Lucena said, staring at the mess. "Oh, oh dear..."

She handed the note to Gydda, who was looking at the two prone figures and obviously wondering whether to take advantage of Beruse's misfortune or help tidy up. She took the note from Lucena and read it over with one eyebrow arched. While she was distracted, Willic slipped down from his perch and turned back into his usual form, only a little ruffled. He came up behind Gydda and gently pried the broom out of her fingers, then began sweeping the books into a pile.

"Hey, be careful with those!" Cobbin exclaimed from the floor. He scrambled up, using Beruse as a handhold, and frantically began collecting books and moving them to safety. "I'm supposed to rebind these while he restores some older volumes—don't move, Beruse, you'll just crumble the pages."

Beruse, who had been trying to roll over and sit up, flopped back down on the floor with a groan. "What's he doing restoring books again? I thought he just gave the library a thorough cleaning!"

"That was fifty years ago," Cobbin answered primly. "Willic, don't do that—he said some of these are very brittle!"

Willic paused in his sweeping, looking down at the mass of books he was in the midst of pushing into a pile. Curiously he picked one up and thumbed through it. "This one's not," he said, letting it fall back into the heap. He tried another one, and another, with the same verdict. "Are you sure he wasn't having a lark with you?"

Cobbin glared and looked offended. From the floor, Beruse gave an exasperated sigh and rolled over onto her back, snatching randomly at a nearby volume. She opened it up and subjected it to her own inspection. Finding it satisfactory she tossed it aside (Cobbin caught it, looking affronted).

"I think Orrus is overworking himself again," she said, scratching herself behind one furry ear. Glancing across at Willic, the two exchanged knowing looks, and Willic set the broom aside.

"He's just being responsible," Cobbin muttered defensively.

"He doesn't know how to relax," Willic said sadly.

"Well why don't you two just *throw him a party* or something?" Gydda suggested, obviously annoyed at the conversation and wanting to have the mess cleared away.

Beruse and Willic gave her amazed looks, as if she had just thought of the most brilliant idea ever, and Cobbin groaned.

CHAPTER 5: *Beruse and Willic Decide to Throw a Party*

It was decided, there and then, that they would throw Orrus a party—specifically a birthday party, since the next holiday wasn't until Midsummer Night (and Beruse hinted that Madgrin would have plans for that anyway), and no one was going to get married just so they could have a party. "Even though," Willic remarked thoughtfully, "I don't know his birthday, or even is he has one."

"He's got to have one," Beruse insisted. She, Willic, Cobbin and Lucena were all crowded into her room, which had become their headquarters. It was a large, plain room, with a sturdy bed heaped with fur blankets and an assortment of weapons hanging on the wall. The floor was bare wood, much worn, with strange discolorations here and there, as though a variety of liquids had been spilled on it. Beruse was sitting on the only chair in whole place (an ancient one of carved oak with a deerskin seat), holding an almanac, while Willic, Cobbin and Lucena were all crowded onto her bed, each with a slate and chalk with which to take notes. At least, Cobbin and Lucena took notes; Willic doodled pictures of mice.

"What makes you so sure?" Willic asked, adding whiskers to his fourth mouse.

"Well, he's *human*, isn't he? All humans have birthdays."

"Yes, but wasn't he one of those . . . what are they called? Magic humans . . . wizards, I think."

Lucena frowned at this. Her adoptive uncle had been a wizard, a very fine one, always doing services for important personages, and he had had a birthday, same as everyone else. She contemplated pointing this out, but Cobbin spoke instead.

"He's not a wizard; wizards are just humans who practice magic. No, he was one of them old Baronian mages: *druids*. They started human, but weren't so much by the time they finished becoming druids, if you know what I mean."

There was a respectful silence while three of them contemplated the insanities of humanity, and Lucena tried to remember what she had been taught about druids. There wasn't much: they had been mysterious people who could walk on water and through walls, and speak to trees. They made human sacrifices to their own set of gods, and had been wiped out by the Crowan Empire, so nobody needed to worry about them anymore

"How about May 26th?" Beruse suggested, placing a stubby finger in her almanac. "That gives us two weeks to prepare, and it's a good day."

"Night," Willic cut in.

"Eh?"

"We should have the party at night."

Suddenly Lucena was aware of all the eyes in the room turned on her, and she blushed furiously (which, in the case of vampires, meant no more than a pale pink). "Oh, you needn't trouble yourself," she said, feeling flustered.

"It's no trouble," Cobbin said, yawning. "Orrus is practically nocturnal anyway. And if we have it from dusk until dawn, you won't have to worry about preparations or cleaning up, so don't complain."

This only served to make Lucena feel more awkward. She wanted to be as much help as possible, and said so.

"Now, now, don't fret. There will be plenty you can do in the nights beforehand," Willic assured her. And there was.

First of all, they had to secure the House's cooperation. As Willic explained to Lucena, one couldn't have much of a party if the room wouldn't let the guests inside. Unfortunately Beruse had set her heart on the ballroom, which was unlikely to comply with their request.

"All because of the *last* time Beruse had a party there," Cobbin said darkly.

"That was a long time ago," Beruse growled.

"What happened?" Lucena asked Willic once they were out of hearing. (Beruse had stormed off to talk to Gydda about the food, and Cobbin had been called away by Grimmach.)

"She invited a centaur," Willic said. "Lovely chap, actually. But he muffed the dance floor and Ballroom sulked for months."

"So what can we do?" Lucena asked. "Promise not to invite a centaur?"

Willic shook his head. "Ballroom is so stubborn, she probably wouldn't listen to either of us. No, in a situation like this, someone's going to have to talk to Himself about it."

"Someone?" Lucena repeated, confused.

Willic gave her a sheepish smile. "Well, I was hoping you could do that..."

"Me?" said Lucena.

Willic twiddled his thumbs, looked down at his toes and coughed. "Yes... well... you see... since you can talk to him through your head, as it were..."

Lucena's eyebrows, which had been creeping downward, shot up again. "Oh! Well in that case, I suppose I *could* ask him now..."

Willic gave her an odd look, with one eyebrow up. "Is it that easy for you?" he asked. "I mean, I can only hear him when he calls me."

"It usually is," Lucena said, surprised. She clasped her hands behind her back and stood up a little straighter, as if she were preparing to make a speech.

"Excuse me, Maker?" she said, poking into the back part of her mind where she often found him. For a moment it seemed like he wasn't there at all, and she felt her stomach twist with nerves.

What is it, Lucena? his voice asked, a little distant and muffled.

"Um, well, you see... Beruse and Willic are throwing a party and they would like—"

"Beruse would like!" Willic cut in.

"*Beruse,*" Lucena corrected herself, "would like to hold the party in the ballroom, only Ballroom doesn't want to have the party in her, and we were wondering if maybe you could, er, talk to her, please. Sir. Ballroom, that is, sir."

Silence. But it seemed Madgrin was just a long way away, and his voice was taking a while to reach her. When it did he sounded amused.

What are they having a party for?

"It's Orrus, Maker. We've decided he's overworking himself and needs a break, so we're throwing him a birthday party."

A birthday party?

"It was the best excuse we could come up with."

CHAPTER 5: *Beruse and Willic Decide to Throw a Party*

There was a tingling in the back of Lucena's mind and some faint laughter echoed around her head. It was not an unpleasant feeling, though it made her rather dizzy. When the voice returned it sounded unusually deferential, almost timid.

Am I invited?

Surprised, Lucena turned to Willic. "Is *he* invited?"

Willic, who had been hopping impatiently from foot to foot, nearly pulled his ears sideways. "Yes *yes*, of course he's invited!"

"Of *course* you're invited!" Lucena repeated.

Madgrin seemed pleased at that. *I'll see what I can do when I return*, he promised.

"Well? Well? What did he *say*?" Willic asked, bouncing on his toes now. Lucena gave him a puzzled look, then realized that to Willic the conversation had been completely one sided, so she relayed Madgrin's answer, at which he bounded off to find Beruse and Gydda and tell them the good news.

Beruse was delighted, but Gydda was furious.

"Do you have any idea what a state that room is in?" she howled despairingly. "Cobwebs and mold, and the best chandelier is all rusty! Who's going to clean all that? I've got dishes to wash, a kitchen to clean, four meals a day to make, and now Beruse wants godlike cakes just for the appetizers! Beruse, I only make godlike food if there are *actual* gods coming, so unless you plan on inviting Telmark or Mahr, you're not getting any—"

"Time to go," Beruse remarked, ushering the two out the door. They hurried away from the kitchen, Gydda's yells echoing down the dark halls. Even Lucena found she did not have the nerve to go back and face the hoblin's wrath.

She spent the remainder of the night drawing up a sensible list of things the party would require, partly for Beruse's sake, since the bear did not seem able to keep organized, and partly for Gydda, who needed something more tangible to work with than just a shower of requests. In the meantime Willic snoozed in a corner of Beruse's room, curled up like a cat, and Beruse snored on her bed. When she felt dawn drawing close, Lucena left her list, neatly folded, on the bedside table, and tiptoed off to her own room.

She woke to the unpleasant sensation of someone forcibly pouring blood into her mouth. At first she thought she would choke: then she remembered she didn't have to breathe, and concentrated on not spitting it back out again. However, concentrating on that made her forget that she had remembered that she didn't have to breathe, old habits took over, and as a result a good amount of coughing ensued, and a sizable amount of blood ended up getting blown out her nose.

"Oh thanks very much for that young miss!" said the person who was administering this strange torture, and the bottle was removed from her face.

Sitting up, Lucena beheld Rhyse, bottle in one hand while the other was wiping a spatter of blood from the front of her apron.

"What did you do *that* for?" Lucena said between coughs and hiccups. Finally she simply blew all the air out of her lungs and held it out, trying to control herself. She wiped her nose with the sleeve of her nightdress.

Rhyse glared at her. "Trying to wake you up, of course!" she said as if this were obvious. "And you should be grateful too! Madgrin's back and having a right row with Ballroom, and Willic says: be sure and go fetch Lucena, she'll love to see this! Only *he* can't because he has to be there, being Housekeeper and all—feh!" she snorted. "And Gydda won't go because she's cranky as a shedding dragon from getting near no sleep last night, and Beruse is hiding like a coward, Cobbin's running errands and Grimmach won't—where are you going?"

All the while Rhyse was talking Lucena had been scrambling out of bed, getting on her slippers, a skirt, and grabbing a shawl to cover the bloodstains on her gown, and finally braving her misty reflection to make sure the rest of the blood had been cleaned off her face. By the time Rhyse had got to Grimmach, Lucena was halfway out the door, and soon the two of them were pelting for the north hall and the ballroom.

A crowd had gathered in the north hall, including North Hall himself, who was standing against the far wall, looking smug. He had never made this much of a fuss. No. Not even when Madgrin had kept a dozen goblins waiting in him for almost three hours. Those goblins had been right terrors: tried to break his windows, deface his walls, and once, when he appeared and asked them (politely) to be more careful, tried to run him through with their wicked little knives. But did he throw a fit and refuse to let goblins in? Of course not! Willic had fixed him up just fine afterwards, and Willic had fixed Ballroom, and would fix her again. So what was her problem? *Really*.

Lucena only listened with half an ear to North Hall, because she and Rhyse had joined the cluster outside the door to the ballroom, and were listening with the rest. The rest included Gydda and Grimmach, and Orrus, oblivious as to why this was happening. (Wasn't Midsummer still months away? what was the occasion? and why Beruse? No one seemed to know quite what to say; Willic was inside the ballroom, and they weren't sure if it was to be a secret.) Soloma was there too, her neck elongated to a horrifying extent so she could press her ear to the door above everyone else's heads. The doors were so thick that they could only hear muffled voices, but Soloma repeated what was going on inside for the benefit of everyone else.

"Ballroom is ranting ... still ... " she was saying as Lucena arrived. "Doesn't want anymore ... oh my, that is *not* a polite word. Well, she doesn't want any more ... disreputable guests ... only ... well ... she didn't say *disreputable*, if you know what I mean."

"Just repeat it verbatim," Grimmach said tiredly. "No one will blame you."

"*I* never use foul language," said North Hall, from the back. "It's degrading."

"*Hush!*" said everyone else.

But they needn't have. At that moment Ballroom's voice rose to such a pitch that it penetrated even the thick oak doors, and everyone shrank away. Poor Soloma's head jerked back from the door with such force that she nearly overbalanced her body and had to reel her head back in.

"I NEVER WANT TO HOST A CROWD AGAIN!" screamed a thin, feminine voice, which Lucena assumed belonged to Ballroom. "THEY MAKE ME

CHAPTER 5: *Beruse and Willic Decide to Throw a Party*

DIRTY AND HOT AND LOUD AND NO ONE HEARS MY PRETTY MUSIC, AND THEY DON'T CARE ABOUT MY FLOOR! ARE YOU *LISTENING?!*"

Soft murmurings. Madgrin was obviously working very hard.

"NO! THAT DOESN'T MAKE IT BETTER! LITTLE PIECES OF MICE-DUNG! FLIPPING, PIP-JACK SQUEAKS!"

Soloma flinched. But Lucena, who had, after all, lived for years at a tough boarding school, had heard much, much worse.

More soft murmurings. Creeping closer to the door Lucena felt a wave of calmness and tranquility roll off it. Madgrin must be using magic. She could hear Willic's voice too, talking reason. Every now and then Ballroom would make an objection, but these slowly became less and less hysterical. Finally, Lucena distinctly heard her say in pinched tones, "It's still not *fair* . . . " and the doors suddenly opened and Madgrin stuck his smooth dark head out to stare down at the crowd. He looked a little dazed.

"Beruse," he said tiredly. "Come along."

To everyone's surprise, Beruse came shuffling out from the shadows beside North Hall. Her shoulders were slumped, and she looked somehow smaller and meeker than everyone else, even though she still towered over all except Madgrin.

"I'm sorry to trouble you," Madgrin said gently. "But all she really wants an apology."

"I already gave one . . . " Beruse mumbled. "Years ago."

"Yes, but I'm afraid it didn't stick. Won't you try again?"

Beruse huffed, and stomped towards the door, which Madgrin held open for her. But before she went inside she whirled around and pointed a stubby finger at Orrus.

"This is all because of you, you know!" she said. "It's *your* party after all!"

Orrus looked bewildered. "I . . . wh-*what?*" he stammered, but the doors had already clicked shut. He turned to Gydda, looking panicked, like a person who learns they must give a public speech and haven't the slightest idea what to say. "But I don't *want* a party . . . " he said.

Gydda rounded on him. "Oh, yes you *do!*" she said loudly. "I haven't been laboring all last night to have you, of all people, pull the rug out from under us!"

Confronted with a red-faced, baggy-eyed, seething hoblin half his height, Orrus recoiled from her and meekly agreed, although he bent and whispered in Lucena's ear, once Gydda had left, "I doubt Ballroom will accept Beruse's apology."

But Ballroom did, and the date was set for the night of May 26th. Beruse and Willic worked around the clock to make everything ready, and there was not a member of the household who, by the night of the event, hadn't been roped into doing something or another. Cobbin helped Gydda in the kitchen. Rhyse insisted Lucena help her clean the ballroom. For this they acquired the assistance of Grimmach, although at first all he did was stand in the middle of the dance floor and give directions about what to clean next and how to do it. Both Rhyse and Lucena found this maddening. Fortunately, Willic wandered in soon after and set Grimmach to work scrubbing the dance floor he had been standing on.

Lucena had not seen much of Willic, nor Beruse, during those nights; they spent their time sequestered in the bear's room working on something secret. Lucena only ever saw Beruse when she put her head inside the ballroom to ask Lucena to ask Madgrin for something. Sometimes it was quite mundane: Willic could not find his golden scissors, and did Madgrin know where they were? (He did; they were on the top shelf of Gydda's spice cabinet.) But sometimes the questions were mysterious indeed, and the answers even more so. Once, when Lucena was hanging from the ceiling, cleaning the chandelier and replacing the burnt-out stubs of candles with long, new, white ones, Beruse barged into the room, neatly stepping over Rhyse, who was replacing a cracked tile, and asked when the golden eggs would turn to glass.

Confused, Lucena contacted Madgrin, whom she expected to be as mystified as she, but he replied at once that the golden eggs would turn to glass when the clocks took their tea break. This pleased Beruse very much and she went away rubbing her hands and chuckling.

The only person who did not immediately become involved in the preparations was Soloma, and of course, Orrus himself. The latter, once resigned to wasting a night at a party in his honor, had offered to help, but was turned down on all fronts: it was his party, and the whole point was to give him a break from work anyway, so what would be the use of him working harder? Soloma was cynical about the whole affair, but when Willic hinted that that no one had the time or skill to make proper invitations, she seized the task for herself. Here Orrus stepped in, saying, "I will see to it that *my* friends get invited to *my* party!" They set up in the library with a mass of papers, ink, parchment, quills and knives, writing lists, revising lists, and when all the lists were done, making the invitations.

These invitations were the most marvelous Lucena had ever seen or imagined; hers arrived early one evening when she was rummaging through her bureau looking for a dress to wear that was shabby enough to do cleaning in, for her original shabby dress was quite worn out.

She heard a fluttering sound behind her, and turning around saw a creature not unlike a butterfly hovering in the air just before her eyes. Not unlike, but three times the size of any butterfly, and made entirely of paper; its wings gave a dry swish and rattle as they moved. Even as she watched, it unfolded itself and became a plain (if heavily creased) sheet of paper, which fell gently into her hands. Holding it up she read:

> Dear Miss Ashmoor,
> You are invited to a special celebration honoring the 1,623rd year of the Druid Orrus, to be held in the Ballroom of the House of Madgrin, night of May 26th to 27th. Do not feel obligated to bear gifts.
> Please reply as soon as convenience allows.
> Yrs,
> Dr. Orrus Abneialaemh

And below this was a little line with the heading "Sign here to accept." So Lucena, still wondering how to pronounce Orrus's last name, took a quill and signed her own comparatively modest one, at which the ink glowed with a flash

CHAPTER 5: *Beruse and Willic Decide to Throw a Party*

of golden light, and her name vanished. The paper then refolded itself into a butterfly and fluttered off.

During the course of the night, she later discovered, everyone received one of these strange invitations, to their delight, and would drop whatever they were doing to find a quill and ink.

By this time they had almost finished restoring the ballroom, and Lucena was looking forward to the work being over. But even before they had finished re-hanging the curtains (a monumental task, as there were curtains all along each side of the long room), Willic came in with ideas for *decorations*.

These included a sea of water lilies made of gold foil to float around the edges of the dance floor, and inside each flower would be some delectable candy or other sweet; also an illusionary dragon to twist and curl around the chandelier, snorting flames; hundreds of floating candles, naturally, and streamers made from moonlight to hang from the ceiling. Listening to this list, Lucena couldn't help wonder if the air would be so full of Willic's decorations that one would be constantly batting them away.

Of course, Beruse had her own ideas, as did Gydda, Rhyse, Cobbin and Grimmach. Beruse wanted dancing mice along all the tables, but Gydda would not hear of that. She had her heart set on a troupe of trained peacocks strutting around the dance floor in formation. Cobbin and Grimmach put their heads together and came up with the most sensible idea: that of inviting the pixies that lived in the ceiling of Madgrin's study to come and watch the party from the shadows in the great arched ceiling. But as their idea did not intrude on anyone else's, no one paid them any attention. It was a mark of how pleased Ballroom was with her cleaning and repair that she didn't complain about any of the suggestions, although she looked a little anxious at the mention of peacocks.

In the end everyone went to Orrus, since it was to be his party after all, and he was the one they were going to ask to do the enchantments anyway. Orrus, who was hiding in a dark corner of the library with a book, looked horrified at first. Lucena pushed her way through the crowd and sat in front of him, filtering everyone's requests, so that he did not simply run away.

After an hour of people talking over one another, and Beruse looking ready to enforce her own ideas with her thick, strong arms, and Willic with his ears flattened down and his hair up in an angry ridge, Orrus stood up declared that *he* would take care of the decorations himself, and they were not to worry about it.

"And," he added as everyone began to walk off, grumbling, "don't even think about hiring musicians, I've seen to that already."

...she and Rhyse had joined the cluster outside the door to the ballroom, and were listening with the rest.

CHAPTER 6:

⁓Orrus and Abneialaemh⸒

THE NIGHT OF THE PARTY APPROACHED. The ballroom was in splendid condition, and everyone was exhausted. Gydda announced that they would have to do without the iced fairy cakes, because she was not spending another minute in the kitchen. Lucena and Cobbin ended up washing all the dishes the night before the party, because Gydda had tottered off to bed. After they finished, Cobbin announced that he too was tired, and to Lucena's consternation she found that everyone else felt the same. One by one they went to bed, and she was left alone.

She went down to visit the ballroom, and found that not everyone had gone to sleep after all: Orrus was there, moving around the room with a single candle floating above his head and muttering to himself. Ballroom was leaning against the wall by the door, watching him intently. She was a tall, thin woman with a severe bony face. The only soft things about her were her flowing auburn hair and fluttering silk gown. Ordinarily Lucena gave her a respectful berth—Ballroom reminded her a little of Miss Smael—but that night she summoned up the courage to come and stand next to the woman. She bobbed a curtsey, but Ballroom's eyes were fixed on Orrus, and she didn't seem to notice. Then, when Lucena was quite certain she was safely being ignored, Ballroom sighed and spoke to her.

"Doesn't it give you the most delightful shivers to see magic being done?" she asked in an excited whisper, very different from her normal, piercing tone.

"P-pardon?" Lucena stammered. She looked over at Orrus again, who at that moment was kneeling by the far wall doodling pictures on it with his fingertips. He didn't seem to be doing anything particularly magical; he wasn't even muttering to himself anymore. Lucena spent some time pondering an answer, but when she next looked up the woman was staring fixedly at Orrus and appeared to have forgotten her.

Then something happened. It was hard to say what, exactly. It was as though a pane of rippled glass rolled before Lucena's eyes: through it the ballroom was transformed from a gloomy dark expanse into a blaze of colors. The change was so sudden she was almost blinded, and didn't notice much aside from the sea of shimmering gold flowers and a twist of red up by the ceiling.

Orrus stood up. Behind the pane of rippled glass he had changed also: he stood amidst the shining, twinkling lights, and was a different person. He was still Orrus, Lucena could tell, but a younger, fiercer Orrus. His hair was much longer, and instead of glasses over his eyes he wore bandages. His mouth was a thin cruel line, and he was wearing an elaborate robe with twisting signs embroidered on it. Lucena got the distinct impression that those signs meant something important, but she couldn't imagine what.

Then the pane of glass rolled away, or simply melted into the world, and everything went back to normal. The ballroom was dark and empty; Orrus had lost his young, fierce look, and was wearing his ordinary plain robes and glasses. But there was still something about the other Orrus around his nose and mouth, even though this mouth was now curved up in a tired smile.

"Good evening, Lucena," he said.

"Good evening," Lucena replied in a small voice. She resisted the sudden urge to hide behind Ballroom, who was watching Orrus as if enchanted. Instead she allowed him to usher her out through the huge double doors and into the north hall, where the long windows all showed different scenes of moonlit beaches.

"It's better to leave it alone now," he explained once they were outside. "Enchantments can be cowardly things, and too much attention can frighten them out of existence."

"Oh," Lucena said, still in her small voice. Orrus bent his head and peered at her curiously through his spectacles. These caught the light from the windows and reflected it, hiding his eyes behind two glowing white disks. It was an eerie sight.

"Did you see something?" he asked gently. "Something... frightening?"

Lucena would have liked to say no, she had not. She would have liked to forget that strange young Orrus with bandages over his eyes. But she couldn't, so she nodded. "You changed," she explained. "All of a sudden you looked different."

Orrus sighed and patted her on the shoulder. "Yes," he said heavily. "That happens sometimes." He regarded her for a few moments with a thoughtful expression, and then slowly, as if it were a great effort, reached into his robe and drew out a small battered book. It was bound in peeling red leather, with a tattered red silk ribbon sewn to the spine for a bookmark. Orrus sighed, and handed it to Lucena. "I do not like to speak of my past, but you may read it here. It is not a happy story, but it may help you to understand. And understanding is the great antidote to fear." Then he walked away and disappeared into the gloom.

Lucena took the little book back up to her room, holding it gently in both hands. Upon arriving she felt the urge to put it away somewhere and never look at it again, but she decided this was unfair to Orrus, so she sat down in her armchair, lit the candelabra on the table next to her, and began to read.

At first she thought it was a diary, for it was not printed by a press, but written by hand. And such writing! Lucena had heard of the illuminated manuscripts of the Old Age monks and magicians, but she had never seen one before. This book, she thought, must have been one of those. The text was inscribed in an archaic (yet still legible) hand, with flourishes and fantastic illustrations worked into the capital letters. These happened fairly often, as the writer was fond of capitalizing nouns such as "Night" and "Shadow" and "Sun." There were also little drawings dancing in the margins of every page, which went along with whatever paragraph they were placed next to. But because the book was so small, and the drawings so numerous, this hardly left any room for the text itself, and there was only a small amount on each page. So although it was a short book, it took some time for Lucena to work her way through. Many of the spellings and expressions she did not recognize, and whole passages of the book were in Cairdric, with no transla-

CHAPTER 6: *Orrus and Abneialaemh*

tions, and she needed the drawings in order to make sense of the narrative. But the story that eventually emerged was fascinating.

Before the Barons and the Kyres, before even the Crowans, before Kyreland was Kyreland; before the goblins and the fae had been driven underground and still lived in company of humans; in those early days when there was not one king but many chieftains, and these were always bickering and quarreling and warring with each other, the real ruling was done not by the nobility, but by their servants, the druids.

One of the cleverest and most powerful of these druids was a young man called Abneialaemh. He had a remarkable talent for reading the lines of fate and predicting the future. This was partly natural talent, and partly because during his initiation ceremony, wherein the novice druid's soul is bound to a demon, the demon consumed his eyes. But though he was blind, his binding to the demon let him see with the demon's eyes, and the lines of fate are as clear to a demon as lines of writing are to humans. Through hard work and study, Abneialaemh learned to interpret these lines, and then to profit from what they told him. He foretold calamities, deaths and disasters, all with astonishing accuracy. He could tell how to avoid catastrophes, and he also knew (though rarely told anyone) how to cause them. But although he was well respected and rightly feared, Abneialaemh was unhappy. He wanted to be a chief in his own right. A chief who was also a druid would be the most powerful in the land, and able to hold sway over an even larger kingdom. He might take a fairy queen, subdue the goblins, perhaps even make war on the giants that terrorized the north.

Such was Abneialaemh's ambition. He contrived for his chief to be killed, as if by accident, in battle. Then, while the chief's relations were fighting for the throne, he quietly took it himself. He had made himself agreeable to the warriors by giving them good advice, so when the dead chief's relations objected to him taking the throne, Abneialaemh simply had the warriors kill a few to keep the rest in line.

At first he ruled well, but as he gained power he was corrupted by it. He became obsessed with power, as those who have too much often do. Then he became mad with it. He proclaimed himself not only chief, but a god. By his magic he conquered the surrounding kingdoms, drove the goblins out of the hills and left them to fry in the sun. He even went so far as to cut down some of the fae trees, leaving the poor fairies homeless and bound to serve him.

Once he had a host of fairy slaves, Abneialaemh set his heart on marrying the princess Brydthien, said to be the most beautiful fairy ever. She was a personage of antiquity even in Abneialaemh's time, and according to legends had died long ago, her bones laid to rest on a small island called the Fairy Tomb, off the coast of what is now Baronia. Undaunted, Abneialaemh called her forth from Dream, that strange nether place where all old stories live on. She came, and he took her up to his castle and wed her in a magnificent ceremony. But even after this his thirst for power could not be quenched, and he treated poor Brydthien very ill, trying first to coax her, and then force her, to teach him her fae powers.

But Brydthien had been a sorceress even among fairies when alive, and clever too. She could not break the enchantment laid upon her by Abneialaemh, but she realized how she could trick him. She told him of her great lords who could grant wishes and reshape the world, and she told him how to conjure one so that it would be bound to his will.

Abneialaemh, blinded by his thirst for power, ignored his demon's warnings and performed the summoning just as Brydthien had instructed. To his delight this caused a man to appear in his court. Accompanied by a giant bear, he was tall and dark of hair, pale of face, with eyes that twinkled with the light of distant stars.

"Kneel before your master, fae creature," Abneialaemh instructed.

The man grinned, wide and eerie, but he knelt. He did nothing else, however, and so Abneialaemh ordered him to make obeisance befitting to a god-chief's presence.

The grinning man did so, though his bear growled disapprovingly. But Abneialaemh was pleased, and told him to rise again.

"Now it shall be seen what wonders you can perform," the druid-chief said, rubbing his hands together.

"Indeed," replied the grinning man. "But not on your behalf. Your conjuring binds me only to three tasks, which I have just completed. And now who serves must in turn be served."

And the grinning man raised a long white hand and said, "My mysteries are mine to keep." Then he took it down, and suddenly Abneialaemh was a druid-chief no longer. The grinning man had stripped him of it, the way one strips off a robe. Then the grinning man went up to Abneialaemh and undid the bandages around his eyes. And when he had peeled them away, he put a glass marble in each empty socket, and raised his hand again. When he took it down a second time Abneialaemh had human eyes, albeit rather glassy ones—and his link with the demon was severed. Finally the grinning man raised both his arms, and then with a great sigh lowered them. When he had, Abneialaemh was gone. He had been plucked out of the world as one plucks the first spring flower.

The grinning man bowed to Brydthien, who had been watching all the time, and bade her go home. She jumped up with a shout of joy, ripping off her queenly accessories, and danced out of the hall, and out of the world. Then the stranger spent some time stripping the power from Abneialaemh's corrupt and greedy courtiers, and when he had all the power laid across his knees he called the children to the hall. They came—trembling human children, and sprightly goblin children, and proud pale fairy children—and all stood before him. The grinning man gave the power of the hills to the goblin children, that they should have the earth to shelter and protect them forever and ever. He gave the power of the trees to the fairy children, so that they could live and play there forever and ever. Finally, he gave the power of the rivers and the fields to the humans, to nurture and live on, forever and ever.

And then he rode out of the castle on his bear. And neither he nor Abneialaemh were ever seen again in the waking world.

Lucena sat in silence with the book on her lap for some minutes after she finished reading. She stared blurrily at the flickering candles, her mind still far away. Abneialaemh had to have been Orrus, and the grinning man was Madgrin. But she found it hard to imagine soft-spoken, polite, considerate Orrus as a corrupted druid mad with power. And just how long ago had this story taken place? Hundreds and hundreds of years, by the sound of it. And what did that make Madgrin, who had been called a great lord by a legendary fairy princess?

"I wonder if Madgrin is king of the fairies?" Lucena said to the flickering candles. To her surprise they were suddenly blown sideways, then they guttered, flared, and went out. There had been no draft of wind, nothing at all. It was as if the candles had been laughing at her, and they had laughed so hard they keeled over and fainted. Lucena sat in the dark and felt more mystified than ever.

"I guess not," she said to the darkness.

When she awoke the next evening and called Madgrin, out of habit more than anything else, she was surprised to hear him answer in person. Sitting up she looked around and saw his pale face staring out at her from a clot of thick, dark shadows by the bookcase. The only light in the room, which came from a single candle on the bedside table, threw his shadow up the wall. Lucena could see it twisting and writhing around the edges, like water plants in a strong current. Every now and then a piece would leap out, briefly taking the form of a bird or a butterfly or a leaping hound, before getting sucked back into the dark mass.

A part of the shadow detached itself from the wall and reached out, slowly blanching until it became one of his slender white hands. This tapped the book Orrus had lent her, which she had left on the reading table by the candelabra.

"I see Orrus gave you his story," he said. "Did you like it?"

Lucena nodded, speechless. Seeing Madgrin again after reading that story was rather like meeting a famous person for the first time, and she did not know what to say. But Madgrin did not seem to expect her to say anything. He emerged from the shadows, and Lucena saw he was dressed in a splendid robe of midnight-blue velvet. Coming over to the bedside table he took up the bottle of blood and the crystal glass that had been set out, and poured Lucena a generous amount. Giving her a meaningful look he went over to her bureau and opened the bottom drawer.

"Since you have been so industriously involved in preparing everything but yourself for this evening," he said. "I took the liberty of procuring you some formal attire." He drew out from the bottom drawer a long flowing gown the color of autumn. He held it up by the shoulders and peeked around at her. "I hope you like it."

Lucena was enchanted. She swung her legs out of bed, heedless of the fact that she was only in her nightgown, and stood up. "Oh, it's *beautiful!*" she exclaimed. And it was: all golden-orange and bronze and creamy yellow fluttering, with delicate white flowing strips hanging down from the shoulders. It was without a doubt the finest, yet most outlandish gown she had even seen.

Madgrin smiled. "Of course it's beautiful," he said, sounding amused. "But it does have a rather... forward... character. It might take some getting used to."

"Sorry?" Lucena looked from Madgrin to the dress. Madgrin shrugged, and let the dress go. At once the the garment took on a life of its own and twirled out of his reach. It stood itself up straight and put its frilled cuffs on its hips, turning to face Lucena in a defiant posture.

"I will wait for you in the hall," Madgrin said, and left, leaving Lucena and the dress to regard each other cautiously. It took her some time to work up the nerve to get herself into it, but after she had one arm in, it decided it liked her after all and wriggled its way onto her body, its laces doing themselves up faster and neater than any maid could have. Looking down at herself Lucena was a little dismayed to find that the dress had no bodice, like the sort she was used to. This let her ample waist spread to its usual diameter which, though more comfortable, also gave her the general shape of a pear on legs.

Chancing a glance in the mirror to confirm her suspicions, Lucena made a face at her transparent reflection. The dress was gorgeous, but the ghostly face that looked back at her was not. Being a vampire had done wonders for her complexion: the prominent acne that had scarred her face for most of her life had dried up and fallen away, but they had left footprints in the form of pockmarks all across her forehead. Her cheeks were still overly round, her nose obstinately stubby, and her eyes disproportionately small and pinched in at the corners. Smiling only made them disappear altogether, and displayed her elongated canines. She looked like some sort of fat, overdressed imp. A ghostly, fat, overdressed imp.

Scowling, Lucena turned away from the mirror, downed a few gulps of the blood on her bedside table to steady her head, and went to brush out her hair. How it looked when she was finished, she had no idea. She didn't look in the mirror again, and went out into the hall with mixed feelings raging in her chest.

Madgrin was waiting, just as he had promised. He stood in the middle of the hall, a living shadow with a pale face. When he saw Lucena, this face was split apart by a wide, warm smile. His eyes glittered, and the light that always seemed to glow inside them spilled out and danced across his cheeks. The effect was dazzling and not a little frightening. Lucena felt her muddled feelings consolidate into ordinary nerves. It was not entirely comfortable, being smiled at like that. But when Madgrin held out his hand she took it without hesitation, and within moments they were whizzing along corridors and through passages, leaving whispers of displaced air in the soft silence of the house.

The north hall was filled with music, but not like any music Lucena had heard before. It sounded as though several musicians had decided to play together, but had not agreed on a single piece, so each one played their own tune. It also sounded muffled, and it took Lucena a moment to realize it was actually coming from the ballroom.

There was a crowd of people outside the ballroom, and as Madgrin advanced they all turned to look at him. Clinging to his hand, Lucena had never felt so embarrassed. All the other guests were dressed in the height of fashion: the men in stuffed silk doublets with starched white ruffles, the ladies in splendid ball gowns with skirts so voluminous they looked like upside-down teacups. Lucena was so preoccupied with their clothes that she barely noticed the guests themselves. When she did she couldn't help giving a start of surprise, for none of them were human.

CHAPTER 6: *Orrus and Abneialaemh*

Certainly, they were all human *shaped*. But one woman had snakes in her hair and wide red eyes that put Lucena in mind of a lizard. As they passed her Lucena saw that her skin, which was a dull greenish-blue and glittered slightly, was made of the finest, most delicate, glistening scales. Another man had fox ears, the same foxy-orange color as his hair, and his companion had a strange headdress with a strip of fur hanging down each side of her head. It wasn't until Lucena looked again that she realized they were rabbit ears.

But she had little time to gawk or make a fool of herself, for as they approached, the ballroom doors were thrown wide, and there, silhouetted for a moment against the blinding light which shone from within, was Orrus.

He was dressed even more splendidly than any of his guests, although his garb was not at all fashionable. He wore a dark green robe, tied about the waist with a heavily embroidered sash, and an embroidered mantle hanging down from his shoulders. It looked as though he was wearing an entire tapestry. From his belt hung loops of delicate silver chains, and from every link of every chain hung a tiny twinkling star. More chains were looped around his neck and shoulders, and these had little strings of stars trailing from each link. This intricate ensemble contrasted sharply with the plain sprig of holly he had tied to his head with a leather cord. In the strange light his eyes were indiscernible behind his glasses, so he seemed to be looking at everyone all at once.

Orrus bowed, making his many chains clink softly together. "Welcome, friends," he said. "I bid you all welcome." He stood aside from the door and held out an embroidery-draped arm, ushering them inside.

The first thing that struck Lucena upon entering the ballroom was the scent of wet grass and roses. It was a pleasant smell, like a late spring evening after a rainstorm, but so unexpected it caused her to stagger. Once she had recovered from that and could look around, she gasped in delight.

Willic's sea of gold-foil water lilies bobbed at waist height all along one side of the room, glittering and flashing in the light of the chandelier and the candles floating beside the walls. These floated so close to the draperies that Lucena worried they might catch fire, until one of them bobbed up next to her elbow, and she saw that instead of a flame at the top of the candle, there stood a tiny shining person. She would have liked to stop for a closer look, but she still had her arm linked with Madgrin's, and so was pulled away.

They were heading for a set of five chairs that had been arranged in front of the little stage where the musicians were still warming up. The two on the right were already occupied by Beruse and Willic, who were dressed in matching cloth-of-gold suits which shone and glittered as much as the foil water lilies. Madgrin took a seat in the chair second from the left, motioning Lucena to sit beside him, which she did.

From her seat Lucena could see all the way down the ballroom, which was slowly filling with Orrus's guests. She saw the people with glistening snake-skins, and the people with soft, luxuriant fur. People in velvet hats, and people in hats that looked like ships. Then there came people who did not look much like people at all: they were small and pale, and wore plain leather clothes with a single shawl of black wool slung over their shoulders. They had straight dark hair and long bony noses, and their eyes were extraordinarily large and bright. They looked a little like the hoblins, only slightly taller, and with normal, human knees. They also did not go barefoot, but wore soft leather sandals.

Lucena stared at them shamelessly as they wandered through the crowd, exclaiming to one another at the grandeur of the decorations, and pointing delightedly at the twisting dragon on the ceiling.

Goblins, Madgrin's voice whispered in her ear. But when she looked he was leaning over Orrus's chair to talk to Willic. She shook herself; when he was close by it was difficult to tell whether he was speaking inside her head or out of it.

Someone plucked at her sleeve, making Lucena jump inwardly. Looking around she saw one of the musicians had come down from the dais and was now kneeling at her side. He had longish, dark brown hair and dark eyebrows, a long straight nose, and pale violet eyes. Like his fellows he was dressed all in black, and he carried a viol.

"Does the lady have a preference for the first song?" he asked in a soft, northern voice.

Flustered, Lucena stammered out that she did not know. The musician raised his eyebrows, making those pale violet eyes shine in the candlelight. Lucena wondered briefly if he was human—he certainly looked more human than any of the other guests, but she had discovered that looks were no guarantee in a place like this.

"Are you sure you cannot think of something?" he asked kindly.

"I'm sorry, but I really can't. I don't know, play whatever *you* like," Lucena suggested.

At this the musician smiled broadly. He stood up, made her a deep bow, nodded to Madgrin's back, and returned to the dais. "The lady says to play whatever we like," he told his companions, and there were happy exclamations.

Curious, Lucena twisted around in her seat to get a better look at them. Up on the dais, they made an interesting picture: there were four, and they were all so very thin they appeared tall, even though none of them were as tall as Madgrin. They all wore simple black suits with no decorations, save the one with the lute, who had a crimson sash tied to his left arm. They were all clean-shaven, save the one who sat next to a pile of assorted drums, who had long bushy sideburns. They were all dark-haired, save the one with the penny whistle, who was ash-blond. And they all had glittering black eyes, save the one who had spoken to her. All alike in some way, but also different.

As she watched, they bent their heads together, muttering, then pulled apart. The one with the penny whistle took a step to the head of the dais, put the whistle to his lips, and tapped his foot four times.

The music started all at once, and took the guests a little off guard. There were surprised glances towards the dais, and from across the hall Lucena glimpsed Orrus shoot the musicians a look that was part surprise, part irritation, and part resignation.

The music flitted about the room like an agitated bird, dipping and swooping, catching people by their feet and coaxing them to dance, all the while chased by the steady beating of many drums. To their rhythm the bystanders were marshaled into lines along the side, clearing the dance floor, which shone invitingly.

As the first brave couples stepped out onto the floor, without a leader or a queue, Madgrin leaned over the arm of his chair and nudged Lucena.

"What did you tell the musicians, La Flein?" he asked.

"What? Oh, I just said they could play whatever they liked," Lucena said. She looked nervously up at Madgrin, but to her relief he was smiling. He tapped one long finger against his pale nose, his eyes glittering mischievously.

"I hope you slept well today," he said. "Because we will be dancing all night."

Lucena looked at him questioningly, but he turned abruptly back to the dance floor. A youth had made his way through the maze of dancing couples, and now stood before them. He bowed deeply to Madgrin and spoke in a language Lucena thought she knew but didn't understand. He had a dark brown face and vibrant red hair twined together with ivy leaves; he wore a velvet doublet the color of forests—all mottled greens and browns, which shimmered and blurred together the more Lucena looked. The only bright piece of his costume was the single gold holly branch he had tied to his right shoulder.

Madgrin didn't answer, but he smiled and nodded graciously. The youth relaxed visibly, and then to Lucena's great surprise stepped sideways to stand before her. He made another deep bow and offered her his hand. He said something, and this time she did understand. He asked her to dance with him.

Uncertain, she glanced over at Madgrin, who smiled.

If you like, he said, through she didn't see his lips move.

Hesitantly Lucena got to her feet, patting her gown to make it straighten. She took the youth's hand with a little more confidence than she felt, and together they stepped out onto the dance floor.

What happened next Lucena had no clear memory of. The music seemed to get into her bones, and she felt itching in her feet. The floating lights grew dimmer, and the world became the shining floor, the music thick in the air, and the dark hands that held hers.

Then they began to dance. It was not a dance she knew, but she followed it flawlessly. They wove in and out between the other partners, whirling, turning, stepping, stooping, then stilling, as the music slowed and the tone changed.

The steady drums came to the front. Growing faster they lost their regularity, beating like a horse's hoofbeats running, like the wild breath of hounds lost in a hunt, like dark things in the night that patter on wet stone.

Looking around, Lucena saw that most of the couples had either paused or dispersed, unsure of what to make of this new piece. But turning back to her partner, she saw a wide white-toothed grin spreading across his dark face. Taking a firmer grip on her hands he began to step and turn and step, faster and faster. The world whirled away with the wild beating of the drums, and Lucena let herself be swept away with it. Dimly she was aware of the music returning, building behind the drums like a stalking beast ready to spring. Everything was moving so fast, it was all she could do to keep up.

Then something snapped: the whole thing made sense; the music, the rhythm, the patterns the dancers made on the floor with their bodies. It seemed as if a fire had lit itself in her belly and now roared up to fill her from toes to fingertips. She grabbed her partner and began to twirl him around the floor with renewed vigor. And when he grew tired, laughingly begging a rest, she left him by the side and bounded back onto the floor, snatching partners at random, outstepping them all, and whirling around the floor so that the floating candles tipped at her passing.

Then the music changed again. The viol was growling, rolling the others away before it, and Lucena paused. There was a commotion at the end of the room, and people were drawing back. A moment later she saw why: Madgrin had stood up, and was walking softly down the hall towards her.

He seemed to bring the music with him. It echoed in his footsteps and gathered in his wake, and when he stopped before her, there was complete silence.

He bowed, low, sweeping a curtain of his robe aside. Lucena replied with her best, well-practiced curtsey. Then, as the viol began to hum, and then to sing, they stepped together and began to dance.

Thinking back, Lucena never could remember what the dance had been, or what the music had sounded like. It was all familiar, yet exciting and new at once. She wondered for a moment how ridiculous they must look; a tall pale man clothed in night and a short, pear-shaped girl wearing a dress the color of autumn; but the music was too strong for such bitter thoughts, and soon they were swept away.

They seemed to float on the music rather than dance; riding it down the room and back again, and it wasn't until their fourth circuit that Lucena noticed they were easily ten feet in the air, slowly spinning and weaving above the heads of the crowd. But Madgrin held her hands firmly, and she was not in the least afraid.

When the viol slowed, they sank and alighted once more on the floor. They stepped apart as the music faded away, and saluted each other. Madgrin took her hand and kissed it, and there was a polite ripple of applause.

But even as Madgrin was straightening majestically to his full, impressive height the penny whistle piped up, and an instant later he had been whipped away to dance by the woman with snake-skin.

After that the dance floor was overrun, and Lucena could no longer keep track of who was dancing with whom: she danced with a string of guests, from the foxy gentleman to one of the pale goblins. She saw Beruse and Willic dancing together out of the corner of her eye, and then Willic dancing with Soloma, Madgrin dancing with Beruse, Madgrin dancing with Willic, and Madgrin dancing with Orrus. She even glimpsed Harga doing a wild, flapping dance with a scruffy old woman in a ragged woolen dress. And still the whistle played, getting into people's feet and making them dance faster and faster. Lucena got a stitch in her side and retired to the sidelines, then remembered she didn't have to breathe anyway, and returned to the dance full force.

At long last the music faded, and the dancers gratefully retired to the edges of the ballroom to clasp aching sides, rub tired feet, drink deeply from glasses of wine and cider nestled in the golden water lilies, feast upon the cakes and breads and puddings that had been hidden under the lilies, or simply collapse on the floor in a tired heap, which was what Willic did.

But the band was not finished yet. Lucena caught a glimpse of them through a gap in the crowd, their heads together. But then Orrus came hurrying over, out of breath and clinking all over from his chains, and spoke to them in a low voice. They leaned forward with a polite air of disappointment, but after Orrus had spoken earnestly for some minutes they shrugged and nodded. The violist, the one with violet eyes, stepped to the front of the dais and cleared his throat for silence. Then he said in his soft voice, which carried a good deal better than it should have:

"We thank you all for your enthusiastic participation in our last song," he said, and here he bowed low to them. From the floor, Willic groaned. "Unfortunately the dance will have to be put on hold for a short while, as we have just received a request from the man of the occasion. It is a song some of you may have not heard in hundreds of years, and many of you have never heard it before. I do not recommend dancing to it," his eyes flitted briefly to Lucena, "unless of course, you have eight legs." A pause, while some of the less fatigued guests laughed. The musician cleared his throat. "This is the Lay of Abneialaemh." And he said it Aub-nay-uh-leff, so quickly and easily Lucena almost didn't recognize what he had said.

When the song began she thought she had heard it before; or at least she got the feeling of knowing what the music was before she heard it. But then the musician with the lute who wore a red arm band began to sing, and Lucena forgot the music. She forgot the words too, as soon as they were sung. She forgot the ballroom, and all the other guests. It seemed as though she had been transported away to a place with rolling green hills and dark twisted woods. Or perhaps that place had come to her. She could smell the grass and the warm earth, hear the crack and rustle of the wood as it muttered to itself. She could hear the wind too: it spoke of secrets and lies, and it came blowing out of the strange new place and into the ballroom. With it came a hundred new voices, singing along. The music filled every nook and cranny of the room, until the air itself was humming.

For ever after that, when Lucena went into quiet places and was very quiet herself, she thought she could hear that song, still echoing inside her head. But she could never remember the words, let alone what they meant.

She spent the rest of the night in a sort of daze: wandering in and out among the guests, trading smiles and polite conversation, her natural timidity forgotten. She made her way over to the shimmering sea of gold water lilies, and although the many treats and sweetmeats in them were nothing she could enjoy, she was delighted to see that the flowers were not made of foil, as Willic had first suggested, but were real living water lilies with soft, cool petals that shone golden in the candlelight.

The musicians began to play again, but it was ordinary music now: pleasing to the ear, but not the sort that made one jump up and dance against one's will, or summoned strange winds from far-off places. A few of the guests who had recovered from the previous dances moved out onto the floor again, but now it was the ordinary, sedate dances, like the ones you would expect to find in the ballroom of a fashionable nobleman, and they held no interest for her. Lucena made her way back to the chairs in front of the dais. Willic and Madgrin were gone, but Beruse was there, slumped back in her chair and rubbing her bare feet. She cast Lucena a rueful look as she sat down.

"I don't know what you told them," she said with a heavy sigh. "But if ol' Orrus hadn't stepped in we'd probably still be dancing. That's their favorite kind of music, and they know all the best tunes." Beruse rubbed her chin thoughtfully, and added in an undertone, barely audible over the music, "They *wrote* all the best tunes."

Lucena fidgeted uncomfortably in her seat. She knew it was probably rude to ask questions about the band when they were standing right behind her, but as they were playing, she couldn't very well ask them. So she tuned to Beruse.

"Just who are they? The musicians I mean?"

Beruse lifted an eyebrow tiredly. "Sons of Dream and Fancy, aren't they?" she said. "They're from the same place as us, me and Willic and Himself and all the rest, though they go wandering in the wider world a lot. They like humans, see? They're an odd bunch." Beruse scratched herself under one tufty ear. Then she turned around in her seat, with her chest up against the back of the chair, and pointed at the musicians like one does a large map. Feeling a little embarrassed, Lucena twisted her head around to see what Beruse was pointing at.

It turned out to be the one with the viol and violet eyes. He caught Lucena's gaze and winked.

"That's Gimbel, he writes a lot of their songs, though he doesn't sing much. He's nice. That," Beruse pointed at the one with the lute and red scarf, "is Tram. He doesn't talk; he only sings. It's hard to tell what he's thinking. That," and here she jabbed her finger at the one with sideburns and the drums, "is Grin. He's not so nice, but he's very clever. And," she waved her hand at the blond one with the penny whistle, "there's Boult. He can seem a little dim, but he's very kind. He *knows* stuff." Beruse sighed and turned back around in her chair. "Taken all together," she said, "we call them the Madders. Don't know why, exactly, but that's what they like to be called."

The night wore on. The guests danced until they could dance no more and then they ate and drank and told stories to each other. The brown man with the red hair who had first asked Lucena to dance came and found her, and insisted on praising her dancing. Lucena was a little taken aback at first, but came to realize she rather enjoyed being on the receiving end of such heartfelt admiration—and from such a handsome person, too.

When the candles were growing dim and the golden sea of water lilies began to sink, they paid their respects to Orrus and tottered out the door. Beruse took Lucena in her strong arms and carried her up to her room and put her to bed.

Lucena never dreamt, but in the dark oblivion of her sleep the next day she heard a humming faintly in the distance that might have been the Madders' song.

He was still Orrus, Lucena could tell, but a younger, fiercer Orrus. His hair was much longer, and instead of glasses over his eyes he wore bandages.

CHAPTER 7:

Keelback,

IT WAS NOT WHAT WOULD GENERALLY be considered a nice night. There was no moon (it had not risen yet), there were no stars (it was overcast), and it was not dry (the clouds above having got the notion that the earth below could use some wetness). But Lucena was enjoying herself immensely.

Seeing in the dark, she had decided, was the best power you got for being a vampire, and now she was testing her new abilities by walking around the lake on a pitch-black night. For her the impenetrable cloak of darkness was swept aside, and she was able to see across the water and even into the trees on the far bank.

Entranced with her newfound powers she dawdled along the shore, gazing at the trees, the rocks, the water, and the sky. Going so slowly, she made not a sound, and the lake was perfectly silent save for the patter of rain upon its surface.

Then there was a sound like *splish*, and a high, piercing mew came drifting across the water. Lucena started, staring around the lake in search of the source of the noise. This was soon revealed to be a small, fishlike creature swimming towards the shore with such speed that it left a thin trail of whitewater behind it. Upon reaching the area of the bank closest to Lucena it began jumping about and mewing, giving off such signs of distress that she lost no time in hurrying over and kneeling down on the mossy bank by the water.

"Whatever is the matter?" she asked the strange little creature. It appeared to be half fish, half spiny dragon, with a pair of pale human arms which it waved about in agitation. It mewed frantically, and dove beneath the water, only to resurface again. It repeated this action so many times that at last Lucena guessed what it wanted and, lying down on her stomach, dunked her head underwater.

It was cold, and she instinctively squeezed her eyes shut and held her breath. Then she heard in her left ear, very distinctly, a small nervous voice.

"Oh young miss, young miss," the voice said. "We beg you come quick: we have found a thing, and we do not know what to do with it!"

Tentatively Lucena opened her eyes. Everything was dark and blurry, like things are under water, but she could clearly discern a bright, dancing blob before her face that had to be the strange little fish creature. She tried to answer, to ask what this "thing" was, but only bubbles and meaningless noise came out. So she had to take her head out of the water, cough, and repeat her question when the creature raised its dragony head above the surface.

"What sort of thing?" she gasped. And then stuck her head back under to hear the answer.

"A big thing, a magic thing. A heavy thing," the creature said. "Maybe evil, maybe not. It fell on Jenshua's house! Oh, please, please come, we cannot lift it by ourselves, and it does not belong here!"

CHAPTER 7: *Keelback*

Lucena considered. She had not the faintest clue how to swim, but then, she could not drown either, so she figured it wouldn't be too difficult to teach herself. The water was cold, but she couldn't freeze to death, and no matter how dark and murky the lake was, she fancied her eyes would adjust, just as they had done to the dark, starless night.

So she slipped off her dress, shoes, and all but one of her petticoats. Then, before she had time to reason herself out of what she was doing, she jumped into the water.

It was very cold, but she had been expecting that. What she hadn't expected was the way she bobbed back to the surface instead of sinking. She floated there for a few moments, perplexed, until she realized she was holding her breath. So against the last shreds of survival instinct she still possessed, Lucena exhaled all the air she could manage, dunked her head, and inhaled the water.

That made the cold much, much worse. Now it was inside her chest as well as all around her. But she was sinking now, and she could see a dim glimmer a few yards off that had to be the little creature. Experimentally she kicked against the water, and found herself moving in that direction. With the aid of her hands she was soon able to get about fairly well, and after a few minutes developed a usable kick, like that of a frog.

She floundered over to the faint glimmer, which did indeed turn out to be the creature, and was about to inquire as to the whereabouts of the thing that needed moving when she realized that now, with her lungs full of water, she couldn't speak at all. Fortunately, the creature seemed to understand this, and she heard its small voice pierce the murky water as it explained that they needed to go down.

So they went down. Down, down, down to where it really was pitch black, and the only thing Lucena could see was the dim golden glow of her guide. Yet she did not fear this darkness; although it wrapped itself around them like an impenetrable cloak, it still seemed to her a safe place. Eventually she began to discern tiny lights, and she wondered if her eyes were adjusting at last. But no, as they drew closer she saw what appeared to be, to her blurry vision, a tiny city built on the lake bottom.

Because of the dark, and the way all the lights seemed to bleed into each other, she only got a vague impression of many little squares of light all stacked together. She longed to swim down and take a closer look, but her guide did not even pause, and soon the lights were thinning out, until they were only specks in the growing black. About when Lucena expected them to disappear entirely she began to see another glow, but this was not a glow of houses: this was the glow of many creatures all clustered together. As they approached she caught snatches of their conversation, which sounded worried and distraught.

"But it is too big to move!"

"How long will it take for Jenshua to get the pulleys and ropes?"

"I tell you it must belong to the turtle, who else could lay an egg so big?"

"Do you really think we should move it?"

"Ah, here's Isshin! Isshin, what have you brought?"

This last was addressed to Lucena's guide, who darted forward and hastily explained that he had found someone from the House who could help them. In the meantime Lucena strained her eyes through the dark and the blurriness, trying to make out what the cause of all the commotion could be.

To her air-adapted eyes there seemed to be the dim glow of a house there, most of which was blocked out by a black lump about the size of a large pumpkin. Perhaps a rock of some sort? But it was perfectly oval in shape, although there were bumps and nubs all over it when she reached out her hand to touch it.

The little creatures were all clamoring at her by this time, begging and pleading for her to remove the object, whatever it was. So she carefully planted her feet on the spongy lake bottom (great clouds of sand and decaying leaves billowed up at this, making the creatures scatter) and took firm hold of the object's nubbly sides.

Lucena expected it to be heavy, but what with being underwater, not to mention her new vampiric strength, it came up quite easily. But then she had not the least idea what to do with it. Isshin would not let her put it down again, as that would ruin what was left of Jenshua's garden, and even though the thing was light enough to carry, Lucena found she couldn't swim up with it. Having dispelled all the air in her body she could no longer float naturally, and with the object in one arm it was impossible to swim.

She floundered helplessly for a while, trying not to step on anything important, until she became aware of a new creature, who had arrived and was tugging a thick, heavy rope. All the little creatures exclaimed over this, but the new creature did not respond. It swam over to Lucena and threw her the rope, then with a shy squeak darted away into the shadows.

The rest of the creatures clustered around her, marveling at it. But Lucena, who recognized opportunity when she saw it, took hold of the rope and jerked it sharply.

Almost at once it began pulling her upwards. Taken by surprise, Isshin and the others were left behind momentarily, but soon caught up with her as she rose swiftly through the shadowy waters, the strange object still clutched to her chest.

Lucena saw the surface long before they reached it; a shimmering grey veil cast over the sky. The rope snaked its way up there, thick and dark, and she went with it. When she broke the surface, instinct took over and she tried to inhale, but with her lungs already full of water this proved disastrous. Clutching the rope in one hand and the object with her arm she felt herself pulled to shore, coughing and choking and spewing froth and bubbles everywhere. She was aware of strong arms helping her out of the water, and Harga's voice saying "Now what have you got here?" but she was too busy emptying her lungs and stomach to answer. For almost five minutes she sat on the lakeshore coughing up water, until at last she was able to take a deep, shuddering breath and reply, with only a few hiccups, that she didn't know.

"Well, whatever it is, the kilips seem happy that you took it off their hands," Harga remarked. He was looking out over the water as he spoke, and following his gaze Lucena saw a cluster of little glowing heads bobbing above the water, and tiny human arms waving at her. She smiled and waved back.

Harga walked with Lucena up to the house. He didn't say how he knew she was in the lake, or how he had sent the rope down after her, but that might have

CHAPTER 7: *Keelback*

been because he was too busy asking questions and poking at the object Lucena had retrieved, which she held tight in her arms the entire way.

"It is obviously an egg of some sort," he declared at once. "Big enough to be a roc's egg, but not smooth enough. See, these bumps are all a natural part of its surface, although there seems to be some algae on it. I wonder how long it was under the water. I don't suppose it could still be alive . . . though dragonturtle eggs take years to hatch. And so strange, I cannot for the life of me recognize it, and I have seen more eggs than you could credit, Lucena."

So enthralled was he that, when they reached the house, and Lucena was whisked away by a concerned Gydda for a change of clothes, he took charge of the egg, saying he would bring it up to the library for Orrus to look at. But when at last Lucena got away from Gydda, who refused to believe vampires could not catch a chill and wanted to give her a hot bath and broth and very nearly succeeded, she found no one there except Library herself, who said she had turned the men out as they were threatening to drip lake water all over her books. Where had they gone? She did not know or care. Lucena was almost mad with frustration when, by a stroke of luck, she found Willic curled up asleep in an alcove of the hall. He was not pleased to be woken, but when told of the excitement he happily led her away, asking old cupboards and empty rooms if they had seen two men and an egg. By these methods they were at last found, having occupied an old workroom which had not been used in ages, judging from the dust.

Orrus pushed his glasses up his nose in surprise when Willic and Lucena burst into the room. Harga had set the egg on a table, where it was making a small puddle of water which had just begun to drip off the edge. The spirit of the room looked at it glumly. He was a shabby old man with scraggily grey hair and an even scragglier beard and didn't even blink at their entrance.

"Oh, hello Lucena," Harga said. He had taken his hat off, and his floppy dog ears were perked up into two mounds atop his head, giving him an unusually alert air. "Sorry we lost you, but just as well you found us; this egg is a right diddle."

"He means puzzle," Orrus explained. "I think it is a griffin egg, but if so it should by rights be dead, as it is completely cold." He rubbed at the scruff on his chin and frowned. "But it is not dead at all, there is something alive inside, and unless I have completely lost my future-sight, it should hatch any day. I don't suppose the kilips mentioned where it came from?"

Lucena shrugged. "They just said it fell on Jenshua's house."

The men had brought candles and lit them, and by their flickering light she was able to get a good look at the egg at last.

It was about two feet long and a perfect oval, covered all over with blotchy brown and green—though some of the green was algae. Its surface was bumpy and nubbly, and around each nub were rings of pale brown, like the ripples a stone makes when it is thrown into a pool of water.

Orrus and Harga discussed the egg for nearly a quarter of an hour, during which time Willic made unhelpful suggestions, and Lucena remained silent. For some reason the sight of the egg filled her with a forlorn, lost feeling, as if she were looking at an abandoned kitten. Obviously whatever had laid the egg was long gone, and the hatchling—when it hatched—would never know its parents.

As if sharing her sentiment, Harga declared he didn't care what creature might come from it, it needed warmth and a safe place to hatch, and to that end he took it away to his den, and Lucena helped him make up some bedding for it out of sand and old blankets, with a pail of water nearby, in case it was a dragon egg.

"Though to own the truth," Harga remarked when they were finished, "if it *is* a dragon a pail of water won't go far."

Soon the egg was the talk of the house, and to Lucena's great consternation, so was she. Beruse was impressed with her daring recovery of the egg and jealous of not being there at the time to see it happen. She contented herself with repeating the story to everyone she met, and soon Lucena found herself being accosted by random rooms, halls, and closets, offering congratulations.

The only person who wasn't impressed by the story was Soloma. Soloma was impressed by the egg. Cool, calm, serpentine Soloma, who rarely left Madgrin's study and practically never showed interest in anything else, was fascinated by it. She was up all hours of the night sneaking out to Harga's den, and whenever she went brought extra blankets, mufflers, and scarves, as if the egg might have worn out the ones Harga had supplied and was in need of new clothes. Harga, exasperated by this, as the interior of his home could only contain so many articles, was obliged to sneak what Soloma brought back up to the house once she had gone.

When not showering Harga with unwanted assistance, Soloma entertained herself by giving him unwanted advice. As a natural reptile she felt herself better qualified on the subject of egg treatment than a mammal, even if, as Harga pointed out, she had never hatched a brood in her life.

Yet for all the attention the egg received from both Harga and Soloma, not to mention Lucena, who often found excuses to sneak down to the den, it never showed the smallest signs of hatching. It remained cold and hard and still as rock, and quite as unwilling to crack.

As the excitement surrounding the egg began to dim, life returned more or less to normal. Lucena took to spending more of her time in the library, where Orrus pointed out all the best books and didn't mind that she preferred the storybooks to those with academic or philosophic content. Indeed, it was partly because of Orrus that Lucena was so drawn to the storybooks, particularly those retelling stories she thought she already knew. For Orrus had a way of talking about stories, not only as if they had actually happened, but also as if he had known the characters personally. Whenever Lucena would finish a book she would bring it to him, and he would take it in his hands and say, "Ah yes, the first story of Timplemeyer Idlewit, later known as both Rumplestiltskin and Tom Tit Tot . . . a charming, clever man. Poor fellow, he never did have a clue with women. Did you know that what he really meant when he asked for her firstborn, was that he wanted to marry her? After all, a man who does a woman's chores without complaint must be infinitely preferable to a rich and greedy king who locks his wife away and threatens to kill her, mustn't he? But no, the girl took it all wrong, and so the whole suit got addled. But this book tells the entire story, doesn't it? Ah, I can see from your face that it does not!" And then he

CHAPTER 7: *Keelback*

would go on to explain how, in the case of Timplemeyer Idlewit, he had gone on to spin gold for another princess, and this one, who was not actually a princess at all but instead a misplaced but charming peasant-girl, eventually figured out what he was really saying, and the two eloped.

"They lived happily ever after, of course," Orrus said, sitting back in his chair with a satisfied sigh. "And they still are, but for some reason storytellers have forgotten that bit. I think they felt it would put wrong ideas into their daughters' heads—though what's so wrong with a woman choosing a man who knows his way around a house? Oh well, it doesn't make it any less true."

Orrus was always insistent on stories being true. Even stories Lucena was certain had never actually happened, like the legend of the farm girl who turned out to be a great dragon, but Orrus said it was true too. When she asked him how this could be he just chuckled and said, "Well, Lucena, there are two different kinds of true stories: there are the stories that are true because they really happened, and then there are stories that are true because they *make* things happen. There's my story, you remember. It's true because it did really happen in your world. And there is Dragonfly's story, which did not happen in our worlds but exists in its own right because it is told and heard, written and read, and resonates with those humans who are not only human but something else as well."

And his eyes lingered a little on Lucena, and Lucena asked if there were more stories like the Legend of Dragonfly, and Orrus answered by giving her a long list.

But Lucena's readings were not confined to fiction. She made valiant headway in *Vampires: A History*, with the help of Willic. Together they read about all sorts of different vampires: vampires who could turn into smoke or bats, or who could steal dreams out of your head, flip them over, and put them back again. They read about low vampires and high vampires, how vampires lost their souls, and how, in some cases, they regained them.

Vampires: A History was fuzzy on this last subject. It seemed the author had been speculating on the possibility of a vampire with a soul, rather than speaking from certain knowledge. He claimed that a vampire with a soul became a different being altogether—that one of the quintessential aspects of a vampire was the partial or complete lack of a soul.

"He's not entirely right, you know," Willic remarked, giving Lucena a thoughtful look. "Some vampires do have souls, and they're not so different. In fact, I think you could say a vampire with a soul is more a vampire than a vampire without one, because a vampire without a soul is just a monster."

"But I don't have a soul!" Lucena protested.

Willic frowned. "Not a complete one, no," he said. "But you've got enough of one to be getting on with. You can just be glad Himself knew what he was doing."

Lucena fell silent, and interested herself in the brocade on the armrest of her chair.

"But he is right about one thing," Willic said quietly. "Vampires can change. Some of them change into bigger vampires, and some of them change into . . . actually, I think he covers that right at the end. I won't give it away."

Lucena gave him a sullen look from across the room. Reading about vampires was all very well, but it still gave her an uncomfortable twisting feeling in her belly to remember that she was one too. And there was something else: a tightening across her chest that was not unlike the sting of shame, although she had no idea why she should be ashamed.

The dangerously morbid silence was effectively dispelled not a minute later when Beruse burst into the room, nearly ripping the door from its hinges. Willic and Lucena jumped.

"The egg!" Beruse gasped, her normally dark face flushed a rosy pink with excitement. "It's finally hatching! Both of you—come *on!*"

Willic barely had time to set the book aside before Beruse caught him with one pawlike hand, hooked elbows with Lucena, and tore off down the halls. She got going so fast that at times Lucena and Willic were lifted clean off their feet. It was almost like traveling with Madgrin!

They went out through the kitchen, where Gydda had apparently abandoned a huge pile of dishes in the sink. Then Beruse was shouting apologies to Frayne over her shoulder as they dashed through the garden, hopped the fence, and pelted along the path towards the wood.

Harga's cottage, when they arrived, was more crowded than Lucena had believed possible. It was a small place, snug enough with two, but now it contained not only Harga, Orrus and Soloma, but Gydda, Rhyse, Grimmach, Cobbin, and even Rusion, the raven of the Day Watch, propped in a corner, looking tired but excited. With the addition of Beruse, Willic and Lucena, it was a wonder the house did not start bulging outwards.

Everyone was crowded around the egg, and Lucena felt like giving up, but Beruse pushed and shoved and eventually got them to the center, where Harga and Soloma crouched anxiously over the makeshift nest.

The egg appeared no different than ever, except now a long dark crack ran lengthwise along it, and it was quivering gently. Even as Lucena leaned forward, trying to catch a glimpse of what was inside, the crack widened, and something pale poked its way out through the top. It was the size of Lucena's thumbnail, and about the same color as her hair (dirty yellow), and for a moment she thought it was a claw of some sort. But then it split in two and began biting at the edge of its shell, trying to chip it away. A hushed gasp went around the room as everyone there realized that whatever was inside the egg, it had a beak.

The egg cracked further open, and for a moment it looked like the whole thing would split neatly in two, but then the beak appeared at the hole at the top, madly pecking at the edge until the hole was quite large. Everyone leaned forward, trying to look inside. And then the beak reappeared, this time followed by a wrinkly, featherless, but unmistakably birdlike head, and then a long neck. Then the egg did split in two, and the rest of whatever had been inside spilled out onto the sand.

It appeared to be a snake. What Lucena had thought was a long neck turned out to be only part of its body. Still, it was bigger by far than any snake she had ever seen—as wide around as her forearm and at least five feet long. Its head was definitely that of a bird, with a strong curving beak and heavy brows. Being featherless, however, and with its wrinkled, scaly skin, it looked more like a dragon.

CHAPTER 7: *Keelback*

It lay in the sand for some time, half in and half out of its shell, breathing heavily through its open beak. There was some shoving at the back of the room as Orrus struggled to the front of the crowd to get a better look. When he did, he adjusted his glasses and leaned down over the strange creature, being careful not to touch it.

"What *is* it?" Harga asked, voicing everyone's question.

Orrus straightened up, took off his glasses, wiped them on his robe and put them back on again. "I don't know," he said at length. When a sigh of disappointment ran through the little house he pulled at his beard in annoyance and added, "I've never seen or heard of anything like this before. It could have been a fourth-order demon, but demons don't hatch from eggs. It could be a sort of dragon, but I've never found a dragon with a true *beak* before. And it's neither a bird nor a snake, that much is for certain."

Rusion roused himself, and looked about to say something, but Soloma cut him off.

"It doesn't matter what it is: it must be hungry. Harga, did you prepare anything to feed it?"

"I, what?" Harga glared at her. "Of course not! I had no idea what it would be!"

Soloma hissed in disapproval, and she looked like she would have liked to say that was no excuse, but at that moment the creature's eyes opened for the first time, along with its beak, and it let out a high, piercing whine. It made Lucena's ears ring, and everyone took an involuntary step back, but what it meant was perfectly clear: the creature was indeed hungry.

"Judging from the shape of its beak," Orrus remarked, his hands over his ears, "I would say it is likely carnivorous. Harga, do you have any fresh meat?"

Harga did, and a few moments later had brought out a dead rabbit and was cutting strips of meat off it with his pocket knife, while Soloma tossed the strips into the creature's snapping mouth. This continued until the rabbit was a bare skeleton, and the creature decided it had had enough. It curled itself into a ball, its head resting on its back, and went to sleep.

Harga sighed, and began putting away the remains of the rabbit, while Orrus leaned over and carefully extracted a broken piece of shell. As he turned it over in his hands, Lucena saw that the inside was smooth and glossy and a pinkish color, rather like the mother-of-pearl in the lid of her aunt's favorite jewelry box. Orrus tucked it away inside his robes and turned to leave.

Most of the crowd followed him, Gydda staggering under the weight of Rusion, who had fallen asleep. Willic, finding the excitement over, left as well. But Lucena stayed, crouched by the makeshift nest, with Beruse looming behind her. Harga went to wash his hands, and Soloma knelt right down next to the creature, her reptilian eyes shining.

The creature's breathing was slow, and Lucena noticed how the skin on its head and back was grey and leathery, while it had smooth, slightly translucent, buff-colored scales all along its chest. It gave the creature a strange, unfinished look, as though whatever had been making it had put the scales on its chest, but then had been called away before providing the same service to its back.

Harga returned, and commented on how late it was, and expressed his desire for some sleep. Beruse and Lucena politely excused themselves, and then waited for Soloma to do the same. But Soloma remained by the creature's side, quite unwilling to move, or even look up at them. Eventually Beruse was obliged to pick Soloma up and carry her, thrashing and protesting, away.

The next night when Lucena went to visit Harga and the strange creature, she found Soloma back at her position, crouching protectively over it. But as soon as the creature saw Lucena it opened its mouth and let out a soft, happy groan. Taken aback, Lucena stopped, but the creature wriggled out from Soloma's grasp and slid over the floor to her feet. There it looked up at her with round yellow eyes and began to make a hoarse laughing sort of sound.

"Oh dear," Lucena said, a little flustered. "Is it hungry again?"

Soloma hurried over; she picked the creature up in her arms and carried it back to the nest, where she stroked it and made soothing hissing sounds. The creature was almost asleep when Harga came back with another rabbit. Then it woke up and began making the high-pitched screaming sound it had before, and Harga had to set it in his lap and feed it strips of meat to get it to be quiet.

Although both Harga and Soloma showed the little creature nothing but the fondest devotion, it was to Lucena that it developed an attachment, much to her surprise and their exasperation. Then, about a week after it had hatched, the creature contrived to follow Lucena up to the house. She was not aware of this until she had been reading in her room for almost half an hour, when she heard a faint tapping sound coming from her door. She opened it, and the creature fairly leaped into her arms. This was no light matter, as it had been growing steadily since it hatched and was now as thick as a young birch and over ten feet long. Fortunately for Lucena it was easy enough to carry around fifty pounds of strange creature, and this she did for the rest of the night until Soloma, waking early, came and took it up to her room. But then Harga missed it and went barging through the house in search, and during the violent row that followed the creature slipped away again. When Lucena woke the next evening it was to a rather heavy weight on her chest, and two round yellow eyes staring at her.

"Oh, good evening to you," Lucena said sleepily, fumbling for the bottle of blood on her bedside table.

The creature opened its mouth wide, made the hoarse laughing noise, and then said in a clear, albeit rather nasal, voice: "Kee-el."

"What?" Lucena asked. She was distracted, being still half asleep and thirsty.

"Baa-ak," said the creature, and slithered off the bed where it began exploring the floor of her room, poking its beak curiously into all the corners, its body coiling and sliding gracefully over the carpet.

Afterwards the creature was always talkative in front of Lucena, although the only things it would say were "keel" and "baak" and various combinations of the two. Because of this she began calling it Keel-baak, which eventually became Keelback, which stuck. But no matter what she did she could never persuade it to speak in front of others. Harga was disappointed about this, and Soloma was bitter and jealous that the creature should behave specially for anyone other than her.

CHAPTER 7: *Keelback*

The fight over Keelback continued, with Harga feeding it rabbit in his cottage, and Soloma stealing it away up to her room to give it baths. But this routine was foiled as Keelback always managed to slip away and find Lucena, wherever she might be.

By the time it had been hatched two weeks it was easily twenty feet long, and still growing. Strange, tube-shaped scales appeared all over its leathery back and head. Lucena could not imagine what they were, but Harga identified them as pinfeathers. And then it seemed the very next day Keelback was covered in soft, sleek feathers, save for its underbelly, which remained smooth and scaly. The feathers were white with black tips, giving it a speckled appearance, and uniformly sleek and smooth, like the feathers on a bird's breast. They started with a crest of white feathers at the head, and terminated just above the tail, which remained bare and scaly.

The feathers were a blow for Soloma, who had wished Keelback to remain as snake-like as possible. But Harga pointed out that it was actually a good thing: Keelback was warm blooded, not cold blooded like a snake, and so having feathers as a means of insulation was a good thing for him. Soloma then asked icily why he was so sure Keelback was *male*, to which Harga just shrugged and said, "It seems to suit him." This sparked another quarrel between the two, which unfortunately happened to take place in Harga's cottage, where he had been feeding Keelback.

Keelback did not like quarreling, and decided to remove himself (though he was on Harga's side in this case) from the scene as quickly as possible. And this he did; moving swiftly through the dark wood until he came out on the familiar path towards the house. There he paused, uncertain of what to do.

Ordinarily he would have gone straight up to the house in search of Lucena, but that night something called to him from the direction of the gate. So he veered off the path towards the main drive, and began slithering along it.

Lucena was in the orchard when Harga and Soloma discovered their charge missing, so she was not in her room when they came banging on the door looking for him. In the end Willic found her, reading beneath one of the apple trees, and explained that Keelback had gone missing.

Lucena was surprised, but not worried. Somehow she felt, in the same place at the back of her mind where Madgrin spoke to her, that no harm had come to Keelback. Even so, when she saw how worried the other two were she decided she had better go find Keelback and show everyone it was all right.

She went by instinct rather than reason or logic. While everyone searched the house, Lucena went around to the front door and began walking out the main drive. She had barely got halfway to the bridge when a familiar figure appeared out of the darkness in front of her. To anyone else he would have been perfectly invisible, for he wore a long dark cloak and hood, and walked like a shadow.

"Maker," she said, stopping. She had intended to tell him all about Keelback, and how he couldn't be found, but at that moment she saw what he held in his arms: it was Keelback, fast asleep.

"Good evening, La Flein," Madgrin said. He held out Keelback as if the creature weighed no more than a down pillow. "This, I believe, is yours."

"I . . . er . . . its not, really," Lucena said, stammering a little.

"Really?" Madgrin said. He sounded amused. "He seems to think so."

"How do you know it's a he?" she asked.

"He told me," Madgrin said mildly. "Now come take what is yours, Lucena."

Slowly, partly because of how heavy Keelback had become, Lucena reached out and lifted him out of Madgrin's arms. He woke up almost at once, and looped himself affectionately around her shoulders. Lucena couldn't help giggling a little as the soft feathers tickled her face.

"Hullo, 'Cena," he said, in a quiet, chirping voice. Lucena stifled a jump of surprise.

"You talked!" she exclaimed.

"Been talking," Keelback replied sleepily. "You just weren't un'standing me. Shadow man fixed it." He yawned a great, beaky yawn, and settled his head against Lucena's chest. In a moment he was asleep again.

Lucena shot a perplexed look at Madgrin, who returned it with a wide twinkling smile.

"Harga and Soloma will be terribly disappointed," she said, sighing.

Madgrin shrugged. He put a hand on Lucena's back and steered her up the drive towards the house. "They must learned to accept it. He really was yours to begin with, and they know it."

"Mine? How is he mine?"

"Well, you brought his egg up from the bottom of the lake, didn't you? If you hadn't he would have died. His life is your charge, and yours his. The two of you will always be connected."

"You know about the kilips and the lake?" Lucena asked. She was surprised. Madgrin had been absent for the past few weeks, and during that time they hadn't spoken at all.

"Yes," he said. "I know everything that happens within the grounds of my House." It didn't sound like a boast at all, only a simple statement.

"So, do you know how his egg ended up on Jenshua's house?" Lucena asked, suddenly very curious. "Do you know what he is?"

"Oh, yes," Madgrin said. "But I'm afraid I can't tell you that. It's a mystery, you see," he added, seeing the expression on her face.

"If you know it, how can it be a mystery?" Lucena asked.

"If *you* knew it, it would not be a mystery," Madgrin said, amused. "I am different. I keep things secret. I keep the mysteries safe."

And that was all he would say on the matter. Lucena sighed, and stroked the feathers between Keelback's eyes, which were particularly soft and fluffy.

"Harga and Soloma will still make a fuss," she told her sleeping friend. "They are both so fond of you."

"To their credit," Madgrin admitted cheerfully, quickening his pace. The lights of the house were visible to them now, glowing invitingly in the gloom. "But it is not as though they will be drastically parted from him. They can still see him as much as he pleases them to. And if all else fails, I am still the Maker of the House. And my word ought to count for something."

Lucena laughed, and agreed it was so.

*. . . Isshin and the others were left behind momentarily,
but soon caught up with her as she rose swiftly through the shadowy waters,
the strange object still clutched to her chest.*

CHAPTER 8:

ꟾGoing Hunting

KEELBACK FOLLOWED LUCENA EVERYWHERE, sometimes wrapped around her shoulders, sometimes slithering behind her, though since he continued to grow at an astonishing rate, the latter became more and more common as the weeks passed by.

He began talking more, though still with some odd mispronunciations, and he had difficulty with the letter L at the beginning of words. Because of this he called Lucena "'Cena," no matter how often she corrected him.

Exactly what Keelback was remained a mystery. Even with Orrus's help she could find nothing definitive in the library—though there were a great many beings which shared characteristics with Keelback, none were a perfect match. When Lucena bemoaned that Madgrin knew but would not say Orrus patted her sympathetically on the shoulder.

"That is his right as a Master of Mysteries," he said. "He keeps his secrets well, else he would not be one. Let it be, that's my advice. It won't be found 'til it wants to be, and as long as the creature knows himself there's no need to break yourself in search of it."

And with that Lucena had to be content, as Keelback knew himself to be Keelback and was happy with that. His favorite pursuit was to spend all his waking moments in Lucena's presence, and many of his sleeping ones besides. Many times she woke to find him using her for a pillow, with his heavy head upon her stomach and his tail trailing off the bed and around the room.

After about a month or so, in early summer, Madgrin called Lucena (and by association, Keelback) into his study. Lucena was unsure if she would be able to navigate the Room of Doors with a giant snakelike creature along for the ride, but to her delight Keelback had no trouble. In fact, the moment they passed through the door and began their slow, dreamlike fall down through the many, many other doors, he gave a happy squawk and darted through the air like a fish through water. Lucena, who had been holding him under her arm, was yanked along and soon had to hold on with both hands as Keelback twisted and writhed and dashed through the air. He would glide up the front of one door, pause, and then glide down the other side, twist, and then spiral down, down, down, before shooting up again, all the while laughing his hoarse, hacking laugh.

After the first few moments of shock Lucena came to enjoy this immensely, and she was able to look around at the room of doors with more attention than she had before. She noticed, with relief, that the door they had come through, the door to the rest of the house, remained fixed. In fact, there was no possible way it could have moved; it was set into the side of an ancient stone wall made of pale grey bricks. Lucena noticed also how the room appeared to have no floor or

CHAPTER 8: *Going Hunting*

ceiling . . . or any walls, besides the one. For that matter, the solitary stone wall faded into misty darkness above and below her, and the doors faded away into the distance, like things do in a fog. The doors themselves were always moving, albeit slowly, though there didn't seem to be a pattern to their movements; they merely floated this way and that, like motes of dust in a beam of sunlight.

If they hadn't had an appointment to keep, Lucena imagined they would have played in the Room of Doors for many hours. But as soon as she spotted the door to Madgrin's study, she began to feel nervous of making him wait. With some effort she convinced Keelback to fly down to it, so she might get off and go in. But Keelback decided that it would not be so much fun playing with the doors unless he had Lucena with him, and so it was that a few moments later they tumbled together into Madgrin's study, startling Soloma so that she nearly spilled her ink.

A cheery fire crackled in the dragon's-mouth hearth, throwing dancing shadows across the banners for the Watch, the Keepers, and the rest of Madgrin's staff. Beside the great oak desk, at her own writing table, Soloma was hastily filing away papers, obviously not wanting to miss this opportunity to fawn over Keelback. But what drew Lucena's attention was the wardrobe that stood in the middle of the righthand wall amid the pictures of strange landscapes. For once, it was open.

Lucena crossed the room to the wardrobe, meaning to peek inside, but she only got a glimpse of dark fur cloaks, before they were shoved aside and Beruse stuck her head out.

"Madgrin," she said in a loud voice, "I couldn't find anything to fit her, so we'll just have to use my old things—oh, hello there 'Cena." She broke off upon observing Lucena. Then she seemed to have an idea. "Oi, you come here a moment," she said, grabbing Lucena by the wrist and dragging her into the wardrobe.

Inside it was all dusty cloaks and the smell of mothballs, but Beruse dragged her straight through them, and she found herself in a bare, circular stone room. There was one window very high up, which showed some faint summer stars. The room was dimly it by a few scraggily candles, set in holders on the wall. In the wall also were many doors, a few of which were open, allowing Lucena to glimpse suits of armor, chain mail, and weapons.

Beruse began picking up some articles which lay about the floor as though they had been tossed there; Lucena recognized some heavy leather gauntlets and thick leather boots. Another seemed to be a sort of bodice with strange inscriptions written all down the front. Beruse held this up to Lucena, frowned, and began fiddling with the laces that ran up either side.

"May I ask what all this is for?" Lucena inquired, eyeing the chain mail warily.

"Well," Beruse said, handing Lucena the leather gauntlets and boots so she could have that hand free. "Himself wanted you to come with us tonight and said I should get you some armor. These are my old things, which may be a bit long and loose for you, but they'll do better than anything else we've got here."

"I see," said Lucena. She examined the gauntlets, noting with concern their worn fingers and the many faded stains. "But where will we be going, that I will need such protection?"

"Where are we going?" Beruse repeated, surprised. "Didn't Willic tell you? You're coming hunting with us tonight."

Then she helped Lucena get into the strange bodice, which felt stranger still once it was on. It covered her from her collarbone to her hips, which made bending over difficult. The boots, once Beruse had provided some thick woollen socks, fit well enough, though the gauntlets made her hands so big and clumsy they agreed in the end to leave them off. Finally Beruse handed her a long, coarsely woven wool cloak with a voluminous hood, and after Lucena had put it on, declared her ready.

Then Beruse went to one of the open closets and pulled out a similar set of armor, only these were much larger and made of black leather, and the bodice had a great "M" in silver inlay over the chest. She wriggled herself into it in a way that suggested she had done it thousands of times. Finally she reached inside the closet that held the weapons and pulled out a short, wide sword in a leather scabbard which she hooked to her belt.

When they returned to Madgrin's study they found Soloma meticulously preening the feathers on Keelback's back. Keelback, miserably bored, saw Lucena and Beruse and surged forward, upsetting Soloma at her work. He wound himself lovingly around Lucena, resting his head on her shoulder. Because of this, the apology that Lucena offered came out a little muffled, but Soloma only shrugged and stalked back to her desk, muttering something about rude children.

Beruse eyed Keelback warily. "You know, I'm not sure Madgrin wants you to come with us," she said to him. "I think you might... er... not like it very much."

Before Keelback could voice an objection he was cut off by the sound of someone laughing from the shadows by the hearth. "No, no, he shall come," the voice said. "By all means, he *should* come."

Lucena looked around and saw Madgrin standing in the shadows behind one of the hearth's carved horns that doubled as a hat or coat hook. But when she looked again she saw that was not quite right: he was not standing in the shadow, he *was* the shadow. As he moved away from the wall and came to join them in the center of the room he left that corner brightly lit by firelight, though the shadow still clung about his shoulders and his feet.

"Now everyone," he said, once they were all gathered together in the center of the carpet. "Look down, if you please."

Lucena swallowed nervously; she remembered this carpet and what it could do, and really had no wish to be engulfed by it. Then to her surprise something soft and warm wrapped around her hand—Madgrin's hand. There were two odd things about this: first, his hand was warm, which didn't seem quite right, as it was the same white tinged with cold pale blue as his face. It came to Lucena's mind briefly that perhaps he was warm from standing next to the fireplace. Second: it seemed like such a sentimental, parental gesture that she almost wanted to throw it off in defiance. But by the time she had realized all this they were halfway into the carpet, and she was glad she had something to hold on to.

Glancing down, her eyes fixed on an empty patch of blue ocean, and soon she could smell the heady, salty scents of the sea and hear the blustering wind in her

CHAPTER 8: *Going Hunting*

ears. Then, before the water became real enough to get her wet, she was hauled sideways, and then the world was flying past beneath her.

It came too fast to see, wheeling colors of blues and browns and greens all streaked and blurred with speed. She clung to Madgrin's hand, even though it seemed to be moving along with her rather than pulling her. Looking ahead she had just enough time to notice a great dark blot moving towards them, and then they were in it. Almost at once they slowed down, and soon they were gliding gently over the steep roofs and narrow cobbled streets of an unfamiliar village. It was night, and the only lights were the golden glow from a few windows and the pale, sparkling stars.

They alighted on the roof of a grand house with spiky turrets and dark windows. At first they were all in the same positions they had been when they left Madgrin's study, but almost at once Lucena stumbled back several paces. Indeed, she nearly fell off the roof, it was so steeply slanted. Fortunately she was still holding Madgrin's hand, and this she clung to for dear life. He stood patiently while Lucena clawed her way up his arm, and Beruse swore loudly in a foreign language; she had landed near the edge and had to drop to all fours to stop herself falling.

The only member of the party—apart from Madgrin—who had no problem with their arrival was Keelback. He had come loose from Lucena during the journey and landed on the roof at her feet. He easily found a grip on the steep, tiled surface, and watched their reactions with curiosity.

After righting herself the first thing Lucena noticed was the smell. During the months of being in and around the House of Madgrin she had grown used to dusty, old smells, and the gentle sweet scents of the kitchen gardens and orchards—even damp, wood-and-moss smells of the forest and the wet, watery smells of the river were familiar to her. She had grown so used to them, she now realized, that she had forgotten what the world outside smelled like.

This particular part of the outside world smelled of smokey air and the contents of chamber pots. And very faintly behind it all, there was a distant spicy scent which might have been pine trees.

The house upon whose roof they had landed was undoubtably the finest in the area, with many turrets rising above them and several layers of slanting roof falling away below. Despite its size it looked to be in a state of disrepair: several of the slates on the roof were coming loose, and the windows were all dark and some were broken.

Beyond this, the rest of the town stretched away below them. It contained houses in the same style as the one they stood upon, but on a more modest scale, all twinkling with lights. Towards the center of the town, where the lights merged together and were the brightest, Lucena thought she glimpsed the spire of a church, and a dark patch next to it which might have been a graveyard.

"Where are we?" she asked.

"Müldif, Elgany," Beruse answered. "The old Hexmason's house."

"Elgany?" Lucena echoed in a small voice. "But, but that's so far . . . " Elgany was one of the strange, foreign countries that lay on the other side of the mountains from Kyreland; Lucena had read about it in school, but all she remembered was that the Elgans were exceedingly clever and very good at witchcraft, and it was fortunate that two other countries and a whole mountain range stood between them and Kyreland.

Madgrin patted her reassuringly on her shoulder. "On the contrary, nothing is far from my house."

All this time Beruse had been standing very straight, her hand outstretched, palm up. Now a small light began to flicker at the tip of her middle finger and, as it grew, traveled down to rest in the palm of her hand. She stared at it intently for several moments. Then, nodding in satisfaction, she fisted her hand, extinguishing the light.

"I found them," she informed Madgrin. "Five miles to the north, in the forest. Shall I go?"

Madgrin gave her a slow, silent nod, and the next moment Beruse sprang from the roof like a jack-in-the-box whose lid has slipped. She landed with a distant thud on the roof of the nearest house, and then was off again, bounding into the darkness.

"Where is she going?" Lucena asked.

"Hunting," Madgrin said. He looked, Lucena thought, a little sad. But she could not think why. He turned away to address Keelback. "Which, now I come to think, is what you should be doing."

"Me?" Keelback said, drawing instinctively closer to Lucena.

"Well, yes." Madgrin seemed amused at his reaction. "You can't live off rabbit forever, now can you? Someone of your size really must learn to feed himself, and the forest over there"—he pointed a little east of where Beruse had been headed—"is full of succulent boar."

Keelback still looked indecisive, but when Lucena gave him a firm pat on the head and told him to give it a try, he slithered hesitantly off the roof.

"Return to us when you are done," Madgrin called after him. "And remember, if you meet any dragons, be polite to them!"

"Dragons?" Lucena exclaimed, suddenly wishing Keelback were not going off on his own. But he was already a pale flicker moving swiftly along the dark streets, and soon he disappeared altogether. "Are there many dragons in the forest?" she asked.

"A few," Madgrin said, not much concerned. "But for the most part, I think they will find Keelback as charming as we do."

"Now," he said, offering Lucena his elbow politely. "We will walk, and see what is to be seen."

Because he was so tall and she so short, Lucena could not hook arms with him the way one is supposed to, but had to hold on rather awkwardly with one hand. At first she felt embarrassed, but then they started walking and all thoughts of shame were wiped clean from her mind.

For with the very first step they took, they were walking on air.

Lucena gasped and grabbed Madgrin's arm with her other hand, just for good measure. But after a few more paces, when she had grown accustomed to seeing her feet firmly planted on nothing and the ground so far away, she removed her other hand and tried to assume a more ladylike posture. This was hampered by

CHAPTER 8: *Going Hunting*

the persistent feeling that every time she put her foot down it would simply fall through whatever they were walking on, and she would go hurtling to her death. But then, she reasoned, she was already technically dead, and would only suffer a great amount of pain if she did fall. But this was hardly any better.

"You may ask questions, if you like," Madgrin said, pulling her attention off such unpleasantries.

"May, may I?" Lucena stammered. With an effort she wrenched her gaze away from the ground and all its grisly prospects, and looked around. They were well into the town now, though still about ten feet above the rooftops. The smells of smoke and various decomposing substances were stronger here, and the scent of pine was weaker. "What... what sort of questions?"

"Oh, all the sorts that you have bumping about in your head," Madgrin said cheerfully. "I know they're there: *Where are we going? How in the world can you walk on thin air? What is Beruse hunting?* That sort of thing." He glanced down at her expectantly over one shoulder, his eyes alight in their dark hollows.

"Well, I can hardly ask them now," Lucena pointed out.

Madgrin laughed. It was a soft, gentle laugh, but nonetheless sounded like something one might hear coming from dark, empty places. Lucena suppressed a shiver.

"Shall I answer them?" he suggested.

"Please do," she replied.

"Well, as to where we are going... currently we are heading towards the center of town. You see the church spire there? I think we shall make a wide circle around it, and perhaps take a rest on the roof of the inn—you can just see its red brick chimneys beyond the church.

"To walking on thin air... in fact air is not at all thin, and if you know where to step, it is quite willing to support your weight.

"As to what Beruse is hunting... well. There is a story behind that...

"Not so very long ago—only about a hundred years—the Hexmason, which is what they call a gentleman-wizard in this country, befriended a vagabond who came wandering into this village one winter night. The vagabond was coatless, shoeless, and hatless, and thin as a rail. The Hexmason pitied him, so he took him inside and gave him a coat and shoes and a hat, fed him hot broth and warm milk and then put him to bed. The next morning the vagabond thanked the Hexmason for his kindness, and offered him anything in the world he liked as repayment. The Hexmason, who for all his learning was still an unobservant man, thought the vagabond was joking, and as a return joke he asked to have an army that could conquer the night. This is in reference to the old wizards' saying that *Day may suffer to bear our sins, but the night will not be conquered.* It has to do with the human fear of the dark. In any case the vagabond promised him this, and then left. Afterwards the Hexmason had a good laugh at the joke, told it to all his friends the next day, and then forgot about it.

"But a fortnight later, in the dead of night, he was visited by a tall, dark-haired gentleman. Behind the gentleman stood all the strongest youths of the village, but strangely altered; their skin was dead white and their jaws hung agape, revealing long, sharp canines. By these signs and others, the Hexmason recognized them as vampires, and the dark-haired gentleman as their master. The dark-haired gentleman said that they were his army to conquer the night, and where did he wish them to begin? But the Hexmason, having finally realized his situation, refused, and tried to defeat them by magic. But the dark-haired gentleman had magic of his own, and he overpowered the Hexmason, and killed him.

"Since then the Army to Conquer the Night, the army of vampires, lurks in the forests, wild with hunger, preying on lonesome travelers. That is what Beruse is hunting tonight."

Lucena's grip on Madgrin's arm had tightened as she listened to his story, and now she gave out a little gasp of realization. "But that's a whole *army*," she said. "Can Beruse defeat them all?"

"I believe so. They have run the length of their story, and are ours to take. And Beruse is strong and skilled, and has been doing this for many centuries." He smiled down at her.

"But, what about the dark-haired gentleman, the master vampire?"

Madgrin sighed. "The gentleman vampire still lives in the old Hexmason's house. Sometimes he comes out to feed on the townsfolk. For a time he was the terror of the village, and stories about him circulated far and wide . . . but those stories are no longer told, and now he is only a local pest. Tonight his story is ended." Madgrin looked out into the darkness, his face unreadable. They walked on in silence for a while, now passing the church on their right and making a wide bend around it. Then he added, almost as an afterthought, "We will meet him soon."

Lucena did not have to ask what they were going to do when they met him. It was written all over the heavy set of her maker's head, the hunch of his shoulders and the arch of his brow. He looked, every inch of him, a predator.

After they had come almost full circle around the church something occurred to Lucena, and she asked, "But who was the vagabond?"

"Hmm?" Madgrin seemed to have been thinking of something else, and he looked down at her curiously.

"The vagabond who the Hexmason took in, the vagabond who promised him the army?"

"Oh," Madgrin said, his brows lowering to cast shadows over his eyes. Like that his face looked more skull-like than ever. "He was a magician. The very worst sort of magician; he made it his practice to go about pretending to be a *daodhé*—"

"A day-o what?" Lucena interrupted despite herself.

"A day-od-hay," Madgrin enunciated. "That is our word for creatures that, if you do them a kindness, no matter how slight, will repay you with favors and good fortune. They often appear as beggars, vagabonds, and other undesirable persons. You hear of them all the time in fairytales. This magician would go about playing the part of a *daodhé*, but no matter what his benefactor asked for, he would twist it about so that they came off the worse for it. He was brutal: once a mother asked that her children never go hungry, and the next day they all died of dragon-pox. We have a word for his type too; we call them *lothrin*, after the most dangerous sort of fairy."

CHAPTER 8: *Going Hunting*

"Well, what happened to *him?*" Lucena asked in a small voice.

"About thirty years ago he summoned me to be his slave for three days." Madgrin spoke the words lightly, but there was darkness in his eyes.

"His slave?"

"Yes," Madgrin said, a tinge of regret in his voice. "Magicians can do that, if they are strong enough, and know the right spells. I am of a caste of beings who are particularly appealing to ambitious mages who wish to have a powerful slave . . . for a short while." He smiled a little. "Appealing, but dangerous; when I left on the third day I took his soul with me."

"His soul?"

"I put it into a pebble and gave it to a demon."

"A *demon?*"

"Yes, a very special demon. Perhaps one day you will meet *her* as well."

They walked on in silence, Lucena sufficiently distracted by Madgrin's story not to be troubled by their distance from the ground. They came to the inn and stepped down onto its roof; Madgrin stood on the chimney, surveying the town, while Lucena sat with her back to it, enjoying the feeling of a solid structure supporting her.

Despite the late hour the inn was a noisy place, and she could hear the sounds of drinking and merrymaking drifting up through the open windows. The few words she caught were all in Elgan, a language she had once been taught in school and forgotten the next summer, so couldn't follow the conversation. All she could discern was the happy rumble and chatter of tired folk with strong drink in their bellies.

As the church bell tolled midnight, the noise in the inn quieted down, and shortly thereafter a string of patrons began to stream forth from the door to make their way home through the night. From his perch on the chimney Madgrin watched them with narrowed eyes, as if he were reading their minds. Which, on further consideration, Lucena thought he probably was.

As far as she could tell they seemed fairly ordinary; there were farmers and craftsmen—even a few who might have passed for gentlemen on a good day, but now with their shirts half undone and arm in arm with their companions and singing fit to raise the dead they looked anything but.

There was a breath of cool air on her cheek, and Lucena looked up to find Madgrin had vacated his station and was now standing beside her.

"Come," he said, helping her to her feet. "We will follow *him.*" He pointed a long white finger down into the ambling stream of people. Lucena could not at first tell who he meant, but Madgrin took her by the hand and led her off the roof. After they had come a little distance away from the inn and the crowd had dispersed it became clear they were trailing a tall, strong-looking youth in modest but well-made clothes. He had a mop of sandy hair, and walked with a mix of purposefulness, as one who knows well where he is going, and unsteadiness, as one who has had a bit too much to drink. He shambled his way through the streets, and Lucena and Madgrin walked silently above and behind him through the soft night sky.

The town grew quiet, and soon the only sounds were the unsteady footfalls of the inebriated young man, and the faint creak and whistle of the wind through the houses.

Then Madgrin stopped. Lucena, uncertain as to their purpose, looked around. After a few moments she became aware of what Madgrin had undoubtably known all along: someone else was walking down the street towards them and the young man.

He was a tall, dark-haired person, wearing black clothes that, while expensive and fine, were also a hundred years out of date. His skin was so pale it almost glowed, and there was a faint scent of wet earth and blood about him just distinguishable through the smells of the town. His eyes were dark and his lips were paper-white, and there was a strange hitch to his gait, as though from stiff muscles and joints.

He was, Lucena realized, the first vampire she had met since becoming one, and she was surprised that of all the possible things she could have felt, it was curiosity. She leaned forward to get a better look, and watched intently as the vampire came closer. By now the youth had seen him, and stopped dead in his tracks, staring at the vampire. But strangely neither of them noticed Lucena and Madgrin, even though they stood in plain sight, albeit twenty feet above the ground. It was as though they were not a part of what happened before them, only observing from the outside. Like watching a play.

The vampire was speaking to the man in a hushed voice, and when Lucena did manage to catch a word it was Elgan, and she did not understand it. Then the vampire's tone changed, and the man, who had been looking increasingly confused, tried to jump away. The vampire caught him by the front of his shirt and held him, struggling, at arm's length. The man put up his hands as if to shield himself from a bright light, calling out and uttering a train of incomprehensible babble. Then the vampire opened his mouth wide, wider than a human mouth should open, and with a quick jerking motion, like a cat pouncing on a mouse, latched onto the youth's neck.

The man screamed. And that scream Lucena did understand. It was in the universal language of pain and fear and anguish, and it sounded hauntingly familiar. It was that scream which suddenly made what was happening not like a play at all, but something real and horrible. She gripped Madgrin's sleeve and stared up at him in astonishment.

"Aren't you going to stop him?" she exclaimed. "Aren't you going to *do* something?"

Madgrin glanced down at her, and although his expression was unreadable, there was something in his eyes that had not been there before. Something that shimmered in the starlight, and for a moment Lucena thought it might have been tears.

"I cannot," he said in a soft voice. "This is still a part of his story. I have to wait."

"But, but . . . " Lucena clung to his sleeve, as if trying to drag him down. She wanted to point out that he had helped *her* . . . saved her, in fact. But then she remembered that by the time he appeared she had already been fatally wounded.

CHAPTER 8: *Going Hunting*

This came as a shock; until that moment she had always assumed Madgrin had simply arrived too late to intervene. It had never occurred to her that maybe ... perhaps ... he had been there all along. That he had had to wait. And watch. Though he had sent her those strange dreams, he had probably done the same for this young man. But what help was a dream if you didn't understand it?

"But ... " Lucena's hand was trembling on his sleeve, and she felt torn between despair and wanting to shake Madgrin to pieces.

"I can't do anything," Madgrin said quietly. "But *you* can." And he drew out from his robes a long, thin, sharp knife, not unlike the one Beruse carried. He offered it to her, hilt first. "If you want to save him, you are more than welcome to."

The youth's cries had become fainter now, and his form hung limp in the arms of the vampire.

Lucena snatched the knife from Madgrin's hand and ran. She ran down the air, out of the night and into the world, stumbling a little when she hit the ground, and sprinted towards the entangled pair. She threw herself at the vampire, shoulders first, with all the strength she could muster. He was tall but frail, and she was short and solid, and for a moment they were balanced, staring at each other with wide eyes. His mouth was covered in blood, and there was an unusual pink tinge to his cheeks. But his eyes were dead and dark and regarded Lucena with morbid fascination.

In that moment something deep inside Lucena's gut turned over and woke up.

The next instant she slashed at the vampire's face. He reeled back, letting go of the man, who crumpled to the ground. Lucena lunged after him, knocking aside the hands that were raised to stop her, and buried her knife in his chest. It was in completely the wrong place for his heart, but she didn't care. All she wanted was to make him spill as much blood as he had taken, to make him feel afraid—to make *him* scream.

He was screaming, now that she thought about it. Horrible, hacking screams, and he was trying to cover the gouge she had left in his face with one hand, while warding her off with the other. Lucena knocked it aside, pulling out her knife, and slashed him again, this time across his throat.

It was enough. His screams turned to garbled wails, and he fled back up the cobbled street, leaving a trail of black blood in his wake.

As he disappeared around a corner Lucena felt a fresh breeze blow by; a breeze that smelt of rosemary and mysteries and old, unopened books. It followed the vampire like a shadow, and soon it too had disappeared around the corner.

Lucena stood, very still, in the middle of the street. She clutched the knife in her hand, and there were splashes of blood all down her front. What a good thing Beruse had made her wear the strange armor, she thought, and looked down at herself to see if she had sustained any injury.

It was difficult to tell—partly because of the blood from the other vampire, and partly because her vision had gone blurry and she felt dizzy. She collapsed to her knees and crouched with her nose almost touching the cold cobblestones, until she could see them clearly once more.

She stood up slowly, and looked around.

The young man lay where he had fallen, one arm flung outwards in an attitude of relaxation, save for the ugly wound on his neck. It was still bleeding too; a pool of blood spread from around his shoulder, and dribbled down the cracks between the cobblestones.

Lucena walked over to him and knelt down, unsure what to do. The something that had awoken in her gut had risen until it rested somewhere under her collarbone, and now it reminded her that she was hungry, and here was a good quantity of blood, fresh blood, no less, and shouldn't she be drinking it? Not off the ground, of course, but from the man himself. He was a big, strong man, and had a lot of blood. The other vampire had barely drained him by half.

This struck Lucena as such an utterly ridiculous idea that she couldn't help giggling. Then, once she started, she found herself unable to stop. She staggered backwards, dropping the knife and leaning against the side of a nearby building while she laughed and laughed, sometimes letting out high, hysterical squeals.

She laughed until she was breathless, and when her mirth subsided she discovered that the something had gone back to sleep in her gut, and was silent once more. Lucena supposed that she should be concerned about having a bloodthirsty entity inside her, but at that moment she realized the really important thing to do was to stop the poor man's bleeding, and move him somewhere safe where he could recover.

Staunching the flow was easier said than done; Lucena had no handkerchief on her, and when she went to look, neither did the youth. In the end she used the knife to cut a strip off the hem of her skirt, and bound his neck up with that. This was not a pleasant business; the vampire seemed to have chewed on his neck rather than bitten clean through the skin.

After she finished her ministrations Lucena picked the man up and slung him, as gently as she could, over her shoulder. She staggered a little, but only a little. Silently thanking her terrifying strength, she began walking in the direction of the lights near the center of town, and the church.

She chose the church on the grounds that it was probably the best place to find help for the poor man at this hour, even though he had been headed in the opposite direction, and even though, as she walked through the silent village, she thought she recalled something important about churches and vampires . . . something that might make things difficult, but she could not grasp it. Like there was a thin golden haze over her thoughts, obscuring her memory.

Despite this haze she found her way easily enough; in this town all roads eventually led to the church, which in turn radiated a gentle light. This it turned out came from the many stained-glass windows, wherein Lucena thought she could glimpse the flicker and flare of bright candles. But she did not get a chance to see any closer, for as soon as she passed through the stone arch that led onto the grounds of the church she began to experience a most peculiar and unpleasant feeling.

It started as a heaviness to the air, as though it were a hot, humid day at the end of summer. As she approached the massive double doors of the church, it condensed into a tangible thickness. It felt like wading through bread pudding,

CHAPTER 8: *Going Hunting*

and Lucena instinctively put up a hand to push it out of her way, but it refused to budge. So she struggled on, leaning forward as one does when walking into a high wind.

Then, when she reached the steps of the church, the air grew hot around her; it burned her skin, and when she inhaled, her lungs too. She struggled up, step by step, until she stood before the door, bent double from the heat and weight. She knew then that there was no way she could bring the man inside, for the door of the church radiated heat like an oven, and Lucena worried that if she touched it she would catch fire. So she laid him against the door, took as deep a breath as she could of the hot, thick air, and shouted. She did not know what she shouted, only that it was loud. Then she turned away from the church and fought her way back to the street. Slowly at first, but then as the heaviness lessened and the air grew cooler, she picked up speed, and by the time she reached the arch she was running flat out.

She shot through at a gallop, and did not stop until she had put several houses and two streets between herself and the church, where she collapsed in an empty doorway, gulping the night air into her lungs to cool her broiled body.

After some time the golden haze lifted, she began to feel a bit more like herself, and she got up and looked around. The houses around her appeared completely unfamiliar, but she could sense Madgrin, in the same back-of-her-head way that she heard his voice, somewhere up and to her left. Away from the church, thankfully. So she brushed herself off, and finding that she still held the knife he had given her, wiped it clean on her butchered skirt and set off in that direction.

She had not been walking long when she came to a small square. During the day it must have been a lively place, for all the houses that opened onto it were shops with colorful banners hung above their windows, but now it was silent and still. In the center of the square stood a lone lamppost, lit, and its light caused Lucena to raise a hand to shield her eyes until they adjusted. When they had she looked again, and saw someone sitting beneath the lamppost, staring at her with great intensity.

He was a small, thin person, wearing good clothes and a fur-trimmed coat. His hair was brown and neatly cut, and he had piercing dark eyes. He looked no older than Lucena at first glance, but something in his eyes made her think otherwise; something that might have been sadness or age, or a bit of both.

They stared at each other in silence for several minutes, during which time the only sound was a dog barking, somewhere in the distance. It occurred to Lucena that morning was coming, and that she should hurry and find Madgrin. So she began walking through the square, giving the strange person in the middle a wide berth, but before she could escape up the road on the other side, she heard him call out to her.

He spoke in Elgan, so she only caught the first word or so, but because his tone was respectful she stopped and turned to face him.

"I'm sorry, I don't understand you," she said apologetically, in Kyrish.

The strange person had left his seat under the lamppost and now stood about halfway between it and Lucena in an attitude of some perplexity.

"Ah, forgive me," he said, in heavily accented Kyrish. "But you are *das Vampirmädchen* who chased away the old man of the hill?"

He asked this in a hopeful way, so Lucena admitted it was so. The strange person seemed pleased by this, and took a step or two closer. In doing so he came close enough to Lucena that she could catch his scent through the prevailing stink of the town. And it was the same as the old vampire had smelled—of grave dirt and blood—although this person was somehow milder and fresher. Still, the realization that he was also a vampire made Lucena take a pace back and put her hand on her knife.

The other vampire noticed this and put his hands up at once in a placating manner. "Do not be troubled," he said. "With you I have no conflict and do not wish one. The Viddengault sends me to—" He paused, as if wondering how to say the last word in Kyrish. After some thought he seemed to give up; he shrugged and continued: "Sends me to the old man of the hill to destroy. To destroy him. In this area I am *dein Bruder*. Er. Brother." He looked at Lucena hopefully, but Lucena still stood with her hand on her knife. The other vampire sighed.

"You trust me not. That is well. You have never heard of the Viddengault? That is poorly. Here," and he took from under his cloak a small scroll of parchment tied with a red ribbon. He then also produced a feather quill and a bottle of ink. Kneeling on the cobblestones of the square he unrolled the scroll, uncapped the ink, and dipped the quill. "Your name, please?" he asked.

"I, oh... er, Lucena," Lucena said, fighting her curiosity's urges to draw closer and see what was on the scroll.

"Lucena," the other vampire said carefully, writing something at the top of the scroll. He then unrolled it all the way to the bottom and scribbled something there. He blew on the ink to dry it, shook it, rolled it back up and tied it fast with the ribbon. Then he put away his quill and ink, and offered the scroll to Lucena. This was a somewhat comical gesture, as she was still over fifteen feet away. He looked a little like a child tempting a shy cat with a piece of fish on a stick.

Lucena considered for a moment, but then she overcame her misgivings and walked forward so she could take the scroll out of the other vampire's hand.

"What is—?" she began, but he cut her off.

"Is invitations," he said. "To next Viddengault. Read instructions carefully. We hope to see you there." Then he bowed, and walked swiftly away into the darkness.

Lucena stood alone in the square for some minutes, puzzling over what had just happened, and wondering if she should run after the other vampire and let him know that the "old man of the hill" was probably long gone by now. But before she could reach a decision something flickered in the corner of her eye, and the next moment Keelback dropped from a nearby rooftop and flung himself at her.

"*Cena!*" he cried in delight, and Lucena had just the presence of mind to stuff the scroll into the breast of her armor before he hit her. "Cena, Cena!" he cried, now in a paroxysm of excitement. "I ate a *boar!*"

"D-did you?" Lucena gasped, staggering a little under the sudden weight. "That is wonderful." She began to walk, slowly because it was difficult to see

CHAPTER 8: *Going Hunting*

where she was going, in the direction she felt Madgrin was. Keelback chattered at her happily for some minutes, but then fell silent, and a few moments later he was fast asleep, wrapped snugly around her shoulders.

Madgrin was waiting for them at the gate of the old Hexmason's house, along with a bloody and tired but satisfied Beruse, who was lazily polishing her knife.

"What happened?" Lucena asked.

Beruse just grinned and gave her the thumbs-up, but Madgrin added, "It is finished. Time to return home." He offered his hand to Lucena, and this time she took it without hesitation.

Coming up out of the carpet into Madgrin's study astonished Lucena. It seemed at first that they would simply sail up into the night sky until they left the whole world behind, but at the last moment it tore apart around them, and there was the bristling, green-crystal ceiling of Madgrin's study, twinkling with its own stars. Then the rest of the sky shattered, and the pieces fell about their feet like leaves, melting as they touched the carpet, and Lucena found herself once more in the study, with the dragon-mouth hearth releasing a lazy, orange glow, and beyond the narrow windows the first birds of the morning were beginning to sing.

"Cena, Cena!" he cried, now in a paroxysm of excitement. *"I ate a boar!"*

CHAPTER 9:

A Parliament of Vampires

"Hallo, what's this then?" Beruse asked, holding up the scroll tied with red ribbon.

They were back in the stone room beyond the wardrobe, and Beruse was helping Lucena out of her armor. That was how the scroll had been discovered.

Lucena was unsure what to say. She had a feeling Beruse would not appreciate that she had been given something by a vampire, but she had never been in the habit of lying, so she told the truth.

Far from being upset, Beruse was downright eager. "Did he really? To the Viddengault? I haven't heard of them in ages... Well? What are you just standing there for, *open it!*"

So Lucena untied the ribbon and rolled the paper out on her knee. The words were a little hard to read in the heavily slanted cursive that ran the letters together, but eventually Lucena was able to decipher it well enough to read thus:

"*To the Vampire, Lucena. I, a member of the most grand assembly of the Viddengault, grant thee the honor of invitation to our next conjunction, to be held upon the night of May 31st and June 1st, in the 1943rd year after the second Wizard's War, under the Palazzo Velevecchio, Milany. Signed*... oh dear, I can't make out his signature. It looks like Raybald or something, but that can't be right. And then there is something written under it in another language: *Kilavk ev durmin deft svilo*... *svilo*... oh I cannot pronounce it!"

"*Kilavk vi durmin deft, svilostrién vi Warsvilkak,*" Beruse recited. She smiled ruefully at Lucena. "It's Osylvanian. The words of the founder of the Viddengault: 'Love the night, and hail to the Beast.' I'm not sure I understand it."

"But what do I do with this?" Lucena said, flapping the scroll helplessly.

"Show it to Himself, I should think," Beruse said with a shrug. "You'll need his help to get all the way to Milany. The 31st is only four days away, after all."

"I see no reason why you should not go," Madgrin said when Lucena shared her worries with him the next evening. They were in the library, and Orrus was puzzling over the invitation, which he had spread out on a table. Madgrin was leaning back in his chair, regarding her uncertainty with amusement. "You have received an invitation, which I understand they do not give out on a regular basis. It would be rude to ignore them."

Lucena fidgeted nervously. "But they are vampires," she said quietly.

"Yes."

Lucena frowned down at her hand. She wanted to point out that, from what she had seen, vampires were evil, and besides, didn't Madgrin kill vampires? Why would he want her associating with them? She glanced up to find him looking at her with a quizzical half-smile on his face, and she realized he had been reading her mind again. She glowered.

"You have been reading the book Orrus lent you?" he asked politely.

Lucena nodded.

"What have you learned?"

She hesitated. She had learned many things, but being put on the spot like that made her quite unable to recall any of them. So she clasped her hands behind her back and glared at the floor.

"I would say," Madgrin continued, "that you have learned some of *what* vampires are, but practically nothing about *who* they are. To do that, you must meet them in person. And who can say? Perhaps you will learn something from them that you would not be able to from a book ... or from me."

He looked expectantly down at Lucena who, though she was still staring at the floor, could feel his gaze boring into the back of her head. But she refused to look up. "I don't understand."

"You don't understand, what?"

Lucena began tracing circles in the library floor with her toe.

"Vampires are ... bad," she began. "You ... hunt them. Why should I ... " she trailed off, unable to find an end to that question.

"As a whole, yes, vampires are very bad," said Madgrin, mildly. "However, taken as individuals, they can be fascinating people. Fascinating and, yes, even good. It is worth getting to know them as such."

Lucena remained staring at the floor as she turned this over in her head. She wondered if this was the reason Madgrin always *waited* for a vampire to finish before he swooped in and ended them. It fitted his mysterious nature, but it didn't help her to understand.

She realized then that she understood nothing at all: not why she was there, nor what she was supposed to be, not even what Madgrin really was. It was like one giant broken picture, and all the pieces were jumbled about so that there was no telling where they should go or how they should fit together. And Lucena knew everything would be clear if she could only see the complete picture. She was on the point of asking Madgrin to put it together for her, but when she looked up he was still staring down at her with the same unfathomable expression he always wore, and she knew he would not tell her. It was one of his mysteries. She would have to learn it for herself. So she sighed and asked the only logical question.

"What should I do there?"

Madgrin shrugged. "Listen to what they have to say. Listen to their stories. Try to see things from their point of view." He rose in one fluid motion, stepped gracefully into his chair's shadow, and vanished. Lucena stared at the spot where he had been with mixed feelings, some of which must have spilled over onto her face, for Orrus cleared his throat politely and touched her gently on the elbow.

"Begging your pardon," he said. "But how far along are you in *Vampires: A History?*"

"Oh," said Lucena, her shoulders sagging. "Only Chapter thirty-two, where he starts on his character theories. Not even half finished," she added dismally.

CHAPTER 9: *A Parliament of Vampires*

Orrus gave her a comforting pat on the shoulder and smiled. "That's quite all right. You can skip most of those chapters, but read the Chapter of the Beast, that's Chapter thirty-seven; it's very informative. And be sure to read the last chapter; it's of particular importance."

Lucena sighed and went back to her room, where she intended to pick up that monstrosity of a book and see what she could make of it. But Keelback was there, having just returned from his evening's hunt, and had brought her the entrails of his last meal as a gift. So instead she spent the next quarter of an hour praising his prowess as a hunter and insisting he eat the entrails himself. By the end of that time she decided that it would be more fun to ride him up and down the endless corridors of the house than read some dusty old book. Eventually Rhyse caught them at it and sent them back to Lucena's room, where they found Willic waiting for them impatiently, and they had barely shut the door before he burst out with demands for Lucena to tell him all about the hunt the previous night. This Lucena did, although Keelback interrupted her so many times with snippets of his own story that poor Willic was terribly confused, so in the end they both had to start over and tell their stories separately.

Lucena had barely finished her part when word came up from the kitchen that Gydda was picking the moonbeans and would anyone like to help? And Keelback, who loved nothing more than being outside at night, dragged Lucena off once more. And so it was, by one distraction or another, that she never did find the time to read anything from *Vampires: A History*, before she awoke on the evening of the 31st of May.

The first thing she noticed, through the haze of slumber and thirst, was Madgrin fast asleep in a chair pushed against the opposite wall.

She stared at him in perplexity for a full minute, wondering what to do. Until that moment she had not known that Madgrin slept at all; she had somehow gotten the idea that he went about in the day just like ordinary people, and then stayed up all night as well. But, she reasoned to herself, everyone had to sleep sometime. So she climbed out of bed as quietly as possible and drank her blood with minimal gulping noises. It was a little unnerving, however. He was so pale and still he resembled a mannequin, or even a corpse. And, Lucena wondered, taking a closer look, was his blue-white skin paler than she remembered? And were the shadows around his eyes darker?

But she had little time to contemplate this, for at that moment the eyes themselves opened, and Lucena found herself staring into black, black pools with tiny sparks of light dancing in their depths. At this she realized that she was bent over him in a most impolite fashion, and with an inarticulate sound rather like a squeak she backed away so fast she tripped on her own feet and sat down.

Madgrin looked down at her in puzzlement, one thin eyebrow arched up on his forehead. Then he started to laugh, and much to Lucena's surprise, she started laughing too. Weakly at first, out of relief that he was not angry, and then as she realized the full comedic side of the situation, with real feeling.

"Why were you asleep?" she asked at length, when their mirth had subsided. She had meant to add "in my room" but then she remembered that this was the House of Madgrin, and it followed that he could sleep anywhere he pleased.

Madgrin yawned, widely, and Lucena noticed for the first time that his tongue was blue, like his lips. He rubbed his eyes and sighed. "I was tired," he said simply. He levered himself out of the chair like someone whose legs have gone numb from too much sitting, and went over to Lucena's bureau. "I took the liberty of arranging a suitable costume for you," he said, withdrawing several articles from the top drawer. "The Viddengault is a formal affair, as these things go. Not something to attend in armor or nightclothes."

"What exactly *is* the Viddengault?" Lucena asked. "You spoke of it as if it were an association; now you make it sound like an event."

Madgrin considered this. "I suppose it is both those things." He shot her a twinkling smile. "When you are ready, come down to the front door; the carriage is waiting. Then you can go and see for yourself." He made her a small bow, and left the room in a swirl of midnight-blue cloak.

The clothes, when Lucena came to examine them, were fashionable, modest things; all black except for a short ruffle of white lace around the collar. Once she had got them all on she felt very somber and grown up, and she walked down to the front door with great conscious dignity.

Madgrin was waiting for her in the shadows by the door, and with a movement of his pale hand it swung open, letting in a soft glow of moonlight.

"Do you have your invitation?" he asked as she approached. Lucena produced the roll of parchment, complete with its red ribbon, from her pocket. Madgrin nodded in approval, and together they walked out of his House through the front door.

Seventeen stone steps led down to the gravel drive, where a four-wheeled coach was waiting. It was not an unusual coach *per se*—made of dark wood in a somewhat old-fashioned style, with a great stylized *M* in silver on the door—but there was no coachman on the driver's seat, and between the shafts stood not a horse, but a great, shaggy bear. And not just any bear; there was something familiar about its eyes and head, and after a moment of staring Lucena recognized it.

"Beruse?" she asked.

"*Hrmph*," grunted the bear, and hunched its shoulders in exactly the way Beruse did when she was impatient. "You look very nice tonight," it muttered in a low grunting voice.

Lucena did not know how to respond to this, so she dropped a curtsey and climbed up into the coach after Madgrin, who had already settled himself among the dark velvet cushions which lined the interior. She barely had time to get settled before they lurched into motion with a jerk and a clatter of chains and the crunch of gravel beneath four large paws and two thin wheels. Looking out the window she could see the dark grounds moving past, first the wide empty park and then the small wood of pine trees after they crossed the river. Kerebryt, the gatekeeper, must have known they were coming, for Beruse did not even slow her pace as she approached the gate, and the next thing Lucena knew, they had left the grounds behind them entirely.

She would have liked to lean her head all the way out the window, but with Madgrin sitting peacefully across from her she felt compelled to restrain herself.

CHAPTER 9: *A Parliament of Vampires*

So she could not see much of what was outside, other than that it was dark and bushy. This put her in mind of a forest, which was furthered by the smells of moss and wood and wet earth which came wafting in. Occasionally a stray branch would brush leaves across the window, making a slithery rustling sound.

Yet strangely, though the trees were ever so close and the earth rose and fell beneath them in gentle hills, the carriage moved perfectly smoothly, without the smallest jostle or knock, as though it were sliding on polished ice.

Then the trees abruptly gave way to a city, full of candlelight reflected in windows, and lantern light reflected off wet cobblestones. It seemed a familiar enough city; all the houses Lucena glimpsed had a reassuringly Kyrish look to them, and all the signs were in good, Kyrish fashion as well. But soon enough they left it behind and passed into more wild lands.

First there were high lonely moors, where the stars lit the open ground with a weak pale glow, and the wind moaned in the distance. Gradually these were broken by great jagged heaps of stone that thrust up through the soft earth, and as they became more frequent so they also became larger, until the carriage was floating serenely through a brutal landscape of sharp rocky mountains, pale in the starlight but with a slight reddish tinge. Lucena thought she caught the smell of smoke and scorched stone, but so faintly it was hard to tell.

Then the landscape changed again; this time shifting abruptly from sharp, rocky mountains to wild pine forests. Lucena could smell the pine, sharp and strong, even in the carriage. But that faded as the pines were replaced by oaks, and then the oaks thinned out to reveal rolling hills, blue-green in the moonlight, cut across with grapevines and decorated with the noble shadows of cypress trees. On some hills Lucena glimpsed the red-tile roofs of villages, and on several occasions they passed right though one. These were small, for the most part, with high houses packed together like fruit on an overloaded branch. When she caught a glimpse of a sign or heard a late-night reveler's shout it was in a foreign language.

The towns became more and more frequent the farther they traveled, until at last they came to a town that was really a city: it was full of tall stony buildings and close, cobbled streets. Lights flared from torches along the road and twinkled in the windows of inns, throwing a soft flickering glow over the frowning houses.

The carriage floated sedately along, first down one street and then another. And though the streets were of tumbled cobbles, never did Beruse miss a step, and the carriage traveled as smoothly as if it were floating.

Finally they came to a halt in front of a grand old building with a spiny, gothic façade and a great spire that rose up in front. From within the carriage Lucena thought it looked like a church, but once she had stepped out she saw it was nothing of the kind.

For a start, there was no unpleasant, hot, thick feeling she had felt around the church in Müldif, and now she got a better look, it was definitely too tall and square to be a church. What she had taken for a spire in front was actually just the smallest of six pointed towers that rose into the sky, their sides lined with a multitude of carved gargoyles and figures in relief. There was no sign of the

Etherealist Arrow, or any other holy device, and the building more resembled some ancient OracÁn citadel than the work of modern humans.

There was a tall, angry-looking doorway just in front of her, mounted on a flight of cracked stone steps. It too was covered in carvings, which conspired to look more like teeth and flames than any recognizable animal. This, combined with the fact that it led into a yawning black corridor, made the whole thing resemble a gaping mouth, and it gave Lucena pause.

"We will wait for you here," Madgrin said, leaning his head out of the carriage window. Lucena turned halfway around to look at him (she did not like to turn her back to the doorway) and managed to summon up a brave smile. Then she squared her shoulders and marched up the cracked steps, her invitation clutched tightly in her fist.

Once she was through the door the darkness wrapped around her like a cloak. It was so dark that even with her vampire eyes she could see nothing, and she was forced to put her hands out before her like a sleepwalker to feel her way along the stone passage. It was just as well she did, for not five feet in, the passage turned sharply, and then her hands met a curtain of soft fabric, which must have been velvet, and this she pushed aside. Beyond it the passage was a little lighter, but still so dim that she had to squint to make anything out. The only light was a sliver of gold some ways ahead, which she soon found was the crack in yet another curtain. She pushed this aside as well, and immediately had to shield her eyes from the flare of candlelight on the other side.

When the pain had subsided enough for her to take her hand down, Lucena found herself in a low-ceilinged hall with a flagstoned floor and stone statues lining the walls. These were of lions and griffins and manticores, all with stone collars with stone chains linking them to the wall. Each one was carved with their paws or claws outstretched, and in each paw rested a lighted candle.

A small group of people clustered together at the far end of the hall, around a raised table behind which sat a bored-looking clerk. As Lucena drew closer she saw he had a long neck and a pointed face, with straggily locks of dark hair falling everywhere. He was busily stamping away at the slips of paper being passed him by the group, and making comments in a sarcastic tone.

As Lucena approached she felt her step hitch when she realized these must be other vampires as well, but by the time she had reached the man behind the table the entire group had filed away through the door at the other end.

"Proof of membership, please," the man said in a nasal drawl.

"Oh, but I haven't got any—I'm not a member," Lucena began, and then hurried on quickly at the clerk's baleful glare, "I have an invitation, though."

A hand the color of parchment reached across the desk between them and made a grasping motion.

"Let's see it, then," drawled the clerk.

Mutely, Lucena handed him the scroll. He snorted at the ribbon and tore it off. He unrolled the scroll, gave it a cursory glance, and then stamped it firmly with a wooden seal dipped in ink. "Guests go left after the second stair. Mind your head . . ." the man trailed off, looking at Lucena for the first time. He frowned, his thin dark eyebrows wriggling together into a knot over his nose. "Though for

CHAPTER 9: *A Parliament of Vampires*

someone like you, that probably won't be an issue," he amended, and then turned his attention to the couple that had just stumbled forward into the light and were tottering down the hall towards them.

Too frightened of the other vampires to take offense at the clerk's tone, Lucena fled through the door and nearly hit her head on the low ceiling. The man had been right to issue a warning, for it was only her diminutive stature that saved her from a nasty collision.

The passage beyond led to stairs, which went down, down and down. It was dark, but not pitch black, being sparsely lit with candles. It was cold and smelled of wet stone and mildew, which put her in mind of the Munsmire School, which made her feel frightened all over again. So when the passage finally ended and she emerged into the room beyond she was visibly shaking with nerves.

But what a room it was. Nothing further from the school at Munsmire could be imagined.

It was a small, circular room, with a ceiling so high that it was lost in shadows. Said ceiling was further obscured by the mass of gold-and-crystal chandeliers that hung down on thin silver chains. Each chandelier was ablaze with candles, whose light sparkled off the crystal and made the gold shine.

Set into the walls all around were balconies, in which were placed innumerable gilded wooden chairs draped in velvet. Four stairways led down out of the shadows of the ceiling, and they were so steep they could not be climbed without the carved handrail. Lucena found this out for herself when she was ushered up one of them by a vampire in an old-fashioned black tunic. Coming to the next balcony up she found another usher, this one dressed in clothes of an even more ancient fashion, who showed her to a seat in the lefthand row. By this time her fear had turned to curiosity about this strange room, and as soon as the usher left she got out of her seat and leaned over the banister to get a look at what lay below.

It was a sea of heads and red velvet chairs. Beyond that she could see, just below where she had first entered, the bottom of the room. It resembled what she had always imagined a lion's pit to look like: a bare brick wall surrounded a circular space filled with dirt, empty save for a single metal post driven into its center. There was an iron ring clipped to the post, with similar rings hung from brackets on the walls. The only break in the wall came in the form of a small iron grill about four feet wide and tall, set in the part of the wall opposite Lucena. As she looked, she thought she caught a flash of movement behind the grill, but it was so dark she could not be sure.

"That's the Beast's pit," said someone to her right.

Lucena guiltily jumped back from the banister and looked around in surprise. The someone turned out to be a young man—hardly more than a boy, really—dressed in clothes that, by Lucena's standards, were only slightly out of date. He was looking at her with his fairish, sandy head on one side, and a grin about his mouth. He was pale, like all the other vampires she had seen, but there was a pinkish tinge to his cheeks and the tip of his nose, which made him look a little like a powdered doll. He was small and slight, but still taller than Lucena, so when he bowed to introduce himself she only just glimpsed the top of his head.

"I am Undergate," he said.

"Lucena Ashmoor," she replied, dropping a small curtsey.

To her consternation the boy, Undergate, laughed at her. "No, no," he said. "Not your *name*, fledgeling, where you are from? That is the way we do things in the Viddengault."

Lucena was a little annoyed at being called *fledgeling* by someone other than Madgrin, but she swallowed her irritation and answered, a little reluctantly; "Munsmire."

"Is that so?" asked Undergate. He leaned forward into her face and grinned a wide, toothy grin. "Then we were neighbors! Undergate is not three miles away, across the bog. We must be friends from now on—where do you live nowanights?"

Lucena was reluctant to answer—something about Undergate struck her as disingenuous, and she was not in a hurry to reciprocate his friendship.

She was saved from answering when, to her relief, a grim usher came along to make them sit down. Then came more vampires, and these seated themselves all around Lucena and Undergate. Lucena felt frightened all over again, but Undergate was acquainted with many of them, and soon he was caught up in conversation with a tall, imposing woman in a medieval dress and bonnet. Still, every now and then he would lean over and grin at Lucena in a way which was probably meant to be friendly, but only had the effect of making her feel more awkward still. The vampires were all pale and beautiful, with distant, cruel, or unhappy expressions, and Lucena would have liked nothing better than to be ignored by them. But sometimes when Undergate grinned at her another vampire would crane their neck around and pin her with a cold stare. And every time they did there was something in their eyes that she rather thought was hunger, and it made her stomach curl in upon itself and her hands start to shake.

The eeriest thing about the place, however, was the silence. When the whole high room was filled, every seat with a grim, black-clad occupant, none spoke save in hushed whispers, which were eaten by the velvet blackness above their heads, making the whole place feel like a crypt full of expectant dead.

To Lucena's acute embarrassment, the only break in the silence came from Undergate. But it seemed the other vampires were used to this, though he received unloving stares. For her part Lucena shrank into the cushions of her chair and tried to be as unnoticeable as possible.

It was, in the end, to no avail. After a few minutes there was a commotion around the lowest ring of seats; a tall man in a black robe that looked like a Crowan toga got up behind a wooden lectern and rapped his bony knuckles on it for silence.

There was already the strange not-silence, of course, but Undergate regretfully broke off his latest conversation and shut his mouth. Lucena noticed that he didn't look embarrassed at all, in fact he seemed downright defiant as he stared at the vampire in the toga, who was shuffling papers together and muttering under his breath. Then the vampire below looked up sharply, and to Lucena's horror, straight at her. His eyes were glassy and pale, and put her in mind of marbles.

CHAPTER 9: *A Parliament of Vampires*

"We have a guest with us tonight," he said in a wheezing voice. "Where is she?"

A ripple of silent interest went round the room. Heads turned in all directions, and there was a hissing sound as the vampires inhaled in anticipation of speech. Reluctantly Lucena stood up. She made a bow, which was all she had room to do, her stomach tight with nerves.

The vampire in the toga narrowed his glass eyes to slits as he stared at her, his lip curling in an unpleasant manner. But when he spoke it was only to say, "And who invited you?" in the same wheezing tone as before.

Lucena opened her mouth to explain that she was not certain of his name, but was saved by the vampire himself jumping to his feet a few rings above her, and crying out in his heavy accent: "It was myself, Lord Minister! I was compelled to, after she defeated *der Hügelmann auf Müldif.*"

"Chased off the Old Man of the Hill, more like," said a lady vampire from the lowest ring. The contempt in her voice was palpable. "That was what you told us the first time, Rabivald."

"But she gravely wounded him," Rabivald continued.

"Yes, and when we reached the Hexmason's house all we found was black powder."

"So it is true *Vampirfräulein* destroyed him?" he asked hopefully.

"Black powder," said the toga vampire, his empty eyes never leaving Lucena, "is only left when the subject is destroyed by magic."

"So she must be magician as well," Rabivald said, and folded his arms as if the matter were settled.

"But you never saw her strike the killing blow," the lady vampire continued ruthlessly. "What proof do we have that she is worthy to join the Viddengault? Does she have a right to be here? We meet here, the finest and wisest vampires of this age or any age, and you invite a babe hardly out of her winding sheet who picks on old men?" She cast Lucena a disgusted glare, and Lucena was quite taken aback by the hatred in it. Yet now that her fears were becoming manifest, the whole situation took on a soothing unreality, and she listened with growing calm as the vampire continued: "Lord Minister, I suggest she be thrown into the dungeon to rot."

To Lucena's consternation, almost the whole crowd voiced muted agreement. The only one who disagreed was Undergate, who jumped to his feet in protest. Lucena felt her misgivings about him fade, just a little.

"My lords and ladies, this is most unfair," he cried, and Lucena began to feel guilty for doubting him. "If she was invited on false grounds it is not *her* fault, and the matter of her steel is easily remedied: give her a chance to prove herself to all of us."

Lucena frowned. She did not like the sound of that—but the other vampires apparently did. They were whispering and muttering together, and the lady vampire was talking earnestly to her neighbor. At long last the Lord Minister shifted his gaze from Lucena to Undergate, and said in a grim voice, "How do you propose she do that?"

"Why, it is simple," said Undergate, a huge smile spreading over his pink-and-white face. "Let her have three minutes alone with the Beast."

Lucena was certain she did not like the sound of this. An interested hush had fallen over the room, and all the vampires leaned forward in their seats, rather the way cats do when they see you have a juicy piece of meat. She saw the lady vampire smiling broadly, and suddenly her calm evaporated and she was frightened all over again.

The Lord Minister rapped his knuckles on his lectern, and all heads turned to him.

"The Beast is only released for executions, with good reason," he said, shifting his gaze to Undergate. "He would destroy any of us easily."

"He did not destroy *Amstrass*," Undergate said defiantly.

There was a sharp intake of breath from all around the room, and the Lord Minister rapped his knuckles (probably becoming sore, Lucena couldn't help thinking) on his lectern again. He leaned forward and gave Undergate a heavy, glass-eyed stare.

"Very well then, Undergate lad," he said, slow and chill. "If you be so assured, then let the vampirina have her time with the Beast. But should he devour her, then we will throw you in next and be done with your unending foolishness."

Silence reigned heavy after this statement. Undergate looked taken aback and was at a loss for words. His confidence in her seemed notably diminished now that his own life was on the line, and Lucena resigned herself to some long hours in the dungeon before anyone rescued her.

Take his offer, Madgrin's voice said in the back of her head.

Everything had been so quiet that for a moment Lucena thought he was standing right behind her, and she had to fight the urge to turn around and look. But she knew most of the vampires were still watching her, so she forced herself to stare impassively forward.

But, the Beast? she asked, forming the words carefully inside her head. *I am no warrior, I could not face it!*

Couldn't you? Madgrin asked. He seemed amused. *You have a beast of your own after all.*

Lucena wasn't sure she was assured by this, and besides . . .

But I have no weapon.

I gave you a stone knife, once. It is still yours.

Lucena stuck her hands inside her long sleeves, and felt something thin and hard and cold bump against her right forearm. Gingerly she closed her fingers around it and felt clearly the handle of the stone knife.

You are no ordinary vampirina, Madgrin said. And now he sounded close enough to be leaning over her shoulder. *You are my La Flein. You hold in your heart more power than all these wraiths combined.*

Without realizing it Lucena had stood up. All eyes were on her, and she looked back at them half-lidded and unreadable. From somewhere around her elbow she thought she heard Beruse grumble that they all looked sickly and frail creatures, and Keelback agreed. *Not even worth a midnight snack,* he said.

CHAPTER 9: *A Parliament of Vampires*

She looked at the Lord Minister, directly into his glassy eyes, and realized he wasn't half as frightening as Orrus had been, when she had seen him with that cruel smile and bandages across his face.

And Orrus was her friend.

"Lord Minister," she said, and her voice came out loud and clear and careful. "I accept your proposal; I will face the Beast."

There was another sharp hissing, this time accompanied by the creaking of seats as their occupants leaned forward in anticipation. Lucena was aware of a great many staring eyes fixed on her, and of Undergate's astonished face. But she did her best to shut them all out, and waited patiently as one of the ushers (no longer so dour and expressionless) came bounding up the stairs to lead her down.

Going down the stairs was worse than going up; they were so steep Lucena had to clutch the handrail and lean back so she would not trip down them. To make matters worse, now everyone was staring at her and hissing as she passed.

The usher led her down two levels past where she had first entered the room, until they stood in the narrow cleft between the outer wall and the inner wall that encircled the sand pit. Before them was a high door with iron bars bolted across it. There were five locks to the door, and these had to be unlocked one by one by first the Lord Minister, followed by the lady vampire who did not like Lucena, and then three other tall, pale gentlemen in black who filed down after them. When all the locks were undone the usher pushed the door open inwards, and Lucena stepped through into the earth-floored pit.

It was strange, she thought, how a place could seem small and insignificant when viewed from above and outside, yet when one steps inside, it becomes vast and intimidating. Such was the case with the pit. Lucena had to crane her neck up just to see above the brick wall, and then all she saw were the undersides of some sharp steel prongs which had been bolted under a slight overhang of bricks, so they were invisible from above but made climbing out of the pit nearly impossible.

The heavy door swung shut behind her, and she found herself alone in the pit save for the metal post with the ring attached. For lack of anything better to do she went over to it, and looked around.

She wished she had not almost at once. Now that she was in the center it was easier to look up at the room above, and she saw a mass of pale faces framed in black, all staring intently down at her. So she looked down again, just in time to see the grill swing open.

A hush fell over the room as complete and silent as a winter field, and for a while nothing happened. Lucena had backed herself up against the metal post, and now had the presence of mind to put her hands up her sleeves again to grope for the stone knife. It was still there, cold and hard against her arm, and the feel of it in her palm reassured her.

Then, from within the darkness, came a soft clinking of chains against stone, a slap and heave of heavy feet, and a snarled breath. Something was moving in the darkness, though Lucena could not tell if it was man or beast, until it emerged from the shadows and she saw it was a horrible mix of both.

It walked on two legs, so it bore some semblance to a man, but its arms looked far too long, and its nails had grown into filthy talons. A shaggy, matted mass of hair covered its head and most of its face and trailed down in scraggily strands over its shoulders. It was naked save for a ragged sheet wound around its loins, and by this Lucena took it to be male, though it was so emaciated it was hard for her to tell. And though its hair covered much of its face, obscuring its eyes and brow, its mouth was clearly visible; this hung open slightly, giving glimpses of long, sharp yellow teeth with something black stuck between them. A smell came off it of mildew and grave dirt, but most of all it smelled of death.

Inside her sleeves Lucena's hands were trembling, but she made herself stay still. Despite the creature's frightening appearance it also seemed confused, and stood just inside the pit swinging its head this way and that, as if looking for something.

"I see ... no victim," it said in a deep, hoarse voice. "Where is my ... victim?"

"There is no victim," Lucena said, holding perfectly still.

Immediately the creature's head swung around at her, and as it did she caught a glimpse of a wide, bloodshot eye. "There is always a victim," it said. "When I am released ... always."

"No, no," Lucena said, hoping that she could keep it confused for her allotted time. She knew it was to be only three minutes, but already it felt like eternity. "You are just having a little ... er ... holiday ..."

The creature balked at this concept. It walked halfway around Lucena and paused, its hands quivering slightly. She took this opportunity to back away and put the post between it and herself, still with her hands up her sleeves.

Moving turned out to be a mistake; the creature's head whipped around and it took several steps towards her, nearly colliding with the post.

"They call on me," the creature said. "I destroy the unworthy. The Beast devours all ..."

"All save those who are worthy," Lucena reminded it hopefully, but the creature shook its head.

From above someone struck a bell and called out, "One minute left!" As if on cue, the creature began to growl.

"The Beast is coming," it said, and its voice filled the tiny pit.

"You could tell it to go away ..." Lucena suggested hopefully.

The creature paused, as if considering the idea. Then it started to laugh. Deep chuckles at first, which escalated into high, manic shrieks. It threw its head back, its mouth opened wide, and it howled with laughter. Then it leveled its gaze on Lucena; for a moment both were still. Then it lunged.

Its filthy, matted hair was blown aside by the movement, and for a moment Lucena beheld its face: a human face, but all the more terrible for it was now devoid of any humanity. It was a boney horror creased with scars, hollow cheeks, and its eyes, set in sunken sockets, were the eyes of something wild and bloodthirsty, beyond reason.

All the nerves in Lucena's body, which had been gradually wound tighter and tighter over the past few minutes, came unsprung in an instant. Out came the

CHAPTER 9: *A Parliament of Vampires*

knife, quick as lightning, and cut a streak through the air as she swung it wide. It met resistance in the form of the creature's neck, and clove clean through it.

A gong struck in the room above, signaling the end of the three minutes, and the door was pushed open. But the creature was already dead; its head came to rest in the sand, eyes still open and staring, as the body toppled to the ground. Lucena stood between the two, her ears ringing and her hands white-knuckled, numb from their grip on the stone knife.

Everything went very still again, but not the nervous, repressed stillness of many people being silent. Instead, she felt the distant serenity one feels on a mountaintop or a secluded glade in a forest. Inside Lucena's mind all was calm and peaceful, but at the same time she was aware of movement around her. The usher came forward, reached for her, then saw the knife and retracted his hand. Above her, the room was alive with vampires leaning forward, exclaiming to their neighbors, or just exclaiming to anyone who would listen. The Lord Minister got up from his seat and gripped the railing until his knuckles were almost as white as Lucena's, and the lady vampire wrung her hands and worked her face into all manner of displeased expressions.

Through all this Lucena stood quietly in the pit until the ringing in her ears had subsided and she relaxed enough to loosen her hold on the knife. But she did not put it away, for she noted its effect on the usher, who could not take his eyes off it and was now giving her a wide birth.

Slowly she walked to the door, passed through it, and climbed back up the steps to her seat. Everywhere vampires drew back from her, some with looks of admiration, some with fear, and some with the same stunned expression as the usher. When she came to her row, the vampires that sat between the aisle and her seat jumped to their feet to make way for her, and Undergate even stood up, as if to allow her more room to be settled.

She sat down with relief, but no sooner had she done so than Undergate tapped her arm and whispered urgently, "The Slayer's Right allows you to ask a question now."

"What?" said Lucena, who only wanted to be ignored for the rest of the night.

"Ask the Inner Ring a question," Undergate said excitedly. "Ask them about Amstrass."

"What is Amstrass?" Lucena asked, bewildered.

"Ask them," said Undergate, with a significant look.

So Lucena stood up again, but she did not ask about Amstrass. It seemed to her that Undergate was taking advantage of her situation so she could ask his question for him. Besides, she had a question of her own that had been gnawing on her mind, so she asked that instead. Pointing to the crumpled hump of tattered clothes that was all that was left of her attacker, she said:

"Lord Minister, I beg of you, what was that?"

Beside her, Undergate groaned and slouched in disappointment, but her other neighbors sat up a little straighter, and seemed ready to answer her question themselves. But before she could be overwhelmed, the Lord Minister rapped his knuckles on his lectern for silence (how they were not purple and swollen by this time, she did not know), and the whole room slumped back in its collective seat in disappointment. He gave Lucena a mildly reproachful look and said, "He was a servant of the Beast."

"And what is this *Beast?*" Lucena pressed on.

The Lord Minister humped his shoulders and withdrew an old mildewy book from beneath his lectern. He opened it to someplace near the beginning of the middle, and began to read.

"'And there I came in upon myself, to the place that should have been my heart. But there was no heart there anymore, only a black void, and in the void was a creature of ragged hair and fangs. I saw it walk in my body and speak with my voice; it drove my every action, it was the source of both my desire and hatred. And it was revealed to me there, in the dark, that this beast had devoured my soul and at the same time kept me bound to my half-life.

"'We vampires are born servants to the beast, and if we hope to survive with our hearts and minds intact we must learn to be its master. So fear the beast, hail to the beast, but do not submit to it. For then we become nothing more than the decrepit weres, ogres and trolls, who live on instinct alone and think nothing of the greater world.'"

The Lord Minister came to a close and shut the book with a dusty clap. "That is how the Vampira D'Amstrass described the Beast in her own words. Even today, nearly three hundred years after she wrote the Book, we still struggle to achieve that goal."

Listening to him, Lucena felt an uncomfortable shiver run down her spine and settle in her gut; memories of the voice she had heard after fighting the vampire in Müldif rose unbidden to the front of her mind, and for a moment she felt so disconcerted she thought she would fall over. So she gave a half-hearted nod and sat down again, a little heavily. Beside her, Undergate was moaning that she should have asked about Amstrass *herself*. This annoyed Lucena, because now she could see he was right; the Beast was common knowledge, and any vampire in the room could have answered her question; but now she was curious about Amstrass, whom she was fairly certain was a person, and she got the distinct feeling further questions would not be answered.

The remainder of the parliament, to her dismay, was tediously boring. The body of the dead vampire was gathered up and carted away with macabre conventionality, and the vampires fell to discussing codes of conduct and laws under consideration. Bickering the way only old people can, with much dragging in of ancient vendettas, grudges and complaints, arguing for argument's sake that dragged on and on until the original point of the dispute was lost.

Keeping Madgrin's instructions in mind, Lucena tried her best to pay attention to all that transpired, but soon found herself bored nearly to tears. The lady vampire who had taken a dislike to Lucena attacked every proposal seemingly out of a delight in causing the proposer to stumble and drop his or her notes. Then there was a wheezy old vampire who sat some rows behind her who could never say anything without relating an anecdote which wound on and on and never had to do with the topic at hand. And the Lord Minister, who was the one person present with the authority to make them all behave, was more interested

CHAPTER 9: *A Parliament of Vampires*

in encouraging them to disagree, often bringing up trivial points at the last moment to give a flagging argument new life.

Lucena sat and glowered at them all. They reminded her of the rare occasions when she had visited her family over Chandarmas. She could easily see her aunt, who also had a dislike for her, as the lady vampire, her great-grandmother as the wheezing, long-winded vampire behind her, and her cousin Rodland as the Lord Minister. Cousin Rodland was always starting fights and then sitting back to watch them with a satisfied smile on his face.

But before her mood could sink much further she felt a pluck at her sleeve, and turned to see Undergate beckoning to her. He had slipped out of his chair and moved a little way down the row to a door set into the back of one of the empty seats. Lucena got up and followed him, ducking and murmuring apologies as she bumped knees with the other vampires.

The door led to a ladder, which they climbed for some minutes before scrambling into a passage hardly tall enough for her to stand up in, and Undergate had to walk doubled over. It led into pitch darkness, but from what little she could see it appeared to have walls of stone blocks, clammy and damp when she touched them. It ran level, neither climbing nor descending, and after only a few minutes of feeling their way through the darkness Undergate pushed aside a grinding panel of stone and let in a faint ray of light, along with a refreshing breath of night air.

They emerged onto a small ledge of the spire, where a thin spiky railing was all that separated them from a fall of fifty feet or more down into the city streets. As Lucena came out of the tunnel she thought she saw a huge dog crouched upon the railing, but on a second glance it turned out to be only a gargoyle. Undergate went over to it and rested his arm upon its back.

Lucena went over to the railing and looked out at the city, which at this late hour was a mess of black shapes and countless pinpricks of light. Smoke and steam rose from the roofs to make a haze through which the more distant lights shimmered. She waited patiently for Undergate, who clearly had something on his mind, to ask her whatever question he had brought her here for, but all he did was stare at her disconcertingly. He had a handsome face, she admitted, with high cheekbones and piercing eyes under strong brows, a full mouth and a sharp nose. And she thought to herself: *He knows he is handsome, and is trying to make me feel uncomfortable.* It made her impatient.

"It is a most pleasing view," she said at length. "But is it all you wished to share with me?"

"Yes," he replied, almost immediately. Then he seemed to realize that the question she had asked was not the one he had anticipated, and he backed himself up. "No, I mean. Of course not. I meant to ask: who are you, really?"

"Who am I?" Lucena said with some surprise. "I already told you that. I am Lucena Clarian Ashmoor, formerly of Munsmire..." she trailed off. There were other ways to describe herself, she realized. The fledgeling of Madgrin and the Mistress of Keelback, but somehow she did not feel like sharing these with Undergate. The more she looked at him the more he reminded her of the first vampire, Miss Smael: something in the way they stood, with their backs unusually straight. And when they looked at you it was always with both eyes, eyes that had a strange hunger in them, as though they would like to devour you. This, Lucena reasoned, had been a rational fear when she had met Miss Smael, but why she should feel it when she looked at Undergate she could not fathom.

A frown of mild annoyance crept onto the latter's brow, as though he had hoped for something more. But Lucena had made up her mind to tell him nothing further, and so remained silent. For his part Undergate become frustrated; he leaned in closer. Lucena resisted the urge to lean away. "At *least* tell me who made you," he said. This time it was not a question.

Instead of speaking she looked down into the street, where it appeared the parliament had let out, and a stream of black-cloaked figures were scurrying away into the dark. Like that, they appeared more like one being, constantly writhing and changing, but despite this, Lucena saw in their midst a single figure who did not move. He stood directly beneath them, the crowd around him parting like water around a rock, and smiled up at her with a pale face which, from this distance, looked more like a skull than ever.

She sighed with relief. Now she knew exactly how to give Undergate what he wanted without telling him anything, and she also knew what to do after that.

Turning to him she pointed down to where Madgrin stood. "There you can see my maker," she said, and Undergate's head snapped up, only to snap back down again when he saw where she was pointing.

"Where?" he asked.

"That is his mystery to keep," Lucena said, and allowing herself a triumphant smile, she picked up her skirts and vaulted the railing.

She heard Undergate cry out as she fell, but what he said was lost as the wind filled her ears and she plummeted to earth. From below she saw Madgrin reach up his hand, so she stretched hers out to meet him. And as their fingers met all heaviness left her body, and she settled to the ground as gently as a leaf.

She did not look back up to see whether Undergate stared after them. Undergate could stare all he wished; he would see nothing Madgrin did not wish him to.

Beruse was waiting with the carriage in an alley not far away. The door sprang open of its own accord as they approached, and Madgrin helped Lucena inside. Only when they were settled, and the carriage was moving smoothly out of the city, did he speak.

"How did you fare?" he asked pleasantly.

Lucena heaved a sigh and told him all about it, though she was certain he knew most of it already. She told him about the vampires, about Undergate, about the lady vampire who had reminded her of Aunt Juprina, and about how they had made her fight the Beast. But when she got there she paused, reached into her sleeve and drew out the stone knife. "Here," she said, "I ought to return this."

"No, no, you *keep* that," Madgrin said. "You never know when you might need it again."

"Thank you," Lucena said in a small voice, "for being there."

CHAPTER 9: *A Parliament of Vampires*

"It is what I am here for," Madgrin said kindly. "I let Beruse come too; I thought you might appreciate her support. And Keelback somehow found his way in also, but I think that was your doing, not mine."

Lucena sat back and let out a shaky laugh. "I don't remember doing anything in particular," she said.

"We often do things we are not aware of when we are frightened," Madgrin remarked, gazing out the window into the rushing night.

Lucena sat back and thought on this, but thinking about being frightened made her remember what it had felt like, being led down the stairs to the door into the pit, which made her remember that horrible, horrible vampire they had called the Beast.

"Maker, what do you know of the Beast?"

Madgrin turned his head from the window and blinked his dark eyes at her. "Which one?" he countered. "There are many beasts, all claiming to be *the* Beast, and it can be troublesome telling them apart."

"Oh, you *know* which one I mean," Lucena said. "The one the vampires were talking about . . . the one inside . . . the one that I fought."

Madgrin pressed his fingertips together. In the gloom of the carriage they looked like bones. "Oh, that beast," he said quietly. "That is the beast of survival. It is the very base layer of a soul; when all else has been stripped away, the beast remains."

"But . . . the way they talked, they made it sound like some sort of demon."

"Demon? Well, maybe it is a little demonic. But no, the beast is only your instincts for survival. It is the power of defiance, of carnage and destruction. In truth there is a little beast in everyone, sometimes stronger or weaker, but most vampires damage themselves so much they lose their heart and their spirit—the very things that keep the beast in check. And so the beast of survival rules them, and they think they are inhuman, when in fact they are only severely wounded."

"But we are—I'm *not* human," Lucena protested.

"Oh, maybe you're not *entirely* human anymore," Madgrin said modestly. "All vampires have a little of us in them, even now, but for the most part they are still human. Which just goes to show you how great the human capacity for delusion and evil can be." He leant his brow against his hand and stared out the window, lost in thought.

Lucena had been greatly comforted by the idea that she was still "mostly human," and was just working up the nerve to ask him who he meant by "us," when she was thrown off track by his last remark. Glumly she looked down at the faint outline which was all she could make of her shoes, wondering if this meant she was going to be evil as well.

"Of course," Madgrin said, no doubt in response to her train of thought, "because of that, humans also have an equally great capacity for good. But . . . but so very, very few of them manage to fill it."

Lucena looked up. He was still staring out the window, but with such an expression of sadness that she felt a little alarmed. So she blurted out another question—a question that she burningly wanted answered—before she had time to be nervous.

"Who was Amstrass?"

"Hmm, who indeed?" he said, obviously still distracted. Then he seemed to remember the question and turned to look at her. "Amstrass is many things," he said. "She is darkness, she is terror. She is the beast incarnate, without sorrow or regret. She has a dark smile, and wears her soul on her face."

Lucena slumped in her seat, for it was hardly a satisfying answer. But it seemed she had succeeded in lifting Madgrin's mood.

"She wrote a book, a little while ago," he continued. "Some vampires took it rather too literally; they were a foolish lot, but in the end it turned out well, for it means I don't have to hunt them."

"Hunt them?"

"My calling, and my penance," Madgrin said. "It has been laid upon me to destroy any and all vampires who pose a threat to the material order. Those who have set themselves to follow the Book of Amstrass, the ones you met tonight, are some of the happy few who do not fall into that category. But Amstrass herself... *she* is a very *different* breed of vampire."

"Are you still hunting her?"

Madgrin sighed so that his shoulders heaved. "Yes, but no. I will have to, but I cannot. She has been very clever, and it will be a long time before I will be able to catch her. But I have been granted an eternity in this world, so I can wait." He laughed softly, and a little ruefully, to himself as he gazed out the window.

"I don't think I like vampires," Lucena said, mostly to herself.

"No one likes to see their worst traits reflected back at them," Madgrin replied in a mild tone. Then he turned his head and smiled at her; a real smile, full of warmth and affection. "But don't assume, just because you share certain characteristics, that you need be like them. Vampires are, like humans, individual, and can define themselves on their own terms. You may define yourself differently from the vampires you met tonight."

A smell came off it of mildew and grave dirt, but most of all it smelled of death.

CHAPTER 10:

Midsummer Night

The story of Lucena's experience with the Parliament of Vampires spread quickly through the House of Madgrin. To her dismay, however, some details were lost, and several were added along the way. A few nights after the incident Willic asked Lucena if she really *had* fought off twenty crazed vampires with flaming swords and a small wyvern at the same time? Lucena told him no. She explained that they did not have flaming swords, there was no wyvern, and only *one* crazed vampire. Willic sighed, and promptly went off and told Gydda all about how Lucena had defeated thirty crazed vampires with swords made of lightning and a griffin. Gydda passed the story on to Cobbin with her own embellishments, and so it went until eventually Grimmach came to ask Lucena how she had single-handedly fought off an army of vampires riding dragons. She was close to tears of frustration when she corrected him. Then she fled to the library and confided in Orrus, who seemed to be the only one unwilling to give her more glory than she was due.

"You have to understand it is in their nature to, hmm, *decorate* the truth, as it were," he said when Lucena had finished explaining the situation.

"B-but an army with dragons!" she wailed.

"Yes, that is a bit extravagant, I'll admit," Orrus said with a chuckle. "But if the truth means so much to you I could write it down for the archives, though that may have to wait until after Midsummer . . ."

It was early June. The windows in the upper reaches of the library had been opened, and from beyond them came the hum and chirp of a thousand crickets, backed by the gentle rustle of leaves in the wind. But these nights, though pleasant, were also painfully short. Lucena had been spending more time asleep than awake as a result, and she had somewhat lost track of time.

"Midsummer?" she asked. "What happens on Midsummer Day?"

"Not the day," Orrus said. "Not Midsummer Day, no . . . it is Midsummer Night that we deal with."

"What happens on Midsummer Night?" Lucena asked.

Orrus's eyes twinkled behind his glasses. "You'll find out soon enough," was all he would say.

Now she knew something was afoot, Lucena began to see preparations wherever she looked. Most notably, Madgrin was everywhere. Usually he could be found if someone really needed him but was often absent for extended periods of time. Now not only was he home, but he was everywhere in it: he was in the kitchen consulting with Gydda; he was in Willic's room, giving him a list of invited (and uninvited) guests; he was walking with Grimmach and Cobbin; he was touring

CHAPTER 10: *Midsummer Night*

the grounds with Harga; he turned up in the library, the ballroom, the east antechamber (where Rhyse had gathered the staff to play cards), and in both the north and south halls. Once, when Gydda sent Lucena to the cellar to get a sack of coal, she found him there staring at an empty patch on the wall as if it had just said something profound. He had the thoughtful, introverted look of someone who has just had a great many important ideas, but is not sure they like all of them. Lucena looked from him to the wall and back again, wondering what to say. In the end she decided silence was the best response and left the cellar with the sack of coal as quietly as she could.

Judging from the preparations, it appeared that a great ball was to be held, but who the guests were no one would say. When Lucena approached Gydda she was either sent on errands or set to washing dishes. Rhyse was cranky and snapped at her to go away. Harga was elusive. Grimmach and Cobbin would similarly put her to work polishing silver and pressing linen if she got too close, and Beruse would make her help set out benches and tables in the orchard. Willic was trailing after Madgrin taking notes, and Madgrin was doing things like holding silent conversations with walls, trees, stones and flowerpots.

In the end she joined Willic on the trail behind Madgrin, in the hopes that she might be able to catch either him or Madgrin in a talkative state and so gain some information. In the end, however, she ultimately learned more from what they did than from anything she was told.

The first thing she deduced was that the guests would number in the hundreds, judging from how many tables had been set out, and that something important was to happen at the arena. Madgrin and Willic were on their way down to it when Lucena began tagging along, and for the next hour or so she followed them in and out and all over the place while Madgrin did things to make the dusty stone seats shine like polished marble, and Willic laid out red velvet cushions on them. Then he walked down into the center, and stood in the middle of the sandy enclosure looking up at the surrounding seats. Lucena did not like it down there; it reminded her all too much of the pit in the Parliament of Vampires, and she was glad when they left.

Something of the nature of the guests she deduced by listening to Madgrin consult with Gydda. Gydda had been asked to prepare stuffed cockatrice, manticore-eye salad, several roasts of similarly unfamiliar creatures, dragons-blood soup, bread in a twenty-foot long braid, an army of miniature chocolate people, and gallons of honeysuckle nectar. It was the gallons of honeysuckle nectar that were the problem; Madgrin had asked for thirty, but she could only get seventeen.

"Better make the rest up in rose-petal wine then," he said when she explained the dilemma. "I doubt anyone will notice."

They left the kitchen with Lucena imagining the guests to be giant, hummingbird people who sipped honeysuckle nectar from flower-shaped glasses with thin wooden pipes. But she also thought they must be very violent if they wanted dragons-blood soup and manticore-eye salad, and she began to feel nervous.

After that they went to find Grimmach, and Lucena did her best to look attentive and busy so that she would not be put to work, while at the same time not actually doing anything. Fortunately Grimmach paid her no attention at all; instead he spoke to Madgrin at length about how terribly overworked he was now that Cobbin had disappeared. But Madgrin was not in the mood to go looking for misplaced servants, so he sent Lucena.

"You know the lay of the grounds," he said. "He is probably hiding in the wood somewhere. Try to convince him to do his duty on Midsummer for once, but remember that he hates fairies."

Lucena had little choice but to agree and scurried off for the kitchen door. She wondered what hating fairies had do to with anything and felt mostly frustration at being cheated of her attempt at finding information.

Sure enough, she found Cobbin after a little searching in the wood, about twenty feet off the trail, curled up in the tangled roots of an oak tree fast asleep. At first she felt hesitant to wake him, but then reminded herself that it was nearly morning now, and shook him gently by the shoulder. He curled into an even tighter ball and tucked his face right down into his belly. Lucena sighed to herself and shook him a little more firmly.

"Cobbin," she said. "Cobbin, please wake up. Himself needs you."

Cobbin's head untucked from his belly just enough so he could open one dark, beady eye and give her a mournful look. This made Lucena angry; clearly he had only been pretending to be asleep.

"Cobbin, *do* get up," Lucena said. "Why are you hiding here anyway?"

"Hate fairies," Cobbin mumbled, tucking his face back into his middle.

"I know that," Lucena said. "He told me. But there are no fairies here, Cobbin."

"Not *yet*," Cobbin said. He unbent his neck so he could glower at Lucena from under his bushy eyebrows. "But there will be. Boatloads of them. It's *Midsummer Night*. The queen and her court come here every year. They sing, make merry, and try to kill us!"

"Kill you?" Lucena gasped in surprise. "Why ever would they do that?"

Cobbin shrugged, and because he was still half curled up this came out as an absurd sort of wiggle. "Fey folk, aren't they? When they're not running off with your brothers and sisters they're trying to kill you. Or make people kill each other. They think it's *funny* . . . interesting, see? They get bored, fairies do. Don't know what to do with themselves so they do things to other people. They like to do this especially in the summer. So, long ago, Himself made the queen promise to come and visit him on every midsummer night so the rest of the world got a holiday. But then *we* have to deal with the worst of them."

"Oh dear," Lucena said, beginning to get an idea of why Cobbin was hiding. "But at least this will make it nicer for everybody else," she said. "And it's only *one* night."

Cobbin snorted. "They'll try to lengthen it. They always do. Fairies can bend time, you know. And stretch it, and twist it and tie it into knots. It's supposed to be the shortest night of the year, and it always feels like the longest."

CHAPTER 10: *Midsummer Night*

"Oh, but I'm sure they can't make it last *forever*," Lucena said hopefully, though she felt certain Cobbin would only moan that *they would probably try* or something like that. But to her surprise this seemed to brighten his mood considerably. He sat up and looked at her with more of the usual twinkle in his eyes.

"No one rules forever," he said. "I suppose I have been acting a bit juvenile. Is Himself very upset?"

"No. But Grimmach is anxious to have you back. He is feeling overworked."

Cobbin sighed as he got to his feet, dusting the dirt and dead leaves off his front. "He probably is," he said. "Rhyse never helps with anything for midsummer; she knows how to hide better than me."

He sounded so resigned, the way he said it, that Lucena felt obliged to accompany him back up to the house and even to help him and Grimmach press and fold miles of silky white tablecloth until sunrise, when she promptly fell over into the pile of unpressed, unfolded cloth that remained.

She awoke in her bed with questions from the night before running through her mind, so the first thought she had when Madgrin's voice greeted her was, *can fairies really tie time into knots?*

Silence. Madgrin seemed a little surprised at the question. Then, at last:

Not that I have ever witnessed. Why do you ask?

It was something that Cobbin mentioned, Lucena mumbled as she rolled out of bed and groped blindly for the bottle of blood. She found she couldn't think properly until she had drunk about half its contents; before that the thirst was so blinding it filled her mind entirely.

They can change the perception of time, Madgrin's voice told her as she sat back to sip the other half. *But never time itself.*

And will they really try to kill us? Lucena asked, lacing up the front of her dress.

Silence. This time it felt more subdued.

Perhaps, he said at length. *But they can only try.*

This was a little disturbing, but since Madgrin seemed to be in a talkative mood Lucena racked her brains for more questions to ask him. But before she could put one into words he spoke again.

Are you dressed?

Yes, she said, slipping on her shoes.

Then come down to the front hall. There is something you should see.

So Lucena pulled her door open and trotted down the darkened corridors, taking turns and sliding through walls into hidden passages as though she had been doing it for years. Indeed, it felt like she had been in the house for years, though it had only been a few months. It occurred to her that fairies were probably not the only people who could change one's perception of time.

Lucena pushed the door open to the front hall and emerged into a blaze of candlelight. It looked as though most of the staff were there, apart from Harga, and they were all staring upwards in amazement.

"Ah, La Flein," Madgrin said, catching her eye. He was standing in the very center, looking like a pillar of midnight. "Your friend seems to have discovered a new form of entertainment," he remarked, and pointed up. Lucena looked, and gaped.

It was Keelback. He was floating just below the vaulted ceiling, twisting and twining through the air like an exotic fish. He curled his snake's body into almost-knots, then pulled himself straight and chased his tail in a circle. He looked thoroughly pleased with himself, and oblivious to the crowd gathered beneath him. But when Lucena stepped forward and exclaimed, "Keelback, what in Heaven's name are you doing?" he froze, looked over at her, and dropped like a stone. Lucena ran forward to catch him and was nearly squashed. She had forgotten how big he was, nearly twenty feet long by now and unspeakably heavy. She collapsed to her knees under his weight, then was forced to sit when he wriggled out of her grasp.

"Did you see? Did you see?" he exclaimed, writhing about on the ground in excitement. "I flew! I really did!"

"Levitation is the usual term for it," Madgrin remarked, looming over them both. But he seemed pleased.

There followed some crowded moments wherein all persons present exclaimed at what a remarkable feat Keelback had performed, and praised him rapturously. Keelback seemed daunted by this at first, but soon grew into it, frilling his crest and glowing with pride. The only person not elated was Willic, who stood apart from the others looking woebegone. Lucena, once she had untangled herself from the crowd, went over and touched him on the shoulder. "What's the matter?"

Willic sighed unhappily. "We'll have to find a way to hide him on Midsummer Night," he said. "The fairies always try to take one of us home as a prize, and I don't think Keelback is ready for that."

The fairies, Lucena decided, sounded like perfectly insufferable guests. She sighed almost as unhappily as Willic. "And I suppose the next thing I shall learn is that they hate vampires," she said, half joking.

To her dismay Willic rounded on her, eyes wide, and clapped a hand over his forehead. "Crimes! I'd forgotten all about that! Oh, they will want to tear you limb from limb. And they will know what you are; you reek of deadness."

Lucena watched, a little offended, as Willic dove into the crowd and fought his way through it to Madgrin, who was viewing the affair with a half smile on his thin face. Lucena saw Willic take him by the sleeve, and Madgrin lean over politely to listen as Willic explained the predicament. When Willic gestured towards Lucena—no doubt complaining of her "reek of deadness"—Madgrin looked too, and she felt something twinge in the back of her head in the place where she usually heard his voice. It felt like a mental wink.

She had no idea what he meant by it, but she was certain he had some solution in mind. Sure enough, the night before midsummer Madgrin brought her and Keelback up to his study, where they stood in front of his desk feeling awkward while he surveyed them with his hands folded under his chin. "I'm afraid tomorrow night will be difficult for you both," he said thoughtfully.

Keelback, who had been looking longingly at the ceiling, snapped his head back down and blinked his wide eyes. "Why?" he asked.

"Tomorrow night," Madgrin explained patiently, "is Midsummer Night; on this night, every year, the Queen of the Fae and her court pay us a visit. It is a

CHAPTER 10: *Midsummer Night*

way of remembering things past, and also a way of providing the poor King with a chance to be alone for a while." His eyes twinkled, and Lucena could tell he knew more than he told.

"Cobbin said it's also to keep them from enchanting or stealing humans away," she blurted out.

"Partially," Madgrin conceded. "That part of the arrangement hasn't always worked out very well, I'm afraid; and that is why I wished to speak with you." He pinned them both with an intense stare. "Fairies, particularly the Fae Ones who will be visiting tomorrow night, are by nature curious creatures. Someone like Keelback would undoubtably capture their attention."

Keelback frilled out his crest in a pleased sort of way. He liked attention.

"Which would be undesirable," Madgrin said regretfully, "because they like to take things that interest them away, to keep them as pets or slaves or trophies."

"I don't want to be a trophy," Keelback said peevishly.

"I should think not. And you would never be able to see Lucena again."

"I shall hide," Keelback declared.

"They will find you," Madgrin sighed. "Though I try to prevent them, they always manage to get into every place they are not wanted. We will be cleaning the fairy dust out for weeks."

Keelback looked truly deflated then. His feathery crest drooped.

"What I can do," Madgrin said kindly, "is make it so that you will not be seen, heard, felt, or sensed by any of our guests in any way at all. Then you would be quite safe, and still able to get about in perfect comfort. How would you like that?"

Keelback looked torn. He wriggled his tail uncertainly, and his crest twitched. Lucena could tell he did not want to be kidnapped by the fairies, and desperately wanted to attend the party at the same time, but he would miss the attention.

"No one will see me?" he asked.

"No *fairy*," Madgrin explained. "To myself, Lucena, and all the staff you will be just as you are now. But the fairies may see things you interact with; so keep that in mind." He offered this last suggestion with a twinkle of amusement in his eye that Lucena thought almost gleeful. And she realized that Madgrin cared for fairies about as much as Cobbin did.

But Keelback could only think of himself, and she saw his eyes go wide as all the possibilities for pranks unfolded inside his head. He nodded vigorously.

"As for you, La Flein, things are much simpler," Madgrin said, turning to her. "The Fae must simply not know what you are."

"Yes," Lucena said. "Willic told me they hate vampires, and will be able to sense what I am."

"Unfortunately," Madgrin admitted. "I do not think it would be wise if you appeared in your natural form. How would you like to be a cat for the night? You could pretend to be Willic's niece. Willic is quite deft at handling the Fae."

It had not occurred to Lucena that she might have to be turned into an animal; but she supposed a cat was not such a bad thing, and she liked Willic. But Madgrin was still giving her a thoughtful stare and tapping his index fingers together in a contemplative way.

"Or," he said. "I could turn you into an owl. Halfain would like that; you do remember Halfain, don't you?"

Though time stretched in uncommon ways within the house, Lucena clearly remembered her meeting with the Day and Night Watch: the raven Rusion and the owl Halfain. She nodded.

"Halfain usually rides on my shoulder during Midsummer Night, and always complains that she has no one to talk to. You could ride on my other, and you would probably see more things of interest that way."

This sounded like a splendid idea, and Lucena agreed at once.

So it was that early the next evening Lucena and Keelback again presented themselves before Madgrin in his study, along with just about every other member of the staff, including Harga and Halfain (Rusion was asleep). Halfain, just as Madgrin had said, perched on his shoulder in the form of a small, tawny owl. She looked at them expectantly out of sharp yellow eyes.

"As some of you may already be aware," Madgrin began while they were still settling down. He spoke softly, yet his voice filled the whole room and cut through the hushed muttering. "There will be changes to two of our number. First, and one that it is important for you all to know, Keelback will be undetectable by any of our guests." He pointed a long, thin finger at Keelback as he spoke, and although there was no outward change in the creature, Lucena felt something about him shift, something she couldn't pin down, and though she tried to think what it was, she was distracted by Madgrin pointing his finger at her and saying, "Second, and this will be obvious to all of you, Lucena will be spending tonight as an owl."

At the word "owl" the changes began. Her body broke out in pins and needles all over, and then went numb entirely. The world turned fuzzy, then stretched, grew, shifted, and snapped back into place again.

She found herself sitting on the floor, looking up at everyone. Looking down she saw a tawny, feathery chest and two rough, horny claws with wicked talons on the end sticking out from the fluff. She went to touch them, and found that her arms were folded along her back in the form of wings. This so confused her that she bent over, half opened her wings, and fell flat on her face.

Sympathetic laughter sounded from above her, and a giant white hand descended out of nowhere and scooped her up. Then followed the disconcerting feeling of being carried helplessly through the air to a dizzying height, where she was set down on a narrow blue hill next to a strange black curtain. Scrambling about to keep her balance, she discovered the hill was covered in woven cloth (she could see the individual threads) which she dug her claws into, and that the black curtain was made of many fine silky strands which, as she tried flapping her wings to keep her balance, she sent billowing every which way.

Once she had regained her balance she looked past the black curtain and found herself staring at the gently sloping curve of Madgrin's cheek. It was then the rest of the world snapped into focus, and she nearly fell over again.

She was perched on Madgrin's right shoulder. Now she brought herself to look, she could see down the cascading fall of his robes to the floor, a sickening distance below. What she had thought was a black curtain was obviously his hair,

CHAPTER 10: *Midsummer Night*

and if she craned her neck around she could glimpse his brow like a cliff above her. In the shadows beneath she could see his right eye, which slid around to look at her as she stared. For a moment it was like looking at the night sky reflected in a bottomless pool of water; she felt as though she would drown in that eye. But then it looked away, leaving her with a prickling feeling all over her body as her feathers stood on end.

With a slithering sound Halfain poked her round owl face through Madgrin's hair. "Stop being so fidgety, do," she said in a small, chirping voice, and disappeared back into the hair.

This made Lucena self-conscious, and she remembered how owls always seemed so aloof and composed. So she sidled up as close to Madgrin's hair as she could and clamped down with her claws. She was quite secure that way, as she discovered when Madgrin walked briskly around behind his desk and sat down again.

"Now," he continued placidly. His voice was a soothing rumble, and Lucena had difficulty picking out the words, they were so big and nearby. He seemed to be giving specific instructions to each member of the staff and answering their questions.

Their questions Lucena heard clearly, as she found when Cobbin piped up from across the room to ask if he could be an owl too (the answer was a great, rumbling "no"). She began to understand sounds better; her hearing was more sensitive than it had been in human form, which took a little getting used to. Sounds now had shape and size, as well as tone and volume. She also found her eyes were much better at detecting movement; Willic's hands as they fidgeted with his handkerchief drew her attention at once, and every time one of Harga's ears flicked her eyes darted towards it.

When all was finished Madgrin stood up, and Lucena clutched at his shoulder for all her little claws were worth.

"And good luck," Madgrin rumbled. Then he left.

This nearly dislodged Lucena all over again, for Madgrin jerked backwards and sideways and out of the ordinary realm of things altogether. The world went hazy and blue for a moment, before, with another sickening jerk, it snapped back into focus (and all the right colors) and they were standing just outside the front door facing down towards the main drive.

So that is how he gets around! Lucena thought to herself. How very handy, but rather uncomfortable.

One grows accustomed to it, Madgrin's voice said.

Lucena felt all her feathers go on end once more. In her head Madgrin's voice sounded exactly the same as it always did, and came as a sudden change compared to the rumble when he was speaking aloud.

"Are you two talking again?" Halfain chirped. There was a scrambling and flapping, and she appeared on top of Madgrin's head, tousling his smooth black hair. "I can tell, it makes my pinfeathers itch."

"Sorry," Lucena said, and to her surprise her voice came out just as chirping and birdlike as Halfain's. For a moment she even thought that she had spoken in a chirping, purring whistle, like the sounds a bird makes, and not real words at all. But Halfain understood. She climbed down Madgrin's hair (it must have pulled terribly but he paid it no mind) and settled down next to Lucena.

"That's well enough," she said. "He talks to all of us like that sometimes, but we can only ever hear if we're the one he wants to hear. Very annoying. But convenient."

"And speaking of whom I want to hear," Madgrin rumbled out loud (Lucena found she was getting better at discerning his voice), "I think it would be best if our guests could not understand you." He raised a white finger and gently tapped both their beaks with it, one after the other. Lucena swayed from the impact, but Halfain just looked annoyed.

"That was unnecessary," she protested. To Lucena she sounded no different, but when Madgrin turned his head again so she could see his profile his mouth was pulled up in a sly smile, and his eyes were twinkling the way they did when he was particularly pleased.

There was a creaking heave behind them as the front door was pulled open. Even though Madgrin did not bother to turn, Lucena found she could twist her neck all the way around and easily see behind them. She watched as Grimmach and Cobbin tumbled outside, out of breath and red in the face from running through the house. Together they took up positions on either side of the door, schooling their pointed faces into trim, statue-like expressions, and pulling their long ears down so they stuck out from their heads like absurd tree branches. There was a rustling of cloth as Madgrin crossed his arms, and Lucena hastily untwisted her neck to see that their long-anticipated guests had just begun to arrive.

They came up the drive in a long procession, appearing one by one out of the shadows until there was a small army of figures walking smoothly up towards the front door. They appeared so suddenly and so quietly Lucena knew at once that they had not come in through the gate but from somewhere else entirely. And though the procession carried ornate paper lanterns which twinkled in the shadows, it appeared that every member glowed faintly with an ethereal light.

As they drew closer they solidified into tall, handsome people, dressed in extravagant fashions ranging from modern to ancient. The first two carried standards bearing the emblem of a dragon coiled around a broken moon with a bough of hawthorn and a bough of rowan beneath, and were dressed in fully embroidered and padded doublets with puffy silk breeches and tight silk leggings. Their cloth-of-gold shoes had ridiculously curled toes, and their long white gloves had gold embroidery around the edges. They had wide frilly collars around their necks which made them keep their noses rather higher than looked comfortable. They also wore wide-brimmed hats with dyed ostrich feathers, which came down almost over their eyes.

After these characters came a whirling, jumping crowd of dancers in flowing Crowan togas with flowers braided into their flyaway hair and then a procession playing solemn music on pipes and fiddles, which clashed terribly with the dancers.

Past the dancers and musicians, only partly visible through the crowd, a tent floated through the air. It was pyramid shaped and made of a cloth that glistened

CHAPTER 10: *Midsummer Night*

in the moonlight. Beyond it more tents kept emerging from the shadows, until they formed an armada of shining cloth and flapping banners. What was carrying them Lucena did not see until the heralds and the dancers and the musicians reached the steps and parted like a curtain before the tents. Then she gasped at the sight of the twisted, twiggy creatures that each carried a tent on its back. Some of them looked like men with two legs, bowed over to rest the tent on their shoulders, while some looked more like elephants or horses, who went about on four legs with their burdens on their backs.

When they reached the foot of the steps the creatures dropped to the ground, scattering twigs and leaves across the paving stones, leaving the tents sitting in the drive. There were near twenty of these, in various sizes and styles. The one front and center was by far the largest, with turrets of cloth and strings of flapping flags. Looking at these, Lucena supposed it must have been enchanted, for little more than a lazy summer breeze drifted across the grounds.

There was a tinkle like breaking glass, and the front flap of one of the smaller tents was thrown back, and a person stepped out. At the same time the heralds called in unison: "Guardian of the Third Look, His Grace the Duke of Last Wish!"

He appeared as a tall, thin person of extraordinary beauty, with flowing ash-blond hair and a circlet of silver over his brow. His clothes were all draping robes that shone like moonlight. Lucena did not like to look long upon him, for his gown blinded her sensitive eyes. Fortunately, no sooner had the Duke of Last Wish fully straightened up, then another tent opened (this time with a sound of nightingales) and a woman, shorter but just as beautiful, stepped out.

"Her Majesty, Princess Lorwen of the Castle Spiral!" cried the heralds.

That name rang bells in the back of Lucena's head, but she had no time to place it, for the tent next to the Princess of the Castle Spiral was blown open, and another, taller woman appeared. This one was dressed in full armor and gleamed in the lantern light.

"The Valiant Knight, Lady Rodamant!"

Well, that explained the armor, but there went another tent:

"His Majesty, Prince Flaxian of Last Wish!"

Yet another tall, beautiful person, but he was dark with flashing eyes. And then the tent next to him...

"The Guard of Envy, Her Grace the Countess of Merlinseye!"

This woman was white haired but still youthful and radiant.

"His Majesty, the King of Highstorm!"

Were there none but beauties here? Lucena wondered as the dashing king practically sprang out of his tent.

"His Majesty, King of Merlinseye, Gradhard the Witchslayer!"

This one had dark hair as well, done in many elaborate braids all down his shoulders. Lucena was so impressed by them that she missed the next tent, and started losing track not long after. There were many dignitaries from Last Wish and several knights of Merlinseye, and one who was called only "Dreadspinner." It was impossible to tell if this person was male or female, for they wore thick black draperies that hung all over their body and their head. Bound about the ankles, wrists, neck and waist by strings of pearls and diamonds, they appeared a bizarre sight indeed. Lucena remembered them in particular, because after Dreadspinner remained only the largest, grandest tent, and there was a pause before its occupant was revealed.

"The Magnificent and Terrible," the heralds said, and the tent quivered, "The Empress of Fae, Supreme Arbiter of Otherwhere"—now the tent was positively shaking—"Mistress of the Distant Wind and Lady of Unspoken Serenity"—and the tent blew open with a bang, revealing an impossibly tall figure (at least nine feet), clad in flying raiments that twisted and whirled like leaves in a high wind, and the heralds finished in a hurry—"her Grand-highness, Queen Titanna!"

There was a deafening silence as the fairy queen stood at the foot of the stairs looking at them. She was so tall that she barely had to tilt her head at all to meet their eyes, and when she did Lucena saw with astonishment that one of them had a diamond in it. At least, it sparkled and shone in a way only a diamond could, spilling flecks of bright light across her face. This face was not like the others; it was an exceptionally long face, with a thin, pointed nose and a small cruel mouth with no lips. Her eyes, especially the diamond eye, appeared too large for her head, and were set rather farther apart than was entirely comfortable to look at. Her eyebrows rose sharply up her forehead on either side of her face to end in little flourishes like the tipped-up wings of an eagle. Their shape and the set of her eyes, gave her face a permanent frown.

She began to walk sedately up the stairs. Though she took normal strides, she was so tall and her legs so long, she took the steps three at once and in no time at all was standing face to face with Madgrin.

Which gave Lucena pause, for she had been certain the queen was taller than her maker. She had to look down, then up again, and finally back down at the front door before she realized that, as the queen had climbed the stairs Madgrin had quietly grown taller and taller, so that when they stood on even ground they were the same height.

Then the fairy queen dropped a majestic curtsey, and Madgrin bowed. Lucena and Halfain had to scurry along his back and then up to his shoulder again as he did so to keep from falling off; fortunately he did it slowly enough that Lucena, who was still having difficulty with her owl legs, was not thrown off in surprise.

"This dream lord greets you, fairy queen, and bids you welcome to the House of Madgrin," he said. Although the words were stiff and formal they rolled off his tongue as if he had said them hundreds of times before. Which he likely had.

"The fairy queen returns your greeting, dream lord, and brings good fortune on this Midsummer Night," answered Titanna. Her voice was strong and brassy, like a sorrowful trumpet, and Lucena noticed that as she spoke, though she blinked her right eye the normal amount, her diamond eye never so much as twitched, and remained fixed on Madgrin the entire time.

Oh, I am so glad I am only a little owl, Lucena thought. *How terrible to be looked at by something like that.*

No sooner had she thought this than Titanna turned her head and looked straight at her. And it was quite horrible. But Halfain remained calm and serene at her side, so Lucena did her best to look so as well.

CHAPTER 10: *Midsummer Night*

"Your owls do not seem to understand the concept of balance, dream lord," Titanna said, her right eye narrowing. Her diamond one continued to stare, wide and glittering.

"I am saving the other shoulder for the vulture," Madgrin answered smoothly. Lucena could not tell if he was making this up or not, but it appeased the queen of fairies. "Come," he continued, gesturing with one arm as the doors swung open. "Enter. You are all welcome in my House tonight."

He turned around then, to Lucena's annoyance, and led the way into the hall. She did not like the feeling of having her back to so many strange people and had to spend most of the next half hour with her head twisted around. Even so it was difficult to keep track of them all. The heralds and the dancers along with the musicians disappeared in a twinkling of silk as soon as they stepped inside and were replaced by an army of retainers and servants she had not hitherto seen. They darted about like hummingbirds in a flower garden, fetching things for their masters or perhaps just running about to look busy. Their masters, to Lucena's consternation, all seemed to feel the need to talk personally with Madgrin. This wouldn't have been so bad if he had remained at the same height, but being Madgrin he thoughtfully adjusted his size to match whoever was talking to him. This meant that along with losing the wonderful view sitting on a person nine feet tall granted her, Lucena also had to put up with her host shooting up abruptly, or shrinking down so fast she almost lost her grip on his robe, as the people clamoring for his attention were packed so thickly around there was no time to do the thing slowly.

After the fifth time Lucena was beginning to feel flustered and would have been ashamed of her loss of composure had she not glanced over at Halfain and saw she looked the same.

"It's like this every time," she told Lucena wearily. "I wish he would just stay as tall as their queen, then he wouldn't have to talk to them all, but he's too kind."

Too kind or not, in between the breath-jerking changes in altitude the conversations provided interesting glimpses of their guests, aided by Halfain's running commentary. This started almost immediately, when they were accosted by the King of Highstorm, now surrounded by beautiful retainers dressed mostly in flowers. Halfain scoffed.

"A fine and dandy image he presents on Midsummer," she hissed to Lucena while the king made a long and eloquent speech on the subject of sharing stars, whatever that meant. "You should see him round the year; all battle and blood and beastliness. He had eight older brothers, you know; he's the ninth son, and that makes him twice as powerful as the seventh son. So he killed them all for the throne of their father, who had the good sense to be eaten by a dragon before his son could kill him as well. He himself has taken care to have all his sons killed as infants, but the problem is he now has ten daughters, and more dangerous by far than either the seventh or ninth son are the powers of the tenth daughter. He will come to a messy end."

Then, when the king had finally gone away, they turned around to find themselves beset by the Duke of Last Wish. He spoke in nothing but rhymes in a language that only vaguely resembled Kyrish, which made him a pleasant listen, though Lucena hadn't the foggiest notion what he was talking about. Madgrin did, and answered him in kind. The way they spoke it almost felt like watching a play, with each actor knowing their part perfectly, working to complete a whole piece.

"He always talks like this," Halfain sighed. "It is a language from so long ago even most of the fae have forgotten it, but Madgrin remembers. So they always take the time to have a conversation in it. I think he tells Madgrin stories for safekeeping, because he isn't allowed to tell anyone else. I like him. He'll talk to us. Watch."

And he did. After finishing his conversation with Madgrin, the Duke of Last Wish turned his pale amber eyes on them, as one equal being to another.

"*Ah ben had mell; Ah wen su well,*" he said, nodding to each of them.

"I know what that means," Halfain said as they watched his retreating back through the crowd. "He said, 'I wish you well.'"

The Duke of Last wish turned out to be by far the kindest of the fae in the room that evening. After him there came a succession of grand fairy ladies surrounded by simpering maids with extravagant hair. One appeared to even have a small ship, complete with little cabin lights, wound up in it. They spoke to Madgrin in faint, whispery voices that Lucena couldn't decipher, and after they had finished he was obliged to give them a long, flowery speech that Halfain had to translate.

"He told them all to go away," she said. "Good riddance, too."

No sooner had the ladies and maids with unusual hair been sent away than the Princess of Castle Spiral descended upon them. Much to Lucena's alarm she threw herself bodily at Madgrin, who was forced to catch her in his arms. The pair swayed like a tree in a gale, setting the owls flapping to keep their balance. Then, to Lucena's continued consternation, the Princess twined her arms around Madgrin's neck, forcing Halfain and Lucena to the very edge of his shoulders. There they sat and glared as Madgrin treated the woman with his usual relaxed politeness. Even when the heralds had announced that a Fae Diversion would be starting soon upon the south lawn the Princess refused to let go.

"Good gracious," Lucena hissed. "Doesn't he ever get annoyed, or angry?"

"Of course he never gets angry," Halfain said. "He's *Madgrin*." She put particular emphasis on the first syllable, as if that explained everything. But Lucena was no more the wiser as her maker, practically carrying the Princess of Castle Spiral, followed the stream of fairies out the postern door.

The Fae Diversion turned out to be a play, performed on the gentle swelling green of the south lawn. The heralds and dancers had strung buttery-gold paper lanterns between the two trees at the top of the hill and erected a wide empty doorway over which they had draped a velvet curtain of deep blue. To the side the musicians gathered, tuning their instruments. Cushions had been set out upon the lawn, and the hoblins and Willic were busily rushing back and forth showing fairies to their seats.

At the back were two mountains of pillows, and it was to these makeshift thrones that Madgrin and Titanna were led. This pleased Lucena, for it meant that her maker was obliged to drop the clinging princess and become nine feet tall again, and thus afforded her an excellent view of the stage. For stage it was now,

CHAPTER 10: *Midsummer Night*

with pieces of scenery set up at the side and a ramshackle throne in the center. There was also a table, which tilted from the uneven ground of the hill, and the fairy who was currently trying to balance a vase of flowers on it was having some difficulty. By the time the audience had all been seated, however, the stage was clear and ready; a hush fell over the crowd as the narrator, a short fairy with a face like a weasel, stepped out from the curtains and made a deep bow.

"Honored and distinguished guests," he said in a clear, clipped voice. "Welcome to the Fae Diversion. Herewith, we shall endeavor to provide you with wit, humor, and a story to lighten the depths of your hearts. Please be seated and be silent, for the comedy soon begins: behold these twenty pixies as they present to you, *The Ballad of Robin Goodfellow!*"

Surprisingly, this was a play Lucena knew well. It was a favorite of children's school houses, and even of some respectable theaters. It concerned a particular fairy knight of great renown who disgraced himself and was forced to serve a human king for a year and a day. It chronicled his numerous adventures and ended with his triumphant return to the fairy court as a hero of kings. The biggest difference, which was immediately obvious, was that all the parts were played by fairies. And since these fairies were not royal or grand members of their race they had not taken much care to appear human. And though they were all human *shaped*, that was as far as they went. Some were foxish, other mouse-like. Some looked downright gobliny. And one (the one playing Robin Goodfellow) had antlers.

The first scene took place in the court of the Fairy Queen, and the players considered this an opportunity to poke some fun at their betters. This in itself was a deviation; whereas in most performances the fairy nobility were portrayed very stiff and proud, now Lucena saw that each actor was parodying a specific person. She saw a rather good impression of the King of Highstorm and the Princess of the Castle Spiral, and all the lines for the Duke of Last Wish had been put into verse. The fairies in the audience picked up on a good many other hidden jokes, and long before Robin Goodfellow was sent packing they were in fits of repressed laughter. Repressed, of course, because nearly everyone in the audience had a parody on stage, and did not wish to offend their neighbor.

But when the play moved into the human world things became truly bizarre. Lucena realized that all the times she had seen this play before it was humans pretending to be fairies, and getting them a little wrong. But now it was the fae's turn to play humans, and it was clear that they were no better at playing humans than humans were at playing fairy. They seemed more inspired by apes than humans, and the characters were horrendously simplified. Combined with the fact that the fairies portraying humans were no more human-like than those playing the actual fairies, they looked to Lucena more like a comical interpretation of a court of trolls than of men and women.

Just before Robin Goodfellow was sent off on his last and most dangerous quest there came a short intermission. The players retired behind the blue velvet curtain, and the audience got up and stretched their legs. All except Titanna and Madgrin, who sat like statues upon their pillows.

A tray bearing wine and cakes bobbed its way through the crowd, carried by one of the dancers. Titanna took a goblet, but Madgrin waved it away. The wave was a peculiar, jabbing wave, and sent Lucena's gaze off in quite a different direction. There she saw Willic, standing beside the stage looking pale and unhappy. He and Madgrin stared at one another intently for a moment, then in a silent flutter of wings, Halfain left his shoulder and went flapping off over the crowd to land on Willic's outstretched arm. They conversed together in quiet tones, then Halfain came flapping back.

"He wants to know who the fae's Champion is," she explained to Lucena. Beside the stage, Willic's pale face twisted in displeasure, and he disappeared around the curtain with a flick of his tail.

"Champion?" Lucena asked.

"The Fae Champion," Halfain explained. "As part of the entertainment every year they pick a champion who is to fight one of us. This year Titanna has requested the confrontation be a bear baiting."

This made Lucena's little owl-gut twist uncomfortably; she knew full well what happened to the bear being baited, and also who the bear would probably be. It made her so nervous that she could not enjoy the play's conclusion at all. But she was obliged to watch with the others as Robin Goodfellow triumphed in his final task and returned to Faerie to find a hero's welcome awaiting him. The audience applauded lustily, and Lucena felt slightly sick.

After the last curtain call the actors passed through the audience throwing flower petals and sweets, causing a general commotion. During this commotion Madgrin left, taking Halfain and Lucena with him.

The transition was not so upsetting this time, and Lucena let herself be dragged through the strange blue nowhere. When again they snapped back into somewhere, it turned out to be the gates of the arena. The arena itself was ablaze with the light of a thousand torches and lamps, and the box seats atop the towers that flanked the gates shone like beacons. But the gates themselves were dark: they loomed above Madgrin and when they opened they made a grinding sound like an angry beast.

Willic was waiting inside. He wore a plain leather smock with red tassels on the shoulders, and carried a baton with red ribbons on one end. He snapped to attention as the gate opened, and then relaxed when he saw who it was. Madgrin nodded to him—a gentle dip of his head, so as not to disturb the owls—and turned to the stairs that led up from the gate to the high box seats atop the towers. These had been furnished in a lavish style with chairs draped in embroidered cloth and cushions and lit with seven bright lanterns. This scene of luxury was blighted by a pile of entrails from a creature the size of a boar. They had been pushed into a corner in a streak of red and brown fluids where they lay smelling of blood. Lucena felt her feathers going on end, and her owlish mind wondered if any of them would make good eating.

Madgrin turned his head and looked at the entrails, which proceeded to shrivel and twist until they were only black little stones, and then shrank away into black nothing.

"Keelback?" he asked, glancing upwards.

CHAPTER 10: *Midsummer Night*

"I was going to eat those," Keelback said reproachfully as he dropped from the ceiling. He looked a little bedraggled, and his crest hung unhappily about his neck. Slithering into the same corner the entrails had occupied he coiled himself up, resting his chin on his back. "I don't like being unseeable," he whined. "I tried teasing the fairies that brought the troll, but they didn't notice—"

"Troll?" Lucena squawked in alarm, interrupting him. She had to turn around on Madgrin's shoulder as he sat down in the cushion-laden chair to keep her eyes on Keelback.

"Oh yes, they brought a troll," he said. "Big fellow. He's not happy. They brought him in a cage to be killed, but I think it's going to be the other way around. I tried to undo the latch and let him out, but there was magic on it and it burnt my beak."

Lucena tutted. Owls, she found, were good at making tutting noises, and it pleased her. It also pleased her to be so high above the ground. Turning around again she looked out through the open end of the box down to the wide white circle of sand, streaked with gold and yellow from the torches on the walls. She could see the doors set into the walls of the arena and the chains that hung across them; they glittered in the firelight. Above the walls rows of planks laid flat upon stilts provided seats for the rest of the audience, and they went up and up to the outer wall in steps of shadow and firelight. There were smaller shadows appearing now, dark shapes of fairies as they made their way to their seats, each with a flickering candle flame to light their way. The empty silence gave way to a gentle murmur which rose and swelled, pierced now and then by shouts and calls.

When the stadium was almost full and the murmur had grown to a low roar Titanna appeared in the box, accompanied by three maids. Where they had come from it was hard to say, for there had been no sound of them upon the stairs nor were there any gusts of wind. They simply stepped out of the shadows and into the lantern light. Keelback watched them intently, his large eyes shining.

As the queen took her seat and the maids arranged themselves about her there came a trumpeting from below, and Willic climbed to the top of the steward's stand (a sort of pillar that jutted out into the arena where everyone could see it, with gaily flapping red flags hanging from the rails). He brought a speaking trumpet to his mouth and announced in a carrying voice:

"Gracious guests, we fairly welcome you to the Arena of—" but here he was cut off by a roaring cheer from the audience. It was not for Willic; one of the doors in the arena walls had begun to shake, its chains rattling. From behind it came muffled thumps and animalistic groans, and these excited the fairy spectators all the more. Poor Willic was forced to shout into his speaking trumpet, so that his voice came out cracked and high, barely audible over the cheering and thumping.

"—of Terror and Delusion," he continued. "We would like to present, without further ado, the first spectacle of the night: from the highest frosted peaks of Svenia, the Arcticus—" and the doors were nearly flung off their hinges as a troll, easily ten feet tall, stormed into the arena. The audience went mad. Lucena's sensitive ears were ringing, so she hunched herself down and sidled up close to Halfain. The troll was similarly put off by all the noise. It swung its tiny head this way and that, blinking dark, beady eyes. Though it did not look particularly intelligent, its air was one of immeasurable malevolence and aggression. It had an evil flat face with a pushed-in nose and heavy brows, huge, bowed shoulders and unusually large arms. It wore a crude leather loincloth which flapped about indecently, and in each hand it carried a heavy stone hammer. It waddled out to the center of the arena and looked around, as if considering what to smash first.

When again there was a lull in the cheering (indeed, the audience seemed so eager, and some were dressed in such warlike attire, Lucena wondered if a few might jump down and begin to do battle), Willic raised his speaking trumpet once more to announce the fae champions who were to fight the troll. The crowd stayed respectfully silent through this, as Willic announced first the Valiant Knight Lady Rodamant and the Champion of Merlinseye, who was a striking fairy with red hair and a wickedly curved battle-axe. These two entered the arena from the opposite side of the troll and advanced together, their weapons at the ready.

Somewhere across the arena a gong boomed, and as its heavy note was overwhelmed by the cheer of the crowd the troll, realizing there were two small, squishable objects nearby, raised its hammers and charged at the fae knights.

At first it seemed all they could do was run hither and thither, ducking and dodging the troll's earthshaking blows. But as the fight wore on Lucena noticed how, no matter how close the knights let the troll get, never did it land a hit. They always slipped away at the last instant. And she became certain they could move much faster if they really wanted to, and were only stringing the fight out to tire their enemy.

The audience apparently thought so as well, and soon grew bored and began a slow, rhythmic clap that echoed around the stadium. Down on the sand the fae knights seemed to agree that they had waited long enough, and a moment later Rodamant neatly stuck the troll's left leg with her lance. A long gush of dark blood followed the blade as she whipped away, and the troll let out an anguished bellow.

The fighting began in earnest then. Despite its injury the troll was moving faster now, and a few times nearly caught the Champion of Merlinseye. But with each near miss it got a nasty slice from his axe, first along its right side, and then on its other leg.

They're wounding it! Lucena realized with a rush of horror. They could have killed it easily right from the start, but they were killing it slowly to provide a better show. It made her insides twist.

"Don't feel *too* sorry for it," Halfain said, guessing her thoughts. "If that troll were ever to catch a fairy it would eat it alive. In little bites. Feet first."

"Oh," said Lucena. She felt ill.

But the audience members were enjoying themselves tremendously. With each swipe the fae knights made, with each fresh spurt of blood, a roaring cheer filled the arena and echoed through the stands. Some were standing on their seats, the better to see, and a few of the bolder ones near the arena were leaning over the rail, shouting suggestions.

Then the troll put on a burst of speed and managed to knock Rodamant off her feet. She flew several yards through the air before tumbling into the sand.

CHAPTER 10: *Midsummer Night*

She got up slowly, using her lance for support, to find the troll barreling down on her. But it had forgotten the Champion of Merlinseye, who took advantage of the distraction to leap onto its back and bury his axe in its spine.

The troll arched in agony, dropping both its hammers, and Rodamant drove her lance directly through its thick neck.

The roar from the crowd overwhelmed the dull thud that sounded as the troll hit the ground, where it lay convulsing until the Champion of Merlinseye hacked off its head. Together he and Rodamant held this aloft as they paraded around the arena, the audience pelting them with posies of flowers and showers of petals as they went. Meanwhile a troupe of fairy servitors came trotting discreetly out with buckets and rakes to clear the carcass away.

"Oh, I don't think that was fair at all," Lucena said weakly. "He was very large, but it was still two on one."

"Fairies rarely are," Halfain said. "Fair, I mean. They're almost as bad as demons. No, worse, actually. Demons are honestly dishonest; a fairy will only smile and say that they think everything is perfectly fine." She clucked disapprovingly.

But there was worse to come. When the Champion of Merlinseye and Rodamant had left the field, and the servitors had come trotting back to rake up the spilled flowers, Willic again took the stand. He was noticeably paler, and he had the pinched look people get when they are trying not to be sick. Nevertheless he put out a bravely steady voice as he once more shouted into his speaking trumpet:

"Thank you fairy gentles, thank you all very much. And now, with the good grace of my Lady and Lord, I will introduce to you our very own Ursa Majora—" but once again the crowd cut him off, this time with a rumbling roar that was almost animal in its sound. At the same time there was a real roar from behind the gate exactly opposite the box where they sat, and it ground open to let Beruse charge out.

Beruse on four legs, covered with shaggy brown fur. Her muzzle was pulled back in a snarl, revealing a healthy row of sharp white teeth, and her hackles were up, making her look even larger. There was a brass plate strapped across her forehead with a strange insignia beaten into it, but aside from that she wore nothing at all; she had become entirely a bear.

"Oh, oh, no . . . " Lucena whispered. After what had happened to the troll, she was suddenly very, very frightened. No wonder Willic was so pale.

"And for her challenger, may I present the brave, the noble"—next to Lucena, Halfain scoffed—"the magnificent"—again the audience's cheer threatened to drown him out, but he seemed determined to get to the end of at least one of his announcements, so he forged on. Lucena heard his voice, high and thin but just audible over the raucous crowd: "The King of Highstorm!"

The King of Highstorm strutted into the arena, the plumes in his helmet swishing to and fro as he turned to survey the crowd. He spared not a glance for his opponent, who loomed, glaring and growling, from across a small ocean of sand, until he had satisfied himself that the crowd was in a good mood, and had made extravagant bows to all the prettiest fairy ladies.

Beruse was getting impatient. She scratched at the ground with one back foot, leaving deep trenches in the sand.

Up in the box, Queen Titanna leaned forward eagerly, and all her maids hurried to the rail to get a better look.

"Do they not tether her?" Lucena asked, hardly daring to hope.

"Of course not," said Halfain. "The fae find that sort of thing boring. Don't expect Highstorm to fight fair, though."

"They aren't . . . are they really going to kill each other?" she asked weakly.

"I don't know," Halfain replied, her voice quiet.

Behind them, Keelback uncoiled himself to slide to the front of the box where he looked out, his crest pressed flat against the back of his head.

Lucena watched the two combatants circle each other, Highstorm with his sword drawn, and Beruse with all her white teeth on display.

Then the fairy lunged. The roar from the crowd was such that it made Lucena flinch and close her eyes, so she missed exactly what happened next. When again she looked they were locked together in a fierce struggle, and there was blood on the king's sword. Then Beruse picked him up, as easy as if he were made of straw, and hurled him at the wall. The crowd "Oooed" and began a steady clap as the King of Highstorm picked himself up again.

The fight resumed, but now both members were injured at least slightly, and they went about it altogether more cautiously. The king was obviously a skilled swordsman, but Beruse was faster than the troll, and smarter too. She obviously felt no need to put him on the defensive when she could dance around the arena making him tired and frustrated. This tactic was frustrating the crowd as well, and they began their slow rhythmic clap again.

Up in the box, Titanna sniffed.

"Your beast does not appear to grasp the proper form of entertainment," she remarked coldly. "Does it intend to play the coward all night?"

"Perhaps she was offended by your majesty's request for a bear baiting," Madgrin replied. At the sound of his voice Lucena turned to look at him, and saw a smile tugging at the corner of his blue lips.

Maybe things weren't so bad after all. Maybe, in his mysterious way, Madgrin was in complete control of this fight as well.

But that thought was shot from her head a moment later when Highstorm waved his hand, and the small doors used by the retainers opened, and a swarm of small, winged animals poured into the arena. In size they were similar to dogs, but shaped more like humans. They had swiftly beating wings that buzzed faintly, and each one carried a sharp little pike.

In the box beside her, Titanna gave out a small, satisfied, "Ah."

In the arena, the swarm of beasts fell upon Beruse, darting in and stabbing at her before flying off again.

Beruse swung about furiously, managing to snatch several out of thin air, snagging them on her claws and crushing their heads in her jaw or beating them against the ground. They were a distraction, however, and while she was engaged, the King of Highstorm lunged forward and landed a blow square in her chest. Lucena saw the blood run, even from her distant perch, and smelled it a

CHAPTER 10: *Midsummer Night*

moment later. It was the smell, she told herself, that made her heart pound and her head spin. It was so strong and sharp.

Up in the box, Titanna sighed in satisfaction.

Beruse staggered. The crowd roared. Then she lashed out, catching Highstorm as he closed in for the finishing blow and sending him flying. She let out a roar of her own that put the crowd's efforts to shame, and with a sudden leap she caught one of the flying beasts and pinned it to the ground, clawing at its face in fury until flecks of blood and flesh could be seen, flying out from under her claws.

The rest of the swarm drew back as Beruse lumbered over her kill, walking slowly to where the King of Highstorm was getting to his feet.

He did not wait, but lunged, and Beruse was too tired or too injured to dodge. The sword slid into her shoulder, but she was herself moving forward with such force that she did not stop until it was buried up to the hilt.

Then she was pushing the fairy over, reaching with her neck, her mouth opening impossibly wide, and there was a sicking crunch as she took his head in her jaws and bit down.

If the king screamed—if he could—the sound was was too muffled to hear. Beruse picked him up and shook him, the way a dog shakes its favorite toy. The way a cat shakes a mouse to break its neck.

She threw him to the ground, where he lay, broken and bleeding. If he were anyone else surely he would be dead.

Lucena had long since forgotten to breathe, just from watching.

But fairy kings must be exceptionally strong and resilient, and as the crowd began to clap the King of Highstorm slowly struggled to his feet again. Though he was unsteady and his face a little green, he drew from his belt a long knife, and began to charge at Beruse.

Beruse stood and faced him, the sword still lodged in her shoulder while the blood poured down her side.

And then Lucena's world slanted sideways, before blacking out altogether as she fainted away.

So she did not see the King of Highstorm falter and, under his own momentum, fall on his face at the feet of the bear.

The resounding thud echoed around the eerily silent arena, covering the small scuffle up in the box as the dream lord fumbled to catch one of his owls as it toppled from his shoulder.

. . . so she did not see the King of Highstorm falter and, under his own momentum, fall on his face at the feet of the bear.

CHAPTER 11:

Somna Ebulis

SOMEONE WAS SINGING. It was not a song Lucena knew, and as she fought off the last clouds of slumber the melody evaporated, along with the words. She lay awhile, trying to recall both, and wondering if it had been a dream. When the last shreds escaped her she sat up and rubbed her eyes.

Madgrin was sitting across the bed from her in the reading chair, his bare feet (she could see them poking out from the hem of his robe) tucked up onto the seat and his knees in his chest. He had his arms wrapped around them and his chin resting on top, his face a white smudge with blue hollows in the darkness and looking all the more skull-like with his eyes closed.

Lucena stared at him fuzzily. She was thirsty. Dreadfully, terribly thirsty, and it was beginning to cloud her vision. She rolled over and felt for the bottle on the bedside table. Someone had already poured her out a glassful of blood, and she drank it off in one long draught. That cleared her head enough so that her hand was steady as she poured herself another shot from the bottle. She sat back to drink it slowly with a sigh of contentment.

You did well, last night, Madgrin said.

Lucena looked up abruptly. He had not opened his eyes, nor was there any sign that he had spoken.

"Er, thank you," she said, uncertain if she should direct her voice towards the figure apparently asleep in her chair, or inwards to the place in her head where she heard him speak. Deciding on the latter, since he didn't stir, she continued. "But I wasn't so well at the end. I must apologize; I did not mean to faint."

Do not be ashamed. Emperors and kings have done the same before you. And likely will again. Inside her head, she could feel him laughing. It tickled. She shook her head.

"Um, Maker?"

Yes?

"Are you asleep?"

Slowly, Madgrin opened one eye. He looked at her from under a heavy blue lid for a few moments, then opened the other one. His eyes were dark, devoid of their usual twinkle. Lucena first thought he looked dead tired, but then she amended that: not tired, sad.

"No," Madgrin said. "Just tired."

Lucena was not sure if this was a reply to her spoken question or her unspoken thoughts. That was the difficulty with Madgrin: she could not tell on which level he was communicating.

A smile tugged at the corner of his mouth, but his eyes remained dark. "Sometimes I find it easier to speak in thoughts. You could too, if you wish."

"Oh, but—" Lucena began, but Madgrin lifted his chin and raised a hand to stop her.

"All you have been doing up until now is listening. Letting me look in on you whenever I please. I don't believe it has ever occurred to you to look back."

Lucena frowned, disbelieving. "Are you saying that I could read your thoughts?" she asked.

Madgrin shrugged, and his left eye twinkled. Once. "I don't see why you would want to," he said good naturedly. "My thoughts are terribly dull, I am sure, compared to yours."

"To *mine?*"

"Oh, indeed. You are always wondering about things. Things I never thought to wonder about . . . not for centuries, anyway. It's delightful. And you have such a fine mind for asking questions. Even now, I can see several, but they are all jumbled up together, and I can't make head or tail of them. You will have to sort them out a bit before I can give answers. Oh, except for one. That is very clear. And the answer is this: Beruse is absolutely fine."

"Truly?" Lucena burst out, her relief flooding over any astonishment at this speech.

"Truly," Madgrin repeated.

Lucena felt a tightness in her chest release her, a tightness that she had until that moment been unaware of. She sat up straighter and took a healthy swig from her glass. Now that she thought about it, she had a great many questions to ask, so she started with the obvious one.

"What happened after I fainted? Was there more . . . fighting?"

Madgrin shook his head. "No, no, the sight of their greatest warrior getting shaken about like a rag doll quite cured our guests of that." He sighed. "But there was a feast afterwards. Much merrymaking, much dancing."

"Was Keelback a terrible nuisance?"

"Absolutely not. Keelback took you up to my study and guarded you for the rest of the evening. He has taken an aversion to the Fae."

"Oh." Lucena felt her heart twinge at the thought of Keelback, as though it were trying to beat again. But the mention of the fairies made her remember Titanna, which made her heart go stone still once more. The terrifying queen of a terrifying race, she couldn't help her curiosity. And if anyone could answer her questions about the Queen of the Fairies, it would be Madgrin.

"How did the Titanna—er, the Queen, get a diamond in her eye?"

Madgrin's eyes flashed at that. She could tell he was beginning to feel better.

"Oh, she merely got it to replace the one that was gone; I believe she felt it would look better than a ball of amber or glass. She has a flair for appearances, as you may have noticed. No, the interesting story behind that is how she lost her eye in the first place. Orrus has the original account written down somewhere, of course, but the fairies will tell you that she has it wander about the Fae Lands so she can see all that happens."

"And how did she really lose it?"

CHAPTER 11: *Somna Ebulis*

"She gave it away, oh, it must be two ages ago now, in return for a favor from the old Svenian Gallows God. Like I said, Orrus has the whole story written down."

Lucena remembered the way Titanna's eye had sparkled with fire when she looked at Madgrin, it had been quite unlike the gentle glint in his eyes. She remembered something else, something Titanna had said that struck her as odd. And not just Titanna—the emotional Princess of Castle Spiral had said it too.

"Maker?"

"Yes, La Flein?"

"Why did the fairies keep calling you the dream lord?"

"A purely honorary title, but it *was* my official position. A little supercilious though; I was not *the* dream lord—no one can claim that title—I was simply *a* dream lord. No one *important*," he added.

Lucena hesitated. Once again she had been given a clear opportunity to ask him straight out who and what he was, but she stopped herself. It was not that she was afraid, nor was it that she did not think he would answer—he seemed to be in an unusually garrulous mood tonight—but that she had the distinct feeling that if she knew what he was, if she knew why he was really here, her whole world would be tipped upside down and spun around until she did not know what was which. She had already died and become a vampire; that had been upsetting enough, and she was only now beginning to get accustomed to it. No, that question would have to wait for another time.

Madgrin had been following her thoughts, she could tell. To her surprise he looked disappointed more than anything else. And here she had been hoping to cheer him up.

Keelback saved them.

He came bursting through the door with all the power his twenty-foot-long body could muster, and tumbled onto the floor beside Lucena's bed.

"Cena, Cena!" he cried, his crest up and his tail whipping about. "Willic says you must come, must come now! Terrible excitement happening! In the laboratory! Come, Cena, come!"

Lucena glanced at Madgrin, intending to apologize for her sudden departure, but he had already risen from his chair and was taking her dressing gown off its hook. He held it out for her.

"Come, La Flein," he said, his eyes twinkling. "You wouldn't want to miss the terrible excitement."

Lucena had barely wrapped the gown around her and tugged on her slippers when Keelback scooped her up and went rocketing out the door, leaving Madgrin behind. Yet when they reached the laboratory he was there before them, a tall blue-black smear in the dusty shadows. He stood in stark contrast to Willic, who was dressed in smart tans and reds this evening, and was darting about in a state of extreme excitement. When he saw Keelback and Lucena he gave out a mew-like cry and hurried over.

"Oh, Lucena, I'm glad you're awake. It's hatching, Lucena. It's actually *hatching!*"

"It was bound to happen sooner or later," Orrus said, standing up from where he had been kneeling in the shadows. "Do come over, Lucena."

With a lurch in her stomach Lucena realized what they were talking about: the not-evil darkness that clung to the shadows in the corner of the room. The darkness Willic had shown her the very first week she had been in the House of Madgrin. She had paid it little thought since then—had quite forgotten it, in fact—so she was surprised to see it now: no longer simple shadow, it was heaving and writhing, as though there were something inside trying to shrug it off.

When she made no move Keelback gently put his broad flat head to her back and pushed her carefully around the cauldron and the bench to where Orrus was standing, his feet hidden in the shadows.

"Why do you need me?" Lucena asked, trying to keep her voice steady. She was frightened of the darkness—terribly frightened, no matter how not-evil Willic had said it was.

Orrus gave her a surprised look. "Well, you're *good* with these sorts of things," he said, his eyes flicking to Keelback briefly.

Oh, Lucena thought. Oh. Well, if she could handle Keelback, then true enough there was not much she could not handle. Unless it was a fairy.

Please don't let it be a fairy, she thought as she knelt beside Orrus and strained her vampire eyes into the dark.

At first she couldn't see a thing, no matter how hard she tried. The darkness heaved about, sometimes flaring up and sometimes folding back onto itself. Whatever was inside was obviously having a difficult time getting out. So, suppressing a shiver, Lucena reached her arms into the darkness and lifted up with all her might.

Like it had done with Willic before, the darkness fled from her touch and flew up into the air, trailing blobs of shadowy cloud. It left behind a gap through which she could clearly see the worn, greyish floorboards, and against these boards were silhouetted three long, spidery legs.

Lucena nearly recoiled in shock. The legs were working frantically against the wood, trying to pull free from whatever they were attached to. Then, with a burst of smoky black dust, another leg appeared. Like the others it was double jointed, black, and dusted with stiff, shiny hair. The owner of the legs appeared to be making progress, and with steady heaving, a face loomed into view.

At first she thought it was a face with two small black eyes and a strange beard. But then the beard moved, and she saw that it was the lower half of a spider's face, its mouthparts tucked up under its chin. As more of it emerged from the darkness, so did more of its eyes. Two large ones appeared above the first two little ones, and these glinted red in the dim light. Then two more on either side. Finally its entire head was out, along with another pair of legs.

Lucena gazed down, fighting the urge to run and cower on top of the bench. She had never been frightened of spiders before, but this one came up to her knees and she could clearly see its terrifying, arachnid face.

Now it had all but its hindmost legs and abdomen free, but this last portion was proving impossible. It struggled and heaved, but the darkness held it fast. It had been struggling for hours, Lucena realized, and was getting tired.

CHAPTER 11: *Somna Ebulis*

The thought caused her to overcome her reservations, and she bent forward to push the darkness back, herding it away with her hands.

With another puff of black smoke the spider came free. It staggered forward a few paces on its many legs, and then collapsed. Which was to say, its body sank to the ground, and it drew all its legs close around it.

Now that it had stopped moving Lucena was not nearly so frightened. Peering closer she saw that its abdomen, like its legs, was sparsely covered in short, stiff, shiny black hairs, though its thorax—which was also its head—was a bare, leathery brown. It had pale spinnerets at the tip of its abdomen, from which hung a strand of silver web.

"Bless my soul," whispered Orrus, who was staring, glassy-eyed, at the spider as though it were a gorgeous woman. "Bless my soul, it is a real shade eater. And a female too, judging from the size."

"A *shade eater*, truly?" Willic put his head around Orrus's elbow to get a better look.

"Shade eater?" Lucena echoed, mystified.

"What's a *shade eater*?" Keelback asked piercingly. The noise disturbed the spider, who shivered all over and clicked her mouthparts together.

In the distance by the door, Madgrin laughed. "It seems our old friend has left us a hint as to his feelings for our choice of decor." His face sobered. "Grimmach will be disappointed; he liked the gloom."

"I don't understand," Lucena said. "What is a shade eater?"

Madgrin glanced at Orrus, who cleared his throat happily. "Shade eaters are a form of *elementavores*. Those beings that feed on nonmaterial things—like salamanders, which eat fire, and therapins, which feed on wind. They are closely related to dumrusks, which absorb dread. Properly, shade eaters are called sombulus (plural sombuli), after the Delpheonian *somna ebulis* which means 'tearer of the veil.' They are called this because they feed off darkness, and so can render dark places bright if they stay long enough. Because of this they have developed a resistance to light remarkable in darkness-bound creatures, and are useful in making the most of what little light you have when you are low on candles. I say, my lord, would it be too much to ask that she be taken down to the library? I am always afraid I will do my eyes more injury if I continue to scrape by with what light the Librarian allows."

Madgrin smiled, and shrugged. "That depends on where she wants to go," he said.

But it became clear that as far as the shade eater was concerned the laboratory was where she wanted to be. No matter what pleading and coaxing Orrus, Lucena or Willic tried (Keelback refused to go near her), she would not budge. And when they became too forward with their advances she reared up her front legs and showed them her bright, yellow fangs, her largest eyes flashing red.

"Ah well, better leave her be for now," Orrus said sadly, and the deflated group left the laboratory.

All save Madgrin. As Lucena lingered at the door she saw him in the shadows, staring fixedly at the shade eater. She suddenly wished for all the world that she could read minds, and to know what he was thinking behind those glittering eyes.

But Keelback was tugging at her sleeve and insisting that *now* she must come see what he had found in the wood. Now, now, now! So she went.

Word of the shade eater spread through house like wind, thanks to Willic's diligent efforts. Soon everyone was pestering Lucena for details, or to take them up to see the shade eater for themselves. They did not pester Orrus because he was far too learned and wise, and Madgrin because... well... he was *Madgrin*. And they wished Lucena to escort them because, Lucena realized with a twinge of amusement, hoblins and transformed snakes and dogs were just as wary of giant spiders that sat in dark places as regular humans.

The only person who did not show an inclination to race up and see the shade eater (pushing Lucena in front of them, of course) was Beruse; she was still nursing two cracked ribs and many other wounds with stitches from her fight on Midsummer Night. She satisfied her curiosity by sitting Lucena down at her bedside and having her tell all about it.

It was the first time Lucena had been in Beruse's room. It was small, den-like, with stone walls, on the ground floor at the back of the house. It had a wide window (open, to let in the summer night air) and a small postern door that led out to a stable where the carriage was kept. It was sparsely furnished with a bed and chair; a large locked chest lay in one corner, and a cracked bit of mirror hung from a peg across from the window. There was also a voracious indoor plant, which showed signs of wanting to become a tree: it had spilled over its pot and climbed up to the ceiling where it spread out its branches and dangled leaves down so low they brushed Lucena's face when she stood. But what most caught her attention (aside from Beruse's bandaged form lying on the bed) were the trophies tacked to the wall. They covered most of the side around the door and window, and overflowed onto the wall opposite the bed. They were a varied assortment: helmets, shields, even one or two broken swords. They glinted in the candlelight, as though on fire. Beneath each one was a name and a date, and these ranged from quite recent... to a very long time ago indeed.

Beruse saw her looking. She smiled, and let out a chuckle that was more like a growl. "You like them?" she asked, nodding her head at the shining wall.

"There are so many," Lucena marveled. "You've been collecting them for a long time, I see. Where did they all come from?"

"Oh, here and there," Beruse said modestly. She seemed pleased by Lucena's interest. "That one"—she carefully raised an arm to point at a dented helm with horns mounted on each side—"I took off a Svenian pirate in 1387. It was one of my first. Oh, but then the sword next to it—the broken sword—that's from a vampire I fought in the Arena in 1066. I only keep the finest ones though... or the ones that were special. Like that gauntlet, the dingy leather one, I got that from one of Amstrass's generals, back when she had an army. They come from anyone I've fought, you see. Vampires, wicked humans, even fairies. Speaking of which, I've a new piece to add to my collection..." Painfully and slowly, Beruse reached under her bed and pulled out a finely carved helmet with a blue feather plume. It had several dents and the feather was still wet and bedraggled. Lucena recognized it immediately.

"That's the King of Highstorm's helm!"

CHAPTER 11: *Somna Ebulis*

"Oh, it is indeed," Beruse said with grim satisfaction. "The loss of this will teach him not to take the Warriors of Dream so lightly. But there will be another champion next year, I suppose . . . there always is."

"Are you made to fight them every year?" Lucena asked sympathetically.

"Most years, seems like," Beruse said. "Fairies, in case you haven't noticed, are a bloodthirsty lot; they like watching that sort of sport, and they're always looking for a way to snub Himself. A member of the Household has to fight a champion of Faerie each year—and it's usually me. Although"—she scratched her chin—"when we had that magician living with us—the one what left that shade eater—he and I would spell each other. Switch off years, you know. And he would always roast them in magic duels. Quite a mage, he was. Miss him, I do. Now it's only me; no one else is warlike enough, and Orrus's sworn off combat magic. Good fun, I suppose, but it gets tiring, you know? I'm not allowed to actually *kill* them."

"Are they allowed to kill you?" Lucena asked.

"Certainly. They all are. Allowed to try, that is." Beruse chuckled, winced in pain, and growled.

"But that's terrible! Suppose they succeeded!"

"You've still some things to learn about this place, haven't you?" Beruse observed. She shook her head. "No, no, as long as I keep my head on my shoulders Himself can patch me up fine. He can fix anything, if he puts his mind to it. Which, for us, he will. He does."

"That's kind of him."

Beruse snorted, and tossed the helmet back under her bed. "Kindness got nothing to do with it—though he is that. He's reasonable, Lucena. *Reasonable*. He doesn't do acts of kindness unless he has a reason."

"Except," she added thoughtfully, "making you. I don't see the reason behind it, so it must have been kindness. But I suppose that's up to you to decide, isn't it?" She lay back on her pillows and closed her eyes with a sigh. "Not that I'm not glad of it," she added. "I think we're better off with you. Now be a dear little cub and fetch me a glass of water."

Though the house was abuzz with excitement over the shade eater, when she did nothing but crouch in the corners of the laboratory, gradually making the room lighter and lighter, the staff began to lose interest. Even Orrus, after he had spent a week taking notes day and night, grew bored and returned to the library. Only Lucena persisted in visiting, which was a source of consternation to Keelback, who was terrified of the creature. He balked at the door of the laboratory and would go no further, but he glared at the shade eater from the doorway as if warning her off from harming Lucena.

But the shade eater did not notice Keelback. Indeed, she did not seem to notice Lucena, even though the young vampire would sit and talk to her for an hour each night. Lucena did this not, as every one else seemed to think, because she was bored, but because she got the strong impression that the shade eater was intelligent. She looked at Lucena in a penetrating manner, as though there were a hundred thoughts and ideas tumbling behind her many eyes.

Lucena kept up these visits, but after a month she began to grow tired of pointless chatter, and she got the feeling the shade eater did too. By this time the laboratory was quite well lit (in a flat, grey sort of way), so Lucena began bringing books to read aloud. This pleased Keelback, because he could listen from the door, and it also seemed to please the shade eater. If a story was particularly to her liking she would come creeping out from her corner to crouch by Lucena's chair, her many legs tucked in next to her body and her eyes shining in the dim light.

Then, one evening in late summer, Lucena awoke to the uncomfortable sensation of being smothered. Something big and long and *alive* had wound itself around her body, raising her to a sitting position in the process. It clenched and twisted, and it was a good thing Lucena had no need to breathe otherwise she would have suffocated.

As she emerged from the haze of unconsciousness she began to discern words pounding at her ears. Words that were unmistakably Keelback's.

"Cena, Cena," he was crying, his high birdlike voice raised to a squawk. "Stop it, Cena! *Stop* it! It moved—Ah!—it moved *again!*"

Keelback was coiled around her, she realized belatedly. But she hadn't a clue what he wanted stopped. Had she done something in her sleep? But after she had wiggled her head and shoulders out of Keelback's grasp she saw plainly what had excited him.

The shade eater was sitting in a corner, all her legs tucked beside her, and every one of her eight eyes glaring at Keelback.

"Oh, hello," Lucena gasped when she caught some breath. "Keelback, please loosen up, I cannot think!"

Keelback obligingly loosened his coils, though he remained wound protectively around her. Lucena worked an arm free and grasped the bottle on her bedside table. She drank down half of its contents to clear her head, and then looked back at the shade eater.

The shade eater extended one long leg, and then another and another. She stepped towards the bed, and said something.

Exactly what she said was drowned out by Keelback going into a fit of squawking and convulsing around Lucena, who felt the blood she had just swallowed being squeezed back up her throat.

"Keelback!" she gasped, and grabbed his beak in both her hands, bringing it shut with a clap. "Calm yourself, *please*." Keelback let out a muffled whimper, but he allowed Lucena to get her upper half out of his grasp and lean over towards the shade eater. "I'm sorry, what did you say?"

"The Keelback is noisy," the shade eater said in a voice full of clicks but trim and clear and easy to understand. "Please make him stop?"

Lucena felt harassed. "Keelback will make what sounds he likes," she explained.

To illustrate her point, Keelback began to whine through her hands, which were still holding his beak shut.

"Keelback, will you calm down? She's not going to bite you—you won't, will you?"

CHAPTER 11: *Somna Ebulis*

The shade eater looked at them. Though her features were anything but human, it was easy to distinguish the scorn written all over them. "No," she said with a heavy click.

"There, you see?"

Keelback whimpered. But after much tedious negotiation Lucena convinced him to let her go, though he remained pressed up against the opposite wall, from where he watched the shade eater warily. Lucena swung her feet out of bed with a sigh of relief and examined her limbs to make sure they were the right shape and working properly. Satisfied, she turned her attention to polishing off her breakfast and getting dressed, pointedly ignoring the two beasts glaring at each other from opposite sides of the room.

Once Lucena had finished her toilette she gathered up the books she had borrowed from the library and went to the door. Glancing back she saw that neither Keelback nor the shade eater had moved, and realizing it was foolish to leave them alone together she said, "Keelback, do come along. And you can come too Miss shade eater... er, you are a lady shade eater, are you not?"

The shade eater swung around and fixed all eight of her eyes on Lucena.

"I am female, yes," she said. "My name is Urgolant."

"Urgolant," Lucena repeated. "Yes, of course. Would you like to come with us to the library? There are many more books there to be read, if you wish."

"I would like that," Urgolant clicked, and her eyes softened. She scuttled from the shadows (Keelback shuddered) and followed on Lucena's heels out the door. Keelback joined them in the corridor, sliding upside down along the ceiling so that his crest drooped nearly in her face.

What a sight we must look, she thought to herself. Walking, crawling and slithering. I suppose all I need now is a monster that swims!

When they arrived in the library Orrus nearly tumbled off the ladder he had been on carefully re-shelving old books. After he recovered he made them all welcome and showed Urgolant to a nice shadowy corner where he would bring her any book she pleased.

But Urgolant did not want to sit in a corner and be brought books. She scuttled up the nearest bookcase and selected a nice thick volume from the top shelf. Then, still perched on the vertical surface, she flipped the book open and held it with her two front legs and began to read, turning the pages with her long mouthparts.

There was no question she was *reading*. At first Lucena wondered how she could read at all, but then, after a few minutes, the giant spider asked, "What does the word *infusion* mean?"

Orrus explained good-naturedly.

"Oh," said Urgolant, and went back to her book.

She read along peacefully until she came to another word that she did not know, and then she asked again (this time it was *susurration*). Each time Orrus was happy to answer, and Lucena soon left her to it and went to stop Keelback sharpening his beak on the bookshelves.

Urgolant spent the rest of the night in the library, and apparently all the next day as well; she was still there when Lucena went looking for her the next evening.

"I have learned three hundred and eighty-two new words," she told Lucena proudly. "Also, I have read all the books on the top shelf of the first bookcase on the right. I think that in another eighty years I will have the entire library read."

Over the course of the next few weeks the household came to accept Urgolant as just another oddity. Since the house was so full of these already it was not a hard thing to do, though the entire staff was more than happy to leave responsibility of the shade eater to Lucena. It was not that Urgolant got into trouble with any frequency (indeed, compared to Keelback she was a paragon of polite behavior), but whenever someone wanted her to lighten a room, or permission to take down the silvery webs she sometimes put up in inconvenient places, they went to Lucena first. As Harga once remarked to Grimmach after watching the young vampire convince Urgolant to take down a very fine web that just happened to go right over his front door:

"It's not that she's malevolent; I don't think there's a harmful hair on her body. But you do get such a feeling of penetration when she looks at you. It's all those eyes. They feel as though they could rip you apart. But when she looks at our Cena they're as soft and kindly as a puppy's. There's no doubt about it, that girl has a way with beasts."

"Oh?" said Grimmach, his pointed face breaking into a smile. "And has she charmed our old Watch Dog then?" He dug his elbow playfully into Harga's side.

Harga put his head on one side and smiled. "Maybe, maybe. I was hoping to introduce her to the Labyrinth once the nights get longer, but what with the season coming on I doubt Himself will give her a spare moment."

The two habitants contemplated this notion in silence while Lucena, happily oblivious, herded Urgolant back up to the House.

If a story was particularly to her liking she would come creeping out from her corner to crouch by Lucena's chair, her many legs tucked in next to her body, and her eyes shining in the dim light.

CHAPTER 12:

Mirror, Candle and Book,

VAMPIRES, IT TURNED OUT, like apricots and apples, had a season. This began the day after the autumnal equinox, when the balance of night and day swung to favor the dark, and lasted until its sister equinox in springtime. Lucena felt the coming of the season distantly. Rather, she imagined, like flowers and trees feel the coming of spring. But the change it worked was dramatic: she found herself waking earlier and staying up later, and yet she was full of energy from sundown to sunup, and her appetite increased accordingly. Gydda began keeping bottles of fresh pig's blood out on the kitchen counter, for Lucena's hungers would come upon her suddenly, and she would stumble into the kitchen with glassy eyes and grope for whatever smelled remotely of blood. Once, she grabbed up a raw steak that Beruse had requested for her dinner and sank her teeth into it, sucking as though it were a ripe orange. When she realized what it was, though, she spat it out and apologized. Then she apologized again for ruining a perfectly good steak. But Gydda just sighed and got her a proper bottle, Keelback ate the spoiled meat, and Beruse settled for a whole chicken.

But there was nothing to be done about her racing through the halls. She would come barreling along, for the pure joy of running. The sliding, dodgy architecture of the house only made it more fun. It was so much fun she sometimes forgot that she, being a solid body, could not pass through other solid bodies. This resulted in some truly magnificent crashes, and after she collided with Cobbin when he was moving a potted plant with glass flowers, Willic sent her outdoors where, at Harga's suggestion, she raked the fallen leaves in the orchard into a huge pile for Keelback to thrash about in. Then she came racing back into the kitchen, still bubbling over with restless energy.

Lucena was not the only vampire to be so affected by the changing season. All the vampires in that hemisphere were going through a similar energy burst, if the amount of time Madgrin and Beruse spent out hunting was any indication. And, after a particularly hair-raising night (Keelback had decided to try and find the longest banister in the house by sliding down all of them, one after the other, with Lucena on his tail), Willic went to Madgrin for help. Madgrin smiled his pleased, secretive smile, and told Willic he would take care of it.

Starting the next evening Lucena began accompanying Madgrin and Beruse on their hunting expeditions. And although these provided a much-needed outlet for Lucena's energy, for her part she felt rather useless.

She was always stuck tagging along behind either Madgrin or Beruse, never taking part in the action herself. When she followed Madgrin it was boring; vampires fled before him, like the ones back at Munsmire. When she followed Beruse, it was terrifying. Vampires saw an enemy they thought they could defeat, and

CHAPTER 12: *Mirror, Candle and Book*

came at her tooth, claw, nail, and whatever weapon they could lay their hands on. And Beruse, though she was an exceptional fighter, after fending off ferocious enemies from all angles, would emerge with a prodigious number of bruises and scrapes.

Then Lucena felt more useless still, since she had been unable to help. And after their third expedition she said so.

Beruse, who had been particularly banged up that night, was not in the best of humors, and replied rather sharply.

"If you want to help, then *help!* You *can* fight, I know you can—I've *seen* you—and Madgrin told me what you did to that vampire in Müldif. I tell you, how about the next time some undead maniac with a hatchet goes after my back *you* take the hit!" And she stomped off wincingly.

Lucena was troubled. The thought of fighting brought back bad memories: those horrifying arena battles, the bloodbath at Munsmire. So she asked Madgrin about it.

Go and fight, he said. *Make new memories. But keep Keelback close to you.*

It was a cold October evening, and the streets of Redling were treacherously wet and slick from the day's rain. The city's inhabitants were bundled up snugly against the chill air and went about their outdoor business with a single-mindedness particular to people who wish to be inside and in front of a fire as soon as possible. This was true at the Standing Seven, where the servants of rich households hurried about doing errands for their masters, and it was also true in the Retching Lanes, where gnarled old women who fancied themselves witches cast golden flames into empty chamber pots for the local street urchins to enjoy. But it was not true in the Theatre District: here was all bustle and noise, and so many people gathered together in one place banished the chill from the air with their combined body heat.

It was nearly ten o'clock, the prime play hour for the more risqué entertainment, and the crowd was busy moving from the World Theatre, the famous, grand playhouse at the top of the street, to any number of smaller, shabbier-looking buildings located along its length. Each building had a crier in front of its ticket window who shouted the name of the play that night, for the benefit of those who could not read the sign above the entrance. These criers each tried to outdo their neighbors, so that their piercing voices were raised to a screaming pitch. But even this racket merged into the pervasive rumble of several hundred people enjoying a night out, warmed by the evening's entertainment and a healthy dose of alcohol.

Beruse stopped at the corner opposite the World Theatre, knocked a clumsy pickpocket who had emerged from a shadowy door into the gutter, and looked about keenly. Lucena, standing behind her, looked too. What she saw was a crowd of people all dressed in their Saturday best (that was to say, the clothes that were perhaps too bright and flashy to be considered Sunday best), hurrying about and fogging the night air with their steamy breath. Beruse, big and warm, breathed out thick clouds around her, as though she were smoking a pipe.

It reminded Lucena of cold winter mornings when she was a girl, when she would breathe out heavily just to see it rise as steam before her face. When she tried the same now, however, there was nothing; her breath was cold. After a few disappointing sighs, she stopped bothering to breathe at all.

"Do you see Keelback?" Beruse asked, disrupting her melancholy thoughts.

Lucena looked. Keelback had been keeping pace with them by gliding along the rooftops, out of reach from the lanterns and the hurrying crowds in the street. Now he was curled around one of the parapets of the World Theatre, looking down at the crowd with great interest.

She pointed, reluctantly drawing in a breath of cold air. "There," she said.

Beruse squinted up at the dark roof and frowned. "You're certain he won't make mischief with the crowd?"

"No," Lucena admitted. "But he did *promise* not to. That must count for something."

Beruse turned to her and raised an eyebrow. She let out a short laugh that sounded like a bark. "Well, it'll be a lesson for him either way," she said, and strode off down the street. Lucena hurried at her heels.

The crowd closed in around them and Lucena lost sight of Keelback in the bustle of ragged silk and gaudy lace. She felt horribly out of place, since both she and Beruse were wearing practical battle attire—Beruse was even wearing trousers!—but if the theatre patrons noticed they must have thought them stray actors from some play.

Beruse stopped again, raising an arm to catch Lucena in the chest. The arm nearly knocked Lucena off her feet, but she grabbed it at the last second and hauled herself upright.

"Do you smell that?" Beruse ask in a tense, low voice, her bushy hair rising into a prodigious mane.

Lucena, who had been pointedly not breathing and thus not smelling either, experimentally sniffed the air. She smelled the near-overpowering odor of many hot humans crushed together, along with a heady tang of alcohol and the pervasive stink of sweat and ammonia. But being a vampire, her nose was particularly inclined to pick out one scent above all others, and this she smelled now, faint but piercingly clear, like a bell in a winter night: blood.

"Did someone have an accident?" she asked.

"Yes," Beruse said grimly. "We did. We're late."

She grabbed Lucena by the arm and dragged her down the road. She went so fast the crowd had no time to part before them, and those unfortunate enough to be in their way were knocked flying as they came through. Lucena's feet lifted clean off the ground as Beruse put on speed, and they tore down the street.

They left the merriment and bright torches behind, finally arriving at a derelict playhouse that was half holes, and the other half patches. One weary lamp illuminated the peeling board above the door, which proclaimed the place to be the Red Theatre. Indeed, what was left of the paint on the door did appear to be red, but what with rot and tar and the pervasive gloom the place was definitely more black.

CHAPTER 12: *Mirror, Candle and Book*

Staring up at the front of the building, Beruse touched the hilt of her stone knife. Instinctively Lucena did the same. It was the same knife Madgrin had given her in Elgany, the same knife she had used to fight in the pit of the Parliament of Vampires, and she found its touch reassuring.

The smell of blood was stronger here.

Beruse drew her knife and kicked the door open. She went inside with a straight back, and Lucena followed on her heels.

Again the smell of fresh blood, now joined by the scent of old, dry blood and the bitter tinge of death. The interior was dark and crumbling, but Lucena had no trouble discerning their target: through the doorway on the right, down wooden stairs and then stony ones, until they emerged into a long underground gallery lit with sickly torches.

It was crawling with vampires. Lucena was aware of their smell, their stink, and their tangible reek of grave dirt, even though she could not see them. What she did see clearly were the three children chained to a stake in the center of the room. They were pale and frightened and one had a nasty graze on her forehead.

Next to her Beruse swore in a foreign language, and she remembered what Madgrin had said that night in Elgany.

This was part of their story. Beruse worked in the same shadowy area as Madgrin; she had to wait.

"Oh no," Lucena groaned.

Beruse looked at her sharply. "Don't get a weak spine now," she growled. "There's only *twice* as many as I thought there would be."

"Oh, but the children," Lucena gestured helplessly, ignoring the general quietness that spread through the crowd of vampires as they became aware of the intruders.

"What about them? They're not dead yet!"

"Maker told me . . . before . . . he said he had to wait. Wait until . . . " but a hard stone in her throat stopped her saying more.

Beruse snorted.

"Not waiting is cheating," she said. "Madgrin can't afford to cheat. But I can. I *do*." And she leapt down the last four steps and plunged into the crowd, her knife glinting in the torchlight.

The room erupted into screams, blood, and violent motion. Lucena exhaled all the extra air in her lungs and followed Beruse into the fray, punching and kicking and slashing randomly. Later, when they compared notes, she and Beruse would deduce that she had done little in the way of killing, but a lot in the way of spreading chaos and confusion, which was a great help on its own.

They got even more help when Keelback appeared in their midst. He brought with him splinters and bits of broken masonry, suggesting the damage he had done to the building above them. He surveyed the scene with innocent befuddlement on his beaky face.

"The children!" Lucena screamed. "Get them out!"

Happy to have something to do, Keelback drifted easily over the fighting, screaming mass, and uprooted the stake to which the children were chained. He helped the children untangle themselves from their bonds and waited patiently while they scrambled onto his back, before carrying them away upstairs, his body undulating smoothly through the scream-filled air.

Lucena caught one last glimpse of the children, looking surprised and pleased to be rescued by such an interesting monster, before something knocked her feet out from under her, and she had to fight her way up through a pile of angry, frightened vampires.

"A splendid performance! Perfectly ferocious, and good thinking getting the children out of the way—I should never have made difficulties with bringing Keelback had I known he would be so helpful—and did you know she practically dug her way out from under a mountain of vampires? I thought for certain she would be buried, but no! Up she came like a volcano, if volcanos ever spit up angry young girls, that is. Whoom!" Beruse threw up her arms to illustrate.

Beruse, Lucena and Keelback were gathered in the kitchen along with half the staff. They were seated around the table in varying degrees of wakefulness and dress; Beruse was still in her armor, in high spirits from the successful hunt. Gydda had been dragged out of her bed early because Lucena had come home in a fearful hunger, and was still in her nightgown and looking half asleep. Cobbin and Willic were wide-eyed attention and admiration, however, and even Harga had come to lean against the doorframe and listen appreciatively.

Lucena sat in a corner on Keelback, who had curled himself into a sort of chair, with his beak resting on her knee. She leaned back and sipped at the pint of boar's blood Gydda had given her, and let Beruse talk. It did no good trying to explain that she had been terrified, that she simply hadn't stopped to think properly and merely did as her survival instincts dictated. Beruse was full of praise for her new partner, and explained at length how Lucena had killed this vampire so cleverly and that vampire so efficiently, even though it was a short list: of the seventy-eight vampires in that room none had survived, but Lucena had killed only three—all the rest was Beruse.

"What did you do with the children?" she asked Keelback in a low voice. In the aftermath she only remembered him reappearing in time to carry her back to where they were to meet Madgrin.

"The what? Oh, the little people," Keelback frilled his crest smugly. "I took them to the river. There were some people with boats there who were going to the ocean, and the little people wanted to go with them instead of going home. They said they wanted to have a proper adventure now."

"Oh." Lucena pondered this and wondered how someone could want more of an adventure after an experience like that. But, she supposed, it was a better outcome than what could have happened.

Despite her initial misgivings, over the course of the next two months Lucena would gradually live up to Beruse's initial glowing report. The all-encompassing terror that before had clouded her brain shrank and faded until it was only a hard knot of nerves which she stubbornly trod under, and she could go into battle with a clear head. This, combined with the sharp learning curve that comes with

CHAPTER 12: *Mirror, Candle and Book*

doing, meant that by their fourth or fifth hunt Lucena could dispatch vampires in the twos and threes.

What she could not get used to, no matter how many hunts she went on, was the animalistic feeling that welled up in her belly whenever a fight was joined. At first she put it down to high spirits and adrenaline, but as time wore on the feeling became more distinct. It felt as though there was a monster in her gut, and it reached out with arms made of liquid fire to guide her movements. It reminded her of the strange impulse she had felt when faced with the bleeding youth in Müldif, and the descriptions in the Book of Amstrass of the Beast.

It proved invaluable at times, however, and saved her existence more than once. One of these near misses happened by accident: Lucena and Beruse had cornered a particularly tenacious vampire in an old mill, and in chasing him all over the crumbling building until someone knocked into the decaying supports for the wheel, which fell into the decaying stonework, which first gave, and then collapsed into rubble and broken splinters of wood. Lucena, who had caught the vampire by his coat, looked up to find shards of wood and stone falling all around her and could do nothing. She was buried along with the other vampire, and for five dreadful minutes was certain she would never get out again. There was something wrong with her left leg; it felt numb and detached from the rest of her. But the fire in her belly kept her hands clawing at the rock around her, pushing it over and down, until she heaved aside a slab of plaster and emerged into the dusty ruin. Beruse dragged her free and found out what was wrong with her leg: a two-foot-long splinter of wood had run clean through her thigh. She pulled it out and asked Lucena if she had any other bits of wood where they shouldn't be.

Then Lucena tried to breathe. She had not been breathing when she had been buried because there was no air, and then once she had gotten out, what air there was was filled with rock dust. But she needed air in her lungs to speak, so she opened her mouth to inhale.

She couldn't. She tried again, and this time some air got in, but that only served to send her into a fit of coughing. Something came up her windpipe and shot out her mouth. It was dark and wet and looked like blood, but it smelled vile.

For hours she could not breathe properly, and after that she could only speak in a whistling whisper. Beruse ended up carrying her home in her arms, and all the way every bump sent jolts of sharp pain through her whole body.

Madgrin was waiting for them when they rose out of the carpet and into his study. He didn't wait for an explanation, but grasped Lucena firmly by the shoulders and did something to make her lungs work again. At the same time she felt something in her lower chest pop back into place.

"Dear, dear," Madgrin said. "Did you get in the way of a falling mountain?"

"Mill wheel," Lucena said in a small voice.

"And a wall of old bricks," Beruse added.

"Goodness." He twinkled a dark smile at her. "How long did it take for you to dig your way out?"

"Ages," Lucena sighed.

"Just short of five minutes," Beruse said proudly. "Didn't even need my help."

"Oh, excellent." Madgrin sat Lucena up on the floor and began picking flakes of rock and wood out of her torn clothing. "Not bad at all. Still, you had eight broken ribs and a punctured lung, not to mention the nerve damage in that leg. I've set them in order, but it will be best to let them heal completely on their own. I'm afraid you must spend the next few weeks in bed resting. I hope you don't mind."

Lucena leaned back into his gentle hands, and thought she did not mind at all. But it is one thing not to mind continuous bed rest when you are tired, and quite another when you are fully rested and on the way to recovery. Lucena awoke the next evening feeling much better (her breathing was practically back to normal) and lunged sideways for her morning drink as she always did—

—and came up short with a strangled cry. Any action that used the muscles of her torso gave her a tooth-rattling pain that ran all across her ribs and up her spine. She lay very still then, her arm tantalizingly close to the bottle on the table, and firmly stopped herself breathing. That helped a little, but a warning tingle remained, and she dared not move. Yet her thirst was nearly unbearable.

Help! She thought.

Eight broken ribs, Madgrin reminded her. *Better to not move at all. Ask Urgolant to help you.*

"Urgolant?" Lucena whispered.

"Yes?" The sombulus crept out of the shadows in the upper corner of the room, her eight eyes a-twinkle in the candlelight.

"Could you . . . ?" Lucena trailed off, gesturing helplessly at the bottle. "I cannot reach."

"Internal damage," Urgolant said knowingly, climbing down the wall and pattering over to the table. "It is a good thing you have an endoskeleton *to* damage. I would have been squished flat." She raised herself up on her back four legs and used the front ones to pour out a healthy glass of blood. This she grasped with her mouthparts and carried to the bed.

Lucena looked at the glass despairingly. How was she to drink it lying down?

"Don't hold it there, you'll spill it on the sheets!" Keelback squawked. He had been curled around and under the bed the whole time, apparently asleep. Now he raised his head above the counterpane, and then ducked down and wriggled under Lucena's shoulders, raising her to a sitting position.

"Oh!" she gasped as another tooth-rattling sting of pain shot through her. But it was not so bad as the first time, and between Keelback propping her upright and Urgolant delicately tipping the glass to her mouth, she was able to drink her breakfast with only a few weak coughs.

Word had spread of her accident. Willic poked his head in on his way to bed and expressed surprise at the fact that Lucena was not covered head to toe in bandages.

"I thought about wrapping her up in silk," Urgolant admitted. "But her maker said that wouldn't help."

"It might have been a good idea when I woke up," Lucena said ruefully.

CHAPTER 12: *Mirror, Candle and Book*

When Rhyse appeared she took the opposite side. The scrawny hoblin stood, arms folded, looking over Lucena's prone form with a critical eye, then declared the only thing that looked amiss was that she was rather pale.

"And that's hardly something worth mentioning to a vampire," she said on her way out.

Gydda was more sympathetic; she turned up around midnight with a bowl of hot blood broth which she spoon-fed to Lucena with motherly care. Lucena was touched by this, and swore to herself she would devote all her energies to helping Gydda in the kitchen as soon as she was able.

That would not be for several weeks, however, as her ribs were slow to heal, and even after she could sit up and turn about with ease, her left leg still gave her problems. Though the wound had been bandaged carefully and healed with surprising alacrity, the leg itself went through periods of numbness, during which time Lucena had to drag it behind her like a stiff log. It was most inconvenient and prevented her from returning to hunt with Beruse for many weeks.

Even when she did feel well enough to go help Gydda her leg was in a sad state: not quite numb but not quite there, full of pins and needles and uncomfortable tingling. The bones itched. All this combined to put her out of temper, and Gydda noticed. Not wanting the serenity of her kitchen upset, even for the sake of clean dishes, she sent Lucena off with Harga the moment he put his head through the door with instructions to "Give it some exercise, there's a good girl."

The night was cold and clear, and above them the stars shone in the sky with that particular brilliance they reserve for winter nights. Together they walked beneath the stars, following the meandering path across the lawns. Harga walked slowly, conscious of Lucena's stumbling gait, and said nothing. Lucena suspected he knew that her temper would only be aggravated by polite conversation, and was grateful for his silence.

At length they crested a rise and stood looking down over the Labyrinth. Its neatly trimmed hedges glinted in the starlight, and the dark paths they formed were perfectly black and empty. Gazing at its intricately twisting paths, Lucena fancied she could discern a picture in them—a beautiful, complicated picture. But whenever it seemed about to slide into focus, something would appear that did not fit and threw her off. Because of this, or perhaps because of the magical starlight, Lucena got the uncomfortable feeling that the paths between the hedges were shifting before her eyes.

"Would you like to go in?" Harga asked quietly.

Lucena eyed the dark passages between the hedges warily. "Is it safe?" she asked.

"Well, no." Harga took his hat off and scratched behind one floppy ear. "Nothing around here is exactly *safe*. But if we don't go very far it shouldn't be too dangerous. Nothing I can't—"

He stopped speaking. It was just as well, for Lucena had stopped listening.

Someone had come out of the Labyrinth.

He had emerged from a break in the outermost hedge and now stood, almost like an extension of the shadowy paths, looking up at them. At length he detached himself from the shadows and moved up the hill with long, rolling strides. He was a tall man, broad-shouldered and thin, and he walked with his head slightly to one side, as if all the world were a picture, and he was perusing it. As he drew closer Lucena saw his skin was the darkest midnight blue, his eyes like glimmering gems set in hollows under his bushy eyebrows. His long, curling black hair was drawn back from his brow and tied at the neck, but loosely; some wisps had broken free and were trailing mischievously around his jaw.

His clothes were black and melted into the darkness like a patch of night.

It was the clothes that drove home to Lucena what this person was. She did not need to hear Harga's sharp intake of breath or feel his elbow in her side. He was kin to Madgrin; another dream lord.

When he crested the hill on which they stood, Harga bowed low, and Lucena tried to curtsey. But she had forgotten her injured leg, and it gave out at a crucial point, and she fell over. Both the new arrival and Harga looked at her in some perplexity. She managed a pathetic half-nod, and lay still (her leg had become completely useless).

Harga gave a little shrug and turned to their guest.

"Welcome, m'lord, how may I serve you?"

"I have business with your lord, Watchdog," the man said. His voice was a hoarse, rich growl, tinged with a northern accent.

"As you wish," Harga said, bowing again. "You may enter through the front door, I will see to it that you are expected." He turned to go, nearly tripped on Lucena, and paused, obviously wondering what was the least embarrassing solution. Then, with another little shrug, he picked her up and slung her over his shoulder. She wanted to cry in protest, but decided that would only be a further indignity. Harga strode confidently up towards the house until, glancing back, he saw they were out of sight of the imposing dream lord. Then he took off at a run.

"*Fearbright* is here!" he shouted when they were halfway through the kitchen door.

Cobbin, who had been lounging in a corner eating an apple, jumped up spluttering, bits of half-chewed fruit spewing everywhere. Gydda looked up from polishing silver, her mouth slightly open. Harga dumped Lucena unceremoniously on the table and rounded on Cobbin.

"Don't just sit there! Tell Grimmach! Warn Willic and Rhyse, too, go on!"

Cobbin hastily wiped apple off his face and dashed into the House, nearly colliding with Keelback and Urgolant as they tried to enter.

This was another extraordinary occurrence: Keelback usually avoided Urgolant, but here he was herding the giant spider through the door and squawking, "Cena, Cena, Urgy's got something *important* to tell you!"

"Yes, yes, I can tell her myself." Urgolant was clicking in annoyance. "Lucena, someone very dangerous has just arrived."

"That's a bit of an understatement," Harga said grimly. "It's *Fearbright*. He just came out of the Labyrinth."

"Who—" Lucena nearly had to shout over Keelback's squawking. "*Who* is Fearbright?"

CHAPTER 12: *Mirror, Candle and Book*

Gydda and Harga looked at her blankly, as though they hadn't the faintest idea how to answer her question. But since Keelback and Urgolant were also looking at them expectantly (and this made a total of *twelve* eyes), Gydda cleared her throat and said thoughtfully:

"Do you ever have that feeling, just as you're waking up, of remembering a dream perfectly, but then when you are fully awake you haven't the foggiest notion what it was?"

Lucena had indeed experienced this as a living girl, so she nodded. Keelback just looked puzzled, however, and Urgolant said, "I always remember my dreams. But what does a feeling have to do with a person?"

"That feeling," said Harga. "That feeling of remembering something, but no longer being able to remember what it was, is a good part of who Fearbright is."

"I don't under*stand*," Keelback said plaintively.

Harga and Gydda exchanged helpless looks. Finally Gydda said, "Think of it this way: Fearbright is a lot like our Madgrin. How would you describe who your maker is?"

Lucena considered this. Lots of ways to describe Madgrin ran through her head: tall, pale, ghostly, gentle, vaguely frightening . . . but none of them described who he was. Then she thought she had it.

"He's like . . . sleeping," she said slowly. "Or not sleeping. It's that heavy feeling you get when you are all relaxed and falling asleep, but still awake enough to *know* you're falling asleep. I think . . . is that what you mean?"

Gydda beamed at her.

"I still don't understand," Keelback said.

"You said he was dangerous," Lucena said, turning to Urgolant.

The sombulus drew all her legs up around her head and clicked her mouthparts nervously. "He's very strong," she said. "And he doesn't like vampires."

"Oh, of course he doesn't like *vampires*," Gydda said. "None of the dream lords do, but that doesn't mean he'll want to hurt Lucena . . . does it?" she turned to Harga for reassurance, but Harga was staring past Keelback and looking grim.

"If Himself doesn't get back soon," he said gravely, "we'll have to get Orrus to talk to him. He has the power to make things very difficult for us . . . not just Lucena."

There followed a tense silence, during which Keelback, though he could not comprehend the idea of people who were experiences, did understand that there was something threatening his mistress, and wound himself protectively around the table on which she sat. Urgolant also unfolded herself and climbed up next to Lucena, one foot resting in her lap.

They were still in these guardian attitudes when Cobbin reappeared, with Willic on his heel. They were both out of breath, and the hoblin was very pale.

"Bad, very bad!" he gasped. "Fearbright wants to speak to Himself now . . . says his business won't wait. We've put out a call, but in the meantime he wants to see *Lucena!*"

There followed in the kitchen such an eruption of voices that Lucena could not keep track of them all. But she heard Harga's deep growl as he said, "He'll not get his claws into *her!*" To which Cobbin snapped, "Why don't *you* tell him that?"

"I don't think he would harm Lucena *in the House of Madgrin,*" Willic said reasonably, but he was drowned out.

"Can't *anyone* find Madgrin?" Gydda demanded.

"Halfain's our only hope for that," Cobbin moaned, "and Soloma says *she* won't be back until dawn—as *usual.*"

"He's usually back by dawn anyway," Gydda said.

"*Beruse* might be back," Cobbin said uneasily. "But who knows how long he'll be gone. Remember 1017? 'I'll be gone a while,' he says, and disappears for a *year and a day!*"

"Oh come, it's *rare* that he lets himself be caught like that," Gydda reasoned. "And he did manage to send word after the first month."

"This doesn't help us," Willic mewed piercingly, "with what we should do about *Lucena.*"

That sobered the gathering. They looked uncomfortably at one another, except for Harga, who glared.

Silence. Keelback twitched his tail.

"If Fearbright wants to see me, I suppose I had better go," Lucena said, and was quite proud to hear how she managed to keep the shake out of her voice.

The room erupted again, this time with protests. Except Willic, who looked at her thoughtfully. Then, when the voices had quieted down, he said: "I think that may be the best course. But I'll also wake Orrus, in case of emergency."

Harga growled. "Not much good Orrus could do against a—"

"He would stand a better chance than any of us." Willic cut him off, bristling a little. Lucena was reminded vividly of a cat puffing itself up to intimidate a dog. "And as long as she has Keelback and Urgolant, why, it might make things even. Certainly the presence of a *shade eater* should give him pause."

And so, with a knot in her throat, Lucena followed Willic up the stairs and through the shifty corridors to the room where Fearbright waited. This turned out to be the east antechamber, and Fearbright was standing next to the piano, regarding it as one might regard an opponent in a contest of wits. As they filed into the room, Keelback and Urgolant trailing in behind Lucena, their mutual dislike temporarily forgotten, he raised his head and leveled his dark stare at them.

"So," he said in a sharp, abrasive tone. "You are Madgrin's fledgeling? I did not catch your name when we met . . . before."

"Lucena," Lucena said promptly. But hearing this only made Fearbright's frown deepen, his eyebrows drawing together like a falcon mantling its wings over a kill.

"Er . . . Clarian Ashmoor," she added.

Fearbright just stared at her. Then he gave a little shrug and glanced, with some interest, at her companions. "I see you have already begun to collect familiars." It was impossible to tell whether he approved or disapproved of this.

"Er, rather, they collected me," Lucena said. "This is Keelback, who is himself, and Urgolant, a shade eater."

CHAPTER 12: *Mirror, Candle and Book*

If Fearbright was impressed by this, as Willic had hoped, he did not show it. In fact, now that Lucena had the chance to get a good look at him, she thought that Fearbright was rather like a frozen pond: all stiff, frigid surface, but somewhere, deep beneath the ice, dark waters flowed. This only served to further the feeling she had of walking on a slippery surface, and she vowed to speak and act with extreme care.

"Well, I suppose you'll have to do," said Fearbright darkly. "I must speak to your maker. As he is not here at present, you are the next best thing."

"Oh, oh, but I am sure *Orrus* would be much better able to help you," Lucena demurred, a little desperately, but Fearbright was already shaking his head.

"You can speak to Madgrin on a level which even *I* am unable to reach," he said, a sneer creeping up one side of his face. "Speak to him now. Tell him Fearbright is in his House, and wishes to discuss an event of dire importance with him. Tell him that. Now."

"Oh, but—" Lucena stammered, unable to explain, in the face of Fearbright's penetrating gaze, how difficult it was to reach Madgrin when she was under such pressure.

"Now." Fearbright's voice was like the snap of a whip in a cold, dark night.

Standing very straight, her hands behind her back and her face screwed tight in concentration, Lucena called out in her mind, with desperation, for her maker. But all she got in return was a faint echo of her own call. It was most confusing, and not helpful in the least. She was forced to open her eyes and tell Fearbright it was no good.

"It may be best to wait, I'm sure he will be available soon," she said.

But Fearbright was not content to wait. He looked as though, if he could, he would have reached into Lucena's mind and pulled Madgrin out through her nostrils.

Then Urgolant spoke.

"Does your maker have any books?"

It was Lucena she asked, but Fearbright who answered:

"He has a library full of them, sombulus," he said, raising an eyebrow.

"I mean," Urgolant clicked, "does he have any that are *his?*"

Lucena frowned. Now that she thought about it, she had never actually seen Madgrin reading a book.

"I expect I could find that out for you," Fearbright said, and he smiled, very slightly. "Tell me what are you scheming, sombulus."

"My name is *Urgolant*," Urgolant said, with more force than Lucena had ever heard from her before. She seemed not in the least intimidated by Fearbright, and as they had been speaking the darkness that clung to the hem of his robes had begun to fade, making him look more solid, less like a talking shadow. All eight of Urgolant's eyes glittered as she said: "We are going to find my mistress's maker with a *spell*. Willic, we'll need a candle ... and is there a mirror in this house large enough to walk through?"

Willic, who had been standing by the door, trying not to be noticed, started in surprise. "Er, yes. At least, I think I can find one."

Fearbright laughed. It was not an unpleasant laugh, being rich and deep, but it had the uncomfortable effect of raising Lucena's hackles, and something in her stomach wriggled up and grabbed hold of her throat and told her to run, run, run away from this *thing*. It was ancient and deadly and had destroyed more of her kind than Madgrin and Beruse put together.

With a huge effort she forced it back down and turned to Urgolant.

"What sort of spell are you planning?" she asked.

"Mirror, Candle and Book," Fearbright said, still smiling. "That is a guaranteed way to find him. But how did you learn it?" This was addressed to Urgolant, with a warm smile, and amusement dancing in his eyes. Lucena felt another pang, this time wishing that she could do something to make Fearbright look at *her* that way. Then reason kicked in and reminded her that she would be quite happy if Fearbright never looked at her in any way ever again.

"*The Fable Book of Magic, Volume II*," Urgolant said. "It's on the third shelf from the top of the seventh row bookcase on the left in the library. I read it last week."

"Studious one, aren't you?" Fearbright remarked. "Very well. Willic, fetch candles and the mirror. *We* will find a book of Madgrin."

So saying he took them straight to the library.

It was not unlike the way Madgrin traveled within the house, but it *hurt*, like being dragged over rough ground. Lucena arrived in the library wincing, rubbing at her arms to dispel the pain. Keelback was similarly annoyed, and Urgolant clicked her mouthparts in irritation.

"You'd no call to do that," she said, reaching out her long hairy legs and raising her abdomen menacingly.

Fearbright ignored her. He moved forward into the circle of sofas and chairs which formed the center of the labyrinth of bookshelves, and held out his hand.

"Come," he said, as if to someone hidden in the shelves. "I know it must be *one* of you."

Slowly, reluctantly, like a weary bird, a book came fluttering through the air from the dark recesses of the room. It alighted on Fearbright's blue, outstretched hand, ruffling its pages nervously.

Fearbright gave a small snort and passed it to Lucena, who caught it clumsily. It was a little book bound in blue leather; the title had been stamped in gold leaf but so long ago that it had mostly peeled away. She could not resist peeking inside to see what it was about but was disappointed to discover that it was in a language and alphabet foreign to her.

There was a scuffling sound beyond the door and Cobbin appeared, panting and pale except for his cheeks which were flushed red from exertion. He snapped to attention on front of Fearbright, and presented him with a candle in a simple brass candle holder. Fearbright looked at it blackly, so Cobbin offered it to Lucena.

With the candle in one hand and a book in the other, Lucena gave a nervous laugh and asked, "Where do I find the mirror?"

"In the cellar, Miss Lucena," Cobbin said, stiffly. "Gydda found one big enough to fit you, but it's also too big to move."

CHAPTER 12: *Mirror, Candle and Book*

"I see," said Fearbright, and Lucena had just enough time to brace herself before there was another wrenching *whoosh*, and they appeared in the cellar.

"I don't like doing that," Keelback proclaimed, and slithered off into a corner between some crates, where he watched the proceedings out of narrow, disapproving eyes.

The mirror was a giant, seven-foot-tall thing set in a heavy wood frame, leaning against a pile of dusty bricks. Harga stood beside it, hanging a storm lantern from one of the rafters.

It was an eerie sight: Lucena stood in the center of the group holding the candle in one hand and the book in the other, but in the reflection there was only a vague, out-of-focus smudge where she should have been, and Fearbright and Urgolant appeared to be standing awkwardly on either side of nothing.

Fearbright's reflection was also a curious thing, for it represented him with a different expression than the one he wore in the flesh. In the mirror he peered down at Lucena, looking tired and faintly amused, but when she glanced up at him directly, all she saw was the same cold, blue-black face as before.

Deep water under a frozen surface, she reminded herself. Her hand trembled a little as she raised the candle so that Harga could strike a spark to its wick, and it sputtered into life. In the mirror a flame blossomed in thin air, its light spilling back out into the room with a soft radiance.

To Lucena it was even more amazing, for as the candle's flame grew and strengthened it cast a spear of light across the glass from top to bottom. This stripe of light was a mere thread at the top, but widened near the bottom until it stretched to either side of the frame, making it look almost like a path.

"A mirror to show you the path," Lucena whispered, remembering a nursery rhyme she had heard as a little child. "A candle to light the way..."

As if in response to her words the light in the mirror sharpened, becoming less a random effect of light on glass, and more of a solid pathway. Beside her there was a mantling of legs, and she felt the weight of Urgolant's many-eyed stare.

"You know it too?" the shade eater asked.

"It is old magic," remarked Fearbright. "The words have traveled far. But do you know the rest?" he asked Lucena, sharply.

Put on the spot, the poor vampire found she could not call up the next line of the verse, and it was Urgolant who came forward and finished the spell, saying: "A book to take you there and back again."

The book fell open in Lucena's hand and all its pages flew out like a flock of startled birds. They flew straight into the mirror, becoming trees lining the path of light, their bare branches intertwining overhead to make a sort of tunnel.

Then at last the mirror appeared to be not a mirror at all, but a doorway, and Lucena mounted the bottom of the frame with as much composure as if she were climbing a stair. She heard a gasp from Harga and Keelback, a soft swish of cloth of Fearbright on her heel, and a hasty scrabbling as Urgolant moved to follow them. Then she was through the mirror completely, and all the sounds and smells of the cellar were cut off.

Inside the mirror—that was to say, on the path, for Lucena doubted they were any more in the mirror than they were still in the cellar—the air was quiet and still and smelled of old paper and ink. Occasionally there were gaps between the trees and she caught glimpses of a velvety blue night sky, and then a soft wind smelling of wet grass and secrets wafted in.

Not so unlike Madgrin, Lucena reminded herself, and walked on. At first she had an urge to turn around and look back, to see if she might wave to her friends in the cellar and see how close Fearbright and Urgolant were behind her, but then she heard the dream lord's sharp voice in her ear:

"Do not look back, or you will never reach your destination."

So she walked on, looking straight ahead, her back a rigid line pricked with pins and needles.

There was nothing much more to see. The trees lining the path of light stretched on and on for what looked like forever, and the path never turned or wavered. The trees themselves were the color of old parchment, and now that she was right next to them, Lucena saw that the dark squiggles she had originally taken to be cracks in their bark were actually lines of writing. The same writing, she assumed, that had been on the pages of the book.

She walked on, her feet making no sound on the soft path of candlelight, though they sank in slightly with every step. She could hear Urgolant clicking her mouthparts, but otherwise all was silent.

Fearbright padded behind her, and she was only aware of him as a deep blue shadow cast from the candle in her hand.

Then, without any particular change in the trees or the light, the path began to go downhill. At least, it felt like going downhill: Lucena found her bad leg did not hinder her so much, and her steps went faster and faster. At last a dark blot appeared at the very end of the light, and this grew larger and larger until it swelled up before them, devouring the trees and the path. Lucena took a deep breath of musty, bookish air, and stepped into it.

There was a sensation of falling, and then her feet hit solid ground, her bad leg twinged painfully, and she collapsed. She would have fallen to the ground—and quite likely lost the book and candle—but strong, cold hands caught her under the arms, and Fearbright lifted her to her feet again.

Shaken more by Fearbright's intervention than by her fall, Lucena looked gingerly around. They were in a wide cobblestone street lined with shops. These shops all had display windows, and it was out of one of these that the pathway ended. Urgolant came skittering out of the window behind her, and daring to look back Lucena could still see the flicker of the candlelight path in that window, and the vague outline of trees. Still holding the candle and book (now no more than two covers and the binding), she looked up and down the street.

"According to the magic, your maker should be nearby," Urgolant said demurely, mostly for Fearbright's sake, who was pacing up and down in front of the shop, sniffing the air like a hound on a scent. At her words he stopped and turned around, but not to look at them; he looked down the dark and stony street, where it disappeared into the shadows.

CHAPTER 12: *Mirror, Candle and Book*

Madgrin was walking up it out of the night. His gait was so smooth it looked like he was floating, and in that silent, darkened street with his pale face he looked like an aspect of Death come to move among the living.

Fearbright went to him, his stride swift and sharp. If Madgrin was surprised to see the other dream lord he did not show it, but he spared a glance for Lucena, and when his head turned to her she saw a light kindle in his eyes that might have been happiness, or might have been astonishment, or might have been the reflection of her candle. But then he blinked and turned away.

"Fearbright," he said warmly. "This is a pleasant surprise. But what has caused you to trouble my fledgeling so that she has seen fit to work such extraordinary magic to bring you to me?"

Fearbright glanced back at Lucena, and the look on his face was perhaps not as cold as it had been. But it was only for a moment, and then he turned to Madgrin and began to speak in hushed, earnest tones.

Madgrin's face fell. He looked so sad that all Lucena wanted to do was run forward and embrace him. But Fearbright stood between them, and so she did nothing.

"I see," Madgrin said, heavily. "Then we must go and do what we can."

The two dream lords bent their heads together, one smooth and pale, the other dark and craggy. Then they were gone, with a soft sigh of air that smelled of old, unopened books, wet grass and secrets.

Lucena was alone in the street, an empty book in one hand and a flickering candle in the other. She took a steadying breath and limped back to where Urgolant was waiting. Gloomily she regarded the window: it was much too high merely to step into, and with her hands full she could not climb.

"I had better give you a boost," Urgolant said.

When they were again on the path of candlelight beneath the trees Urgolant remarked, "Interesting. Your maker did not seem concerned with how you would get home."

"What?" Lucena, who had been occupied in trying to tell if the writing on the trees had gotten bigger, was not fully attending.

"He did not offer to take you home," Urgolant elaborated. "Either he was confident in your abilities to find your own way . . . or the news this Fearbright brought is so important it put everything else out of his head."

Lucena chewed her lip and did not answer. She liked to think it was the first option, but when she thought of Fearbright she got the uncomfortable feeling—like not being able to remember a vivid dream upon waking—that there was something dreadfully important about him that she was unable to see. But it did not change the fact that she would have been stranded if not for Urgolant's magic.

"Well, I'm glad you knew about the mirror path anyway," she informed the sombulus. "It was a good idea."

"We're not home yet," Urgolant pointed out, but she sounded pleased.

Despite Urgolant's reservations the only surprising incident on their return journey came when a man walked out of the trees and stopped in the path, looking around him in bewilderment. He was a tall man with a narrow chin, a hawkish nose and long dark hair. He was wearing the robes of a wizard, but in a fashion easily two hundred years out of date, and instead of the ordinary greys and blacks, these were all shades of purple. He too carried a pageless book in one hand and a candle in the other, and as they drew closer Lucena saw there was another path of light that crossed their own, and it was on this other path that the gentleman stood. When he saw them the bewilderment left his face, and he smiled politely.

"Ah," he said in a cultured voice. "Good evening to you, lady vampira, somna ebuli. Sorry to interrupt, but paths crossed—didn't mean to. Good night." And he strode off along his path and out of sight before Lucena could say a word.

When she drew even with the other path she had the strangest sensation of being two places at once. There were two visions of an endless pathway made of light, and two tree-lined tunnels. It was most disconcerting. No wonder the gentleman had looked bewildered. But her own pathway burned brighter, and with another step she was back on it. She heard Urgolant clicking in annoyance as she passed through, but then they continued on their way as peacefully as before.

A square of light yawned before them, spilling onto the trees and sending tendrils of pale fire out along the path. Sensing the end of their journey, Lucena and Urgolant hurried forward together, half blinded by the light and by their desire to reach their destination. Lucena broke into a hobbling run, and in that last moment she thought she saw a line of writing un-stick itself from a tree, and reach out into the corridor like a malformed hand. But the next moment she slammed into the wall of light, and just had the presence of mind to put out her good foot to land on before she tumbled back into the cellar, Urgolant practically on top of her.

Lucena only had a brief glimpse of the stony cellar walls, the dusty packing crates, Keelback's glad smile and Harga's surprised face, before the air was filled with pages. Pages flew out from the still shining mirror, flocking around the book in her hand, struggling to get back inside. Handing her candle to Harga she held the book open until all the pages were once again neatly settled. Harga blew the candle out, and the light went out of the mirror. It became once again a piece of glass, and no door at all. The only door in the room was the archway at the top of the steps, and standing in it, looking sleepy and worried, was Orrus.

"What is all this?" he asked, rubbing his eyes. "First Fearbright is here, and I must protect Lucena, then he is not here, but Lucena has gone with him... now here is Lucena back, but I do not see Fearbright anywhere. Grimmach, what has been going on?"

The hoblin butler was standing very straight behind Orrus, his hands behind his back, but he could only shrug and mumble something about, "Sorry sir, misunderstanding..."

Orrus sighed, rolled his eyes, and tottered back to bed.

Lucena was far from sleepy, and it was just as well, since she was obliged to spend the wee hours of the morning telling the assembled staff all about her adventure with Urgolant and Fearbright on the mirror path. And then repeated the entire story for Beruse, who dragged herself in the kitchen door (where everyone

CHAPTER 12: *Mirror, Candle and Book*

had assembled) at four in the morning and complained loudly that she had been forced to walk home since Madgrin had disappeared. So Lucena explained.

"Oh, well that's all right, then," Beruse said once Lucena had finished. She took a deep draught from a mug of hot cider and sighed contentedly.

"Do you have any idea what it is Fearbright wanted him for?" Lucena asked.

Beruse shrugged and shook her head. "You'll have to ask Himself," she said. "But more like as not he'll just *smile* and not answer you."

Lucena went to bed that morning with the pent-up, nervous feeling that she had done, or perhaps said, something wrong. Perhaps it was this feeling—or perhaps it was the excitement of the evening—that kept her up longer than she was used to; for she lay in her bed in her windowless room, and felt the tendrils of sleep wind around her, but still she remained awake enough to hear—or thought she heard—the sound of voices in the back of her head.

One of them was Madgrin. The other was Fearbright. And, to Lucena's dim surprise, they seemed to be talking about *her*.

Then she fell asleep.

Madgrin was sitting across from her bed, in his usual darkened corner, when she awoke the next evening. But unlike the last time, he was wide awake and watching her with amusement glinting in his dark eyes.

"You made quite an impression on Fearbright last night," he said as Lucena poured out her breakfast. "He has taken a fancy to you."

"Taken a fancy?" Lucena nearly spilled her glass of blood in surprise.

"Oh yes," Madgrin's eyes were sparkling now, and a smile was tugging at the corners of his mouth. "Ever since you fell down trying to curtsey to him. 'Madgrin,' he said to me, 'I never thought you of all of us would be the one to sire a vampire with real charm, but you seem to have done it.' Charm, Lucena. He found you *charming*. And he was impressed by the magic you worked last night, with the help of a sombulus, no less."

Lucena took a long draught from her cup, hoping it would clear her head. "Impressed?" she echoed. "I thought he was thoroughly angry with me for being a vampire, and was only looking for an excuse to burn me to a cinder."

But Madgrin was shaking his head. He laughed softly. "Many vampires have good reason to fear Fearbright, but it seldom occurs to them to do so ... until it is too late. But he works in shades of twilight, and relates to vampires as individuals, rather than as a whole race. If he gave you any admonishments, *la flein*, I'm certain it was only in excess of his temper, which has been piqued by recent events."

"He did seem anxious to see you," Lucena mused. "May I ask what it was which so concerned him?"

Madgrin's face grew dark, and retreated within the curtains of his night-black hair. He seemed to dislike the question—or to dislike the thoughts it brought to his mind. When he answered it was in a low voice. A sad voice.

"One of our number has become involved—through no fault of her own—in an unfortunate situation. Fearbright hoped that I, having myself once or twice been caught in similar trouble, might be able to . . . disentangle her."

"And did you?" Lucena asked.

Madgrin was very still, sitting in the shadows, looking and his hands. Then he smiled, just a little. "We . . . helped," he said in a soft voice. "These things are best left to run their course. But it will come out our way in the end . . . it always does."

And with this cryptic statement, Madgrin faded completely into the shadows, leaving Lucena alone in the windowless room.

"Ah," he said in a cultured voice. "Good evening to you, lady vampira, somna ebuli. Sorry to interrupt, but paths crossed—didn't mean to. Good night."

CHAPTER 13:

℧ndergate

Time in the House of Madgrin passed at the same pace it did everywhere else. The seconds, minutes, hours, days, weeks and months—even years—came and went in their due course. What it lacked were the usual results of said passage: the staff did not grow older, nor were they replaced. Surrounded by such consistent company, and with her night bordered by the unconsciousness of day, Lucena's early years in the House of Madgrin appeared to pass more rapidly than the few she had spent on Earth.

Change, when it did occur, was slow and subtle. When she arrived it had been a dark, silent place, but in her presence it began to shake loose from the clutches of its somber cloak. Rooms that had not allowed anyone inside for centuries opened their doors of their own accord; mirrors and windows grew clean and bright without any help from Willic, and mean little doors and archways expanded to become wide and welcoming. To an outside observer it might have been obvious that these changes were the direct consequences of having a young vampire rampaging about the place, bringing life and excitement wherever she went. To Orrus and Willic, and others with a more intimate knowledge of the place, the actual change in the House itself did not reflect Lucena's influence on the building, so much as on the lord of it. For it was the House of Madgrin, and reflected what its maker felt. Though Madgrin did not change outwardly (indeed, he remained more changeless than anyone) the entire attitude of the House indicated his higher spirits.

All of these changes were lost on Lucena. For she was going through her own strange metamorphosis, considerably longer and more complicated than anything that came over the House or its Habitants.

Lucena was becoming a seasoned veteran of combat.

In December of 1943, on her first hunt after being nearly squashed by a mill wheel, she threw three vampires off the roof of a four-story building, then jumped down after them to finish the job. The building was a house in a long row of houses, faced by a row of equally tall houses, and Lucena leapt from one vertical face to the other on her way down. Her pale hair had come loose in the scuffle, and it blew about her head, and in the flaring lamplight, Beruse told her afterwards, she almost looked like an avenging angel descending from heaven.

Beruse was not the only one with this opinion. Apparently they missed a vampire on that hunt, and it got away and told its story, which was then exaggerated tenfold, but all in whispered rumors that never reached Lucena's ears, and if Madgrin heard the whispers he only smiled to himself and said nothing.

Two years later she walked into an opium den run by the worst sort of exploitative vampires, set the place on fire, and walked out again. Against the

CHAPTER 13: *Undergate*

leaping flames and inhuman screaming, with her expression set in the blankest, most unpleasant of masks, she appeared more like a demon walking straight out of hell.

A true warrior she became, Beruse proclaimed proudly, when in late February of 1950 she slaughtered a hundred vampires in the greatest rising northern Kyreland had seen in decades. Granted, she had Keelback's help; she rode upon the monster's back as he dipped and curved and darted about the battlefield, taking her in one instant to the thick of the fighting, then whisking her away to safety the next.

This performance generated more rumors and stories than all her previous exploits combined, which spread throughout the countryside (and beyond) in a matter of months. They were whispered in covens and crypts, told around dying fires, sometimes in frightened murmurs, sometimes in quiet satisfaction, and one enterprising scholar even went so far as to commit them to writing. And if the book they were written in went missing, and if soon after, Madgrin could be seen chuckling to himself, no one knew or noticed, least of all Lucena, who remained oblivious to her growing fame until one night in late May, several years later.

She had been in the House of Madgrin for a decade. The battle of the northern rising had left her with several broken bones and a scar around her right eye that proved reluctant to heal. Even though she could not see it, she could feel it whenever she frowned or put her hand there: the rough, delicate skin that never smoothed over like the others scars. Because she could not see it herself (her faint, blurry reflection was not clear enough) she was forced to accept Beruse's judgement of its appearance, which was that it looked very becoming. Which was to say, Urgolant later told her, it was becoming to a warrior. Which was to say, it looked hideous.

Hideous or not, she refused to feel self-conscious about it, and made no attempt to hide it. Because of this she drew many a sidelong glance whenever she went out into the world to hunt. She grew accustomed to this, and to the way people tended to avoid her. So when someone looked, and then kept on looking, and then started following her, she noticed immediately.

He was a young man—hardly more than a boy—with a fair, sandy face and a slight frame. Lucena knew him at once; for in the same way that time had passed her by, all her important memories had remained fresh and clear.

What a difference ten years and a hundred battles made, she thought as she stopped and turned to face him. When we last spoke I was terrified, but now I see he is hardly bigger than I am. Why, I could send him flying with one good shove.

"Hello, Undergate," she said with a cold smile. This smile, she knew from experimenting with Cobbin, twisted the scar around her eye something terrible, and made her look quite savage. To her satisfaction, Undergate—for it was he—stopped in his tracks as though someone had struck him.

"So it *was* you," he said, swallowing so it made his throat bob.

"Yes, it is I, old Munsmire," she replied. "But you must call me Lucena now, or Ashmoor. Those are my names."

"Yes, I know," he said, coming a cautious step closer. "I knew it to be you at once. No, I mean, it was you. The Snake Rider, from the rising three years ago."

There could only be one rising he spoke of, Lucena knew, but had it been three years? It shocked her. She stared at him.

Mistaking her shock for incomprehension Undergate continued. "There were tales of a maiden warrior who rode a giant, flying snake and killed vampires by the score. She saved a whole village single-handed. They said she was the same as the Falling Angel who hunts down wicked men and sets them on fire. There are stories about her too, how she descended from Heaven ten years ago in Kirkdale."

Lucena remembered Kirkdale also: her leg had not quite healed from the mill accident, and the jump from the building had been incredibly messy. It was a lucky thing she did not do herself another injury. But ten years? It was staggering. Until then she had been oblivious, to some extent, of just how much time had passed. She had noticed the inevitable changing of the seasons, how the nights grew longer and shorter and longer again; she had noticed how the trees outside the house shed their leaves, and the frigid beauty of the landscape when it was cloaked in snow; and she had observed in a distant manner how Keelback had matured into a truly magnificent beast. But the staff had remained unchanged, and no birthdays had been celebrated since Beruse and Willic's arbitrary party for Orrus. It had left her adrift in a sea of endless time with no point of reference.

Until now.

"Ten years?" she said in a whisper. "It has been *ten years?*"

Undergate looked flabbergasted. "Really Munsmire, I know it can be easy to lose track of time, but have you not noticed the changes?"

"Ashmoor, please," Lucena insisted. Then, catching what he had said, "What changes?"

Undergate gestured at their surroundings. They were standing in a deserted thoroughfare beside the Reid where it ran through the center of Redling. During the day and early evening this was crowded with people, but now it was getting on to the small hours of the morning, and not a soul was about save the two cold vampires. The river smacked against the pier with a resentful slushing sound, while broken reflections of the spring stars twinkled in its depths. The houses lining the other side of the thoroughfare were dark and brooding, shuttered for the night. To Lucena it was just another dim night scene, one of thousands she had seen in every city across Thamber. Each one was different and strange in its own right, and in that they were all the same. So with everything being new all the time, she could hardly notice any changes.

Undergate felt differently. He pointed down river, to where there was a mass of dark scaffolding stretching almost entirely across the water.

"That bridge," he said. "They began building it last fall. They say it's going to be the biggest yet. And that"—he pointed at a gap in the city skyline—"is where Old Basil's Tower was, until the revolutionaries blew it up two years ago. There"— he waved in the direction of a tall church spire—"was where the Tall Oak was, till it cracked in half in a storm in '49. Changes," he repeated, "everywhere."

Lucena looked dutifully around her. She had to admit, if you lived in one place and got to know it, surely you would notice the passage of time and its effect on things. Unless that place happened to be the House of Madgrin.

"Do not say you have not noticed," Undergate said sternly.

CHAPTER 13: *Undergate*

Lucena sighed. "Where I have been living . . . we do not have such changes."

Undergate stared at her. "Where, may I ask, do you live, Munsmire?"

The question was an unwelcome one. Lucena had no more desire to answer his questions now than she had ten years ago. Fortunately he had given her the perfect opportunity to change the subject.

"Ashmoor," she said. "You would please me better to call me Ashmoor."

Undergate looked unhappy. But he was also deeply curious to learn more about her. While he was trying to formulate an ingratiating reply, she turned smartly on her heel and walked away. She had promised to meet Beruse before the sign of the Red Prince Inn at three o'clock and had little time to spare. But, to her dismay, Undergate trotted after her.

"No, don't you go disappearing on me again," he said. "Not when I've been searching for you all this time!"

"You've been searching for *me?*" Lucena exclaimed. "Why go to all the bother?"

"I was worried," Undergate said. "One little vampire in this big world all alone." He put a hand on her arm.

Lucena stopped walking and looked pointedly at his hand, but he did not remove it. Indeed, he tightened his grip. Lucena was not afraid. She thought of Keelback, twisting through the sky over the river. He could be at her side in a moment, if she needed him.

"Why do you think I am alone?" she asked. She curled the hand of the arm he held into a tight fist.

Undergate looked down, saw the fist, and took his hand away. He retreated a tactful step.

"You pointed at an empty stone square and said, 'There is my maker,'" he said. "And you came unaccompanied."

"Perhaps you could not see my companions," Lucena suggested, and put out her mind to call Keelback.

"Don't be ridiculous, I have very keen eyes," Undergate said, puffing his chest out a little. "And a keener mind than you, if you are so oblivious to change. Perhaps I ought to make you promise to meet me here a year from now, just to make certain you can keep track of time." He said the last words mockingly, and the tone grated on Lucena's nerves. Then Keelback alighted behind her, and anything that Undergate was preparing to add never left his mouth. He gawked at Keelback.

Lucena swung a leg over Keelback's lithe body and took a firm hold of his feathery mane. "To Beruse," she told him. Turning back to Undergate she added; "I go where my enemy is. If you are in ill company a year from now, we may very well meet again." Keelback shrugged himself into the air, and they left Undergate in the deserted street, gazing after them in astonishment.

It was to be more than a year before she saw Undergate again. Lucena kept count, as she realized she should have been doing all along, by keeping track of Midsummer. This was easy enough, since the fairies were always unpredictable and the same thing never happened twice. To make doubly sure, Lucena began to keep a record. At the celebration following her encounter with Undergate the entry read:

"Midsummer, 1953: The Fairy King came. He seems kind; he gave everybody gold pieces, but they all turned to flowers the next day. Still, they are very pretty flowers."

And the next:

"Midsummer, 1954: One of the fae crossed the river and offended a roc. They chased him all the way to the front door, and then flew away. Bits of stone everywhere; one nearly squished Urgolant."

And the next:

"Midsummer, 1955: A fae princess tried to kidnap Willic, but he bit her. Big mess, the Queen turned the river to ice for a few minutes before Himself calmed her down."

That year proved memorable in more than one way, for in the autumn that followed, Lucena acquired another friend.

How it happened was this: on a crisp October evening Madgrin had taken Lucena to a lonely castle in the Svenian mountains, and there before the gate was a shadowy warrior mounted on an equally shadowy horse. This horse was large and broad chested, with long feathery hair about its wide hooves and an equally impressive mane and bushy forelock. It wore a heavy bridle with a long-shanked bit in its mouth, and its eyes glowed like a dying fire.

Madgrin did not wait for the warrior to offer his challenge; he merely rose up until he was as tall as the man on the horse and plucked the sword from the warrior's hand. Once he had done so the figure crumbled to dust and the horse's head shot up, as though it had been released from a spell.

Then Madgrin went inside, leaving Lucena and the horse to regard one another with equal wariness. At length, when the horse did not attempt to trample her to death, Lucena walked up to it (very slowly) and (even more slowly) took its bridle off. To her horror she saw the bit was even crueler than she had thought; with spikes that must have dug into the beast's tongue and long shanks to make them bite, it looked more like a device for torture. She threw the contraption to the ground in disgust. Then she relieved the horse of its saddle and other entrapments, and gave it a firm pat on the neck.

The horse looked around at her with its flaming eyes and twitched an ear. And then something odd happened.

The moon was near to full that night and would have shone brightly indeed but the skies were blotched with clouds. At that moment it managed to find a gap, and its light washed over the gates of the old castle, casting long shadows from the jutting spires, the tall thin trees, and Lucena herself.

In that moment the horse gave a soft snort and dissolved into smoke, which flowed into the shadows behind Lucena, and vanished. She turned this way and that, trying to find where it had gone; she examined the ground and a part of the nearby forest, but there was nothing.

Not one sign of the strange horse did she see until they had returned to the House and Lucena was in the well-lit kitchen, telling her story. Urgolant had just pattered in, when all eight of her eyes fixed on Lucena's shadow and she

CHAPTER 13: *Undergate*

nearly backed right out again in alarm. Willic peered over Lucena's shoulder, and she saw his eyes widen. Turning to look behind herself she saw her shadow stretched on the floor and wall, just as it should have been. Only her shadow no longer held any resemblance to her own human shape: instead it was the shape of a huge, hulking horse. And in the place where its head would have been, two small embers glowed like a dying fire.

The immediate reaction in the room was pandemonium. Keelback squawked loudly; Gydda took up a soup spoon and held it like a club, and Willic flashed to the upper shelves in a whirl of fur and tail.

Lucena remained calm. She looked sternly at her shadow and said, "So *that's* where you went. Now, now, come out and introduce yourself properly."

The shadow quivered. The burning eyes flashed. Then with a wheeze and a snort the horse surged out of the shadow and into the room, like a beast rising from the ground. The table went skidding across the floor, and a chair was thrown up against the wall. Keelback rose into the air in alarm and plastered himself to the ceiling; Urgolant skittered out the door and Gydda leapt to the countertop.

The horse stood in the middle of the kitchen, its neck arched and tail swishing, while its ears jerked this way and that. Even in the bright room its eyes blazed, and its fur was black as coal. It looked around in apparent bewilderment and stamped an ebony hoof.

"Who are *you*?" Lucena demanded, her hands planted firmly on her hips.

The horse said nothing. It flicked its ears forward attentively at the sound of Lucena's voice, then shook its head and snorted. It took a step forward and breathed hard into her chest. Its fur was cool, Lucena found when she reached up to stroke its nose, but its breath was warm and wet, and sent flecks of goop flying into the air, just like a real horse's.

"*What* are you?" Lucena asked, more gently.

"What is it doing in my kitchen?" Gydda growled.

The horse laid its ears back along its neck and shot her a nasty look. But before the situation could deteriorate further the garden door opened and Harga walked in. He stared at the horse, then at Lucena.

"She," he said.

"What?" said Gydda, still clutching her large spoon.

"That's not an *it*," Harga explained. "She's a *night-mare*." He beamed at Lucena. "An excellent addition to the family. Where did you find her?"

"Svenia, Castle Orlssen," Lucena told him. "Only I didn't mean to take her back. She came out of my shadow."

"Well of *course* she did," Harga said. "I expect she didn't want to get left behind. But she does look a little thin. If you don't mind I'll take her down to the wood and see she has a proper breakfast."

"Breakfast?"

"Oh yes, it's almost five in the morning."

Lucena glanced worriedly from the clock to the night-mare, but satisfied that Harga would take good care of her, she went up to bed, collecting Keelback and Urgolant on the way.

She had hoped, in a distant, unrealistic sort of way, that the night-mare would become Harga's responsibility. He seemed quite taken with the creature, and she liked him well enough. But the next evening Lucena rose from her bed to find her shadow was once again that of a huge horse, and the eyes were brighter this time.

"Ah well," Lucena sighed. "If you mean to stay, then so be it. But we must see to it you can get on with the others."

So she went out into the orchard with Harga, Keelback and Urgolant. Harga lit a good torch to give her a shadow, and she called the night-mare up out of it. Since he knew what was coming, and he was still larger than she, Keelback bore the transformation with remarkable calmness. But Urgolant, no doubt afraid of getting squished, made several attempts to escape into the trees.

Introducing Urgolant to the night-mare proved even more problematic, when it became apparent that the night-mare was just as afraid of Urgolant. Lucena managed to get Urgolant to hold still, but the night-mare refused to come within ten feet of her. She stomped her hooves and tossed her head, eyes flashing, and she danced about the orchard, trampling fallen fruit and narrowly avoiding collisions with trees.

The only good thing that came out of this was it gave Keelback a feeling of superiority. *He* was not afraid of Urgolant! And he curled himself protectively around the huge spider, to show just how not-frightened he was. Lucena didn't bother pointing out that he had, in fact, been very frightened of her in the beginning, and arguably worse behaved.

After what felt like hours, Lucena and Harga managed to coerce the night-mare into coming up to Urgolant and getting a good look. The two dark creatures stared at one another for some minutes while the night-mare puffed steamy breath in and out. Lucena wondered if it was an insurmountable difference: if Urgolant's nature of consuming darkness might prevent her forming a friendship with a creature with such an affinity for shadows. But then the night-mare worked up the nerve to touch the tip of her nose to Urgolant's front legs. She jerked her head back as though she had been burned, but when Urgolant did not rise up and attack her, she bent her head again and peered at the spider with obvious curiosity.

She took a few heavy breaths that rustled the spiny hairs on Urgolant's body, and then visibly relaxed. She dropped her head to the ground and began to graze, completely unconcerned with the huge spider squatting beside her.

Everyone breathed a sigh of relief.

From then on the night-mare was Lucena's shadow, both figuratively and literally, and for some time Lucena found herself glancing nervously over her shoulder at it. Since she had no meaningful reflection, she had relied on her shadow to reassure herself that she was still her own self, but now half the time she turned around, it was huge and horse-shaped, with glowing, fiery eyes. But since she did not have to look at her shadow all the time, she could easily ignore it. It was worse for the others, who had to put up with the incongruity of a small plump girl with the shadow of a giant warhorse. Willic remarked that it was like

CHAPTER 13: *Undergate*

her shadow had taken on a life of its own and decided to become something else. Which, Lucena allowed, was more or less the case.

If it was odd for Lucena, and a little disturbing for the Habitants, it was a source of amusement for Madgrin, who was delighted that she had acquired another familiar.

"A nightmare is a good friend to have," he told her, smiling. Lucena noticed that he said it as one word. "Nightmare." But like the word meant something different to him than it did to other people, and soon she began to think of it that way as well. Lucena found it exciting, because it meant that something she thought of as bad might be a good thing after all.

Beruse also warmed to the idea of having a monstrous horse hidden in Lucena's shadow, especially after said horse surged to life in the middle of a hunt and went about trampling vampires and snorting tongues of fire. Because of this, and because the nightmare never did give her name, Beruse took to calling her Intok, which meant "little fire" in the ancient language of the arctic bears. The name stuck, and soon even Lucena was calling her that.

It was partly because of Intok that she met Undergate for the third time. They had chased a trio of vampires to ground in a field on the outskirts of Redling, and Lucena was walking back along a country lane, Intok frolicking in a field beyond the hedge, when there came a startled snort from the nightmare, and a terrified shriek filled the night air.

Lucena was over the hedge in an instant and pelting over the grass to where Intok was dancing and snorting. There was something lying in the grass, and it was rolling around and moaning. For one mad moment Lucena thought it was an injured gnome, but then a hand flailed and Undergate sat up. His eyes were wide and bloodshot, and he was staring at Intok with abject horror. Intok was staring at him as well, obviously in the process of recognizing a vampire, and wondering whether to step on him. Before she could make a decision, however, Lucena rushed up and put a hand on her big shoulder, pushing her away.

"No, no," she said. "You needn't trample this one. Oh, do calm down," she added as Intok snorted in protest. Keelback, seeing the excitement on the ground, descended with a great *whumph*, and peered at Undergate curiously.

Poor Undergate. He was bone thin, and his eyes were sunk in deep dark hollows. He had obviously fallen on hard times, and after being rudely awakened by a great beast treading on him, when faced with Keelback's beaky countenance he gave a little cry and tried to wriggle away.

Lucena pushed at Keelback's head. "Stop that, you're frightening him," she said. To Undergate she added soothingly, "Don't worry, it's only Keelback and Intok. They won't hurt you. Not now, anyway."

Undergate looked around, eyes wide, but recognition flashed in them when he saw Lucena. "M-Munsmire," he croaked, his voice hoarse from disuse.

"Ashmoor," Lucena corrected automatically. The poor vampire looked so pitiful she could not find it in herself to be annoyed with him. Taking him by the arm she half led, half carried him to a break in the hedge, and thence through to the road. In times long past someone had laid a large slab of stone on the verge for weary travelers to rest upon, and here they sat while Lucena searched her pockets for something to drink.

Her efforts yielded a small bottle which Gydda had filled with a potent mix of ox blood and brandy. Beruse made her carry a bottle of it ever since the incident with the mill wheel, and she knew well the effect it caused. So she unscrewed the cap, tipped a healthy dose down Undergate's throat, and put the cap back on again. Almost half came right back up and out through his nose, but after gulping madly like a fish he managed to swallow most of it. Slowly, some of the color came back to his cheeks, and his eyes did not look quite so dead.

"What was in that?" he asked hoarsely.

"Brandy," Lucena said. "And ox blood. Undergate, when was the last time you ate?"

Undergate shuddered and passed a thin hand over his face. "I cannot remember . . . what is tonight? Wait, no. Do not tell me. You do not even know what *year* it is."

Lucena could have told him with reasonable confidence that it was December 18th, 1955, but she chose to remain silent.

"It is winter," he said, staring up at the cold stars. "When last I ate . . . fed . . . drank, the trees had leaves of every color. The mornings were not so cold."

"Autumn," Lucena said. "The last time you ate was autumn. No wonder you are so poorly. Well . . ." she looked up and down the road, wondering what to do. It was a long walk to anywhere from where they were now, but she knew there were butchers in Redling, and lots of rats. That gave her an idea.

"I can take you to a city," she offered. "Hide you in a cellar. I'm sure there will be many juicy rats there, and when you have got up your strength you can convince a butcher to give you something more substantial to drink."

Undergate only shuddered and hid his face in his hands. "No," he whispered. "No, no, no, no! I cannot . . . oh, I cannot go near humans! There is a burning here," he touched his belly, "and a haze here," he tapped his temple. "And when I am close to humans it becomes unbearable. I will surely—no, I already have . . ." he trailed off.

"Have what?" Lucena asked.

He looked at her with eyes wide and frightened. "I drank a human," he said in a small, hoarse voice. And, having confessed his crime, he began to weep. But there were no tears in his dry, dead body, so the sobs were empty and grated like grinding rock.

Lucena regarded him with some perplexity, and eventually (if only to make him stop the terrible noise) offered him the bottle again. He took it, downed a large gulp, and nearly choked on it. The sobs turned to coughs, and the coughs to weak, humorless laughter.

"It was an accident," he said. "Or, perhaps not? Is it not inevitable that we will be drawn to what we once were, what we desire to be again? And in pursuing that desire, we lose what little we have left of our humanity."

Lucena looked at him blankly. "Humans kill other humans all the time," she said bluntly. "Most often for foolish reasons."

CHAPTER 13: *Undergate*

"Not to *eat*," Undergate grated out. "Not to feed off of, not to live on. We are monsters."

Something that Madgrin had told her, years ago, flickered in the back of Lucena's mind. She smiled. "And what makes you think that is a bad thing?"

Undergate turned his sullen gaze upon her, and scowled. "You have never drunk human blood," he said. "You do not understand . . . it is . . . a curse. You cannot fight what you are."

Lucena sighed. Deciding that Undergate was beyond her help she got up and, beckoning to Keelback and Intok, began to walk down the road.

"Wait," Undergate called out, half rising from his seat and holding out the bottle. "When will I see you again?"

"I do not know," Lucena called back over her shoulder. "Perhaps never. Keep the bottle, but do not drink too much at a time or you may do yourself an injury." She left him upon the stone at the side of the road and did not look back.

When she returned to the House the first thing she did was find the copy of *Vampires: A History* that she had borrowed years ago and return it to the library. She decided she was sick of vampires and wanted to think on them no more.

But it was not to be. Because her main livelihood was destroying them, they found their way to the forefront of her mind no matter what she did. But she repressed thoughts of Undergate and all the uncomfortable feelings he brought with him, until they met again.

That happened in February of 1957, more than a year after the encounter in the snowy field, and at first Lucena did not recognize him. They were in Efranta at the time, a long way from Kyreland, and she was not expecting to see him. Walking down the Rue de Pavillion, which led through the most fashionable part of Serais, the capital of Efranta, she was lingering in front of shop windows to admire the goods on display when she caught the unmistakable smell of fresh blood. Hurrying on she found that down the street the shops turned into cafés and stylish restaurants, each of which produced their own fragrant aroma, but none so strongly as La Daria Rouge, which stood across the street from her. It was a perfectly respectable establishment, with a brightly lit sign and a small courtyard filled with tables and happy patrons. These all appeared to be ordinary humans, drinking ordinary alcoholic beverages and eating very elaborate (but quite conventional) sweets and pastries. Yet from this building came the smell of blood, and in stronger and stronger waves the closer Lucena got. Then, when she was standing just outside the courtyard, one of the patrons stood up and beckoned to her. Not until she had entered and was nearly at his table did she recognize him.

"Undergate," she said, the relief in her voice tempered by a degree of reservation.

"Munsmire," said he, smiling all over his cheerily flushed face. "So good to see you again, pray take a seat. Some refreshment, perhaps? My pleasure."

And while Lucena was making her usual protestation that he was to call her Ashmoor, not Munsmire, Undergate signaled to a waiter and spoke to him in rapid Frantan. It went by so fast that Lucena, though she could read and write Frantan perfectly, did not understand.

"This is the most wonderful place in the world, Munsmire," Undergate said. He certainly looked a good deal better than before: his face, though still hollow about the eyes, had lost all other similarities to a skull, and the body beneath his neatly tailored clothes had filled back into its usual size and shape. His cheeks were rosy, and he had a glint in his eyes that had been missing the last time. Looking at him in his high spirits, Lucena could not help feeling wary and began to wish she were elsewhere.

She listened with polite interest while he told her about Serais, extolling the city's virtues. The best of which, according to Undergate, was La Daria Rouge.

"The best linens, crystal and glass," he said. "And all the fashionable Seraisian patrons. I hear they keep some very fine spirits and brew a good coffee, but they also cater to our very own particular needs." He leaned forward and winked.

"They serve blood?" Lucena asked, only moderately surprised. She had smelled it, after all, and still the scent addled her mind a little. She was getting hungry, and there was something new and exciting about the smell of this blood that caught her interest. Probably because it was Frantan, she told herself. Everything about that country was rich in textures that delighted her senses.

"How quick you are," Undergate said with a chuckle. But there was a metallic ring to the sound, and it held no real mirth. It made Lucena look at him sharply. "But you have always been a very quick one," he amended, seeing the look. "So let me get directly to my point. I have been thinking, Munsmire, thinking very seriously, about finding *Amstrass*."

"Amstrass?" she said blankly. "Why would you want to do that?"

Undergate twisted his fingers and glanced nervously over his shoulder. Then he leaned across the table and continued in a confidential voice: "It just doesn't feel right, out here," he said. "All this," he gestured around the place he had, moments before, been loudly praising. "There's got to be *more* to it than just us."

"Pardon?"

"More to being a *vampire*, Munsmire. More to us than this beast under a mask of civility. There are mysteries in the Book of Amstrass that not even the Viddengault understand." He leaned back in his chair, regarding her with hard eyes. "I mean to find out. I mean to find Amstrass and make her explain. There are so many questions I need to ask her. Did you know, Munsmire, that none of the Ministers of the Viddengault knew how vampires came to be in the first place? They have no more idea of where we came from than humans do!"

Lucena felt a chill begin working itself down her spine, for Undergate was coming uncomfortably close to those questions that she did not want answered. Not yet. But fortunately for her she could see he was going about it the wrong way: Amstrass was not the answer to his questions. Madgrin was. And as far as she could tell, Undergate didn't strictly know Madgrin existed.

She cleared her throat. "One theory is we are a form of the undead," she said, trying to steer the subject in a safer direction. "Created by the demon Lif to punish Man for rejecting her."

Undergate waved his hand dismissively. "That is what the Chandrics will tell you. I have done a good deal of reading on the subject. According to Induit

CHAPTER 13: *Undergate*

teachings vampires were the bastard children of a demon and a woman; in Svenian tradition it was the Batwitch, Orolga, who bit a man and made him the first vampire; the Urvians told of dancing shadows that turned men crazy and sucked the life from livestock; everyone has a different explanation." He sat back in his chair and crossed his arms. "None of them I believe for a moment. We are more than common monsters, I know it. We can rise above all of this, this plain, mortal world. This is not where we belong. So I mean to find Amstrass and have her show me the way. But I need your help for this; you have walked darker paths than I."

Lucena set her jaw. Inside she was writhing with discomfort and confusion. One part of her wanted to jump up and run away as fast as she could. Another part wanted to slap Undergate for even toying with the notion of pursuing such knowledge. And another, smaller part of her, was just as curious as he, and a little flattered that he had asked for her help.

Stymied in this way she did not notice the waiter approach, carrying a tray laden with crystal glasses and a decanter of dark red liquid. But she noticed the mouthwatering smell, and it cast all thoughts of Undergate and Amstrass and everything else out of her mind.

The waiter set out the glasses, and Undergate poured her a drink. He pushed the glass across to her. "Think about it," he said. "I am sure you wish to learn the truth as much as I do."

Lucena wasn't thinking about truth at that moment. Indeed, she hardly heard his words. Her mind had focused on that crystal glass of thick, warm blood. She took the cup and drank its contents down like someone dying of thirst, then set it back on the table and sucked in air to clear her palate.

Something was different. Something was wrong. Her mind was still in a haze; sounds had gone far distant and even her vision was blurred. But there was nothing wrong with her sense of taste, and this sense told her clear and loud that what she had just drunk had not been ordinary blood. It was too sharp, too sweet (or was it too bitter?) and it set every nerve in her mind ringing. Most disturbing of all, its taste was too familiar. Lucena knew it, but not from her years and years as a vampire; this was a taste from her childhood, when she would fall and cut her lip, bite her own tongue by accident, or suck on a small cut.

She stood up slowly, pushing her chair back. Her mind was spinning, and a terrible ache welled up in her gut that felt like shame and horror and guilt rolled together. She put her hands on the table to steady herself, and focused her eyes on Undergate. He looked back, all surprise and innocence.

"That was human blood," Lucena stated, thickly.

Undergate smiled, pleased with himself. "I told you it was a wonderful place," he said serenely. Lucena wanted to throttle him.

"You tricked me," she said, still thick and slow.

"I did nothing of the sort. Don't look so *betrayed*, Munsmire. No one has died from it. I tell you, the doctors here are most viciously stupid. They are all too happy to let blood out of perfectly good humans, and all one need do is be there to cart it away for them. If the human does die it's their fault, not ours."

"The human?" Lucena echoed hollowly. "The *human?* Undergate, that came from a *person!*"

Undergate shrugged. Lucena stared. She could not make him comprehend what was going on in her mind. He did not understand how she had strived to avoid this very thing since she became a vampire. It was what separated her from the beastly way of living that she fought, tooth and nail, every time she went hunting. Which was why she enjoyed the hunting. It made her strange un-life worthwhile. She had used all the evil strength in her body to do good. To rescue innocent people, not to harm them.

Now she was angry. Dreadfully, fearfully angry. The rage burned up all her other feelings and left her staring at him in blind fury. It was this blind fury that led her to do what she did next. Looking back, she realized she never would have done so in a normal frame of mind.

She let out a high, hard laugh that rang throughout the courtyard, leaving silence in its wake. Then, while heads turned and hushed voices whispered, she bent forward across the table and said to Undergate:

"If you really want to find Amstrass, *fine*. I will help you. I will help you with all the power I have. But I do not promise you answers, or truth, or understanding. I wish you every sort of pain from this endeavor. Know this."

She stood up. The many candles set about the courtyard cast her shadow in several different places at once, but one shadow stretched out behind her, darker and larger than the others. And this shadow was not the shadow of a woman, but a horse. And in its shadowy head burned dying embers. Undergate saw, and the rosy flush left his face.

"I will see you in one year's time, at this very place," she told him. "Then you may tell me your plan for finding Amstrass, and I will aid you as best I can." She turned to face her shadow. "Come, Intok. We are leaving."

Chairs were tipped over and tables sent sliding as people surged away from the giant black horse that sprang from the paving stones. Taking a firm hold of her mane, Lucena dragged herself up onto Intok's back, and with a haughty glance down at Undergate, rode off into the night.

The horse looked around at her with its flaming eyes and twitched an ear.

CHAPTER 14:

Amstrass

LUCENA STOOD IN HER ROOM, obstinately facing away from the useless mirror, doing her best to keep her mind shut. Never before had she been so set against Madgrin reading her mind, and never before had she been so terrified of him.

Over the years Lucena had learned a few things about her maker. One was that he detested vampires. It was in a distant, cold, polite sort of way, but that only made it more terrifying. The other thing she had come to accept with the passage of time was that somehow she was different from other vampires. Somehow he did not hate her in the slightest. And Lucena had convinced herself this was because she didn't harm humans.

And perhaps she hadn't harmed anyone. Perhaps the person whose blood she had drunk had made a complete recovery.

Or perhaps not. And then Lucena would have that blood on her conscience for the rest of her existence. And her maker would hate her for it. It made her feel ill.

She would tell him, of course. He would know eventually, as he eventually knew all secrets, but she knew with rigid certainty that her only way to salvation was in being honest, and that knowledge tormented her.

Wary of their mistress's mood, her familiars had backed themselves up against the far wall of her room, where they made a comical sight. Keelback had stretched himself out against the ceiling, and Urgolant was huddled in the corner. Intok had fled Lucena's shadow and was standing across from Urgolant, contriving to look as insignificant as a large horse in a small room could.

"Maker," Lucena began for what felt like the hundredth time. But there was a tightness in her throat that did not allow her to speak.

Someone knocked on her door. Lucena turned towards it as though facing the gallows.

"Come in," she said, her voice hardly more than a whisper.

The door opened a crack, and Madgrin's face appeared in it. After a moment he glided through it and shut the door behind him with a click. Silence reigned again.

Lucena's mouth had gone dry, but she had to say something.

"I'm sorry," she began. "I—"

Madgrin stretched out his arms. The long sleeves of his robe made curtains of midnight blue. "Come here," he said.

To Lucena it looked as though his beckoning arms were a gateway into a starless night sky. But she made herself move—first one foot, then the other—until she stood between his outstretched arms and teetered on the brink.

CHAPTER 14: *Amstrass*

Then, to her astonishment, he pulled her in and embraced her. The illusion vanished as she discovered there was a real, solid body under the cloth, and real arms around her shoulders holding her there, and he was not a portal to oblivion at all.

In the stillness that followed she could feel his heart beating, slow and steady.

"La Flein," he said gently. "Tell me what troubles you."

Lucena could not find the words to describe her feelings. She just opened her mind and let them spill out of her. It was such a relief not to have to bottle them up that they came out in a torrent. On and on, gallons of uncertainty, guilt and shame chasing each other round in circles. Madgrin bore the onslaught in patient silence, his body perfectly still against hers except for the beating of his heart.

"Am I very detestable?" she asked at last in a small voice.

"No," he answered. "Not at all."

"I feel horrible."

"That will pass."

"I feel as though I did something wrong. I made a terrible mistake..."

Madgrin sighed. He was so much taller than she that his breath barely brushed the top of her head, but she felt his chest rise and fall under her hands.

"There are some acts so terrible they cannot be forgiven," he said, "but even to these there are always counteractions that can be taken—even if they do not perfectly ameliorate the original crime. This I know well. As I know you have done no such thing."

"I am still sorry for it," Lucena whispered.

"I forgive you," Madgrin said, "for what that is worth."

It was worth quite a lot, Lucena thought, even as she felt cold tears running down her face. Though they were tears of relief she turned her face into Madgrin's robes to hide them, and these he graciously accepted as just another secret to be protected.

"There are some things that cannot be undone," he said after a time, speaking to the empty air over Lucena's head. "Some choices cannot be unmade. But such a choice is yet before you. There may come a time, La Flein, when you must make a choice that will forever change what you are. But this is not that time. Nothing has changed but that you now have a broader experience of the world."

Silence. Slowly the heavy emotions began to lift; she felt the tension in her limbs begin to ease, and she extracted her arms from between their bodies to wrap them around his waist. They stood so entwined for several minutes, until the familiars, sensing the storm had passed, crawled out from the corners of the room and insinuated themselves into the embrace as well as they could. Keelback rose up, draping himself around Madgrin's neck and resting his head on Lucena's shoulder. Intok stood on one side, enfolding both of them in the huge dark curve of her neck and head, and Urgolant got as much of herself between their legs as she could. It was awkward, but also touching, and Lucena found she was smiling as she spared a hand from Madgrin to stroke Urgolant's head.

"I was a little foolish," she admitted. "I met a vampire from the Viddengault in Efranta. He is determined to find Amstrass, and I promised I would help him."

"Ah," said Madgrin, and by his tone she knew that he already knew this.

"I was angry," she explained. "He wants Amstrass to tell him secrets I don't think she has, and because he had tricked me I wanted to trick him. But now I see it was a foolish notion. Amstrass is one of those people who can't be found unless she wants to be, isn't she?"

"Not always," Madgrin said. "She can be difficult to find, but there are ways of summoning her. I can show you, if you wish."

Against his chest Lucena shook her head. "No, not now. I'd rather he not find her, to tell the truth. I have promised to meet him again in a year, but that gives me time to think."

"A year is not a very long time," Madgrin said.

Lucena was obliged to agree with this, a little ruefully. "Yes, but not now," she said. "I am too overwrought. I want to think about other things."

"Willic has found a nest of gremlins in the attic," Madgrin offered. "I believe he was hoping someone would help him catch them."

Lucena smiled against his chest, still wet from her tears. "That sounds like just the thing."

"Amstrass?" Orrus asked in surprise, one bushy eyebrow raised. "Yes, we have several books about her. But I thought you'd sworn off vampire studies?"

Lucena clasped her hands behind her back and rocked forward on the balls of her feet. "Well, yes," she admitted. "But I feel I ought to know more about her ... she seems interesting."

"Interesting is too light a word for her," Orrus said. But he shuffled off among the towering cases and a while later returned with no less than five formidable volumes, ranging in age from crumbling and dusty, to almost new. Lucena eyed them warily.

"I think I had better take them one at a time," she said.

"Oh, then start with this." He took one of the newer ones and passed it to her. It was modest compared to the others, bound in dark purple cloth that was almost black. It had no title, but Orrus explained: "The magician that used to live with us wrote it. He was well studied on the medieval characters. Wrote a book on Machalion Draconicus as well."

"This was written by the man who left us Urgolant?"

"Yes, that one. I can't recall his name at the moment, but it wasn't important. He merely called himself after the town he was born in. Felpines ... or Felis ... " Orrus trailed off.

"Felpass," Urgolant said, causing both Orrus and Lucena to turn in surprise. She raised herself halfway onto the table and extended one dark leg and tapped the purple-bound volume. "I read that years ago. Good, if you can decipher his handwriting."

Felpass's handwriting was indeed something to be reckoned with. It was spidery, with sharp dashes and letters with legs and flourishes sticking off in odd directions. This made the pages look like they were filled with strings of madly dancing figures rather than words, and the words themselves did not help with understanding: Orrus had said the magician was well studied in medieval characters, but what he had failed to mention was that he was himself medieval. His grammar and spelling bore all the familiar hallmarks of *Vampires, A History*, and in addition he used many letters and symbols Lucena had never seen before. She was obliged to borrow a runic dictionary from the library as well, just to understand the glyphs he had put on the title page.

As it turned out they spelled, in mage's runes, the Svenian phrase "Hail to the Beast."

Lucena suppressed a groan, wondering if the whole book would be this way.

She was saved by Urgolant, who apparently had no difficulty deciphering ancient writing, and had besides read the book before and already unravelled some of the more tangled bits. These barricades overcome, Lucena found it was actually a very good book, with all the most famous stories about Amstrass in the front, and then in the back several chapters on what had actually happened (according to Felpass).

These stories Felpass had collected from legends and rumors he had encountered all across Thamber—and some from as far away as Crowa—and which he had preserved in what he considered their truest form, although he had included extensive footnotes detailing their myriad variations. Lucena found these distracting, since the stories themselves, as far as they were stories, were actually quite good, if somewhat haunting and gruesome.

One which struck her in particular was the tale of how a little Svenian village had disappeared, and this clung to her long after they had finished the book.

What had happened, according to Felpass, was that one day the bells placed over the graves of the newly dead began to ring. They rang quietly at first, but became louder and more desperate as days went by. Finally some men went to see what was the matter; they walked up the hill to the graveyard, and several people saw them open its gates and go inside. They never came out again. The bells continued to ring. By and by, more and more people went up the hill to the graveyard. None of them were ever seen again either. And still the bells continued to ring.

Then the old men and women lost patience with their sons and daughters; they heaved themselves out of their chairs and tottered slowly up the hill. But when they reached the gates of the graveyard they found them overgrown with ivy and nettles and thorns. Defeated, they went home and died of disappointment.

The village became a ghostly town as more and more people disappeared into the graveyard or fled the place entirely. No one ever visited, and though they sent messengers for help, none of them came back. At last, the only people who remained in the village were the children. And on that day the bells in the graveyard finally ceased to ring. Instead there came an unearthly, beautiful music that drew all the children first into the street, and then out of the village, and finally to the gates of the graveyard itself. These now stood open, and inside they could see a pleasant garden with soft green grass and many good things to eat. The children at once surged forward and ran inside. All except one.

She was the last to go. She was a small girl with a game leg and a blind eye. Because of this she looked more closely at things, to make up for the loss, and so she noticed what all the other children had missed: the woman who stood by the gates and held them open. The woman saw her looking and beckoned.

She was a tall woman dressed in red with long pale hair, a pale face and a dark smile. She asked the girl her name. The girl replied. The woman said her name was Amstrass. Then she gave the girl a glass eye, a pair of shoes, a warm cloak and a small purse. She told the girl, "Turn around, walk down the hill, through your village, and away. Do not stop or look back until you come to the next village. Then you are free to do as you like, but always remember to tell your story to whomever you meet."

The girl did exactly as she was told. She came safely to the next town, and passed on the story to everyone she met in her long life, and though many tried to go back to her village, it could never be found again.

Felpass had put a note at the end of the story, which read: *"I have this from an old woman who claimed to be that very girl. She had a limp and a glass eye, and showed me the old shoes and cloak that Amstrass had given her. I asked where her village had been, and she told me it lay halfway between Öluskas and Tvin at the mouth of a valley. I went there, and found an old scar where a large portion of the land had been pulled into Dream, and the rift sealed over. I have no doubt that village still exists, but it is no longer a part of the material world."*

This was the most concise of all the stories. The rest had at least two versions that had to be told from beginning to end, and many had much longer, more involved notes trailing after them. The one that told how Amstrass became a vampire had no less than five variations, each one completely different. Impatient, Lucena began skimming the notes and only reading the first rendition of each tale. Nevertheless, this was enough to thoroughly quench any desire she might have had for meeting Amstrass in person. The stories told how she tricked families into eating their neighbors, how she impaled her enemies on wooden spikes and then hurled them off cliffs. She also had a penchant for kidnapping children, and no one (not even Felpass) could find out what happened to them.

Then she came to the second half of the book, and here things became even more interesting.

The first section, "A Nice Record of the Unhappy Trials of the Wife of the Last Count of Amstrass," told, according to Felpass's own research, the true events of Amstrass's transformation. The title, however, was misleading; there was nothing *nice* about it. After finishing, Lucena was obliged to stare into a dark corner of her room and concentrate on squashing the nightmarish images out of her head, and she concluded Felpass must have been using the word to mean something else entirely.

"Accurate," Urgolant told her. "*Nice* can also mean accurate and precise. It can also mean stupid, unlikable and pretty."

"Well," Lucena said dubiously. "It certainly is precise and unlikable."

Several hundred years ago (by Felpass's reckoning), there was a castle overlooking a prosperous town in the Svenian mountains. Both the town and the castle were called Amstrass, and the master of the castle traditionally took the title of Count d'Amstrass. They had kept the castle time out of mind, and were expected to keep it for many long years to come. But in those dark times there were dangerous folk about, and on a cold winter day a pack of marauding werewolves attacked the town.

Driven to distraction by cold and hunger the werewolves fell upon the town and killed all who did not flee before them. Enraged, the count sent out his soldiers, but night was falling, and they were soon defeated by the werewolves.

After they had satisfied their hunger upon the town, a strange madness came over the werewolves (as will sometimes happen after a bloodbath) and they ran up to the castle, snarling and howling. Some in the form of wolves, some in the form of men, and some in strange combinations of the two, they forced their way inside and killed whoever stood in their path, overrunning the castle. They killed guards and tortured servants, and when they found the Count of Amstrass they cleaved his head in two. Then they dragged the Count's wife and children up to the highest tower and threw all seven children one by one out the window. The distraught Countess they forced out the front gates which they locked behind her, no doubt with the intention that she should die from the cold.

The Countess of Amstrass went away through the snow in a daze of pain and grief until she came to the edge of the forest that stood all around the town. This she entered and walked until her feet were numb, and the cold air burned against her skin. Then she came upon a starving vampire lying in the snow who, upon seeing a living human walking towards him, got up with the intention of feeding upon her. But no sooner had he sunk his teeth into her than she bit into him. And since hers was the stronger heart, even as he drained her life away she sucked the life out of him; he fell to the snowy ground a shriveled dead husk, and she rose again, a vampire.

Then the Countess of Amstrass went back to the castle and set it on fire. She stood at the gates and killed any who came out. Then, just before the late winter dawn, as the fire was dying, she went inside. She found the leader of the wolves and the ones who had killed her husband and children hiding in a stone crypt where the flames could not reach. Taking a stone axe from the tomb she cut the leader's head in two, then dragged the rest up to the highest tower and threw them out the same window her children had passed through earlier.

It was said among the people that all had died that terrible night, and now the castle was deserted. Yet in the years that followed few who went to the castle ever came back again, and those that did returned so addled with fear that no sense could be gotten from them. The people recognized the signs of a vampire, and the place acquired an evil reputation. The creature that dwelled within the castle was called the Vampira d'Amstrass, but after a few generations this was shortened to Amstrass, and the vampire kept that as her name ever since—the name she had been given in life long forgotten.

There were several entries after this of less interest. Felpass noted that the famous animosity between vampires and werewolves appeared to have originated with that event, contrary to what most folklorists contended. Then followed a lists of dates and locations where Amstrass had been active. These were mostly Svenian villages with hard-to-pronounce names, and Lucena skimmed over them until she arrived at the last entry in the book.

It was short, and written in red ink as opposed to black. The title read (in mage's runes, naturally): *"How Amstrass came to Wear her Soul on her Face,"* and told how in the winter of 1378 Amstrass came upon a magician and his apprentice living in a small hut high in the mountains. Though they were poor, and though the magician recognized Amstrass for what she was, they did not force her outside, but fed her boar's blood and gave her a place to sleep, for it was a cold and snowy night. The magician was also a practitioner of black arts, and preferred to have vampires as allies rather than enemies.

Amstrass stayed with the magician and apprentice for the rest of the winter, learning odd spells and a little magic. In the spring when the snow had melted and it was time for her to leave she asked the apprentice, whom she had grown fond of, to come with her. The apprentice politely declined, not having finished his training. Amstrass in her irritation killed him and then disappeared without a trace.

This atrocity did not go unnoticed: both the angel Tumiel, who governs hospitality, and the demon Macheval, who guards dark magicians, were angered by Amstrass's actions. Tumiel declared that from thence forth no vampire might cross the threshold of a home unless explicitly invited by the resident and went away in a huff, but Macheval sent his hound, Bryfang, to find the apprentice's soul and return it to the magician who, by his own dark arts, was able to resurrect the poor boy. Then he went and confronted Amstrass, and finding her to have no remorse for betraying her host's hospitality, he took out her shriveled, dead heart and replaced it with a burning coal. This caused her such pain that she fell to the floor and begged him to destroy her. But Macheval only took her withered human heart and used it to reconstruct her long-lost soul. This he wrote on the left side of her face, telling her that if she could conquer the beast that had destroyed her human heart she could quench the burning coal. He remarked that if she did, the lump of coal might even be an improvement over her old, twisted human heart.

After this Amstrass disappeared for several centuries, the only sign of her existence being the appearance some years later of the *Book of Amstrass*, which garnered a following of idealistic vampires, who took its philosophical essays as literal commandments.

The current whereabouts of Amstrass were unknown, though Felpass noted that a new story about her seemed to crop up every twenty-five years or so, and that he might have to return in a few more centuries to compile a second volume.

Lucena closed the book and put it away. She felt cold inside, and a little dizzy from squinting at the candlelit pages for so many hours. But one thing was quite clear in her head: she did not want to meet Amstrass.

She did not ask Madgrin about ways to summon the vampire, and returned the book to Orrus the next night. Then she contrived to put Amstrass and Undergate out of her mind. This was not a difficult task: the vampire season was almost over, and with the coming of spring and the sun came the usual springtime

CHAPTER 14: *Amstrass*

distractions, and Lucena had less and less time to spend carefully not thinking about vampires.

The rocs were breeding, which meant territorial fights between the males, which meant slabs of stone flung everywhere, which meant that everyone with a strong back was roped into tidying up. In addition, Gydda was seized with a fit of spring cleaning and systematically worked her way through the House, airing out rooms and dragging heaps of old junk into the halls for disposal. Lucena woke one night to find the place filled with the smells of a spring night, for Gydda had opened all the windows to let out the dusty air that had accumulated over the winter. This also served to let all sorts of things *into* the House; mostly mundane things like mosquitos and moths and some small animals, but also a mischievous wind that blew in through the kitchen door and played havoc in the lower rooms. Orrus, Willic and Lucena spent all night trying to herd it out again.

So it was by one means or another she managed to put the matter of Amstrass entirely out of her mind until nearly a year had passed, and she found herself compelled by her promise to Undergate to meet with him again.

It was with reluctance and trepidation that she approached La Daria Rouge on the appointed night, and she had brought Urgolant with her to be safe. Madgrin had been kind enough to cast a misdirection spell on the sombulus so she would not attract attention from the other patrons, and so they walked boldly through the tables set out in the courtyard until they came to the one more or less in the same place where Lucena had met Undergate the year before. Undergate was not there, and she was tempted to turn away at once, but common politeness dictated that she wait at least a few minutes. So she sat down and, when accosted by a waiter, ordered a perfectly innocent fruit drink.

"There you are!" Undergate exclaimed, pushing his way violently through the crowd, a large and predatory smile on his face. He sat down opposite her and proceeded to spill an armful of books and scrolls and a few sheafs of loose paper over the table. Lucena surreptitiously moved the candle to the very edge, where it was less likely to set the whole thing on fire, and looked in despair at the huge amount of material Undergate had collected. One of those documents probably held the key to finding Amstrass, there were so many.

"It is the most frustrating endeavor," Undergate said, shoving the books into some semblance of order. "There is no lack of *material* on Amstrass, but authenticated fact is scarce."

"Is that so?" Lucena said, hope flaring in her chest.

"I've collected all the more reliable sources," Undergate continued. "Plus some of the more believable stories. I want you to help me go through them. Together I am sure we will discover a way to find her."

"Oh," Lucena sighed, the little hope going out. The last thing she wanted was to read more about Amstrass, but since there was no way of getting out of it politely she dutifully pulled a sheaf of paper towards her and began. She contrived to pass most of the papers to Urgolant under the table, so her companion would have something to do.

* * *

"It was *fascinating*," the shade eater said, her four front legs tapping eagerly on the table. All eight of her eyes were sparkling, and her mouth pincers moved enthusiastically as she talked about her night out.

Lucena was less animated; she slumped in a corner of the kitchen sipping a glass of boar's blood and trying to think of something—anything—that did not have to do with Amstrass. They had spent four hours with Undergate at La Daria Rouge, and Lucena had read so much in that time it made her head spin, but they had not made any progress. True, they had found some informative writings in his collection (a detailed account of how Amstrass butchered a group of nyskies in 1538, which Lucena had only scanned and passed hurriedly on to Urgolant) but no concrete evidence to build on. Anything that seemed solid enough, like the first-person account of a ten-year-old girl who had seen Amstrass walking on the beach near Clipping Head in 1930, was also vague and unreliable. After all, there were many tall, blond women in the world, and who was to say an imaginative child might not mistake an ordinary woman for an extraordinary one? Lucena had made this point, and others besides, throughout the evening, which had put Undergate into a cantankerous mood, which hadn't helped their search. In the end they had parted ways after agreeing that they would meet again in a year's time, and having successfully put off an encounter with Amstrass, now Lucena wanted nothing more than to not think about her.

Urgolant, unfortunately, had no such notions. She told a rapt audience of Willic, Soloma, all the hoblins and even Harga, who had come to lean against the kitchen door, about her own conjectures and ideas, and some of the interesting facts she had uncovered.

It was one of those facts that eventually drew Lucena's reluctant attention.

"What was that?" she said, rousing herself.

Urgolant paused her eager tapping on the table and rolled three eyes in Lucena's direction. "I said, there are no credible accounts of Amstrass massacring humans since Macheval put the soul on her face."

"But the nyskies..." Lucena protested.

"Felpass alluded to the Macheval event as being quite recent, and his book was completed in 1564—Orrus told me."

"Oh," Lucena said, turning back to her cup. She wasn't sure if this changed her mind or not, but she listened patiently while Urgolant finished her speech.

But it was not enough to make her desire Amstrass's company, and the next year she approached La Daria Rouge with no more enthusiasm than the last, and with similar results. This time Undergate had brought some divining runes in a velvet pouch, but neither he nor Lucena could get them to work. Urgolant was eager to try, but Lucena didn't let her.

In the third year Undergate thought he had deciphered an old map that showed where Amstrass's Frantan house was, but when they went there it was only a sparse wood. Lucena spent several uncomfortable hours stomping through the undergrowth ostensibly looking for secret gates or doors while Undergate went back to his divining runes.

They spent their fourth meeting tediously translating an old Svenian document which turned out to be a list of the Seven Deadly Sins as applied to elves and how to trick them into committing them. Lucena often wondered where Undergate got his material, but because he never made any further attempt to interrogate her about where she went or what she did between their meetings, she never asked.

By the fifth year the meeting had become a routine annoyance, and by the sixth it felt as though her existence had always been this way: every February she would take Urgolant (or Keelback or Intok, depending on who wanted to come) and go through the carpet in Madgrin's study to La Daria Rouge in Serais. And, while she noticed some subtle changes in the patrons from year to year, the staff of the café never changed, nor even seemed to grow old: by the time they had been meeting there for ten years the only noticeable changes were in the new chairs and tables the proprietor had been obliged to purchase, and in Undergate himself.

He was growing thin again. The harrowed look in his eyes had returned, and his clothes were patched and frayed. Lucena remembered when those clothes had been new, and she realized that while she had been doing her best to forget about their quest for Amstrass, Undergate had been obsessing about it. This was no whim or mad idea to him, but an all-consuming endeavor. And she had promised to help him. So with a sigh she dragged the latest paper towards her, with the honest intent of making the best of it—if only to appease her conscience.

Lucena soon discovered, to her annoyance, that the frustration of trying *not* to get somewhere was nothing compared to the frustration of actually trying and being stumped at every turn. Though she bent her mind earnestly to studying the papers Undergate provided, and even read all the books the about Amstrass that she had sworn not to read, she found herself none the wiser, and a good deal more aggravated.

It took another two years and the approach of their thirteenth meeting before Lucena finally relented. Undergate had been a withered husk of a vampire the last time they had met, his eyes lit by a feverish light, and she felt nearly repulsed with pity for him. So she went and asked Madgrin how to summon Amstrass.

He gave her a twinkling look from over the heaps of books on his desk. "That is simple enough," he said. "For someone like you, all you have to do is call her by name."

"By name?" Lucena exclaimed in surprise. "You mean her original name?" she added cautiously. For Amstrass's original Svenian name was very long and difficult to pronounce.

Madgrin shook his head. "No, no. She discarded that name a long time ago; it means nothing to her. Call her by her chosen title: Vampira d'Amstrass. Do it with clear intent, and she will not hesitate to come."

"Oh," said Lucena, taken aback. She had never thought it would be so simple. But now she had been hurled from one dilemma to another: should she attempt to summon Amstrass purely for Undergate's sake, or go back to avoiding the subject? *She* certainly had no wish to meet the famous vampire, but that seemed to be the only way to divert Undergate's downward spiral, and it seemed she was an integral part of summoning her. In the end she decided to wait and see what state Undergate was in this year, and not to do anything rashly.

LUCENA IN THE HOUSE OF MADGRIN

* * *

"I think we should summon Amstrass," Undergate said evenly. He was a terrible sight, all sagging eyes and hollow cheeks with a greenish tint to them.

Lucena had been tipping close to making the suggestion herself, but hearing it spoken aloud by Undergate made her reverse direction in a hurry.

"Do you really think that's a good idea?" she tried cautiously. "She's a very powerful person, by all accounts. I do not think she would take kindly to being summoned."

"She doesn't want to be found," Undergate said matter-of-factly. "That much is clear. The only way to deal with people like that is to summon them . . ."

That sounded dangerously authoritative, and Lucena narrowed her eyes. "Do you have a means?" she pressed on, hopeful that he would not ask her for suggestions.

But instead Undergate took a leather satchel from his side and dumped its contents over their table. Candles, scrolls and small vials of liquid rolled every which way, and Lucena had to scramble to save them. Undergate paid no heed to the mess and drew out a sheet of paper written all over in red ink. He handed it to Lucena.

It was a simple enough incantation, and required only that the summoner set a place for the summonee and offer them a boon of some sort. Reluctantly Lucena got up and moved around the table to stand next to Undergate, and they set out her chair as the place Amstrass was to appear. They put the glass of wine Lucena had ordered in front of the chair as the boon she was to receive. Then they stood back and studied the paper.

"You hold it," Undergate said. "I have it memorized."

So Lucena took the paper and held it so she could see the writing clearly. It was a good deal more elaborate than simply calling the vampire by name, which gave her conflicting feelings. She took one last look around the courtyard of La Daria Rouge, and then gave all her attention to the spell.

As they spoke the first line it seemed to Lucena that nothing was happening at all; that they were only speaking words and nothing more. She did not even get the hair-on-end tingle that happened when Orrus did magic. But then they came to the part in the spell where they had to name the summonee, and together they said:

"Vampira d'Amstrass, Vampira d'Amstrass . . . Vampira d'Amstrass!"

All at once it felt as though her tongue had turned to lead. She struggled to make the words, to form them in her mouth and push them out. Her head was in an iron vice and she could not think from the pain. Somehow she forced herself on, and suddenly the pain and heaviness stopped. Instead she felt light-headed and the words flowed freely out of her. They flowed so freely that she found she was speaking words that were not in the spell at all. She did not know the language they were in, or what they meant, but they begged to be spoken and so she spoke them.

When at last the tide ebbed and she came back to herself Undergate was staring at her. Lucena coughed nervously and handed him the paper.

CHAPTER 14: *Amstrass*

"My apologies," she said weakly. "I got carried away."

Undergate opened his mouth, but whatever he meant to say was lost in the collective gasp from the other patrons as all the lamps in the courtyard went out. They were followed by the lamps inside the building, and the lamps on the street, and finally the lamps of the surrounding establishments, until the city was plunged into an eerie gloom.

Somebody screamed and knocked a table over. There were angry shouts, and the proprietors were hurrying hither and thither trying to resurrect the lamps and candles. In the darkness she felt Undergate grip her elbow in excitement. Then there was an almighty *crack* and the table before them was split asunder and the chair opposite smashed to kindling.

A rip appeared in the air above where the chair had been, and it was pushed open impatiently like someone thrusting aside a curtain as Amstrass stepped through.

There could be no mistaking her. She towered over both of them, easily six feet tall or more, and her wild, pale hair tossed about so that it stood straight up in places. She wore a dark red gown that buttoned up to her chin and came down to her toes, its sleeves flared out at the wrists, obscuring her hands. There was a strange discoloration across the left side of her face which looked rather like curlicues and dots one moment, and a pattern of frosty leaves the next.

She looked exactly as Lucena had imagined her from the stories she had read. Her face was set in a blank grim mask, and her fine, strong brow cast shadows into her glittering eyes. She raised her right hand and pointed a long waxy finger at Lucena, who took a step back.

"You called me," she said in a voice that reminded Lucena of frozen mountains and desolate peaks, her mouth a cruel curl. "I have come."

Lucena knew she had to answer; she knew that to stand in silence was a terrible insult, but she was having difficulty speaking. For as soon as Amstrass had pointed at her, strange visions started pushing their way into her head: a holy arrow pointed down, the symbol of Hell; a great pale hound with hungry eyes, grinning at her; a lonely castle silhouetted against the full moon; an open grave on a windy hillside; a gaping window. It seemed as if that window was where Amstrass stood, and Lucena was falling into it.

Undergate's voice, hard with nerves, brought her back to reality: "We have summoned you, Lady Amstrass, because we wish to know the truth of our cursed existence. I beg that you may counsel us, so that we will be enlightened."

It was a good speech, and one he had no doubt had ready for years. Unfortunately it was completely wasted on Amstrass, whose clear, cold eyes remained fixed on Lucena. Lucena swallowed, trying to get her breathing going so she could speak, but before she could, Amstrass's left arm reached out, cracking as it stretched to twice its normal length, and she grabbed Undergate by the neck, lifting him clean into the air. He made a choking sound and kicked his legs, but he could not get free.

All the while she never took her eyes from Lucena, and then her right hand with its pointing finger stretched out across the table as well. Lucena backed away, but the arm made a vicious dart, like a cat pouncing on a mouse, and caught her by the neck. She let out a strangled cry as she was lifted into the air, and clasped her hands around Amstrass's bony wrist. It was waxy and cold, and hard and strong as a live oak branch.

Now the images were coming so thick and fast they were overwhelming: a blood red dawn; a hut on fowl's legs; the yawning mouth of a dark cave; a young girl limping along an empty road; a flayed human corpse laid upon a bed.

This last image was so terrible that Lucena wanted to scream, but she had no air left in her lungs to do so, and no way of getting the air through her throat even if she did, for Amstrass's hand was like a cold noose around her neck.

"Two young vampires mean to make me their tutor," the icy voice said. Amstrass spoke in hardly more than a whisper, yet her words blared in Lucena's ears, loud enough to wipe all the images clean away, and now Lucena could see Amstrass regarding each of them in turn with equal dislike. Slowly she raised Undergate higher into the air and brought him across to her, his toes brushing the surface of the table.

"This one is ignorant by circumstance," she said thoughtfully. "And the knowledge he seeks will lead to his demise."

Lucena felt the fingers around her neck tighten a fraction, and she found herself hovering above Amstrass, the great vampire looking at her through a fringe of pale hair.

"This one is ignorant by choice," she said, sounding a little irritated. "And turns her back on the knowledge that will save her."

Lucena squirmed. Amstrass glared at her. She glanced back and forth between the two of them for some moments, before her mouth cracked into an evil grin, and she chuckled darkly.

"I wonder," she mused to herself. "You're not very sturdy little fledgelings, are you? Hmm? If I were to bash your heads together I doubt either of you could put your brains back in. Or, if I were to squeeze *really* hard . . . "

The hand around Lucena's neck tightened again, and for one ghastly moment she thought her head was going to come right off.

There was another tear in the world, one which Lucena felt more than saw. From it there came a brief touch of cold night air and the scent of old, unopened books, secrets and wet grass; and then Keelback was there.

He lunged forward and clamped his beak around Amstrass's wrist and, with an almighty heave and twist, tore her arm right off. With a snap of tendon and bone Lucena was thrown through the air. Keelback broke her fall, and she collapsed to the ground in a heap, clawing at the arm still clutching her throat. But no sooner had she taken hold of it than it burst into a cloud of dark flapping wings. In her confused state Lucena did not recognized them as bats until they were streaming back to Amstrass, flapping around the severed stump until, as one, they solidified into a whole arm once more.

Amstrass bent her re-formed arm this way and that, examining it carefully. She seemed to have forgotten poor Undergate, who was still thrashing and kicking in the grip of her other hand. Lucena was at the point of asking Keelback to free him as well, but then Amstrass noticed she was still holding him, and dropped Undergate onto the remains of the table. She turned to Lucena and

CHAPTER 14: *Amstrass*

smiled broadly. So broadly, in fact, that it looked as though her mouth would split her face in two, and Lucena thought she could see every one of the vampire's pearly white teeth, with her elongated canines gleaming devilishly.

"Well fancy *that*," Amstrass said through her smile. "You have a *familiar*. Maybe you're not such a waste of flesh as I thought."

She neatly stepped over the wreckage of the table and chairs, ignoring Undergate, who tried to snatch at the hem of her dress, until she stood above Lucena. Keelback, his crest bolt upright, raised himself until he towered over Amstrass, and hissed. But Amstrass only gave him an annoyed glance and bent to speak to Lucena.

"I have familiars too," she said confidentially. "Would you like to meet them?"

"I have no wish to fight," Lucena croaked, her voice ragged. "Or to offend you."

"Oh, but that's not the point!" Amstrass exclaimed. "Do you know how *long* it's been since I last found a vampire who could summon familiars?" She bent close over Lucena so that their noses nearly touched. "Seven hundred years," she said, carefully enunciating each word. "Seven hundred, forty-three years, eight months and eleven days. That's a long time—Oh, will you *desist?*"

This last was addressed to Keelback, who had grabbed her by the other arm and was attempting to lift her off the ground. Though he was holding her thin, boney arm in his beak, the moment she spoke those words he found himself holding the nape of a huge shadowy dog. It grew and bulged out of the place Amstrass's arm should have been, its dark fur coiling about its face. At least six red eyes glowed in its head, and its breath smelled of something awful. Keelback dropped it with a disgusted shriek and coiled himself protectively around Lucena.

Amstrass, and her dog, regarded them thoughtfully. With her remaining hand she scratched herself lazily behind one ear, and the dog shook its head. Then her face cracked into a smile again, and she began to laugh: great, cackling cries that rang out through the night and raised the bile in Lucena's throat. Then, without warning, they lunged forward, the dog opening its mouth wide to reveal rows of sharp yellow teeth.

But before they could reach Lucena, strands of heavy black shadows darted forward like so many ravenous fish and twined themselves around the pair. Lucena gazed in bewilderment, until she felt a soft hairy foot come to rest on her shoulder, and looking up she saw Urgolant, staring hard at Amstrass with all eight of her eyes.

"You mustn't harm Lucena," Urgolant said in her clear, clicking voice. "It's not fair."

Amstrass, picking bits of shadow off her face, glared at Urgolant. Then she smiled. Lucena was coming to dread those smiles. The dog stretched and grew, so that its head was as big as Urgolant, then twice as big, and finally it seemed as though it could swallow the entire café.

It descended upon them, and Lucena could see every one of its teeth and the dark pink interior of its mouth with the rolling tongue and gaping throat.

She felt a surging, boiling beneath her, and a second later Intok surged into life, carrying the three of them into the air and out from between the dog's jaws.

Below them, Amstrass laughed. One arm stretched up, impossibly long and thin, and a cold, hard hand clamped itself onto Lucena's shoulder.

"Don't you go running off so fast," Amstrass said, her voice loud as if she spoke into Lucena's ear. "You're much too fascinating to let go so easily."

Lucena looked down and found Amstrass was just a smear of red against a pitch-black world. The tables and café were gone. Undergate was gone. The city was gone. The world as she knew it was gone, replaced by a heavy black ocean of night.

It began to roar, and then the roaring became a rushing, and then Lucena was swept away, pulled down into the black abyss. She clung to Intok and Keelback, and Urgolant clung to them, and together they forged their way forward, cutting through the current, until at last they broke free from the strange black world, and the only darkness around them was the natural dark of the night, pricked by faint stars.

"You called me," she said in a voice that reminded Lucena of frozen mountains and desolate peaks, her mouth a cruel curl. "I have come."

CHAPTER 15:

The Two Vampires

THE FIRST THING LUCENA FELT WAS RELIEF: they had escaped Amstrass and her strange magic, and now they just had to figure out where they were and how to get home. Then a hand like an iron claw grasped her hair, and she heard an impossibly loud—yet whispery—voice in her ear, and she realized they had not escaped at all.

"You fool!" Amstrass said angrily, jerking Lucena's head this way and that. "You've taken us *east!*"

"I—what?" Lucena cried, grabbing at the hand in her hair and trying to get up. Amstrass lifted her bodily into the air and set her on her feet, then turned her head to face the eastern horizon. There, sure enough, was the telltale lightening of the sky, the sky that had been so dark in Serais. And as always, Lucena began to feel the heavy fuzziness inside her head which signaled the onset of unconsciousness.

"Oh dear," she said thickly. It was already becoming difficult to speak.

"'*Oh dear,*' she says," Amstrass echoed mockingly. "Haven't you got any sense in that dense, enchanted head of yours?"

"'m not enchanted," Lucena mumbled, twisting around in Amstrass's grip. "Keelback? We need to go."

Keelback obligingly came forward and latched his beak onto Amstrass's arm, looking at her hopefully. But she only gave him an annoyed glance and did not let go of Lucena.

"We're in the Lindish Alps," she said. "There will be no going anywhere until tonight. Until then—" She looked across Keelback's beak to where Urgolant and Intok stood, uncertain what to do. "You two," Amstrass commanded, "start digging."

Lucena awoke that evening to the unpleasant sensation of being underground—not just in a cavern underground, but buried under the earth. Cold, wet soil pressed in on her from all sides, and she dared not open her mouth or eyes. She dared not breathe, either, and despite the raging, pounding thirst which always greeted her upon waking, she held perfectly still.

By shifting her body about she discovered that the earth was fairly soft, and gave easily under her touch. So she worked one arm up to her chest and began to carefully push upwards. The earth gave way immediately, and her hand met air. Realizing how shallow her burial had been Lucena thrust herself upwards, spitting dirt as she emerged.

She spent the next five minutes getting soil out of every conceivable orifice. Being buried got you dirtier than anything.

CHAPTER 15: *The Two Vampires*

Lucena had struggled into a sitting position and was shaking her head vigorously, trying to dislodge dirt from her ear, and was considering the benefits of getting to her feet and jumping up and down, when Amstrass came back. She took one look at Lucena's predicament and gave her head a good whack one way and then a good whack the other. It left Lucena with the feeling that her brain was no longer in its usual place, but her ears were perfectly clear.

She took a breath to say thank you, and then had to spend the next few minutes snorting dirt out of her nose.

"Thank you," she said at last, a little hoarsely.

"I don't hold with saving things," Amstrass said, sitting down beside her. "But your bird-snake wouldn't let go of my arm."

Lucena took this to mean "you're welcome." She nodded and looked around a bit hazily. She was thirsty, and there was no sign of Keelback. "Where?" she began.

"Your bird-snake went hunting. The nightmare is behind you, and your sombulus is reading," Amstrass informed her.

"*Reading?*" Lucena said, incredulous.

"I gave her a book," Amstrass said, folding her arms and looking pinched. "She wouldn't stop asking me questions, otherwise."

Good old Urgolant, Lucena thought happily. And none of them had been killed or eaten while she slept. She wondered if she dared ask Amstrass if there was any blood to be had.

As if in answer, a bottle that smelled of whisky and blood was pushed under her nose. She recoiled.

"I'm not *that* thirsty," she protested.

"I know," Amstrass said, harshly. "It doesn't matter."

She watched intently as Lucena forced down a few swallows, a small frown creeping over her painted face.

"That's an odd kind of enchantment you've got," she said. "It's worn off."

"I'm *not* enchanted," Lucena retorted, thrusting the bottle back.

"You *were*," Amstrass maintained. She took the bottle and tucked it up her sleeve. "It wore off many years ago, but you've kept the effects about you. I can't imagine why; it's not convenient, and nearly got you *killed* last night."

Slowly Lucena began to comprehend what Amstrass was talking about. Her habit of falling unconscious at first light, of course.

"That's not an enchantment," she said. "It's a . . . a compulsion. My maker's fault. He said it would wear off as I got stronger."

"Ha," said Amstrass. It wasn't laughter: she just said it, like it was any other word. "It wore off indeed, a long time ago. I can only imagine you *like* it this way . . . for some reason." She spat and turned away. "Sheltered vampires," she muttered contemptuously, shuffling through the dead leaves and twigs that coated the ground.

They were on the side of a low mountain, on a relatively flattish swell surrounded by black oaks that cut out the view, but Lucena could smell snow and the sharp scent of pine on the air and gathered they were quite a ways up.

Amstrass wandered off past Urgolant until all that could be seen of her was a flying mane of pale hair and a smudge of red. But then she came marching back, sending leaves flying before her, and knelt down so that her nose was almost touching Lucena's.

"You said compulsion," she said. It was not a question.

"That's what my maker called it." Lucena struggled to back away, but Amstrass kept crawling through the leaves to close the distance.

"No vampire can lay *compulsions* on people, not even their fledgelings," Amstrass continued. "Glamours, yes, but not compulsions. The only ones powerful enough to do that are . . . " she trailed off, studying Lucena's dirty face closely. Then, without warning, she darted forward and bit Lucena on the neck.

Lucena kicked and punched and said some very nasty words she had learned from Beruse, and Amstrass withdrew, smiling, as the markings on her face worked themselves furiously.

"I *knew* it," she announced triumphantly. She stood up, grabbing Lucena by the hair again and dragging her along. "You're a *Lamphra's* Child, you really are!"

Lucena barely heard. Her skin stung where Amstrass had bit her, and she feared her hair would start coming out. So she did the only thing she could think of: she grabbed Amstrass by *her* hair and pulled, viciously.

"Please stop that racket," Urgolant whined as Amstrass yelled in pain.

Then there was a great shadowy body between them, and both Amstrass and Lucena were thrown to the ground as Intok charged in and broke their mutual hold.

Lucena lay in the leaves and twigs, trying to sort out which parts of her body were hurting and which parts were not. It turned out most of her body was hurting, and while she was deciding whether or not any of the hurts were the serious kind, a strange sound filled the air. It was a hacking, whooping, shrieking that sounded like a deranged bird. Only when Intok moved aside and Lucena could see the source of the noise did she realize what it was.

Amstrass. Laughing.

The vampire laughed in great, heaving breaths with her head thrown back and her mouth open wide. Lucena noticed that the markings on her face—her soul, if Felpass was to be believed—had worked themselves into something that might have been writing. But it was a writing in a foreign language and a foreign script, and Lucena could not read it.

Sometime during Amstrass's fit of mirth Keelback returned. He brought with him a freshly killed boar which he dumped beside Lucena.

"I'm glad she's feeling better," he remarked cheerfully, with a nod in Amstrass's direction. The laughter had died down to a wheeze, but Lucena failed to see the improvement.

"Better?" she asked.

"She was all gloomy doomy all day," Keelback sighed dramatically. "Would only talk to Urgolant about all the men she'd killed and never did anything interesting. But I did something good, see? Brought you dinner—or breakfast. Please don't look sad, Cena, it's fresh." He nudged the boar carcass invitingly.

CHAPTER 15: *The Two Vampires*

Lucena was so touched by this act of kindness that she threw her arms around Keelback's neck and hugged him soundly. Then she reached in her pockets for her jackknife and bottle. It was the replacement of the bottle she'd given to Undergate years ago, and the recollection made her think of Undergate, poor boy, left all alone in the wreckage of the café . . . but his plight still seemed favorable to hers.

Before her thoughts could descend into self-pity, however, Amstrass came over and snatched the knife from her with one hand and picked up the boar with the other.

"Don't eat off the ground," Amstrass chastised. "It's uncivilized."

Lucena didn't feel bothered enough to point out that simply being a vampire was uncivilized, but she did wonder aloud, "What, besides the ground, is there to eat off of?"

For answer Amstrass set the boar down, stuck the knife in it, clapped her hands, and then pulled a small table out of thin air. It was a square, wooden table, the sort used for holding flower arrangements in expensive homes. Amstrass turned it around, found it satisfactory, and planted it firmly in the ground so that it was at an incline. Then she placed the boar on the table with its head hanging off the downhill side and made a neat, practiced cut in its neck. Quickly she grabbed two mismatched wine glasses out of the air as well, and held them below the thin stream of blood.

Lucena went over and sat in the dirt uphill of the table, where she didn't have to watch the torturously slow work. After a time Amstrass stood up, unceremoniously pushed the boar off the table (to Keelback's protest), and set the glasses in its place.

"Come," she said to Lucena. "Drink with me."

It was almost polite by her standards. Still, Lucena gave Amstrass her best glower and considered sitting right where she was. But that would be dangerously close to sulking, and would probably lead to more hair-pulling on both sides. Besides, she *was* thirsty. So she got up and went downhill to the table, where she stood opposite from Amstrass.

Because of the incline Lucena found herself eye-to-eye with Amstrass, and this was a small comfort. But she was prevented from regaining her composure completely by Amstrass's soul, which was still in the form of dense, black writing, and she kept distracting herself trying to read it.

"I would apologize for my lack of manners," Amstrass said stonily. "But I have made a practice of not apologizing anymore, and I won't start now."

Lucena decided it would be diplomatic to consider this an apology. She inclined her head ever so slightly.

"The fact is," Amstrass continued, her tone becoming more thoughtful. "I was surprised. I am not easily summoned, even by the spell you and your partner used, which is a strong one. I couldn't understand how I came to be stuck in that pretentious, frilly little den, and it put me in a temper. I have a fierce temper; you may have noticed."

"I noticed," Keelback cut in. "You're worse than Rhyse."

Amstrass rolled her eyes sideways at Keelback, but otherwise gave no acknowledgement. "It was you," she continued. "*You* were the one that called me.

Not that silly spell. That should have been enough to tell me what you are, but as I said I was in a temper and not inclined to be observant." Her eyes narrowed. "*Do* you know what you are?" she asked sharply.

"I'm a vampire," Lucena answered.

"That is like saying, 'I am a body,'" Amstrass snapped. "Which I am, but I'm more than that besides. You are not just a vampire, you're a *lamphramine* vampire."

"What is a *lamphramine*?" Lucena asked, coldly.

Amstrass stared at her in unmasked astonishment. "You mean you were not told? Well, of course you weren't. Those dream lords always play things close to their purely metaphorical hearts... but you should have been able to recognize the signs. You really are ignorant by choice, aren't you?"

Since this was more or less true, Lucena chose not to reply.

"*Well?*" Amstrass asked. She had, Lucena decided, a horrible way of saying that word. It demanded an answer, and implied that the lack of that answer was the recipient's fault. "Do you know which one your maker is? Dreamsad? Badman? Highdark?" When Lucena looked bewildered at each name Amstrass sighed. "Fearbright?" she offered. Lucena shook her head.

Then, "It *can't* have been Madgrin," she said, looking intently at Lucena. Lucena did nothing. No nod, no shake of the head. She glared back at Amstrass and defiantly sipped her blood.

"It *was* Madgrin," said Amstrass, her eyes growing wide. They were so pale they shone in the darkness. She finished the contents of her glass, pulled a chair out of the air, and sat down. She rested her elbows on the table and her chin on her hands, all the while regarding Lucena with great interest.

"Well, you're not very pretty, and you haven't got a killer's instinct," she said. "But you seem brave, and you've got a warrior's heart. I suppose that must count for something. Maybe Madgrin can see more than I." She frowned. "What's your name?"

"I am Lucena Clarian Ashmoor," Lucena said, with great firmness.

Amstrass shook her head. "Names given in life are transient; they die with our human bodies. Where are you from?"

Lucena was unmoved. "My name is Lucena Clarian Ashmoor, and I will answer to any of those three. It does not matter where I came from."

Amstrass's eyes narrowed, and the writing on her face wriggled into angular spikes. But she did not move, and the corners of her mouth perked up in something resembling a smile.

"Very well, Lucena Clarian Ashmoor," she said, showing all her teeth as she spoke. "I have a *proposition* for you."

A strange tale began to circulate among the people of Thamber that spring. It told of two ghostly women, one tall and beautiful who rode a blood-red stag, and one short and ugly who rode a shadowy, black mare, who could be found wandering in the mountains at night, but who always disappeared with the first breath of dawn.

CHAPTER 15: *The Two Vampires*

Some said it was Grúnemalder, the wood witch, and her princess-daughter. Others said they were the ghosts of a fae queen and her retainer. Still others thought they were an elfin knight and her squire gone adventuring in the human world. None of them suspected vampires, and Amstrass found this most amusing.

As it turned out, Amstrass found a great many things amusing, often in a darkly humorous way Lucena didn't think was funny at all. Still, she made interesting company, even if Lucena sometimes regretted her choice.

"Come with me," Amstrass had said. "Travel by my side for a year and a day. Let us be companions; I will show you the ways of the world which your dream lord never could. I will tell you all my secrets, and in return you will tell me yours."

Lucena was not particularly tempted by this offer. She wondered aloud what Amstrass would do if she refused.

"Oh, I'll chain you to me by your collarbone," she said pleasantly, "and take you with me anyway."

Lucena had given in and agreed. Almost immediately afterwards she had been uncertain if she had done the right thing, and went stumping off through the forest to sulk.

She had found Madgrin waiting for her at an outcropping of rock, leaning against its side with his arms folded. He looked up and smiled when he saw her, and Lucena realized how different smiles could be. His was full of humor and delight, and after all of Amstrass's grimaces that passed for smiles it was a wondrous relief. And not until she saw him, leaning casually against the mossy boulder, did Lucena realize just how nervous she had been.

"Did I do wrong?" she asked fretfully. "It did not seem that I had much of a choice."

Madgrin shrugged. "That remains to be seen," he said, but he did not seem particularly worried. "You can learn a lot from Amstrass, if you remember to ask questions. I think it will present an interesting challenge for you. And for her."

Lucena was uncertain about this, but she said nothing. Something that Amstrass had told her was digging at the back of her mind and refused to go away.

"Maker?"

"Yes, *la flein?*"

"Amstrass said you put an enchantment—no, a *compulsion* on me. The thing that puts me to sleep every morning, and causes me to wake from hunger in the evening. Only it's not on me anymore. Only I act like it is. Are her words true?"

Madgrin smiled ruefully. "She is half right," he said. "There was a compulsion on you, but I did not put it there. It was a . . . side effect. Truth to tell, it wore off many years ago, but you seem to have been more comfortable continuing your usual . . . habits"

Compared to all that had happened in the last twenty-four hours this new revelation barely shocked Lucena at all. In fact, she found it amusing.

"So you're saying," she said, "that all those years of dropping into a dead faint at sunup, all those evenings going blind with thirst, I was just doing that out of *habit?*"

"Habits can be strong," Madgrin pointed out. "Though I think now would be a prudent time to work on breaking that one. Amstrass is clever, but she is not always concerned with the safety of her companions."

They stood in silence for some minutes, listening to the gentle whisper of the mountain wind. Then Lucena asked: "How long since the compulsion wore off?"

Madgrin stroked his chin thoughtfully with a slender, pale finger. "It is difficult to say. But I know for certain you were well out of its sway by the time you visited the Viddengault."

This did surprise her.

Madgrin just smiled. "Strong habits," he said.

The forest was silent. To Lucena it felt that she stood in the trees, in the brambles and the pine needles, but Madgrin was someplace else entirely. Though they were close enough to touch each other, it seemed a great shadowy chasm had opened up between them, and all at once she felt very far away from the House, from Willic and Beruse and Harga and Gydda, and all the people who had ever been kind to her. There was a tugging feeling under her breastbone that ached at the thought of not seeing them again for so long, and for a moment she thought of leaping the chasm and running away with Madgrin. But that would make Amstrass angry—very angry. And though Lucena was afraid of what Amstrass might do if she really lost her temper, she *had* promised. So she resigned herself, but it was still a hard egg to swallow.

"A year and a day," she said.

"Not a long time at all, really," said Madgrin.

"I shall return to you."

"I do not doubt it."

Then, coming forward and bending almost double, he took her chin in his hand and laid a gentle kiss upon her forehead. It tingled a little, but left a pleasant, warm feeling. He turned her head to one side and whispered into her ear, "Amstrass was wrong: my heart is not metaphorical. And if you ever need to speak to me, no matter where you are, do it through yours. I hear you better that way." Then he stood up, gave her one last twinkling smile, and walked off into the darkness.

A wind rattled through the trees, and Lucena knew she was alone.

Then there had come a smashing, crunching noise as Amstrass rode up the hill, mounted on her blood-red stag. "*There* you are!" she cried, the mad glint in her eyes ablaze. "Summon your steed! The night is young, and we have ghosts to chase!"

Madgrin was right; habits *were* difficult to break. No matter how hard Lucena tried, she found herself dropping unconscious at the first light of dawn. Sometimes she managed a sort of half wakefulness, where she could not speak or think clearly, but she could move. This, Amstrass pointed out, was better than nothing, though Lucena could barely remember those times, and even then the memories were grey and vague.

CHAPTER 15: *The Two Vampires*

Amstrass, Lucena was not surprised to learn, had no such shortcomings. Her mental powers were not affected one jot by the rising and setting of the sun, and direct sunlight, the universal bane of vampires, did not even singe her. One of the earliest images Lucena was able to tease from the vague after-dawn memories was the sight of Amstrass walking angrily towards her though streaks of bright morning sunlight. As she passed from shade to light she seemed to flicker in and out of sight, for when the sunlight touched her skin it took on a luminous, translucent quality, like the wing of a bat or a fish's fin. Then she would pass into the shadows and be solid once more. Sitting and thinking this over the next evening, Lucena also remembered the angry expression on her face. Now why had she been angry?

"You were standing right next to a cliff in all your wool-headedness and blundering about like a bear with its head in a beehive." Amstrass told her when she asked.

Lucena pointed out that her mind and body did not cooperate in the morning, and that she had not known about the cliff. Amstrass sniffed. "You've no right to let it rule you so. Snap out of it."

But try as she might, Lucena did not find it so easy. She spent what felt like an eternity (though Urgolant later told her it was only a week), blundering about in the mornings after sunrise in a woolly headed cloud. Gradually, with consistent training and encouragement from her familiars, Lucena achieved a sort of cognizance, though she was always slow of thought and stiff in limb, and it would be several months before she could think clearly in the mornings. But during that first week she nearly did herself a serious injury many times, and it was with amazement that she learned that Amstrass had been her repeated savior.

"The light was coming, and you were standing there, staring at it dumbly, saying you'd lost your foot or something," Keelback told her confidentially. "So Strass"—he always called her Strass—"she picked up a boulder—yes, *that* boulder—and plunks it down right in front of you. And kept on piling them up until she had made this cave we're sitting in now. Don't believe me? Fine, ask Urgy then, she spun the webbing to catch the shadows so it would be nice and dark inside all day. See? *Tell* her, Urgy!"

Then Urgolant came and explained things as well, and then Lucena had to admit that perhaps Amstrass was not as uncaring as she seemed. Yet for the first few months that they traveled together she saw not one single act of compassion, and she began to suspect that Amstrass's heart was indeed made of hard, black coal.

During those months winter broke, and spring came slowly to the mountains of eastern Thamber. Amstrass took her up and down all the alps from Niérlind to Gell, into hidden dells and valleys and reaches of countryside. They visited several interesting places, including a Fae battlefield. This was a wide glacial valley overgrown with soft grass and moss and dotted with shattered pieces of white stone. From a distance they almost looked like bones, and Lucena said so.

"They are," Amstrass replied. "Mountain troll bones are made of stone. They acted as vanguard, and the casualties were horrendous."

"You saw?"

"Oh, yes, I stood just there." She pointed across the valley to a tumbled heap of brownish rock. Then she went on to describe the battle in enthusiastic detail, but Lucena did not attend. Thinking of trolls and fairies had reminded her of Beruse, which had made her think of home, which made her homesick, which made her sulky. She contrived to be depressed and bored, though if Amstrass noticed this change she did not appear to care. She pranced across the valley, telling how she had seen a particularly bloody engagement here, or how she had seen a troll fall there, or how she had witnessed a clash of heroes here, responding to Lucena's half-hearted "Oh's," and "Ah's," as if they were enthusiastic encouragement.

Just as grim, though not as conducive to homesickness, were the ruined castles they found. These were ancient buildings, empty of life but full to the brim with stories. Lucena and Amstrass would sit in the throne room, or the grand hall, or royal chamber, and Amstrass would tell her all the sordid details of the castle's past. These were usually fascinating, and in the more intact buildings where she was safe from the light, Lucena found herself staying up later and later into the day listening to Amstrass's tales.

One castle, however, was different. It stood on a cliff overlooking a small farming village, and was considerably less ruinous than the others. It had its chapel intact, and though the forest had grown up all around it the interior was untouched by weeds or decay. To get to it Amstrass led Lucena through trees that grew so tightly together that she had to turn sideways to squeeze between them, and when they reached the gates, they were bound shut with ivy and briars. Lucena's mind flashed back to the story of the bells in the graveyard on the hill, and how those gates had also been bound shut with briars.

So she was hardly surprised when Amstrass rapped on the gates, and with a slithering and rustling, the ivy and briars retreated of their own accord, and the gates swung open for them.

Magic rushed out like a fresh wind. In fact, anyone else might have mistaken it for a wind, but Lucena had not lived for years in an intensely magical house without developing a sensitivity to its presence. This, combined with her observation of the enchanted briars, served to put her on guard as she entered. After she had taken the time to examine the castle further she found her suspicions confirmed; the place was not ruined at all, in fact it was in such excellent condition that it almost seemed to be lived in.

Tapestries hung on the walls, warming their cold stone faces with scenes of hunts and royal processions, and carpets padded the floors. The bedchambers had beds in them, neatly made, with washbowls on the side tables. In the dining hall cups, plates and cutlery were laid out as if for a meal, with a magnificent candelabra in the center of the table.

It was this candelabra that made Lucena realize exactly what was wrong with the castle: it was lit, but the flames of the candles never wavered, never guttered, and the candles themselves never grew any shorter, or shed drips of wax onto their holders. It was as though an image of a lighted candelabra had been put there in its stead. But when Lucena put out her hand she could feel the smooth wax of the candlestick and the heat of the flame.

CHAPTER 15: *The Two Vampires*

Then she examined the plates and cups for further discrepancies between image and reality, but found none until she came upon a silver goblet with an intricate design etched into its surface. Curious, she went to pick it up to get a closer look, and found that she could not. It was not, as she had first thought, that the goblet was heavy, nor was it rooted to the table by magic: it simply slipped through her hands like a wet eel, and she could not take hold of it.

Perplexed, Lucena went back through the castle to reexamine everything: sure enough, she could not lift the tapestries to see behind them nor peel the carpets from the floor. There was hot water in the washbasins, which was warm to the touch, yet no steam rose and her hand was perfectly dry when she removed it from the basin. Similarly she could not lift the counterpanes off the beds, though she could lie on them, but they were hard and stiff, and did not give under her weight. All in all it seemed the castle was under some sort of spell that fixed it in place forever.

Lucena sat on the side of one of the beds and thought about the magic. It was old and strong, though not as old and strong as the magic in the House of Madgrin. It was not malevolent, but unbending as a cold iron bar. And unlike the magic in the House, which pervaded every inch equally, this magic was centered in a place downwards and to the left. The cellar, perhaps? Lucena got up to go find it.

It was not the cellar but the chapel. Lucena recognized the uncomfortable, prickling sensation she got around holy places, and with trepidation she approached the arched doorway. Yet when she arrived she found that the Heavenly Arrow, which usually guarded the entrance to all holy buildings, had been torn down, smashed to pieces, and the pieces scattered across the floor. Lucena didn't bother trying to see if she could pick them up. Where the Arrow had been, someone had painted another arrow, this time pointing down. The symbol of Hell. It did not give Lucena comfort, but she was able to go inside.

The room was empty and dim, save for Amstrass, who sat at the foot of the altar, a red patch in the cool grey morning. She was slumped over, and appeared to be asleep. Lucena had never seen Amstrass sleep in all their time together, so she approached cautiously. As she did so she thought she saw tears running from her eyes. Red tears, which left faint streaks across her cheeks.

Lucena stood over the sleeping form and pondered the sight of a vampire weeping blood. Eventually a rustling sound and a soft moan drew her attention away from Amstrass, and with a thrill of horror she realized the room was not empty after all.

It was a long, narrow room, typical of a chapel; there was an altar at one end on a raised dais, and along each wall were row upon row of high-backed, wooden benches. And every seat was occupied by a sleeping child.

They ranged in age from lanky youths to toddlers, with some of the latter resting on the former's laps. They were dressed in clothes of an ancient fashion, though they too varied in style and quality: some were of fine make and expensive material, while some wore little more than rags. There were robes and jerkins, trousers, dresses, and suits. The children were dark and fair; pale, freckled, and every shade of brown; some were rotund, some boney; every size, shape and color

Lucena could imagine. And they were, each and every one of them, fast asleep. Sometimes one would shift, turn their head from one side to another, or snore softly, but otherwise the place was silent as a tomb.

The strange atmosphere created by all the sleeping children, the eerie sight of Amstrass weeping tears of blood, and the haziness of morning combined to give the place a dreamlike quality, and Lucena felt a dreamlike fearlessness come over her. She leaned forward and touched Amstrass gently on the shoulder.

"Amstrass," she whispered, so as not to wake the children. "Amstrass, what happened here?"

For a moment Amstrass did not respond, and Lucena wondered if the strange sleep had extended to her as well. Then her eyes snapped open and she looked up.

They were not red or swollen or any of the things eyes are when they have been crying, and Amstrass did not look particularly taken with grief or sorrow. If anything she looked annoyed.

"What is it?" she asked sharply.

Unable to voice her thoughts, Lucena gestured at Amstrass's cheeks. Amstrass wiped a hand across her face and then stared at it in puzzlement when it came away with blood on the fingers. She frowned.

"That hasn't happened in while," she said in a low voice, almost to herself. Taking out a red silk handkerchief she carefully cleaned the rest off her face and then wiped her hands. "Did you want something, Ashmoor?"

Seeing that Amstrass was not gripped in some paroxysm of sadness, Lucena took a step back and gestured at the rows of sleeping children. "What is this place?"

"This is the chapel," Amstrass said, giving her a bland look.

"I mean the children," Lucena said. "What happened to them?"

Amstrass looked around as if she had only just noticed that they were surrounded by sleeping bodies. She shrugged. "Nothing. Nothing happened to them. They came here, that is all."

"But why are they asleep?"

"So they can dream," Amstrass said. She glanced at one of the high chapel windows, where from outside the light was growing stronger. "It's getting late," she said. "There is no shade here, you can sleep in the crypt today."

For some reason the sight of so many sleeping children had quite cured Lucena of any desire to sleep. She felt wide awake and energetic, so even though she followed Amstrass down to the crypt she peppered her with questions all the way.

"How did they come here?" she asked as they passed though the dining hall. "Did *you* bring them?"

"I help," Amstrass said. "But they come on their own, sometimes."

"How long will they sleep?"

"Until the enchantment is broken."

"When will that be?"

Amstrass paused at the head of the stairs that led down to the crypt. She seemed troubled by the question, as though she were not certain of the answer. "When Dream lets them go," she said at length.

CHAPTER 15: *The Two Vampires*

"Did you put the enchantment on them?" Lucena asked as they walked down the stairs.

Amstrass glanced back at her, smiling. "I helped," she said, and pushed open the door to the crypt.

Lucena did not go through. She stood opposite Amstrass in the tiny passage and braced herself against the wall. "I'm not sleeping down there," she said flatly.

Amstrass raised an eyebrow. "Why not?"

"I don't want to sleep in this place."

Amstrass laughed. "You nincompoop, the spell only affects humans," and she grabbed Lucena by the collar and pushed her through the door, locking it behind her.

The crypt was underground, and there were no torches. It was black as pitch, and even Lucena's vampire eyes had difficulty seeing. It smelled of dust and moldy cloth, and in the distance there was the sound of water dripping. It was also cold as the belly of a cave.

Lucena sat on the step by the door and prepared to be thoroughly miserable all day, for she was certain this was the day she would never sleep. And she did spend what felt like several hours huddled against the cold wall, cursing Amstrass and cursing enchantments.

Then, out of the dark and the quiet, she heard the sound of footfalls coming closer. They were soft, and accompanied by a faint clicking sound. But not until the great shaggy shape loomed into sight did Lucena recognize Amstrass's hound. It came and sat at her feet, and she felt its warm, moist breath on her face.

"Little Vampira cannot sleep?" it asked. Its voice was rumbling, with a hint of a growl, not unlike Harga's, but stunted in a way that suggested it was not accustomed to human speech. But it sounded sympathetic, and she answered readily.

"I don't want to."

"Little Vampira is frightened?" it suggested.

Lucena glared at it. That is, she glared at the lumpish patch of blackness at her feet that was darker than the rest of the dark room. But the dog was unperturbed.

"I tell a story, maybe? Hmm? Will story help?"

When Lucena still said nothing it whined and nosed at her knee.

"Am I allowed to ask you questions?" Lucena asked.

"Always allowed to ask questions. I not always able to answer, but asking is good. It helps you learn."

"All right then. How did all those children get there?"

More whining. Lucena thought the dog would not answer, but after a time it spoke again. It said, "They were unhappy. They ran away from home and came to this castle, because they thought fairies lived here. But Vampira and I were here instead. But Vampira likes children, and she wanted them to be happy. So she put a spell on the castle to keep them safe, and to keep them always children. So they sleep, and they dream of playing in the forest, in the gardens and in the castle. They dream of feasting and games and of being happy. Maybe one day they wake and must grow up, but not for long time. Vampira's magic is strong, it lasts.

"Is Little Vampira better now?"

"Hmm," was all Lucena said. But she was grateful to the dog for answering her question, so she added: "Thank you. Perhaps you could tell me a story now, if you like."

So the dog told her one. It was not what she expected. It concerned an acorn that wanted to be a tree and tricked a squirrel into planting it instead of eating it. But it soothed her sore feelings, and without realizing it Lucena fell into a soft slumber, sleeping soundly until the evening, when she awoke with a start as Amstrass opened the door she had been leaning against, and she fell over backwards.

They left the castle three nights later.

"Why?" Lucena asked as they rode through the dark, dripping wood. "Why collect children?"

Amstrass gave her an odd look: it was full of sharp edges, but her soul made the shape of tears pouring down her cheek.

"I like children," she said, with leathery softness.

In the silence that followed Lucena remembered those first seven children, lost so long ago out a tower window on a cold winter night.

She did not ask any more.

All through the summer and into autumn they worked their way west, out of Niérlind, through Gell, along the southern border of Hyberia and across Ossylvania, until they reached the southern border of Svenia just as the first winter storm arrived. It was long and cold, and left the world under a heavy blanket of treacherous snow and ice. This was of no concern for Amstrass, however; her red stag could walk as easily upon snow as upon turf, and of course Intok simply took the snow as an excuse to fly, carrying Lucena clear over the frosted treetops.

The nights were bitterly cold, and at times during their long rides Lucena felt like her nose and ears would fall off. She was obliged to borrow a great many scarves and wraps from Amstrass (who handily pulled them all out of the air) so that she looked more like a bundle of mismatched knitting than a person. By contrast Amstrass didn't seem to feel the cold; she always wore the same high-necked red dress which, though it covered her from wrist to toe, was made of such thin wool that it was hardly warm enough for the freezing Svenian nights. These grew even colder as winter deepened and they traveled further and further into the northern mountains, which were at once breathtakingly beautiful in the moonlight and terribly bleak and forbidding.

In late November they came to a small village nestled deep in the mountains below a craggy castle. It was a lonely place, yet some houses bore lights and there was a fiddle player on the street corner by the only inn. He was bundled up as thickly as Lucena, and his violin sounded plaintive in the empty streets. He nodded at them, and Amstrass dropped some coins at his feet as they passed. As he

CHAPTER 15: *The Two Vampires*

tipped his hat, Lucena caught a glimpse of bloodshot eyes and a pale beaky nose before he tucked into his fiddle once more and resumed his mournful wailing.

"Who was he?" Lucena asked as they left the village and started up the winding road to the castle.

"A vampire," Amstrass said carelessly. "An old one. They are all old vampires here."

"And this place is?"

Amstrass shot Lucena a piercing glance. "This is Amstrass. My old home."

Side by side, the two vampires rode up to the forbidding castle, and Lucena felt colder than ever.

They passed through a gate halfway through the process of falling down, and entered a mean, stone courtyard choked in snow. Here they dismounted, and Amstrass forced open the ice-bound door.

Inside was as great a contrast as ever Lucena could have imagined. The derelict entrance gave way to a grand hall with columns of sculpted marble and an arched ceiling with a cloudy night sky painted on it. Their footsteps echoed on the polished stone floor as they walked across and, by the time they reached the far side of the hall, sounded as though an army had marched through it. Beyond was a staircase, and here was another drastic change: in times past the staircase must have been as grand as the hall, but now it had fallen into decay and the steps were treacherously cracked.

This harsh juxtaposition of opulent splendor and utter ruin proved to be a recurring feature throughout the castle. Amstrass had a suite of rooms near the top of the west tower that were fit for a queen, but you had to watch your step as you left because the stairway was pockmarked with holes and loose stones. Then you rounded a corner and were faced with a cascade of steps clothed in rich velvety carpet, and illuminated by ranks of candles in ornate holders. This would, in turn, lead to a room in which the ceiling had caved in, and it was nothing but heaps of rubble bathed in winter starlight.

Once, when Lucena went exploring, she thought she saw Madgrin standing in the middle of the wreckage, as if waiting for her. She went to him filled with glad surprise, abruptly cut off when she realized it was just a slab of rock that had fallen at an odd angle, and the glittering lights she had thought were his eyes turned out to be nothing more than moonlight reflected on some bits of glass embedded in the stone.

The encounter put her out of temper for several days. It had made her realize just how much she missed her old home. She sat up in her little room near the cellar late into the day trying to reach Madgrin. She tried with her mind, and when that didn't work, with her heart, as he had asked her. That didn't work either. No matter how she tried she ended up feeling ridiculous, and she wondered how on earth she was supposed to use her heart, when it didn't even beat. In the end she gave up and went to ask Urgolant for advice.

Urgolant was in the castle library, which she had discovered minutes after their arrival. It was a modest collection compared to the one at the House of Madgrin, but the room itself was extraordinary. It was a condensation of the ruinous grandeur of Castle Amstrass, being comprised of a checkerboard of rich, luxurious tiles containing polished wooden bookcases, walls draped in tapestries and richly carpeted floors, and squares where piles of books were stacked one upon the other on bare stones, heaped against cracked walls that barely supported the crumbling ceiling. It was as though the ruins and the riches had minds of their own and were determined to fight it out here. But Urgolant had a different theory, which she began expounding upon the moment Lucena found her.

"It is the books themselves," she said. "See here, all these," she led Lucena to a warm, homely tile and swept a foot across a shelf of books gleaming with care and attention. "These are all histories, mythos compilations, fairytales, that sort of thing. But these—" she scurried around a corner to where the dust was caked thick upon the haphazard piles of books, and starlight shone down through cracks in the walls. "These are all instructions. Guidebooks. Magic books. You see, this one is bleeding, that one is glowing. There is one here somewhere that I cannot open. These books *want* this place to be in ruins."

"Why would they want that?" Lucena asked. She was getting tired of ruins and was feeling homesick.

Urgolant worked her mouth feelers up and down uncertainly. "I think raw magic likes ruined things. It gives it something to build on. I read that in a book once too. There is a certain magic that can only exist in death and destruction and ruin."

Urgolant meant it kindly, but it did nothing to improve Lucena's mood. Too grumpy to even voice the query which had brought her, she went away to one of the not-ruined patches and sat down with her back against a bookcase. She closed her eyes and breathed in the smell of old bindings, dust and paper. If she pretended very hard it was almost like being back in the House's library, but there was something missing. Or something different. Castle Amstrass was all hard edges, and even the air held a sharpness to it that never let her forget where she was.

Perceptive as ever, Urgolant came crawling over and crouched beside her, going through the titles of the books on the shelf behind them. "There's a copy of *Elegy for an Elf*," she remarked in a conversational tone. "That's interesting. And here's the first volume of the *Rat-Wizard Chronicles*, but you'd need a magnifying glass to read that. Oh, would you look at this? She has a copy of *Vampires: A History* . . . " and she trailed on, expounding upon Amstrass's collection, most of which she had already read back at the House.

But Lucena's mind had stopped at *Vampires: A History*. That one brought back such memories (Willic reading it aloud in the kitchen; Madgrin kindly recommending it to her) that although she was no fonder of the material than she ever had been she suddenly desired to read it, if only for the memories it stirred.

"Hold a moment," she said, interrupting. "Can I see her copy of *A History*?"

"Certainly, certainly," Urgolant said. "It's right here," and she plucked it neatly off the shelf and handed the volume to Lucena. This copy was well worn, with raw places in the leather binding and several pages coming loose. Lucena took it carefully up to one of the nice rooms with good chairs, and began to read.

CHAPTER 15: *The Two Vampires*

At first she read only the parts she already knew, since it was not knowledge she desired but familiarity. But as she went on she found herself more absorbed in the book, for unlike the copy at the House, this one had been annotated.

These notes were in rough black ink and a sharp, jagged hand that Lucena knew could only belong to Amstrass. Some of the notes were so hastily scribbled they were illegible, but others (particularly the short ones) she could make out with little difficulty.

The first one that caught her eye was scrawled in the margins of the section devoted to the deep and abiding hatred between werewolves and vampires, and how their common heritage as former humans set them apart. The note was only two words: "NOT TRUE."

Lucena remembered how the magician's book had said that Amstrass's terrible vengeance on the werewolves had sparked the vendetta between the two races. She knew that *A History* was old, but was Amstrass yet older? Intrigued, she read on.

The notes came thick and fast now, and with practice Lucena became adept at deciphering them. Eventually she came to read the notes before the manuscript, and then the notes alone.

"DIFFERENT VAMPIRES ARE VULNERABLE TO DIFFERENT THINGS," read the note above the section devoted to religious artifacts and their effect on vampires. And beside the heading of effective weapons against vampires: "HAWTHORN STINGS MORE."

Often the notes left Lucena wishing Amstrass had written more, but she could not get up the courage to go and ask in person.

However, some entries begged explanation, like the one above the entry for sunlight: "IT DOESN'T ALWAYS WORK." But Lucena kept plugging along, now entertained by Amstrass's minor vendetta against the author. Inspired, she began comparing the firsthand knowledge she had of hunting vampires against the facts in the book.

Then she got to the last quarter, and found it wasn't there. The pages had been torn out, and on the inside of the back cover was written a single word: "RUBBISH."

Lucena was dismayed. It had just gotten to the point where the author examined the various origins of vampires, and she had been looking forward to reading Amstrass's opinions of his disturbing and melodramatic theories.

It was morning by then, and she was forced to leave the little tower room. Whatever Amstrass said about sunlight, Lucena knew she felt hot and feverish as it drew close. So she retired to her room for the day, but the next night curiosity drove her in search of Amstrass, and answers.

Amstrass was nowhere to be found in the castle, but her dog was sitting by the door: a big shaggy black mess with three red eyes. It saw Lucena coming and thumped its tail.

"I'm looking for Amstrass," Lucena told it. "Can you take me to her?"

The dog thumped its tail once again and nosed the door open. Lucena followed it out into the frigid night. The sky was clear, and the hard icy snow gleamed in the starlight; a set of footprints led away from the gates and disappeared into a gathering of trees that marked the outskirts of the great wood that surrounded the castle. The world was silent save for the distant whining of the violin down in the village. The dog set off after the lone tracks, and Lucena followed. In her hands she carried the crippled copy of *Vampires: A History*.

Amstrass had not gone far into the wood. She was standing in a small clearing, statuesque in the cold night. In the starlight her red gown was almost black, and her hair was frosted silver. The writing on her face that was her soul glowed faintly when it was cast in shadow.

Slowly she turned to look at them. Her expression was blank. But she was also, Lucena reminded herself, a real and solid person. She swallowed down the lump of fear in her throat, and went boldly up to her and held out the book. Amstrass looked at it unlovingly.

"It's missing some pages," Lucena said, by way of beginning.

"You came all the way out here to tell me that?"

Lucena was silent, but she held the book tightly in both hands.

"I know it's missing pages," Amstrass said. "I tore them out myself, and burned them."

"Why?"

"Because they were *wrong*."

Lucena felt a strange wash of disappointment and relief. But a little part of her remained cynical: Madgrin had wanted her to read this book. Orrus had wanted her to read this book. That had been so, and it followed that there must have been something in it worth knowing.

Amstrass must have read her feelings from her confused face, for she gently pried the book out of Lucena's hands. She paged through it, pausing now and again when something caught her eye.

"You read it?" she asked.

Lucena nodded.

"And now you want to know where vampires came from."

Lucena was silent. It had not been a question, which was just as well. The feelings that swirled inside her were too conflicted to allow her to answer.

"It's an understandable interest," Amstrass said. "Every being capable of it desires to know why they are here. But . . . I think you already know why *you* are here."

Lucena shook her head. She fiercely, definitely, certainly did not know what had made her. It was a mystery, and she liked it that way. But she was teetering on the brink of the cliff of her knowledge, and Amstrass was behind her, crowding her towards it.

"Don't be ridiculous," Amstrass said, her mouth working its way into a grin. "You've met them, spoken with them. You were made by them. You're an *original*."

That caught her off guard. "An original?"

Amstrass tossed the book from hand to hand. "An original vampire," she said. "Rootstock. Wellspring. Missing link. All vampires descend from people like you, in one way or another. The blood gets diluted, the powers are hidden,

CHAPTER 15: *The Two Vampires*

but it's all there. I had to dig find mine, but in you they're right at the surface. In a way, you're less human than me."

"But you're a *vampire*," Lucena blurted out.

Amstrass shrugged. "A vampire is just a human given an unusual choice and put in strange situations. Maybe that's all you would have been if he had just let you alone. But no. You've been too long on the edge of his world, it'll only take a step—or two—and *whoof!*" She threw up her hands.

Lucena felt cold, and not just from the night air.

Amstrass was smiling, but inwardly, as if laughing at herself. "I could have gone over to their side," she said. "I nearly did, once. You need a soul, and I had mine. But there's a freedom in humanity that they don't have. I didn't want to give it up. Still don't." She looked piercingly at Lucena. "Why haven't you simply asked *him* yet?" she demanded.

Lucena shook her head, and mirrored what Amstrass had done with her hands. "Whoof," she said. "Like you said. I'm afraid."

Amstrass gave her a tired look. "There's nothing for you to be afraid of. You've been living in their bosom for years. With *Madgrin*, of all people. You won't get any trouble from them, not if you're with him."

Lucena opened her mouth to explain that that wasn't what she was afraid of at all, but it was no use.

"The lamphra were never the enemy of humanity, anyway," Amstrass said. "In a way, they have been their greatest allies."

"Allies?"

"They walk the silver line between the conscious and the unconscious. Dreams and promises gather around them; they are the magic of the night, of mystery and inspiration. Lucena, do you know what Dream is?"

"What?" Lucena blinked, confused.

"Dream," said Amstrass. The way she said it, Lucena was certain she did not mean the mundane flights of fancy and sleeping visions most people meant when they used that word.

She shook her head.

"It is one of the four Great Realms, along with Matter, Demos and Ether, and between them flows the Wider Realm: Faerie, the Dragon Lands, all the Heavens and the Hells. Every afterlife you've ever heard promised, and a few others besides."

Amstrass paused, to see if this enlightened her audience. When she found it had not, she continued. "Matter is where we are." She stamped the snowy ground to illustrate. "The tangible and the finite; the place where time and space run straight, and life and death are separate.

"Demos is where the old demons come from. I don't know its rules. Nobody does. But I think they must be very different from ours. I think that is why you don't see the old demons in this world anymore; the Realms have grown apart over time. But there used to be demons everywhere; before humans, before the dragons, before life as we know it; first there were demons.

"Then there is Ether, and Ether is everywhere. Have you ever heard the saying *tree speaks to wind*, or some other such nonsense? Well, Ether is where that happens. Everything has thoughts in Ether, and everything just is. Time means something else there. I hear there are some parts of Faerie that are close to Ether, but the truth is Ether is always close, just beneath the surface."

"And Dream?" Lucena prompted, not seeing where this was going.

"Dream is what binds them all together," said Amstrass, her soul flashing on her cheek. "Dream is where gods go when they die. And to be born. Dream is where the ideas and thoughts of all knowing life arise. Dream is where fear has a body and hope is a river. Dream is all the tales you've ever heard and all the ones you haven't. There is even a place in Dream called the Sea of Stories, where every story ever told is preserved in its one island of reality. Some of the older stories have several islands stacked one on top of the other, like stones, because there are so many different versions."

"Have you ever been to Dream?"

"Once." Amstrass's eyes were shining, but in a soft, wistful way. "But I can't go back there. The lamphra aren't fond of me, you know. My story should have ended a long time ago, but I decided to go on. That is how they get you; once your story is complete they can take you away. So I keep making more stories. More and more. I'm the only vampire that has figured that out, so far. All the rest disappear eventually. But I remain; more than a vampire, less than a lamphra; still human. I like it this way. There is a magic in being human that they don't have."

"The lamphra created the vampires," Lucena said, realization dawning.

Amstrass shot her a long-suffering look. "Yes. They don't follow the normal rules of life and death, so they can reanimate a dead thing, even bring a soul back and remake it with some of their powers. It doesn't always take, but humans mostly respond well.

"We get some of their powers, and weaknesses: lamphra are mostly feelings and ideas, which are easier to shape in darkness. That's why they disappear in sunlight, and why vampires will often be killed by it; we lose the power that keeps us in existence. But we also got a little mixed up in the process.

"Lamphra feed off half-made dreams and ideas. They absorb them from thinking minds, shuffle them around a bit, and then send them out again as inspiration. They feed off the *process*, you see. But vampires feed on life. We, who are bereft of physical life, must feed on the life of others. And we don't give life back; we can't. Lamphra are creatures of dreams, but vampires are creatures of nightmares. That is the first twist. Then, we *proliferate*."

"Proliferate?"

"A lamphra can make a vampire, but so a vampire can also make another vampire. I can't imagine why the lamphra started making vampires in the first place. Companions? Slaves? Entertainment? I don't know. But once vampires started making more and more of ourselves we began to cause problems for the world. We are walking death, and death does not mix well with life. There is a balance in this realm, and we tipped that balance. We are still tipping it, and ... bad things found their way into this world because of us. Because we and death walk in life where we do not belong. That is why the lamphra hunt us. That is why they must hunt us. That is why even I—" Amstrass broke off. She had become

CHAPTER 15: *The Two Vampires*

excited by her speech and was pacing to and fro. Clenching her fists she shook her head as if to clear it.

Lucena came forward and put a hand on her arm. "I understand now," she said. And she did, though she was not sure she wanted to. Now it was clear that Amstrass had not pushed her off that cliff, but merely drawn aside a veil so Lucena could see what lay beyond. And far from it being a gaping, dark chasm, it was as though she beheld an entirely new country where before there had been only void.

"Come," Lucena said. "You have answered all my questions candidly, it is time I returned the favor."

Amstrass gave her a quizzical look, as if she doubted this, but she walked back to the castle with Lucena. Once there she led the way up to her own rooms, which were at the top of a crumbling tower filled with bats—all hibernating. The rooms themselves were the height of luxury. Amstrass and Lucena sat on velvet-lined armchairs with their feet on a thick Dahlsan carpet. Amstrass provided them with glasses of brandy and blood, which were their winter rations. Amstrass drank her glass down in a moment, but Lucena only stared at hers. She rolled the fluid around in the cup, watching it slide down the side in long red legs.

"Where are you from, originally?" Amstrass asked at length.

"My family lived in Haywitch," Lucena answered, "but I spent most of my life in a girls' school at Munsmire."

"How did you become a vampire?"

Lucena told her. About Miss Smael. About the girls in the dormitory. About the vampires in the hall, clawing their way through the door. About the battle, and about Madgrin. Amstrass said nothing, asked nothing; made no comment. She sat with her chin resting in her hands and watched Lucena like a dog who is fascinated yet puzzled by what it sees. Her soul twisted across her face in lazy curlicues, and her hair drooped.

When Lucena had finished she asked, "Where did he take you?"

So Lucena told her about the House, and about Willic, Gydda, Rhyse, Grimmach, Cobbin, Harga, Soloma, Beruse and Orrus. She told her about the living rooms, about the vast grounds with hidden distances, about the river that ran in a circle and about the roc colony. A part of her was astonished that she would share so much information with a woman who, if not an outright enemy of her maker, was in no way a person to be trusted so. Yet as she spoke of her old home and all her old friends a great yearning washed over her, and she recalled every memory of her home, no matter how small, to try and assuage the pain. All that happened, however, was what had begun as a dull ache below her collarbone migrated down and to the left and intensified. It felt like someone had put a hard, cold stone inside her breast, and something was tugging at it, trying to pull it free.

When Amstrass asked what she did in the House of Madgrin, Lucena ended up telling her more about the funny little quirks of everyday life than about the exciting hunts with Beruse. She missed those too, but more acutely she missed Willic and his catlike ways, reading books together in the kitchen with Gydda, or the long night walks with Harga across the grounds. She missed Cobbin and his misguided worrying. She missed looking out the windows in the north hall. She even missed Soloma, in all her dry, sarcastic ways. She missed the subtle smell of wet grass and secrets and old, unopened books. She missed everything about her old home, and wanted it all back so much it hurt.

Then Amstrass asked her about Madgrin. She asked it in the same hard, direct way she had asked all the other questions, but she gave Lucena a sideways glance after she said it, as though she wasn't sure of Lucena's reaction.

Lucena did nothing at first. The hard, cold ache had suddenly gone soft and turned to bitter longing, and she couldn't move for the pain of it. At length she raised her head and began to speak.

"Have you ever had that heavy sort of feeling when you're falling asleep when you really are asleep but still awake enough to know it?"

Amstrass frowned, then nodded.

"That's my Maker," Lucena said. It gave her a thrill to say those words again, and she went on. "He's kind. He's never angry, or harsh, or cruel. But he's frightening. He looks like a shadow with a skull for a face if you see him from a distance. He has a straight nose and blue shadows below his brow, and when he's very interested or happy his eyes glitter. Otherwise they are dark, you see. Black as night, deep as the sky. His hands are long and slender, not bony or knobby, and they're very strong. He has a heart, too. You wouldn't know right away to look at him, but if you put your head right up against his chest you can hear it . . . beating . . ."

Something wet rolled down Lucena's cheek, and to her embarrassment she found herself crying. Hastily she wiped at the tears with the back of her hand, but when it came away she saw it was stained with blood. She stared at it. She was still weeping, too; she could feel the tears welling up in her eyes and streaming down her face. Oddly enough the only thing she thought was *Bother, now I shall ruin Amstrass's nice chair.*

Then Amstrass reached over and handed her a large handkerchief. There was a look in her face that was not quite pity, not quite embarrassment, and a good deal of sadness. It confused Lucena, but she took the handkerchief gratefully and buried her face in it.

They sat for some time in silence while Lucena tried to stop the flow of bloody tears, and Amstrass asked no more questions. When at last the torrent had abated Amstrass got up and went to one of the high windows, where she stood surveying the silent winter night. Then she laughed, a sharp, bitter laugh that held no humor, and gestured at Lucena.

"You should go," she said, turning with a sad smile on her face.

Lucena rubbed at her eyes, which were very hot and puffy, and gave Amstrass a confused look.

"You may leave," Amstrass clarified. "I release you from our bargain. Go home."

Still Lucena stared. She could not quite believe what she was hearing, since it had been exactly what she was wishing for. She stood up.

"I don't understand."

CHAPTER 15: *The Two Vampires*

"Neither do I. Not exactly," Amstrass admitted. "I had planned to keep you here all winter. It gets lonely, you see. But I think you should return to your maker."

All at once the cold homesick ache came back, and it was all Lucena could do not to run from the room that instant—down the treacherous stairs, out into the snow, to find her way back home by any means she could think of.

But she stayed a little longer. She had grown familiar with Amstrass during their time together, and unreasonable though it was, she knew she would miss her. And it was all so sudden; it took a little getting used to.

"I'm afraid I have not been sufficiently helpful," she said. "You have told me a great many things I needed to be told, and in return I have bored you with trivial matters."

Amstrass waved a hand dismissively. "I told you my secrets, you offered to tell me yours not knowing that you had none." She pointed to the door. "Go."

Still Lucena stayed. "Thank you," she said.

Amstrass looked at her sharply, almost as though she had been insulted. It made Lucena smile.

"Perhaps we will meet again sometime, and I will have secrets to tell you then," she offered.

"Ha," said Amstrass. "Vampires rarely get along. Next time I expect we shall hate each other and come to blows. But you know how to reach me." She turned and wandered off into the other room, out of sight behind a bookshelf and a large embroidered chair.

"Goodbye," Lucena told the empty air, and left.

A strange tale began to circulate among the people of Thamber that spring.

CHAPTER 16:

Beyond the Teeth of Dream

THE CRUMBLING, MAGNIFICENT HALLS echoed with Lucena's footsteps as she pelted down from Amstrass's tower, the sheer joy at the prospect of going home driving clean out of her mind the problem of how she was going to get there. It wasn't until she was out on the snow-covered drive that the reality of the situation sank in, and she slowed to a contemplative trudge through the white drifts.

Going home had felt like an easy thing to do when she was not allowed to do it. Now that it had been given to her as an option, however, Lucena discovered that she had no ready means of getting out of Amstrass's cold, harsh world, and back into her own comfortable, mysterious one.

Keelback and Urgolant, who had joined her as she was was running out of the castle, now clustered around her; Urgolant walking carefully through the snow, and Keelback twisting through the air above them. Intok, as always, was a black, horse-shaped smear stretched on the ground.

"We could use the Labyrinth," Keelback suggested, when they had gotten around the first twist in the road, and the castle was lost behind a dark cliff.

"No," Urgolant said. She was having difficulty with the snow, and it put her out of temper.

"How *would* we do that?" Lucena asked, taking a step and sinking up to her knee.

"Harga told me, once," Keelback explained. "He told me that all labyrinths are connected to the one at home, and if you get lost in one maze you can come out there!"

"But how are we to find a maze here?" Lucena asked.

"We could make one," Keelback suggested. "Harga did say *all* the mazes, so I would think that includes the ones you make yourself."

Lucena and Urgolant exchanged glances. They were both tired of trudging through the snow. Lucena glanced back at her shadow, and she saw Intok snort and nod in agreement.

"Could you make a labyrinth for us?" she asked Keelback.

"Absolutely," Keelback replied, his crest frilling with importance.

So when they reached a part of the road where the snow had formed a good, wide drift, Lucena and Urgolant stood back while Keelback traced a labyrinth in the snow with his tail. It was a very good maze, albeit a bit wobbly, save the fact that the path was a mere scratch in the snow and impossible to get lost in.

Lucena eyed it skeptically, but she did not want to criticize Keelback after all his hard work. So after he had finished she set off along his line-path, carefully putting one foot in front of the other so as to keep strictly to the path. She heard Keelback and Urgolant scramble to follow her, with Urgolant snapping that Keelback must stay on the ground for this to work.

At first it seemed utterly ridiculous. Lucena carefully stepped along the groove in the snow, and all around her the silent pine trees watched them scornfully.

"Think of home," suggested Urgolant. "Think of the *House*. It probably wants us back, and will help us if it can."

This made sense, in the nonsensical way of things with the House of Madgrin. Lucena pictured it as best she could: its shadowy bulk and shifting face, and its rooms full of candlelight and secrets.

She remained firmly rooted on the rough path drawn in a drift of snow.

"Think of dreams," said Urgolant. "Think of Madgrin."

So Lucena thought of dreams, and of her maker. Not only how she knew him, but what she knew of him.

What was Madgrin?

The feeling of falling to sleep when you are just awake enough to know it.

And with a feeling much like falling, the harsh world of the cold, snow-covered forest slipped aside and she entered an ethereal, blue world.

"Hey, wait for us!" she heard Keelback cry, and she was back in the snowy trench. The stars were sharp above her head.

"Hush!" she heard Urgolant snap. "You're distracting her!"

Lucena shut her eyes and concentrated on that ethereal blue world, like one does on a fleeting dream, while at the same time trying to relax her mind. To relax her own hold on the tangible world.

With a jerk she felt her foot go through the crust of snow, but when she looked up she was no longer on the drawing of a maze Keelback had made with his tail, on a road through a forbidding winter wood, but in a low tunnel made apparently of ice.

There was shouting and protests above her as her companions arrived, Urgolant landing in a heap of legs next to her, and Keelback clinging to the walls before sliding sedately to the ground.

Lucena inspected their new surroundings cautiously at first, and when they did not dissolve into the winter forest, with more intensity. The tunnel was not carved, as it would have been if humans had made it, but smooth and clean, like something had melted a path through it. There was a ragged hole in the ceiling where Keelback and Urgolant had broken through, and ahead the ice glinted with reflected light from some far distant place.

Lucena stepped carefully, testing the icy floor. It was slippery, but firm, and made a pleasant change from the thick snow. Putting one hand on the wall to steady herself she began to walk slowly forward.

Keelback loved it in the ice tunnel. He slipped and slid about, giving little squeals of delight that echoed off the walls. Lucena and Urgolant crept along after him at a more sedate pace, with several setbacks when they came up against rises in the tunnel. Time and again they were obliged to use Keelback as a living ladder, which thoroughly ruined his fun, and he would dart off again as soon as they were finished with him. Lucena had entertained the idea of riding him, but

CHAPTER 16: *Beyond the Teeth of Dream*

she had the strongest feeling that the dreamlike magic would not work properly unless they each walked the path themselves.

All the while the light was growing stronger, and after what felt like miles, the slippery ice gave way to wet rocks and stone which, though less slick, were still treacherous. They were loose and moved about unexpectedly when you trod on them, but Lucena and Urgolant greeted the change with relief.

The rock tunnel was wet; water dripped from the ceiling and pooled on the floor, and all the rocks shone with reflected moonlight that filtered in through cracks in the ceiling. Then they rounded a corner and Lucena saw before them a shining arch of white light, and it took her a few moments to realize they had reached the end of the tunnel.

They emerged onto a flat, grassy field. The air was warm and filled with the smell of wet plants, which stretched on around them as far as the eye could see. The sky was black; there were no stars, only the lone white moon hanging directly above them. In the distance, against the black sky, Lucena thought she could see the blue silhouette of a mountain ridge, and a grey smudge of cloud.

A gentle wind blew across the grass, but other than that all was still and silent. Keelback held no appreciation for it.

"Where do we go from *here*?" he screeched. But his voice was quiet and small, dwarfed by the size of the landscape.

Urgolant looked like she would have liked to scold him, but she had no more idea than he. They all turned around, looking for a path, but there was only the even grass and the black, bleak sky. There was not even a tunnel mouth to show where they had come from; it had disappeared into the earth.

Finally Lucena looked down at her feet, to where her shadow crouched, and Intok's glowing eyes looked back up at her.

"What do you think, Intok?" she asked.

Intok surged out of the ground with a rush. She sniffed the grass, snorted, and tossed her head. She trotted about for a bit and then came back. She put her big, soft nose in Lucena's face, then turned around and walked away with determined purpose.

Without a word, they all followed her.

At first it appeared Intok had picked a direction at random, and Lucena couldn't help having some doubts. Then she caught a scent on the wind that was not grass nor stale air; it was the thick, soft smell of secrets and old, unopened books, mixed with the clear scent of a lake at midnight. It was only for a moment, and nothing about the scenery had changed, but it gave her heart.

Intok walked on, over the even, level grass, and it seemed they were at it for hours. But slowly the silhouette of the mountains drew closer, and Lucena could see they were headed for a place where the mountains rose up into jagged spikes and towering spires, with deep valleys in between.

Intok drew ahead of them, her long, lunging stride easily outdistancing even Keelback. As though she walked on firm land, and they trudged through deep mud. After a while she was only a dark smear in front of them, then she was a speck in the distance, and then she disappeared into the mountains. Yet all the while Lucena thought she could hear the steady clump and thump of her hooves on grass, as though she were only a few feet away.

The grass gave way to loose sand and rocks, and there were Intok's tracks, leading straight towards the mountains. They followed them, and Lucena hoped Intok had waited, had looked around and found them gone, but the sound of her hooves went on and on, this time with a sharp clack now and then as she hit a rock, and after a time even they faded into the quiet night.

Around the time Lucena lost the steady rhythm of Intok's hoofbeats, they reached the mountains. These rose up on either side, steep and silent and black, somehow blacker than the sky. They followed Intok's tracks up a dry, sandy riverbed until they came to a cliff. Keelback quickly slithered up it, while Urgolant and Lucena climbed the treacherous face. When they reached the top he was gone, though Lucena could hear the soft whisper of his scales against the stone.

"Put your hand on me," Urgolant said.

Lucena did.

The path was clear now. It was cut out of the black rock of the mountains, and wound its way through the towering peaks.

Lucena and Urgolant walked on, side by side, into darkness. They had left the moon behind: now there was no light, and no sound but their feet on the stony path. It was the first time since she had become a vampire that Lucena had been in a place so dark she could see nothing at all, and with the darkness came all the old uncertainties. Suppose she were to slip? Or there were a rock she did not see? Or another cliff?

They slowed to a mere shuffle, and it seemed they were once again in a tunnel, this time a tunnel made of darkness. How long they were in the darkness was unknowable. Five minutes? Ten? A few hours? A day? Lucena stopped reckoning time and simply walked.

Then the thing she most feared happened. She took a misstep on a loose stone, and with a clatter she went skidding sideways. She landed sharply against a cold, dry slab of rock and lay for a while, stunned. After a minute she sat up and called out to Urgolant, but there was no reply, only the faint sound of eight nimble feet pattering away on a rocky path.

Lucena sat in the darkness and struggled against the grip of despair. She was alone, utterly alone, and had no idea where she was or where she should go. She felt like all her friends had deserted her, or she had lost them somehow. Worse, she was homesick. She longed for her old room and her old, comfortable bed— the one that Willic liked to nap in. And thinking about Willic brought out the hard, cold ache in her chest, right around where her heart was.

The feeling reminded her that she had a heart, even if it didn't beat, and that reminded her of something Madgrin had said . . . how long ago? Months? Years? Centuries?

Speak to me through your heart, I can hear you better that way.

She had tried before at the Castle of Amstrass and failed. But this was a strange, dark place, and Madgrin never seemed very far away in strange, dark places. So Lucena reached out with her heart; she reached out with all the hard

CHAPTER 16: *Beyond the Teeth of Dream*

misery of homesickness and the despair of being lost. She wasn't sure what she said.

Warmth answered her. It was soft and kind and gentle, and it held her heart in its long, pale hands and smiled.

You are not lost. You are coming home, La Flein.

Where am I?

You are in the Teeth of Dream. You must come through them. Come beyond them. Come home.

Lucena sat up. The darkness was as impenetrable as before, but then she caught a whiff of secrets and rainy nights, and knew where to go. Slowly she leaned forward and felt around. She found the embankment of rocks she had slid down, and climbed up them. She found the stony path and stood up. She began to walk.

I lost Intok, she said with her heart. *I lost Keelback and Urgolant.*

You lost no one, Madgrin said. *All must walk the path, and it runs differently for all. They are ahead of you. They are coming home.*

Light crept back into the world. At first it was a pale glow in the darkness, but then it came through in hard, slanting rays. It was a strange, unearthly sort of light, and very bright. Lucena raised her hand against it and went forward with more speed. There was a narrow gap in the cliffs of darkness before her where the light blazed through, and she ran towards it.

She nearly fell again, for the light marked the end of the mountains. The path stopped in a precipice of twenty feet, below which lay a sloping hill of pale sand. The high cliffs on either side gave it the feeling of a door, and Lucena peered out of it in wonder.

The mountains ended all at once, as though someone had cut them off with a knife. High, jagged peaks, sharp as blades, ended in a smooth, sheer wall. On either side of her they stretched away for what seemed like forever, but before her was only the gentle swell of the sandy hill, and beyond that a thick, dark forest. In the unearthly light Lucena had trouble seeing; the colors were washed out and everything far too bright, but for a moment she thought she saw Intok as a tiny shadow, just before she disappeared into the trees. Keelback was following, and Urgolant just behind him.

Needing no more encouragement, Lucena jumped. She landed in the sand at the bottom of the cliff with a soft thud and sank up to her knees. Pulling herself free she began to make her way towards the forest. It took longer than she would have thought, because the distances seemed wrong here. Nevertheless she came upon the three unmistakable tracks of her familiars leading into the trees, and she followed them without hesitation.

It was much better under the trees. They were mostly thick oaks with heavy branches, and they sheltered her from the harsh light. Growing so close together they made a pathway with their trunks and branches that was impossible to miss. The ground was even and firm, coated with dry leaves, and Lucena marched along as fast as she could.

Then she thought she saw the wisp of Keelback's tail disappearing around a corner. She broke into a run. The trees gave way to wild hedges, but she hardly noticed. The sky above was a deep, deep blue pricked with countless glittering stars, and the air was chill but fresh. Frost crunched under her feet, and the bushes grew more and more tame. They were trimmed into neat boxes ten feet high, and made the path turn in sharp directions. Once or twice Lucena felt like she was running in a circle.

The frost was slippery, and to continue running Lucena was obliged to look at her feet. She saw the ground pass by, saw the mark of Intok's hoof or Urgolant's foot. She ran. The hedges closed in around her, and she had to turn sideways to fit through. Twigs caught at her clothes, at her hair and face. She put down her head and charged.

She emerged into a snowy maze with neatly trimmed hedges that rose up just above her head. A thin layer of snow lay upon everything. The ground under her feet and under the snow was stone flags, and in the distance she thought she could hear the sound of trickling water.

She was tired, so she walked. The stars above her twinkled, and a pale glow appeared to one side. The east, Lucena remembered. Dawn was coming. Up ahead the path turned sharply to the right, and a great deal of starlight fell across the ground.

Dragging her feet a little, for it seemed the path would go on forever, Lucena wearily swung around the bend, and stopped.

The hedges had ended. Before her, the snow-covered grass ran up in a smooth swell to the top of a hill, where two tall trees stood guard on either side of a stone bench. Lucena knew that bench; she had stood beside it once before, watching Fearbright come out of the Labyrinth.

And now the bench vanished as every member of the Household gathered around it, waiting for her. Harga was there, in his squashed mushroom hat. Willic stood on the bench itself, resting his paws on the shoulders of Beruse, solid and leather-clad. Even Soloma was there, bundled up to her nose in scarves. Rhyse and Gydda stood arm in arm, and Gydda's other hand held a messy wooden spoon. Cobbin and Grimmach stood behind them, collars on crooked and looking like they had been dragged out of bed a moment earlier, but so happy that this did not dampen their excitement at all. A ruffled, shaggy mass of black cape marked where Rusion stood, and beside him pale Halfain in a tawny dress waved. Orrus, wearing his thickest winter robe and uncharacteristic furry boots, had come halfway down the hill to meet Intok, Keelback and Urgolant, who had only been a little ways ahead of Lucena after all. And in the center of the whole gathering, like a blue shadow streaked across the snow, was Madgrin. He smiled at her.

Lucena picked up her skirts, and ran to him. He held out his arms, and she threw herself into them, crying out as she did:

"I've come home—we've all come home! I missed you all so much!"

She thought she saw Intok as a tiny shadow, just before she disappeared into the trees. Keelback was following, and Urgolant just behind him.

CHAPTER 17:

Through the Sea of Stories

THE HOUSE HAD CHANGED LITTLE IN LUCENA'S ABSENCE, and it was almost as though she had never left. Her room was ready and waiting for her, dusted and clean, with the bed neatly made. All the old familiar quirks of the House were the same, and the comforting smell of secrets and old books hung in the air like a gentle veil.

Which suited Lucena, who wanted nothing more than to return to her old habits. So though she was obliged to recount her adventures many times at the request of the household, otherwise she rarely thought of them. Her time with Amstrass seemed distant after her journey through the Teeth of Dream, and Lucena pushed it firmly to the back of her head.

But though she returned to hunting with Beruse, accompanying Harga when he inspected the grounds, and helping Orrus clean the library, she found that though the House and its habitants had remained largely unchanged, she had not. First, her submission to daylight was thoroughly broken, and she found herself lying awake in bed more and more. While she lay she wondered about things. Now that Amstrass and pushed her to the edge of the cliff of her understanding and torn aside the curtain, Lucena couldn't help peering at what it revealed with growing curiosity. She wondered where the hoblins had come from, and Willic, Beruse, Harga and Soloma. She wondered where all the doors in the Room of Doors went, and she wondered what was inside Madgrin's private garden. And she also wondered if Madgrin knew she wondered these things, for he was always silent in her head when she stayed up into the day, and Lucena got the feeling these were questions that needed to be asked in person.

So she did nothing, said nothing, and wanting nothing more than her old life, she returned to her routine as best she could. Then, in early spring, she and Beruse discovered a body in the road as they were walking back from a successful hunt. It was a man, and he lay on his back, proudly displaying the wound that had killed him. Beruse walked right past him, but Lucena stopped.

"Oughtn't we to, I don't know, move him?" she asked.

Beruse looked over her shoulder at the body. She shrugged. "It could save someone an unpleasant accident," she conceded, and stooped to pick up the body.

She stopped. Lucena, who had gone to take hold of his arm, stopped too. His shirt had been ripped aside, and on his bare forearm she saw clearly what had been obscured before: the Etherealist Arrow, pointed up to his elbow. Now she looked, he had others on his hands and chest, and wore a metal one on a chain around his neck. Their combined force was enough to stop her hands from touching him. Beruse seemed to be having the same problem. She frowned.

CHAPTER 17: *Through the Sea of Stories*

"Paranoid old bastard," she muttered. "Fat lot of good these did you."

Lucena frowned. She put out her hands once more to touch the body, but it was as though the man had an invisible shield around him. And it burned. Lucena took her hands away.

So in the end they left him in the road, being unable to offer him the last dignity of the dead without injury to themselves.

Walking away, Lucena was struck by a question that had never occurred to her before.

"Beruse, why do those marks burn?"

"What marks?"

"The Arrow. It burns, and it makes my head hurt sometimes. I used to think it was because vampires were unholy creatures, but that's not quite it, is it? For there are other faiths, other deities, whose signs do not affect us so."

Beruse was silent, and her shoulders drooped. "No, it isn't."

"Do you know why?"

Beruse shrugged. Then she shook her head. "It has always been that way. Madgrin can defy the Arrow, though it pains him to do so, but we are not as strong as him."

Lucena frowned. Time was when she would have been satisfied with such a weak answer, but now she found her ignorance distressing rather than comforting. So when they got back to the House she marched up to Madgrin's study and asked him the same question.

Madgrin was rearranging the books on the shelves behind his desk. It was something he did now and then; he would take them down, open them gently, and then put them back in a different place. He said it kept them happy.

At Lucena's question he paused. He turned the book he was holding over in his hands, examined the cover, and then turned it back again.

"There was a war, a long time ago," he said at length. He passed a hand across his face and suddenly looked very tired. "One side held a grudge." He smiled at her. "It is not your fault."

Lucena went around the huge desk and sat down on the steps that led up to the shelves. "I want to know *why*," she said.

Madgrin walked over, though he moved so smoothly it looked more like floating. She heard the soft whisper of his robes as he sat down beside her and handed her the book he had been holding. It was a collection of Thimble Tales, small stories seamstresses told each other while they were working.

"A long time ago," Madgrin began, and as he spoke the world shifted: it was as though the stones of the hearth turned around to listen, like the very air was paying attention. "Before this world took on its current face, before the dragons, before the fae, when the continents themselves were in different forms..."

"Before God?" Lucena asked in a small voice.

Madgrin inclined his head in a half nod. "Before *human* gods." He was silent a while. "When I was young, there was a war. It was a foolish war, as all wars are, but it involved three proud and powerful ... what to call them? *Races* does not justify. Let us say they were three different orders of being.

"There were the demons—the old demons, the ones that exist beyond human comprehension. They do not live easily in this realm now, but they used to come into it often. It caused... problems. Demons are beings of change, of chaos, and when they came here their nature manifested itself in floods, earthquakes, and droughts. Once, they caused a volcano to fire, to spit out the guts of the earth and burn the land for leagues around, and afterwards it sat and coughed black smoke into the air, so much that the earth was cloaked in heavy clouds for an entire year. For a whole year, all over the world, there was no sun. Many things died. But it was an unintentional side effect of their presence which caused the destruction, not their intent. Some of them brought life into this world, or spurred that which already existed to new and incredible forms.

"None of us were inherently evil, Lucena, remember that. We didn't mean to do so much damage."

He fell silent. There was an expression on his face like sorrow, but his eyes were alight and burning.

"There were the sarlef. You may already know of them, though not by that name. Humans in particular have always been fascinated by the sarlef. They seem to enjoy worshipping them. But the sarlef were also invaders in this realm. They came here from the Ether-lands, which also have a different set of rules, and again this caused problems. Sarlef have... an interesting effect on time. They can bend it, mold it to their own desire.

"And then there were *us*." Madgrin gave Lucena a very intent look, and she couldn't help leaning away a little. "*La Flein*, do you know what I am?"

Lucena swallowed. "I think you are called *lamphra*," she said in a small voice.

A little of the hardness eased from Madgrin's face. "That is the word people use nowadays," he said. "Do you know what it means?"

"I *think* it means ideas," she replied. "It means dreams... the important kind of dreams that help you figure stuff out. It means inspiration; and the wonderful feeling when you suddenly remember something important that you thought you had forgotten."

Madgrin was smiling now, broadly, and his eyes were twinkling. "That is *part* of what we are," he said. Then he become more somber. "It also means nightmares; it means the powers of creation behind the worlds, it means the 'what if' of every story you have ever heard. We are the mirror that reflects the hopes and dreams of the world. In the darkness we make them real, and in the darkness we preserve them forever. That is what lamphra are... that is what I am."

"And you fought in a war?"

Lucena was sorry as soon as she asked, for his face fell and the light went out of his eyes. Despite this she leaned into his shoulder and clasped his hand in hers. "Tell me about it," she said. "I want to know. I want to understand," she said, admitting as much to herself.

Madgrin turned their hands over, so Lucena's were on top, and placed his other hand over hers.

"I don't know why we fought anymore. I'm not entirely sure we ever had a reason. We were three equally powerful and completely different orders of being, each confident in our own rightness, and the wrongness of everyone else. Per-

CHAPTER 17: *Through the Sea of Stories*

haps that was all it ever was. But like I said, it was a useless war: though none of us could triumph, none of us could be defeated. In the end the thing that suffered most from our pointless conflict was the battleground. That was this world ... your world. And for that I am sorry." He squeezed her hand gently. "So sorry."

Lucena wanted to tell him not to be sorry; that her world was doing quite well! But he went on:

"Towards the end we began to go about things in what we thought was a more sensible manner. Each side retreated to its own realm: the demons to chaos, the sarlef to the ether, and the lamphra into dreams. We then created armies, armies that could be defeated, and sent them into this world to fight. Whichever army won the most battles, won the war for their creators. But it was to no good end, for those armies did more lasting harm than anything we ever did directly.

"You're smiling and shaking your head, does it trouble you to see me sad? I can be sad, sometimes. But let me explain: the remnants of those armies are still here, and they are still causing this world harm. Our contribution, vampires, are a part of that. They weaken the wall between life and death and let bad things pass through; more than once this world has been on the brink of collapse because of what we did. You are no longer smiling, do you have a question?"

"What about me?" Lucena asked. "*I'm* a vampire, am I hurting the world?"

Madgrin smiled sadly. He extricated one hand from her grasp and reached around her, pulling her close. Again Lucena could feel the warmth of his body against her face and, faintly, the beating of his heart.

"A drop in the ocean, *La Flein*," he said. "A drop in the ocean. One drop doesn't know what the whole will do. But it wasn't the vampires we made that caused the problems, nor the vampires they, in turn, made. It was the generations and generations of vampires that came after. It was when they spread to every corner of the earth, when every human could find their nightmares in the waking world ... that was the great wrong. That is why I am still here ... "

"Here ... where?"

"Here in your world. The world of humans and flesh. The world of physical material. Here ... in exile," Madgrin said with a sigh, releasing her. "After the war was ended, when it became obvious how much damage we had done, those of us most directly involved were banished here, to help right the wrongs we had caused. Some of us have done better than others. The sarlef, like I said, have problems being worshipped. They become gods. The Etherealist god is a powerful sarlef who hated lamphra, and he takes it out on every single one of our blood descendants. I know it is a rather roundabout way of explaining it, but that is why his Arrow burns you. That is why vampires cannot enter places holy to sarlefine gods, or suffer the touch of their blessed water. It is a grudge from a war long past, for which you bear no blame or responsibility.

"Have I caused you grief, *La Flein*? That was not my intent. You have nothing to grieve for; the guilt is on my head, not yours. Come, that was a poor story; let us find a better one to cheer you up."

* * *

Despite the somber nature of the revelation, Lucena felt much better after hearing Madgrin's story. It was as though a great weight she had not known she carried had been lifted from her shoulders, and for a few days afterwards she felt like she was walking on air. She went out with Harga to see the grounds again, saw the river and the lake, and even went climbing on the rocs, who were hibernating for the winter.

She visited Orrus in the library, where she helped him reorganize one of the shelves that had been disturbed by a fairy the previous Midsummer, and she helped Cobbin dust off a pile of old books that had been found in a corner the previous autumn. She lounged about with Willic, playing cards and taking naps. Even dry, humorless Soloma could not dampen her spirits.

She went and helped Grimmach repair the laboratory. The room had been deserted since the magician, Felpass, had left, and Grimmach had decided it was high time to put it to use. What use that would be was uncertain, but Grimmach figured the best way to go about it was to start by getting rid of all the junk. He roped Beruse into the operation as well, and together they made short work of the piles of furniture and broken tools. For some of the more curious artifacts, however, they had to bring in Orrus: the jar with three tiny, sleeping heads, for example. No one wanted to wake them up. Also the set of vials full of strange, glowing liquids troubled the hoblin. But Orrus scooped everything up and took it away, muttering to himself about what should be done to magicians who left their magical projects unfinished.

Lucena returned to her comfortable, if surreal, existence. Though every time she went out hunting she could not shake the fear that she would run into Amstrass again, or worse, Undergate, and that they would spoil her good times. Especially Undergate, though she could not understand why. Undergate seemed so small and insignificant next to Amstrass.

But she never saw him, not even the one time she was in Serais (though she avoided going anywhere near La Daria Rouge), and gradually her fear of an encounter faded with the reestablishment of her routine. Only now Lucena could look at the House, with all its eccentricities and quirks of character, with a fuller understanding of why it was there. And it did not destroy her vision of the world, let alone her understanding of it; rather she felt relieved. The cliff she had thought she stood on was no cliff at all: merely the border of another realm. And now she was curious about this realm. Dream, Amstrass had called it. With the sea of stories, where every story that was ever told had its own island. One night she went and asked Madgrin about it.

Madgrin was walking in the grounds when she found him. Against the night sky he was almost invisible in his dark robes, and his face seemed hang in the air above her like a moon. A smiling moon, for her questions pleased him.

"It is true that all stories make their own reality," he said. "Within themselves, all stories are real: but if it is a particularly strong story, a true story, even if the events in it never actually happened, then its reality takes shape in Dream. A good story lasts forever, and this is why: even if everyone on earth who ever heard it has died or forgotten, even if no one read it save the person who wrote it, it still exists in the depths of Dream, and from there it will flow back into the waking

CHAPTER 17: *Through the Sea of Stories*

world, in some form or another, to be told and retold, and rebuilt upon itself in the Sea of Stories."

He trailed off, and walked away across the grass. They were on the lawn, pale and dry and patched with snow which glowed in the moonlight. Lucena went crunching across it after him, and when she caught up she found they had crested a rise overlooking the river, and Madgrin was staring down at it with a rueful expression on his face.

"There are rivers in Dream too," he said. "They flow out of the sea and into this world, carrying sparks with them."

"Sparks?" Lucena asked.

"Sparks are the means to an idea," Madgrin explained. "They are what make ideas happen. Some people can create their own sparks, but most of the time they get them from the rivers. This river used to flow past my old home..."

He stopped. Lucena glanced up at him, but his face held so much sadness that she had to look away again.

"There are places within Dream, as well," Madgrin said, firmly changing the subject. "Countries. Worlds within worlds. The kingdoms of Heaven and Hell are both in Dream, so is Elysium, and the Neverlands."

"What are the Neverlands?" Lucena asked.

"They are a particular kind of heaven," Madgrin said, his face softening. "It's different for everyone, but generally only children can get there.

"And there is the Endless Wood."

"The Endless Wood?" Lucena echoed. Madgrin had turned and left the hill, walking so smoothly over the grass it looked like he was floating. She had to trot to keep up.

"The Endless Wood binds the worlds of Dream together," he explained. "It is in every world and every story. Like the Labyrinth is connected to every other labyrinth, so the Wood is connected to every forest or grove that ever existed, or ever will. The Labyrinth was built, you see, as a means to get about places. The Wood grew itself, and has a mind of its own. It has no boundaries, and it is forever: it will exist, in some form or another, as long as there are worlds for it to exist in."

They reached the orchard, and Madgrin passed under the shadow of the trees as serenely as an owl into the night. Lucena, hearing this talk of woods that went on forever, hesitated a moment, then dove in after him.

"If you go far enough in," Madgrin remarked, flitting from shadow to shadow, "if you follow the right paths, you can come out in a completely different world, or not come out at all. You can enter it from the most insignificant coppice, and miss it in the most ancient forest. But our wood, our Forest, is very close to it. That is why you must be careful which paths you take."

Walking as they were in the orchard, this began to give Lucena all sorts of uncomfortably exciting ideas. Even though these were ordinary trees, bare of leaves, with thin, neat trunks, she couldn't help feeling that if she were to turn *there*, then she would find herself in a completely different wood. A wild, ancient place, terrible in its wonders. It was worse than the Labyrinth, and she stuck close to Madgrin's trailing robes.

She could see the lights of the House through the trees, glowing a warm welcome orange, but Madgrin deviated from the path and went to pass the high stone wall that surrounded his own garden. The garden Lucena had never entered, nor seen. The garden, Harga said, that smelled of home. He had been speaking of Dream, Lucena realized now, as Madgrin stood before the wall, pressing a hand against the cool rock.

"One must always take care which path one takes," he said under his breath, and Lucena wondered if he was speaking to himself. Then he turned and walked quickly into the shadows and disappeared, leaving Lucena alone before the stone wall.

Spring came slowly that year, with blizzards and snowstorms raging day and night. During the short calms Keelback would go frolicking in the snow, gouging huge blue tracks in the white blanket. But when the clouds rolled in again he would flee to the House and curl up in front of the kitchen fire.

Urgolant loved the weather. That is, she loved to sit inside next to a window with a pile of books to keep her company and, from the comfort of the House, watch the storms raging outside. Willic would often join her with a cup of steaming hot tea, and together they would marvel at the snow.

Harga did not like the snow. It lay so thick in the forest that he had to dig a tunnel to his den, and then had to keep digging as the snow banked up deeper and deeper. Eventually he gave up and camped on a blanket in the kitchen, to Gydda's dismay.

Around late April the snow abated, followed by a long, slow thaw. The river was bloated with freshmelt, and the lake swelled to cover the entire beach and some of the smaller trees. But the weather was mild, and Lucena took her first walk outside for months with Harga.

The grounds were still thickly coated in snow, though there were a few places where the bare earth peeked through. Passing one of these bald patches Harga stopped abruptly and went to kneel at its edge. Looking over his shoulder Lucena could see two strange flowers growing in the center.

Barely four inches high, with dark glossy stalks and sharp, narrow leaves, they each had five roundish blue petals with ragged brown edges and a spray of white stamens in the middle. One long, red petal curved out from the bottoms, like a tongue.

Harga examined them closely, then with a sharp, decided motion, he plucked them neatly off their roots. He folded them gently into his hand and set off towards the House without explanation. With an exasperated sigh, Lucena followed.

Harga went in the front door, which was almost unheard of. He marched straight up to Madgrin's study and so sudden was his entrance that Soloma cried out in protest.

Madgrin looked up from the map he was studying. Seeing the look on Harga's face he smiled.

"Has the invitation bloomed?" he asked. "I felt it take."

CHAPTER 17: *Through the Sea of Stories*

"Yes, my lord," Harga said, taking a deep breath. "Only it's not just one, there are *two* this time," and he held out his hand with the strange flowers in his palm.

Madgrin's face went perfectly blank and skull-like. He plucked the two flowers from Harga's hand, and laid them delicately on his desk.

"Thank you, Harga," he said quietly. "I will take care of this."

Harga made a curt bow, turned on his heel, and left. But Lucena remained. She stared at the flowers, and the more she did, the more they looked like beckoning hands. Invitations, Madgrin had called them. Invitations to what?

"You've never seen a flower like these," Madgrin said, perceiving Lucena's fascination.

Even though it was not a question, Lucena shook her head.

"They are very rare. They only bloom here once every century or so, and even then there is only one. For two to bloom..." he trailed off, looking at the flowers in puzzlement. "I can only guess she wants to meet you," he said quietly. So quietly Lucena hardly heard, and pretended she had not. Then he looked up and she was met by his dark, fathomless gaze.

"*La Flein*," he said. "I shall be going on a journey shortly, would you come with me?"

"Come where?" Lucena asked, her breath catching.

"To my old home," Madgrin said. "To Dream."

Lucena hesitated for one moment. Just long enough for her heart, had it been alive, to beat once. Then she said:

"Yes."

They left quietly the next evening. Madgrin was waiting for her in the hall just outside her door, half hidden in the shadows, and when she spotted him he turned without a word and walked away. She followed him, turning first here and then there in places she had never seen before. The corridors grew older and less familiar, the wood paneling giving way to stone masonry, and finally to roughly carved bedrock. They were left walking along what felt like a tunnel that had been cut through a mountain. The smell of old books had long since gone, and instead there was a sharp, tangy scent in the air. It reminded Lucena of the pungent herbs that grew along the riverbank.

The tunnel began to climb, and as it did the little lanterns that had lit their way ended, and they were plunged into darkness. Or not quite darkness: silvery starlight glowed up ahead, and it grew and grew until the end of the tunnel was visible, a wide jagged oval of white light.

The tunnel ended in a gaping mouth of tumbled rocks, and Lucena and Madgrin stepped out into a garden she had never seen before.

Water trickled down from a great stone urn in the center of an ornamental pond in front of them, and all around, hydrangea bushes were in full bloom of whites, pinks, purples and blues. Beyond the pond Lucena could see neatly pruned hedges and rose bushes, also in bloom, with beds of pansies walled off by rings of stone. Turning about she could see the great hulking shape of the House behind them, some of its windows still aglow. But it seemed somehow distant from the garden, as though she were seeing it through a curtain of water, or thick smoke. They had come far away from the House, she realized, though they stood practically in its shadow.

Madgrin had put his hands into his sleeves and was looking for something. A moment later he produced the two invitation blossoms, and handed one of them to Lucena.

"Hold on to that," he told her. "You will need it to enter."

Lucena held up the flower to get a better look at it. Sometimes, depending on the way she turned it, it looked more like a face with its tongue sticking out. She stuck her tongue out at it, just for good measure.

"It will be easier if you hold my hand," Madgrin said. So Lucena slipped her free hand into his, and together they started through the garden.

They passed the ornamental pond with the trickling urn, through the neatly trimmed hedges and rose bushes. These became more wild the farther they went, and the bushes rose up around them to cut off any view of the outside world. The path was winding, and sometimes it felt like they were going in circles. On the ground were little stones that glinted and sparkled with all the colors of the rainbow, and tiny lights hung from the inner branches of the bushes, lighting the leaves from within and throwing their twiggy tangle into sharp silhouette.

There was a sound of water, and with the next few steps Lucena found her feet sunk in it. The water came up to her ankles, and it was frigid. The fiery stones burned beneath the surface, their light reflected against the water in darts and whirls. Soon the water was up to her knees and she was having problems keeping hold of Madgrin's hand. This was, she found, because he was walking on the surface of the water, rather than through it. When the water came up to her waist she let out a yelp, which made him pause and look down.

"Do you still have your invitation?" he asked.

Lucena held up the little flower in answer.

"Try smelling it," he said.

So Lucena did. It was a heady scent, strong and tangy but also soft. It made her head spin, and along with the spinning came the disorienting feeling of rising to the surface. She held tight to Madgrin's hand and looked cautiously down at her feet. Sure enough, they rested firmly on the surface of the water, making pale ripples that spread out in rings. Hesitantly she took a step, found the water solid enough, and took another. Together they set off again through the bushes, though now these were growing smaller as the water submerged them, and soon only the topmost leaves were peeking out over the surface.

Chancing a glance behind them Lucena half expected the House to have disappeared, but it was still there, a black lump against the night sky, with a few welcoming lights burning. Around them the water stretched on and on, to either side disappearing into darkness, while ahead Lucena thought she could see some faint lights in the distance.

The water was still, the only ripples coming from their footsteps, and there was a soft wind blowing against them. The lights in the distance grew closer but hardly any brighter, and it took a while for Lucena to recognize them as reflected starlight. Starlight reflected off dark glass windows set into high stone buildings.

CHAPTER 17: *Through the Sea of Stories*

Ahead of them a city rose up out of the water: a great, empty city made of dusty stone. They came to a stairway leading up between the houses, and they stepped out of the water and up into the city.

It was hard going; the stairs had been built for people with much longer legs than either Lucena or Madgrin, and it felt more like climbing a series of waist-high walls than a stairway. The houses too were built on the same generous scale, though Lucena never glimpsed any of the giant occupants.

Once, though, when they were passing a house with an awning over its front door Lucena stole a glance inside and saw that the shadows were teaming with roosting ravens. They crooned to each other in their sleep, and occasionally one would rouse itself to resettle its wings.

Madgrin saw her look. "This is a Titanic ruin," he explained, his voice strangely muffled by the silent air. "Your ancestors built it, a long time ago. It was a very great city once, but it fell into ruin and was taken back into Dream. Now it is kept by the King of Ravens, who guards all ruined cities in Dream."

Silence. They clambered up another giant step, and made their way across the wide expanse of pale stone to the next one. "Our raven, Rusion, comes from here," he added quietly.

Up and up the steps they went, and slowly the city fell away below them. The stairs continued climbing into the sky until they had left the city far behind. Looking up, Lucena found it impossible to see the end of the stairs (the steps were so huge she could not see past the one in front of her), but she could faintly make out a strange pattern on the air above them. It reminded her of the way light reflected off the surface of rippling water, only inverted, as if she were looking at it from beneath the surface. The darting patches of light grew stronger the higher up they went, and indeed they seemed to be getting closer. The world became lighter, and more and more Lucena felt that they were in some dreamlike sea, and they were getting closer and closer to the surface.

Then it was upon them; the inverted surface came right up to one of the steps, casting strange shadows against the pale stone. And as Lucena scrambled up over the ledge she burst through into a new world filled with light.

They had reached the top. Before her the stone stretched away into a landing about twenty feet long, and then ended. But the first thing she noticed was the moon: it hung before her in the sky, so huge and close she thought she could touch it if she only stretched out her hand. Its face was pockmarked with craters, and strange ridges ran across it, like mountain ranges with hills and valleys. Unlike the moon she remembered, this one shone with a light of its own, and instead of being the pale, black-and-white sort of light she was used to, this one held all the colors and all the warmth of the sun. But it was soft and gentle, and didn't burn at all.

Lucena took a breath to ask Madgrin about it, but as she inhaled she discovered the air was extremely clear; it was cold too, and smelled of clean water and starlight. Then it struck her.

"We're in the sky," she said.

"Yes," said Madgrin. He had walked some distance away, and it was then that Lucena looked around; she found they were surrounded by the glinting, softly lapping surface of an ocean, the ocean they had just climbed up through. Crawling to the edge of the platform Lucena could see down, impossibly far down, to the bottom. There was the giant city, and beyond it was a strange country, bleak and open, crossed with lines that could have been roads, or walls, or canals—Lucena wasn't sure. There were also white puffy things that were probably clouds, but they were so far below they looked tiny, like little sheep running across the ground. The effect was so discombobulating that Lucena was obliged to scurry away from the edge and find something else to look at.

Madgrin had gone to the far side of the platform, where for the first time Lucena noticed the strange boat that was docked there, rocking a little on the ocean of the sky. It was long and narrow, with an open top and a high prow. There was a little deck in the back in the shape of a chair with oars mounted on either side, and a flag that drooped lazily in the clear night.

Madgrin was speaking with a figure who stood by the stern, a shorter, broader someone than he, but a someone with likewise night-black hair and pale blue skin. Lucena could see a great deal more of this skin because he was naked to the waist, wearing only a dark blue kilt.

As she approached they broke off their conversation, and the ferryman leaned around Madgrin's elbow to stare at her in amazement. Lucena bobbed a short, uncertain curtsey. There was a strange, swirling pattern tattooed on his left shoulder that trailed over his chest. It reminded Lucena a little of Amstrass's soul, only this pattern did not move.

Without a word the ferryman ushered them onto the little boat, which dipped and rocked as Lucena stepped into it. She had to grip both sides to keep herself steady, though Madgrin walked composedly to the front seat and sat down without so much as checking his balance. Lucena crawled up and sat beside him, clutching the armrest as the ferryman cast them off and began rowing out to sea.

The not-water lapped at the side of the boat, glittering in the moonlight. Where the prow broke each wave they split into a thousand tiny droplets, each one flashing with a different color of the rainbow. It gave Lucena the feeling of plowing through a sea of glittering diamonds, except that when she looked down she could still see, through the surface reflections, the strange lonely land at the bottom of the ocean. It was pale and ghostly, broken by mountains in places and patched with deep forests.

"The Teeth of Dream," Madgrin said, seeing her look.

"The teeth?"

"You crossed them once, on foot," he said. "They mark the the border of true dreams, the what-ifs, maybes and the nightmares."

Lucena shivered, remembering those eerie mountains. The sky was a cold place, and though she was naturally resistant, the air still bit at her nose and cheeks. She huddled down in her seat, even though this restricted her view to the prow of the boat. Madgrin, however, sat very straight with his neck stretched forward and an eager glint in his eye, like a dog on a cart that is going home.

"Where *are* we going?" Lucena asked.

"To the Garden at the Top of the World," Madgrin answered. "The heart of my Queen's realm."

CHAPTER 17: *Through the Sea of Stories*

"Your Queen?"

"Yes. She calls us home now and then. And she wanted to meet you."

Lucena felt her stomach twist uncomfortably at the thought, and she asked no more questions.

The ocean of the sky was vast, and for a time it felt like they were hardly moving at all; how much time it actually was Lucena could not say: the moon hung in the same position (a little above and behind them), and the dark blue distance stretched on and on.

Then, in one of her rare peeks over the side, Lucena saw that ahead of them and to their right was a strange sort of hump floating on the ocean. It looked a little like a soap bubble, only instead of being swirly pinks and whites and yellows, this one was clear and faintly tinged with blue. And it was huge, easily ten times bigger than the House, and inside it Lucena glimpsed a low, rocky island.

They passed the strange bubble-island, and left it far behind. Then another one appeared, this time to the left, and much bigger. This was more the size of a city, and it towered above them. After that the islands came thick and fast, sometimes alone, sometimes clumped together. Sometimes a large one had several smaller ones surrounding it like frozen ripples, and one Lucena saw had another island stacked on top of it.

Unbidden, Amstrass's words sounded in her head, cold and clear as the night when they were first spoken:

Some of the older stories have several islands stacked one on top of the other, like stones...

She had wondered then, how this could be. Now she was seeing it, and she gasped in amazement. "This is the *Sea of Stories*," she breathed.

"Yes," said Madgrin.

Passing the stacked island the boat put on speed, and the islands slid by and disappeared behind them with increasing rapidity. Though perhaps that was only because they were becoming more and more numerous—giant bubble islands with little bubble islands clustered around them, with other bubble islands stacked on top. Sometimes an island had as many as three, and each one of those also had little bubble islands floating in midair around them. Their undersides were lumpish and rocky, and some trailed roots or tentacles.

Sometimes Lucena could see inside the bubbles to the islands themselves: these were unfamiliar lands, with strange mountains and hills; sometimes she saw cities, and sometimes the entire island was a city. Some of them had an odd, compacted look, as though they had been folded in on themselves in order to fit inside their bubble.

Lucena was so fascinated by the islands themselves that it was a while before she thought to look beneath the surface of the sea, and when she did she was surprised to find that most of the islands appeared to be floating. Only a few were supported by the mountainous terrain below the ocean surface, in which case they appeared to be resting on islands that had sunk into the sea.

When Lucena pointed at these and asked, Madgrin smiled.

"Each island is a story," he explained. "Some stories are built off of nothing but imagination and whimsy, but others are made from actual events; those are the ones with islands beneath the surface. The island below is what actually happened, while the island on the surface is the story that was made out of it."

"And what about the islands resting on islands?" Lucena asked, pointing at one such island towering on their right.

"Retellings," Madgrin said. "Stories change over time, just like people. When a story has changed enough it grows a new island on top of itself."

Lucena considered this. "What about all the ones around them? The little ones..."

"Diversions," Madgrin explained. "Extensions. Stories that were derived from the greater story, not made whole on their own. Sometimes they sprout retellings and diversions of their own, if they're strong enough.

"You can see one there," and he pointed to a small floating island with another island perched on top and several tiny specks floating around it.

Lucena appraised the oddity solemnly.

"How are stories made?" she asked quietly.

"How are they made?" Madgrin echoed. He stroked his chin thoughtfully. "They are made in many different ways, I suppose. Sometimes they are told, sometimes they are made up, and sometimes they happen on their own."

"Yes," Lucena said. "But how does a story make an island?"

Madgrin shrugged. "How does a river make a riverbed? How do trees make a forest? They do it by being. Every story makes an island simply by existing. I told you; all stories make their own reality within themselves, and that is what is preserved here in Dream. And so they can be told over and over, and never be forgotten."

"But..." Lucena began, thinking of all the stories that had ever been told, not to mention all the ones that would surely be made up in the future.

"The sea is wider than what we can see," Madgrin said, anticipating her thoughts. "Space is infinite here."

As time went on, and they passed island after island with no sound but the gentle dunk and splash of the oars, Lucena began to believe this. At some point she thought she fell asleep, if indeed it was possible to sleep in Dream, for the next thing she knew Madgrin was gently squeezing her shoulder and telling her, "Awake, *La Flein*. Awake."

Rubbing her eyes Lucena discovered they had come to a veritable forest of bubble islands, rising all around them with multitudes of diversions and retellings. But that was not what caught her interest: in front of them a low grassy bank broke the line of the sea, before sloping so steeply it shot up in an almost vertical wall whose top was lost in the dark sky.

At first Lucena thought it was a flat wall, but then she saw that to either side it curved away, and so concluded it must be a very wide circle or oval. A cone shape, perhaps?

The boat ran aground on the grass with a slithering sound, and Madgrin stepped lightly out and held her hand while she disembarked. He bowed to the ferryman, and Lucena dropped a curtsey. The ferryman saluted them and pulled his boat off the shore. He paddled away through the sea, a little bobbing figure amidst the dancing light of the waves.

CHAPTER 17: *Through the Sea of Stories*

Something was waiting for them on the grass by the hill. Two somethings, now Lucena thought about it. She knew they were there before she turned her head to look; their presence burned in her mind like a hot iron, and it was with great trepidation that she turned around to face them.

They *appeared* to be lions. At least they were very lion-*like*. But they were each easily the size of a small horse, and had four twining horns winding out from their heads. Eagle wings adorned their backs and their tails were particularly long and snake-like. It took Lucena a second glance to realize that they actually were snake tails, with soft glimmering scales.

Their eyes glowed like molten gold in the moonlight, and they regarded Lucena and Madgrin with all the prepossession of a pair of cats. But Madgrin was not daunted by their appearance, their attitude, nor the way they made the air around them blurry, as though they were in fact much larger creatures that were only allowing small portions of themselves to be visible. He approached them, bowed deeply, and said with genuine gratitude, "I am honored you came to meet us."

One of the creatures bowed its head in return. As it moved, it left golden shadows behind in the dark, as a candle does when moved quickly.

"This is my fledgeling, Lucena," Madgrin said. "Lucena, two cleons of Dream."

"Very pleased to meet you both," Lucena said a little shakily, bobbing a curtsey.

She couldn't tell if the cleons were pleased or not. Their lion faces, surrounded by thick shaggy manes, were open and placid, but somber. All they did in response was to open their wings wide, which made them look three times as big, and advance slowly.

Lucena wanted to run away and hide behind Madgrin, but Madgrin had come forward and was sliding onto the back of one of the cleons, tucking his knees up so they wouldn't interfere with its wings. So Lucena took a deep breath of sharp, clear air, and went to the other one. She found it was easier to lie along its back with her arms around its neck, though she was careful not to cling too tight.

It was how she always imagined sitting in the sun would be; surrounded by the soft golden flames of the cleon's fur and feathers, which were warm and tingled pleasantly.

The cleon shook its head, fanned its wings, and took off. Then everything was rushing air and whirling feathers. Lucena was vaguely aware of the grassy wall passing by on their left, and a great bubble island falling away to their right, but mostly she saw cleon fur and cleon feathers and the wide night sky around them.

Upwards they soared, and Lucena began to wonder how high the hill rose: they left the islands far behind, and the moon was level with her shoulder when she realized that the top of this sky was not the surface of an ocean, but a thick blanket of dark blue clouds.

The cleons plunged into the clouds, burning a patch of warm gold through the veil of night. And then, with a suddenness that nearly knocked Lucena off her mount, they burst out of the clouds and into sunlight.

It was afternoon sunlight, long and slanting and warm. The air was blissfully soft and fragrant, but everything was so bright Lucena had to clamp her eyes tightly shut. When she could open them again she saw they had surpassed the top of the grassy hill, and beheld a sight that drove all other thoughts and worries from her mind.

It was indeed an oval, surrounded on all sides by frothy clouds, white and gold in the light of the sun. Inside was a garden, full of bright green grass with thick dark trees and rolling hills with many rivers and hidden dells. The fields were frosted with red and orange wildflowers, and dotted with chalk-white rocks that made strange patterns, like writing, on the grass. Lit by the sun hanging low and close in the sky the place glowed like the cleons.

Like the cleons! If they had glowed in the moonlight, now they blazed. It was truly like sitting in the sun, and to see anything Lucena had to squint through blinding yellow fur.

One of the cleons spoke then. Lucena did not know which, for its voice filled her head and seemed to come from all around.

"Welcome," it said in a voice like a hundred cellos playing in harmony. "Welcome, lost ones, to the Garden at the Top of the World."

*When Lucena pointed at these and asked, Madgrin smiled.
"Each island is a story," he explained.*

CHAPTER 18:

Grimbald,

THE GARDEN AT THE TOP OF THE WORLD was larger inside than out, as Lucena discovered the moment the cleons alighted on the grass and she slid to the ground. From above, it had appeared to be no bigger than the grounds of the House, but once inside stretched on forever.

Madgrin thanked the cleons gravely, and they bowed their shaggy heads in turn before leaping into the sky again, where they joined their brethren twirling in and out of the white clouds that crossed the thin blue sky, flashing with golden light.

"What were they?" Lucena asked Madgrin as they set off up the hill into a nearby forest.

"Cleons," he said. And then he added, "They were some of the first to come here out of void. They were the guardians of the first dreams."

Lucena tried to give this information the solemn consideration it warranted, but the grass was so soft, and the ground was so moist and springy, that she soon forgot the cleons in her delight of it. She longed to take off her shoes and go barefoot. But Madgrin had gone very serious the moment they landed, so she kept her silly wishes to herself.

One of the more disconcerting things about the garden was the sunlight. Although it did no visible damage to either of them, and certainly it caused her no discomfort, it had the effect of making Madgrin partially transparent. He looked like an image of himself reflected in water: all the light parts clear and opaque, but in the shadows of his robes and hair Lucena could see straight through to the grass on the other side. Holding up her hand she noticed the same effect, but upon poking at the transparent part she found it still quite solid. That was comforting.

They passed under the trees, and there the long slanting shadows caused Madgrin to flicker in and out of sight as he passed through them. Lucena hurried through the grass to catch up, sending clouds of white butterflies swirling into the air around them. For a moment she thought they were forming some important shape (that of a person or a face) but when she looked again they were only butterflies, glinting in the sunlight.

The grass grew short under the trees, patched with moss, and the air smelled thickly of flowers. In the distance Lucena could hear snatches of music, but it was so disjointed and faint she could not pick out any melody. If anything, it reminded her of an orchestra warming up and tuning their instruments.

Through the trees she glimpsed a structure made of white stone with many columns. It had no walls but a magnificent domed ceiling to make up for it. There were statues on the roof, draped in ivy and holding gold instruments. For one

CHAPTER 18: *Grimbald*

surreal moment Lucena thought they were the orchestra, but then they came out of the trees entirely, and she saw that the structure was surrounded by people, and there on a little dais by the steps was the real band: four tallish, thinnish men in black suits, three dark, one fair.

It was The Madders. Gimbel, Tram, Grin and Boult, all busily working their instruments, except Grin, who was reclining lazily behind his drums and admiring a flower. They looked as though no time at all had passed since they had played at Orrus's not-birthday party, though Tram had replaced his red scarf with a sort of turban that hung at a lopsided angle off his head.

Amazed as she was to see the Madders there, Lucena was more amazed at the group of people gathered on the soft lawn below the structure.

About half of them were human shaped, albeit with pale blue skin; she thought she saw Fearbright among them, but his form was eclipsed when one of the *other* people danced into view. These people did not look human at all, though they walked on two legs and wore clothes of the same fashion. They were covered head to tail (for they all had tails) in soft short fur. Their faces, though open and intelligent, bore more resemblance to rabbits, cats or foxes, with sensitive noses and cleft upper lips. Many of them had fine long ears, and several had strange, double-jointed legs.

Then one of them, who looked like a combination of rabbit and cat, came hopping over with cries of delight. His fur was golden, his ears were very long; his eyes were wide and purple-violet, and one of them twinkled through a monocle. Lucena felt a tug on her memory: of Willic, long ago, showing her a battered old hat and telling her it belonged to . . .

"Greetings, Tobius Leander," Madgrin said, bowing.

"What, what, how now?" Tobius Leander danced nimbly past Madgrin and came to lean into Lucena's face. He had a spray of whiskers around his muzzle, and they tickled. "You're an interesting conundrum, if I do say so myself."

"P-pleased to meet you," Lucena stammered.

Tobius Leander smiled. It was a strange smile, as he did not show any teeth but scrunched his face into a heart shape and beamed at her. "Pleased indeed as a friend in need," he said. And bowing he took her hand in his furry, paw-like one, and planted a whiskery kiss upon it. "Your arrival has been most anticipated," he told them. "The queen is not yet beside herself, but she is working on it."

"Then we had best find her and make sure she keeps herself together," Madgrin answered with perfect seriousness, but Lucena could tell he was laughing behind his eyes, and some of his gravity had lifted.

"Excellent!" cried Tobius Leander, and took off across the green, plowing through the blue, grim-faced crowd that had gathered around where the band was setting up. They scattered before him, and at the same time there was a commotion from behind, where apparently someone was trying to get their attention.

"Confulscators and tweezelbusters!" screeched a hard, high voice. "What do I have to do to get things *organized* around here?"

Madgrin stopped in his tracks. He turned around and, face breaking into a wide smile, spread his arms out: "Grimbald," he cried joyously. "My Queen!"

What Lucena was expecting, she did not know. But after her encounters with Titanna and Amstrass she had imagined someone tall and slender with graceful legs and arms and a proud and noble face. She had had a vague idea of someone with flowing night-black hair, perfect moon-white skin, and a soft voice.

In these expectations Lucena was completely wrong.

The woman who stood in the center of the lawn, at the head of a confused herd of deer laden with food, was not tall. In fact she was shorter than Lucena, and perhaps because of this stood very straight, her feet slightly apart, chest thrust out and her neck elongated to add every possible inch to her stature. And she was not slender.

Her hair was dark brown (it shone copper in the sunlight) and hung in wriggling strands around her face, which was bright blue. It was a round face, which would have been pleasant enough had it not been for the expression it wore; her dark blue lips had been pulled into a perfect upside-down 'U' and her soft button nose was scrunched up into her face as though she smelled something foul.

She had her eyes closed, and because of the dark shadows around them this made them seem a little too big for her face. But then they opened, and Lucena saw that they were in fact small, beady eyes, bright white and without pupils or irises. They shone in her head like twin glass moons, and their gaze pierced everything.

The moons turned their pale stare on Lucena, and they blinked in surprise.

Lucena met them and was lost. The world fell away and she was consumed by the milky white glow. In it, her mind was filled with possibilities, ideas, plans, hopes and dreams. They poured through her head—too fleeting to grasp but as substantial as boulders being hurled at her. Under their weight she staggered back and bumped into Madgrin. She felt his hands on her shoulders, and his voice came out of the white and said, "Steady, steady. She is your queen too, she will not harm you."

Lucena came out of the white world of dreams and chances and into her own head to find Grimbald had turned her gaze to stare up at Madgrin.

"I am not hers *yet*," she said. Her voice had changed: it had become a rich, smooth voice; deep for a woman but high for a man. It reminded Lucena of a stringed instrument made to purr. But then Grimbald turned her strange, writhing-haired head to where the Madders had at last been left to set up their show and shrieked again in her grating, hoarse voice: "You pillow-heads! Not in the Southeast! Move your drums Grin, and don't smile at me like that!" and she stomped off to deal with the wayward musicians.

After that things came on in a blur, and Lucena lost track of their proper order. It was all very dreamlike, fittingly enough, and she wandered away from Madgrin across the lawn, staring unashamedly at the people she found there. A deer offered her a drink in a carved wooden mug, and she took it without wondering how a deer could hold something without hands. She sipped the drink, which tasted like honey and sunlight and burned her throat like whiskey.

Someone very like Tobius Leander walked by. They had black fur and a white tuft at the end of their tail. Lucena stared after them, and as a result nearly walked right into Fearbright.

CHAPTER 18: *Grimbald*

In her dreamlike state she felt no need to apologize, but stared up at him in unabashed awe. He met her gaze with a sharp, sarcastic one. He raised an eyebrow:

"So, you have decided to come out of the shadows?"

Lucena shrugged. She did not feel compelled to answer him.

Surprisingly, Fearbright was satisfied by this. He gave her an unexpected smile and moved on.

Lucena came to a shady corner of the lawn where an oak tree had grown up next to the stone structure. The drink had made her warm and sleepy, and the shade looked cool and soothing, so she sat down.

Something else was sitting in the shade next to her. At first she thought it might have been a cleon, for its presence burned on her mind in a similar way. But when she turned her head to look she found it was nothing of the kind.

The first impression she had was of a lithe, feline body with short blue fur; the next was of long black claws, clacking and scratching at the earth; two long black horns like scythes; bony wings with stars inside; a flowing blond mane. Three red eyes stared at her from this jumble of visions, and they were the only things Lucena could see clearly; all the rest carried a distortion, like something reflected in a wobbly mirror, and they came in bits and pieces, as though someone had drawn pictures of several different animals and then pasted them together. Or, Lucena thought on later consideration, like a very large creature that had folded in on itself many different parts in order to fit into the available space.

The red eyes blinked. Lucena did not see them blink, but she felt it. Like something coming between her and an open flame for a moment; the heat lessened, then returned.

"You're a demon," she said, dreamlike and unafraid.

"Yes," the demon said. Her mouth was very red, with fine white teeth. Her voice was hard and raspy.

"I didn't know demons came to Dream."

"We go wherever we wish."

"Why are you here?"

"I have come to hear and watch my grandchildren play." The demon jabbed a piece of wing at where the band was putting itself back together after Grimbald had forced them to move yet again.

Lucena looked at the Madders in their trim black clothes and happy human faces. She chanced another glance at the demon.

"They are your *grandchildren?*" she asked, incredulous despite herself.

"After a fashion," the demon said. "Not unlike your father."

"My father?" Lucena said in surprise. "But my father is dead."

A smile spread beneath the eyes, long and curling and white. "I mean the Mad Shadow."

Lucena opened her mouth in question, but it died in her throat as the band finally began to play.

It was different from any music she had ever heard. Different, somehow, from the music the Madders had played before. If Lucena had to choose a word to describe it, it would have been *alive*. Not in the sense that it was lively and fast (though it was that too) but that it felt to her as if the notes, the beat, and the rhythm had a spirit of their own. As if this was music that was always there, always moving: the Madders had simply become the door through which it passed, and danced a while among them.

The demon—all the strange, distorted pieces of her—sat up and watched the band eagerly. But when all Lucena did was stare with her, and at the players, and at the dancers lining up on either side of the green, the demon prodded her in the side with a paw.

It felt like being burned by something cold, and left her side numb and tingling. Lucena yelped and looked around reproachfully.

"You should dance," the demon said, unapologetically.

Lucena took another look at the dancers lining up. Both animal and humanlike appeared very organized, and Lucena had not the faintest clue where she would fit (though she did see Madgrin in the line, and that made her feel less afraid).

"I do not know my place in it," she said.

"No one does," the demon replied, "until they dance it."

Silence. The paw waved menacingly.

"Go," the demon said.

Lucena went.

She took a place at the end of the line, next to a tall woman with rabbit ears and across from a cat in the shape of a man.

Grimbald came to the head of the lines, and then sprinted down between them, her black skirts flying. The music changed. It became the dance. And Lucena found all she needed to do was follow along.

It was unlike any dance Lucena had ever seen, let alone participated in. Some grabbed a partner, others grabbed several; for a while Lucena was caught in a whirling ring of dancers that spun across the grass, knocking other participants flying. Some people also danced on their own: the cat man, who wore a tight-cut black coat with long flowing tails, never took a partner at all, but twirled around with leaps and bounds that made Lucena dizzy to watch. Tobius Leander changed partners so often it looked like he was dancing alone, flitting from one to the next in a mad scatter of golden fur and flowing horsetail.

It was dancing, pure and simple, with no other reason than for the joy of the movement. For the ecstasy of putting the strange, living music into motion. The dancers became the music embodied, and they wove and dipped and leapt between each other as nimbly as the notes. Blocks of dancers formed and reformed with the progression of the chords, while others took up the beat, marching or jumping in place.

For a time Lucena became the music. It flowed through her limbs and animated her, moved her, without thought or worry.

In her whirling and twirling she somehow got pushed to the center of the mob of dancers, and here the music left her, and she stopped.

It was like being in the center of a storm: while the tempest raged all around, in the middle it was perfectly calm. And in the middle Grimbald was waiting.

CHAPTER 18: *Grimbald*

The Queen of Dreams stood with her arms folded across her bosom and her feet planted firmly apart, regarding Lucena with narrow white eyes.

The music changed again, and Grimbald began to circle round her. It would have looked predatory, except her motions were carefully exaggerated—clearly a dance step. Lucena followed her example, keeping pace so she stayed on the opposite side of the circle.

Grimbald smiled, a bright smile that curled up both sides of her face and stuck there. Lucena felt her stomach clench: one would have expected someone with a face like Grimbald to have a charming smile, probably with dimples. And though she did have dimples, the smile her face made was anything but charming.

It was the smile of someone with secrets. It was the smile of someone with passions. It was the smile of someone who had seen empires rise and fall, and had a hand in both. It was a smile to make the Devil pause.

Step and step, around they went. The music quickened its pace. Grimbald laughed, and then she dashed, a black streak across the green. But Lucena was quick and nimble of foot, and she skipped out of her reach. They danced around each other, chasing and tugging this way and that. The music drove them on, and Lucena got the feeling that while Grimbald wasn't playing the music herself, she was directing it somehow. As though it was her movements driving the music, and not the other way around.

Faster and faster they whirled together, until the world outside the inner circle was a blur of colors and sounds. Always Grimbald was stepping towards her, and always she was dancing away. Every challenge in step and stride she matched, bringing them closer but never touching.

The music was ringing in her ears, humming in her veins, driving her onwards to a place she did not know. It got into her bones, a vague buzzing inside her skull that made her vision blur. She saw nothing but swirling colors, a flash of gold, and then a large blue hand appeared, palm before her face.

Lucena stopped. Instinctively she put up her own hand to meet the other, and as their fingers touched the world slid back into place.

The music had stopped, and so had all the other dancers. Lucena and Grimbald stood in the center of a watching crowd, their hands raised to meet each other as though in greeting, or a truce.

It lasted only a moment: Grimbald took her hand down and stepped away. Then she raised both hands and clapped softly.

Applause broke out amongst the crowd, and Lucena nearly stepped on her own foot turning around to look at them all. Everyone was smiling, and she saw Tobius give her the thumbs up.

"Well played," Grimbald said, her voice soft as velvet and hard as stone. "Well played indeed, little Badgrave."

Lucena turned around to protest that she was neither of those things, but Grimbald had wandered off and the music began again.

Immediately she was swept off her feet by first one partner and then another, until she tumbled, confused and dizzy, into Madgrin. He took her by the hand

and led her confidently around the green, weaving in and out between the other dancers.

"Well done, *La Flein*," he said, stooping so he could speak into her ear. "Well done."

Lucena was not sure what she had done, or how she had done it well, but she allowed herself to feel the warm glow of satisfaction as Madgrin led her away into the dance.

The music ended gradually, releasing the dancers gently from its spell, and one by one they began to mingle more casually. Lucena clung to Madgrin's elbow, feeling progressively more tired and sleepy. The faces slid by, none of them sticking in her memory, until a devilish blue one appeared to her left, accompanied by a beckoning hand. With a sigh Lucena released her hold on Madgrin's arm and went.

Grimbald was waiting for her sitting under a tree, holding a very strange instrument. It looked like a sort of fiddle, but when Lucena got closer she saw it had no strings but a gaping mouth filled with sharp teeth in the middle. There were horns around the upper edge, with two glistening black stones that looked like eyes set on either side of the neck. As Lucena approached, it gnashed its teeth at her.

Grimbald smacked it bodily on the ground. She laid it across her lap and tapped its neck with the bow thoughtfully. When she saw Lucena she patted the ground beside her.

"You certainly took your time," she said as Lucena sat down.

"I'm sorry," Lucena said, uncertain.

She was rewarded by a gentle tap of the bow across her back.

"Never apologize," Grimbald told her. "Especially to me."

Lucena opened her mouth to say sorry, stopped herself just in time, and ended up making a choked noise.

"Better," said Grimbald, twiddling her fiddle between her fingers. "Well now, let's see them."

"See who?" Lucena asked, confused.

"Your friends," said Grimbald, the smile creeping across her face. "They're not far off. They never are."

Lucena stared at her. Grimbald set her fiddle aside and clasped her hands around her knees expectantly. Then, when Lucena still said nothing, she sighed with exasperation and pointed at Lucena's shadow.

"There," said Grimbald. "Come out, you."

Lucena turned around; at first her shadow looked like an ordinary shadow, if a bit larger than it should. Then it shrugged, opened two glowing eyes, and surged out of the ground.

Intok shook her head and mane and snorted, obviously surprised. Lucena was surprised as well; she thought she had left her familiars back at the house. But here was Grimbald getting up to prod at her shadow some more, and now with a frantic scrabbling and scuffling a disheveled Urgolant clawed her way out onto the grass. Finally Grimbald reached her hand into Lucena's shadow and pulled Keelback out by the beak, almost like a conjuring trick.

CHAPTER 18: *Grimbald*

Lucena wondered if it *had* been a sort of conjuring trick, since she had never known them all to fit into her shadow before. But from the guilty looks Keelback was shooting her, she suspected they had been there all along.

Grimbald clapped her hands with delight, and actually squealed a little when Intok condescended to sniff her outstretched hand.

"Oh, wonderful. Wonderful!" she exclaimed, giving Keelback's beak a friendly tap. "So many already! Why, you are practically the *Mistress of Monsters*, aren't you? I like that, 'Badgrave: Mistress of Monsters.' It suits you."

"My name is Lucena," Lucena said, the old protest bitter in her mouth.

Grimbald paused and looked at her thoughtfully, suddenly quiet.

"Yes," she said slowly. "Yes, I suppose it still is. Well, it won't last forever, you know. You'll need a stronger name if you keep at it like this. But Lucena could last you a century or more, so you have time. But when you need a new one, come to me."

She wandered off around Urgolant, who skittered in a circle to keep all eight eyes on her. But Grimbald seemed to have lost interest in Lucena's familiars; she went over to a tree and idly picked some leaves.

"How do you like Dream?" she asked.

Lucena looked around at the late evening sky, the streaked gold and green grass, and the unusual persons there. "It is interesting," she said, carefully. "I don't quite understand it."

"You'd be wrong if you thought you did," Grimbald said. "So that's good." She came back holding a leaf between two fingers and sat down across from Lucena. Holding the leaf between them she said: "Make a wish."

"Sorry?"

"Make a wish," Grimbald said. "I can grant wishes. Big ones, small ones, anyone's. No one's. Just tell me."

Lucena looked at the leaf, wondering if it had anything to do with this. She shook her head. "I can't think of anything," she said.

Grimbald huffed. "Think of something," she said. "It doesn't matter what it is."

So Lucena thought some more. But everything she thought of that was trivial she could get for herself, and anything that was big she didn't feel like having yet. And it seemed foolish to waste a wish on something she didn't really want or could get for herself. So in the end she shook her head, and because she couldn't apologize she tried to explain:

"There's nothing for me to wish for," she said. "It's all just there, and I can get it myself if I need to."

Grimbald raised her eyebrows. It made the dark shadows under them stretch so it looked as though her face was getting tugged out of shape. She smiled shortly.

"Well that is something," she said. "But someday, Badgrave, I do owe you a boon. A real wish. And I don't like being on the owing end, so better start thinking what it could be. But I'll give you a hint: the best wishes are not your own—they're made for someone else."

She tossed the leaf aside and rolled over to sit next to Lucena, took up her fiddle, and lazily began to play.

For a violin with no strings and a lot of sharp teeth it made a very pleasant sound. Sometimes it was deep and humming, sometimes it was high and soaring. Slowly everyone on the green ceased what they were doing and came to listen, and Intok, Urgolant and Keelback, who had been crowded in a guilty huddle behind Lucena, crept forward. With a soft whisper of cloth Madgrin sat down on her other side, and put his arm around her shoulder.

There, surrounded by her friends and in the soft evening sunlight, listening to the strange music of Grimbald's fiddle, Lucena thought of a wish. A wish to remain here, in this time and place, forever. But she knew that such a wish was foolish, and so she did not make it.

After their return Madgrin never spoke of what had happened in the garden. He did not speak of Dream or of Grimbald, either to Lucena or to anyone else. If she hadn't known better she would have thought she dreamt it all. Except that sometimes she would pass the wall around Madgrin's garden and catch the sharp, tangy smell of the ocean; or she would come to a particularly secluded part of his House where the dust lay deep and the air was still, and when she closed her eyes she could imagine she was again in the giant ruined city filled with black ravens. And sometimes, when she was walking in the Wood with Harga, she would see other paths leading off, twisting away into the night, and from them she could sense the presence of far off secret places and old, towering stories.

But always it was distant; behind a veil of dust or beyond a twist in the road. Ever she was on the edge of Dream, living on the silver line between the solid land of what was, and the churning ocean of what could be.

*Faster and faster they whirled together,
until the world outside the inner circle was a blur of colors and sounds.*

CHAPTER 19:

Madgrin.

A S A HUMAN CHILD Lucena had thought of time as running in a circle, or at least a spiral; with certain events inevitably repeating themselves, like the cycle of the seasons and the nights and the days. After she had come to the House of Madgrin, however, these cycles had become less and less significant. And after her visit to Dream they became almost unnoticeable. There were two great milestones in her memory: her adventure with Amstrass, and her meeting with Grimbald. Each had left her with an expanded view of her world, and when no further revelations were forthcoming it felt like time solidified in that state. Not that it stopped, but became compressed. So although her vampiric memory could recall every minutia of the daily events that followed, so it also kept her visit to the Garden at the Top of the World fresh in her mind, like it had happened just the other day, or week, or month.

Time flowed into a great, meandering river, and in it she lost track of the days and the nights and the years, and it was the most unbalancing thing to discover that over a hundred years has gone by.

She found out because Willic and Beruse had taken it into their heads to throw another birthday party, and this time it was for *her*.

"It's been a hundred and fifty years since you came to live with us," Willic, who had always been good at counting years, told her. "That's a good number to celebrate."

"One hundred and fifty years?" Lucena echoed, feeling her knees go weak.

"And sixty days," Willic amended. "But I hardly think that signifies."

Lucena let it pass. It was in keeping with the character of Beruse and Willic's parties that though she had been born in February and come to live in the House in April, that her party should be thrown in July.

"Are they indeed, how excellent," was Madgrin's reaction. He had smiled and went away immediately afterwards. Lucena had grown accustomed to his occasional disappearances, but in the past few months these had become longer and more frequent, and when he was gone there was a strange block on her mind which prevented her from contacting him. When he returned he would be tired and quiet, and sit in his study and read. But he always came back. So she could only hope that he would magically appear for her party. And in this she was not disappointed.

Not only did he appear, as calm and serene as could be in the hectic preparations beforehand, but he also brought with him the musical entertainment for the night in the form of none other than Tobius Leander himself, who stood at one end of the Ballroom and played on his pipe for three hours straight without a rest. And while he played, the room was full of dancing paper butterflies in

CHAPTER 19: *Madgrin*

yellow and blue and pink which, when he at last retired, turned to flowers and fell to the ground in a thick blanket of petals.

Sitting at the far end of the room in a high-backed stone chair, Madgrin watched the proceedings with his usual placid expression, but Lucena got the distinct impression that he was very tired, for he never joined in any of the dances.

Soon after that, in early August, he disappeared for even longer than usual. Everyone got into the doldrums then, even Willic, who spent hours as a cat curled up beside the oven and did not respond to anything. Beruse sulked, Soloma hibernated, Harga hid in his den, and the hoblins all contrived to be as grumpy as possible.

Only Orrus seemed unaffected by their lord's absence. So Lucena took to spending time with him in the library, reading books with Urgolant, and sometimes trying to teach Keelback to read. It was not a promising endeavor, and it was only the lack of anything else useful to do that kept them at it.

Then one evening she came up to find Orrus poring over a book which appeared to be on fire. Then Lucena looked again and saw that its pages were glowing, a warm yellow glow not unlike a young fire. Orrus bent over it, his glasses shining in the light and obscuring his eyes, while his mouth worked open and closed, forming strange words she did not recognize. At last he made a few decisive sweeps with his hand across the open book, tapped it sharply, and the light disappeared. He unbent and regarded Lucena gravely, his glasses still glowing faintly.

Then the look was gone. He closed the book and tucked it under his robes, gave Lucena a short smile, and went away among the shelves. Lucena did not ask what he was doing, but she had the strongest suspicion that he had been trying to locate Madgrin. And had not been successful, judging by the results.

For the first time Lucena began to seriously worry about her maker, and wondered if she should again attempt the Mirror, Candle and Book spell that she had used so many years ago. But she feared that whatever forces were keeping Madgrin away would also defeat her, and what good would that do?

So she waited and worried, until one evening in September she was shaken awake by Beruse, who loomed over her bed, shaggy and more bearlike than ever.

"Something bad is coming, I can smell it," she said.

Sitting up and peeling her eyes open Lucena regarded her dully for a few seconds while the meaning of her words sank in. Then: "Bad?" she asked.

"It's dangerous. Kerebryt let it through the gate, but we'll see what Frayne does."

Lucena rolled out of bed, and as her senses slowly returned she became aware of what Beruse had already felt: a twisted knot of malevolence practically outside their front door. It was enough to get her dressed and armed in record time, out of her room and down the stairs.

Most of the staff had gathered in the Entrance Hall, and as Beruse and Lucena came out onto the balcony that faced the door she saw that Harga had dropped to all fours and was growling. Gydda, armed with a cleaver, stood next to him. Grimmach and Rhyse stood opposite them, and to Lucena's surprise Rusion was there as well. He looked bedraggled and tired, but he stared at the front door as though it were about to come alive and bite him.

The something outside had reached the door. It stopped. Tendrils of darkness that looked like black slime oozed in around the frame and between the cracks. It smelled vile.

Next to Lucena, Beruse took out her crossbow and primed it.

With a bang the door was blown open so that both sides bounced off the walls. A seething mass of writhing black slime tumbled inside, splattering the floor and making terrible squelching noises.

It smelled of things dead and decaying, mixed with the pungent odor of rotten eggs. The smell alone made Lucena gag, but what truly made her recoil was the thing's presence. The black slime seemed to well up in her mind, threatening to drown her.

She clutched the banister and tried to keep from retching.

The glob of slime stopped once it got inside the door. It seemed to look around, and then began to slowly ooze forward.

Everyone retreated; from the smell, and from the sheer reek of evil that the thing gave off.

Next to her, Lucena saw Beruse aim her crossbow.

And then the thing looked at her.

It was like an icy cold hand had closed around her throat; her chest froze up, and the oozing slime in her mind surged forward. For a moment she was lost, drowning in it, and then:

Don't be afraid, La Flein.

His voice was weak and muffled, but she recognized it in an instant. Fighting her way out of the darkness in her own mind she grabbed Beruse's arm.

"Don't fire!" she gasped. "That's him, that's our *Madgrin!*"

Beruse froze, her aim still locked on the massive black blob slowly oozing closer. Without thinking Lucena vaulted the railing, plummeted twenty feet, and landed heavily upon the tile floor. The darkness loomed above her, and in its depths she thought she saw writhing tentacles and wormlike creatures, constantly turning in and devouring themselves.

The smell was almost overpowering. Lucena swayed forward and backward, fighting the dizziness that threatened to overcome her.

"What have you done with my maker?" she demanded.

The thing paused, seemed to consider her, and then advanced. Lucena took a step back, but caught herself. She reached out and grabbed one of the writhing tentacles of darkness, pulling it away.

It stung, burning like fire without being hot. Lucena gritted her teeth.

"Where is my maker?" She repeated.

The thing lunged at her. She put out her hands to stop it, but it engulfed her in foul-smelling black ooze that stung and burned. She might have screamed, but any sound that escaped her lips was swallowed in the dark. She reached inside the thing and tore at the slimy black worms. They wriggled under her hands and tried to escape, but she ripped at them with all the ferocity and tenacity that

CHAPTER 19: *Madgrin*

hunting vampires had taught her. When she felt them twining around her legs she kicked, she squirmed, and still she dug in, farther and farther.

She felt something that was not slime. It was soft and cool and didn't burn, and felt like it could be someone's hand. She grabbed it around what might have been its wrist, and held on, pushing at the slime around it to tear it free.

All of a sudden the hand came to life, clutching her arm like a drowning man grasping a rope. She pulled, desperately ripping at the slimy worms that clung to it. And then a large glob came away, and she was face to face with Madgrin.

He looked as she had never seen a living man look. His eyes were nearly lost in deep dark hollows, his face so emaciated it looked like something that had died in the desert and been left there. His mouth was open, and there was a dark liquid running from it.

"Maker," Lucena gasped.

Intok surged out of who-knew-where into the burning, slimy darkness around them. Lucena felt her, the soft brush of her mane and her warm, wet breath, and then her ears were pierced with a terrible scream as the nightmare charged forward, trampling and kicking at the muck until Lucena could work her other hand forward and grab Madgrin by his bony shoulders.

By this point she was almost entirely engulfed in the slime, save her feet. But Intok's appearance jerked the rest of the staff into action. Strong hands closed around her ankles and pulled, and after a lot of thrashing and screaming and hauling Lucena managed to drag Madgrin out of the burning muck, whereupon they both collapsed in a heap on the floor.

Lying on her back Lucena caught a glimpse of Intok, larger and fiercer than she had ever seen her, mane flying from her neck as though she stood before a gale, as she reared up and struck at the glob of slimy worms with her forefeet.

The glob shuddered, hissed, and then collapsed in on itself. Intok snorted, and proceeded to trample it into the tiles until there was nothing left but a dark smear.

Lucena sat up, was nearly overcome by nausea, and had to turn over and vomit on the floor. She wasn't sure what came out of her except that it smelled as bad as the slime had, and she wondered if maybe she had swallowed some.

Still dizzy, she was vaguely aware of a cluster of people who surged around to help them, of hands and arms that picked her up and half led, half carried her away. Lucena tried to protest, but her stomach was still making objections and she was forced to keep her mouth closed. In the end she needn't have bothered, for she was deposited on the floor in a corner of the kitchen while everyone else dragged Madgrin up onto the table. She wanted to protest this; to say that he didn't need help, he was fine now, and why did he need to go on the table anyway?

Eventually she realized it was because he appeared to be unconscious. And when she prodded experimentally at the back of her mind where he usually spoke to her she found it empty and dark. Cold. Dead. A bubble of panic began to billow up inside her chest.

Beruse appeared in the doorway with a long stone knife and a grim expression, followed closely by Orrus. Together they came to stand over Madgrin's prone form, and Lucena struggled to her feet and joined them, for she did not like the look of the knife.

At first glance Madgrin looked as though he were sleeping peacefully, but the shadows under his eyes were too dark, and his face still more resembled a dead husk. And, upon closer inspection, she discovered he was no longer breathing.

"Is he ... dead?" she asked, her small voice ringing around the silent room.

"Not yet," Beruse said grimly. "Orrus?"

Orrus was bent over Madgrin's chest, apparently listening for something. But when he stood up he shook his head. "Too many layers of enchantments; but the one that's hurting him is the Sarlefine worm. Better get it out as soon as you can."

Beruse grunted in acknowledgment. Then she noticed Lucena. "Oh good," she said. "You can hold him down."

"Hold him down?" Lucena repeated faintly.

For answer, Beruse took Lucena's hands and planted them firmly on Madgrin's neck. "Don't let him get up," she said. "Not even if he bites you."

Lucena opened her mouth to protest, but then Beruse was tearing away Madgrin's robes, cutting at them with her knife at times, until his entire chest was bare.

There was an open wound that ran along the center of his chest, from his navel to his collar bone, and the skin had been pushed back around it so that the raw flesh was exposed. But like in a dream where nothing is quite right, Lucena saw that his blood was indeed blue; so it followed that the terrible cut looked like someone had spilled blue paint all over his chest. But what made her shudder were the maggots.

There were hundreds of them, all inside. At first they were invisible since they were the same dark slimy black that the ooze had been, but once Lucena recognized them she had to turn her head away to keep from being sick.

She found Beruse's face. Beruse stared down, her mouth a thin line and her jaws clenched.

"Someone get a bucket," she said, and raised the knife.

After that everything became a nightmarish blur. Madgrin convulsed violently the first time Beruse went in with her knife, and nearly sent them all flying. Lucena ended up climbing onto the table and holding him so that his head and shoulders were in her lap, and she had him by the arms. Even so, every time Beruse pulled another wriggling, slimy handful of maggots out he would thrash so violently she was almost thrown off.

When he did, his face changed. Lucena saw it elongate, with heavy spiky brows, a curved snout, and a mouth full of sharp teeth. He looked more like a dragon than a man, but always with the same skull-like features.

"Maker?" Lucena asked in a horrified whisper.

"Hold him!" Beruse shouted. She was up to her elbows in Madgrin's chest, and had hold of something big. She tugged. Madgrin convulsed. He screamed, a horrible, dragon scream that made Lucena's teeth hurt. Beruse, her own teeth bared, pulled harder. Lucena tried to hook one arm around his neck to keep him from biting Beruse, so his snapping jaws came down on her instead.

That hurt. But Lucena had been hurt before in worse ways, and she held on.

CHAPTER 19: *Madgrin*

With a sick squelching noise and a shout of triumph Beruse dragged something out of Madgrin's chest. It was a bloated sack as long as her forearm, slimy black and dripping in blue blood. Out of it protruded a multitude of wriggling tentacles and suckers, which snapped and spat as Beruse raised it at arm's length above the table.

Without hesitating Beruse ran it through with her stone knife, cutting a terrible gash in its side. But still it writhed and squelched, alive and furious.

"Orrus!" Beruse cried.

Orrus came forward, a sprig of evergreen in his hand. There was another flash, as though a glass pane had been slid in front of him, and through the pane the two versions of Orrus could be clearly seen. One of them, the Orrus with glasses, held out the sprig of tree and gently touched the dripping sack. The other, the Orrus with bandaged eyes and strange robes, took a spiky dead branch and ran the sack through. And as he did the sack lurched, curled in on itself, and then shriveled away until nothing was left but a withered black husk. The pane of glass broke, and the Orrus Lucena knew stepped forward and took the shell out of Beruse's hand.

Beruse returned to picking bits and pieces of slime and worm out of Madgrin, but he no longer responded. He lay, a man's body with a dragon's head, as still as if frozen while Beruse washed the wound, neatly stitched the flaps of skin together, and applied a bandage. Only when she was finished did he relax. Closing his eyes, his face shrank back on itself until he was again the human Madgrin Lucena recognized, and she was able to remove her bleeding, mangled arm.

"I want to stay with him," Lucena objected when they tried to move Madgrin. She was still dazed from the fear and the pain, and barely noticed Gydda bandaging her arm. Madgrin was unconscious on the table, but from what Lucena could see he was breathing now, though slowly.

"We could move him to his bedchamber," Grimmach suggested, oblivious to her request. "But I don't know if it will let us in."

"I can reason with it," Willic said. He was pale, and had not quite come out of being a cat; he still had the whiskers in addition to his ears and tail.

"I'll stay with him," Lucena insisted, and she made a half-hearted attempt to get free of Gydda.

"You're in no condition to look after anyone," Gydda chided, planting her firmly on a stool. "Besides, it's almost morning."

"I'll be okay." She reached out and grabbed a fistful of Madgrin's robe. "I'm used to staying up now."

Gydda opened her mouth to let out more admonishments, but Beruse cut her off.

"Let her stay," she said. "She'll be the first one to know if he takes a turn for the worse."

So once Willic had convinced Madgrin's bedchamber to let them all in, and once Gydda had Madgrin tucked away in the giant bed, it was Lucena who stayed in the quiet room after everyone else carefully tiptoed away.

It was a large room, so filled with shadows that the only thing that could be easily seen was the bed, which lay in a pool of gentle light cast from a basketed candle. There were two long windows beside the bed, and unlike the windows of the north hall, these looked out onto the real grounds. Standing before them Lucena could make out the lake, the wide pale expanse of lawn, and the twisting silver strand of the main drive. In the east she could see the lightening of the sky that heralded the day's approach, with thin misty bands of clouds stretched across the horizon.

The windows had no curtains to draw, to her surprise, and so Lucena went around to the far side of the bed, where she would not be inadvertently burned in her sleep, and sat down with her head next to the mattress. If she craned her neck she could just make out the contours of Madgrin's body and the pale peak of his nose.

At first she thought she would never get to sleep. And her excitement and nerves did serve to keep her awake for all of perhaps five minutes. Then exhaustion truly came on, her head fell back against the side of the mattress, and she slept.

And for the first time in a hundred and fifty years, she *dreamed*.

She dreamt that she had stepped out of her body and was watching the room from up near the ceiling. She saw Madgrin; she saw herself; and she saw the brightening of the windows as the sun crept up into the sky. She saw the beams of light, how they were thrown across the room, but at such an angle that they never touched the bed, nor its occupant. And, she was relieved to see, neither did they touch her own body.

At noon Madgrin sat up. He arose in one fluid motion, as though he did not have a gaping wound in his chest. He looked around, and seemed puzzled to discover Lucena's body asleep beside the bed. He got out of the bed, and stepping around he carefully lifted Lucena onto it in his place. Lucena felt that, in a distant sort of way, as though it really were happening to her. But she also saw it happen. It was all very dreamlike and unreal, so perhaps she was not as surprised as she would have been otherwise when he leaned over and kissed her on the forehead, like an affectionate parent putting a child to bed.

She felt that too, so acutely in fact that it nearly pulled her out of the air and back into her body. For a moment she was strung between the two, and then she snapped back into the dreaming world, where Madgrin had left the bedside and was limping towards the door.

Lucena hovered above him, wanting to usher him back to bed. There was an unhealthy deadness in his eyes, and he was hunched over with one arm across his midsection. She remembered the worm, and she wanted to yell at him to get back in bed and lie still. But somehow she knew he would not hear her; it was one of those dreams where one could scream and scream and never make a sound.

Madgrin opened the door, went through it, and shut it behind him. Lucena followed him into the hall, drifting behind his head as he made his way through the house.

It was a much brighter place during the day, Lucena observed. There were many windows she had never noticed before, now with their curtains drawn back

CHAPTER 19: *Madgrin*

letting in strong beams of sunlight. She carefully avoided these, even in her strange, disembodied state, though Madgrin walked right through them. Unlike Amstrass, he didn't go transparent, but took on a fuzzy, indistinct look, as though he were on the other side of a misty pane of glass.

Eventually they came to the steep, narrow staircase that led to the roost where Halfain and Rusion lived, and Madgrin climbed up it. He opened the little wooden door and stepped out onto the roof. In the noon sun everything was blisteringly bright, and Lucena hung back in the shadow of the eaves, squinting at the dark blur that was Madgrin as he advanced onto the roof.

When he was about halfway to the feathery huts he stopped, turned around, and looked straight at Lucena. He brought one finger to his lips in the sign of silence, and smiled. Then he turned his back to her and, lifting his arms, turned his face up to meet the sun.

At first it appeared nothing happened, but then she saw that the image of Madgrin was slowly fading, like a steamed-up window as it clears. She could see the edge of the roof through his back, then his shoulders, and finally his trailing robes and outstretched arms. At the last moment all she could see was the outline of him, his arms still raised, and then it wobbled and billowed out like a curtain in the wind and flew to pieces that evaporated in the sun. The rooftop was bare save for the huts of the Watch and a soft summer wind.

Then Lucena did scream, and as she had anticipated, no sound came out. Forgetting herself, she ran forward into the sunlight.

There was a horrible jolt all over her body, and the world went black.

She came back to herself slowly, like an exhausted swimmer rising to the surface. She was in a bed—a large, luxurious bed, and someone was singing, though the words and music flitted into and out of her mind like butterflies. It was beautiful, sorrowful singing, and she strained against the bonds of sleep to sit up and see whose voice it was.

But it wasn't until the song was finished that she at last found the energy to turn her head sideways towards the source.

It was Madgrin. Whole and alive and not in the least transparent, he was standing facing the darkened windows, his arms folded across his chest. The last few notes hung on the air, and when they faded he turned his face to hers.

It was in all respects his old face; softer, not so skull-like. But there was something wrong about it all the same. Some spark or twinkle was absent, leaving his face like a piece of carved marble. But he smiled his old smile, and that melted away all of Lucena's doubts. She sat up.

"You," she began in a small voice, suppressing a lump in her throat. "You're... whole?"

For answer he drew back a fold of his robe, revealing his chest. His clean, unbandaged, unmarked chest. There wasn't even a scar.

Lucena slid out of bed. Walking slowly, she crossed the few feet of distance and touched him gently. He was solid.

"How?" she asked.

"I remade myself." Madgrin said simply.

Lucena looked at him, puzzled.

"This body is an idea," he explained. "I can change it, and remake it if needed."

Lucena thought of the skull face and the dragon's head. She suppressed a shudder.

"I have grown used to *this* idea," Madgrin passed a hand over his face. "But I could change it, if you like," he added with a twinkle of his old smile.

Lucena shook her head. Unable to speak she put out her arms and embraced him. She felt his long arms go around her, and she settled herself into the warm folds of his robes.

But there was something amiss. Something she couldn't put her finger on and didn't want to. She wanted everything to go back to normal now, but there was something that was very clearly not. And after a while she realized it wasn't something wrong, it was something missing.

He had no heartbeat.

Pulling away she looked hard at Madgrin's chest. She put her hand over the leftish place where she had always felt it beating before. But nothing. She frowned up at him.

"Maker, what happened to your heart?"

Madgrin drooped. He removed Lucena's hand. Holding it between both of his own he sighed heavily and said, "It is not my own anymore."

Lucena continued to look confused. He smiled at her sadly.

"Oh, *La Flein*," he said. "Things are going to be rather difficult for a while."

Madgrin disappeared into his study for most of the night after that, despite the protestations of every one of his staff. But he merely smiled and shrugged them all off. With nothing to do but worry, Lucena went to her own room and sat with Keelback on her bed.

Keelback had grown over the years; slowly, inch by inch, and now it was difficult for him to fit all his coils on the bed, but somehow he managed. His eyes were deeper too, and he did not squawk as much; but his feathers and scales he shed in abundance, so he always appeared sleek and young.

Not so, Urgolant. She had grown larger and fatter, with fold upon fold of wrinkled black skin. The skin was tough, and proved impervious to most weapons and sharp objects, as Lucena had come to appreciate. Yet Urgolant still enjoyed nothing so much as reading; she now sat in the darkest corner of Lucena's room surrounded by piles of old scrolls.

Only Intok remained unchanged, being always the same shadowy nightmare. Lucena watched her shadow now. Cast upon the far wall by the lone candle of her table, it stretched almost to the ceiling, the shape of a looming horse; and from the shadow of her head two orange flames stared back.

"What's wrong with Madgrin?" Lucena wondered aloud.

"His heart is missing," Urgolant answered, not looking up.

"I know that."

"There is a strange smell about him," Keelback said. "Like bad dirt and swamp."

CHAPTER 19: *Madgrin*

Silence. Lucena had *not* noticed that.

Intok put her head out of the shadow and blew wet, warm breath at Lucena. She meant it to be soothing, but it did not answer Lucena's question.

Then in the small hours of the morning Madgrin himself appeared. He seemed to come through the door, though she did not hear it open or close. He was simply standing there, waiting for her.

Lucena got up and went with him. They walked out of the house by the front door, down the steps, and out along the drive. They did not speak a word, but walked in step together. They went through the forest, crossed the river by the bridge, and then turned to walk along the riverbank. It was a warm summer night, and the air beside the river was refreshing and sweet.

A hundred questions flitted through Lucena's mind as they walked together, but as each one came to life it crumbled back to nothing. She had the feeling now was not the time for questions, or perhaps the time for questions was over for good.

They walked along the river, upstream and towards the Roc City. It loomed above them, craggy and pale in the moonlight. But there was a small path that wound in and out between the steep mountainsides, and they followed this, while the silent stony birds roosted far above.

Coming out of the city they found a ferry by the side of the river, and Madgrin took them across. They walked up the path, crossed the lawn, and came into the orchard. The apples were small, hard, round things, but the peaches were plump and ripe. Madgrin reached out and picked one, white-and-pink with a soft snowy fuzz, and handed it to Lucena.

She looked at him in confusion; they both knew she had no more reason to eat fruit than to eat grass. But Madgrin smiled. "Keep it," was all he said, and that was the only thing he said to her until they were standing just outside the kitchen gardens. There he stopped, his shoulders drooped, and he looked more tired and sad than Lucena had ever seen him.

"*La Flein*," he said quietly. "I'm afraid I must go away for a while."

"To where? For how long?"

"I do not know. It might be a very long time."

"Will you come back?"

He looked down at her. His eyes were shining, but there were tears in them.

"Oh yes," he said. "I always come back."

It was almost dawn; they embraced; he kissed her goodbye on the forehead, and then walked off into the dying night. Lucena stayed by the gate and watched until he faded away completely into the weakening darkness.

The next evening when she woke, he was gone.

It was not just that he was not anywhere in or around the house, nor that he was in a distant part of the world: He was gone. The corner of her mind where his voice spoke to her, and where she spoke to him, was empty. It was frightening. She got up without even looking at her breakfast and went to find Orrus.

He was not in the library as usual, but in his own rooms. He had all the cupboards open and was wrapping up books into a bedsheet.

Lucena stared at the scene in dismay.

"You're leaving *too*?" she asked.

"I'm afraid so." Orrus sighed. He tied a bundle of herbs together and tossed them into the pile. "It's not safe for me here anymore," he explained. "I'll have to go wandering for a while."

"When will you come back?"

"When *he* comes back."

And that was all he would say. Lucena went away to find Beruse, and instead found the entire staff gathered morosely in the kitchen. Even Rusion, looking very unhappy, was perched in a corner, and Halfain was sipping tea at the little table.

The sight of the Watch, who she hardly ever saw, sitting together in the kitchen, only served to further drive home the fact that something had gone very wrong.

"This doesn't happen often," Beruse explained sadly. "But sometimes he has to go away. I'm not sure why. He never says. But he always comes back." She gave Lucena a brave smile, but there was no comfort in it.

Lucena took a seat across from Halfain and next to Willic and gave herself over to misery.

Sometime later Soloma entered the kitchen. She seemed as dejected as the rest, but before silently taking her place among the moping crowd she went over to Lucena and tapped her gently on the shoulder.

"Himself left you something in his study," she said. "Said to tell you it was there, but you have to get it for yourself."

Lucena watched her retreating back in confusion. If Madgrin had wanted to give her something why hadn't he done so the night before? But her curiosity was piqued, and it gave her something to do, so she left the kitchen and walked slowly up through the house, past the ballroom and the antechambers, and through the north hall and the twisting, misty passages. She passed Willic's room and her own, the library, and finally she came to the room of doors.

Only there were no doors in it now, save the great carved one that led to Madgrin's study. Lucena's hands were shaking as she pushed it open and stepped inside.

It was dark beyond the door; the fire had sunk to a grill of tired embers, and the only other light came from the glowing spots among the leafy, crystalline ceiling. The carpet had been rolled away to the side and all the pictures turned to face the wall. There were no books in the bookcases, and the desk was empty save for two things: A folded letter, and a large vial of blue liquid, stopped with a cork.

Lucena took up the letter and, spreading it out on the floor by the hearth where the light was strongest, she began to read.

CHAPTER 19: *Madgrin*

Dearest La Flein, *Lucena,* [it said in Madgrin's clear, serpentine handwriting]

I am very sorry but I have to go away for a while. I am not sure how long it will be. I will return—I always do—but it may not be in the form which you have come to know. It is my hope that, when that time comes, you will have also changed, and so may better understand my predicament.

This is something I still find difficult to talk about, and here, now, when I have little time to spare, I shall not even try. Suffice to say that during your stay in my house I have afforded you certain protections, and now that I am gone, so are they.

I am not tremendously worried. You have protections of your own, after all. But I am leaving you with something that should render you beyond the reach of any conceivable danger.

By rights it has been yours all along. I have merely been keeping it safe for you. You will find it in the vial beside this letter.

It is your life. Your death. It is the blood of dreams. The soul of a lamphra. Claim it, as it is yours, and you may live again. Not a return to the life you once lived, but a step forward into a wider world. A change, moving forward. Change is life, after all, though it be frightening. So is living, in my experience.

I recall telling you once that a time would come for you to choose what you were to be. In truth I think you made that choice many years ago. This is merely the culmination of it. A conclusion, but one that blossoms into a new beginning, I should hope.

Though I am bound you are free, and of all things, I am most proud of that.

So fly free, free as a young dream,
and I shall remain

        Madgrin

Then exhaustion truly came on, her head fell back against the side of the mattress, and she slept.

CHAPTER 20:

Dawn,

LUCENA SAT IN THE DIM, QUIET STUDY, reading and rereading the letter. She took down the vial and looked at it carefully. In the bottom, where the liquid was the darkest, deepest blue, there glinted something bright and fragile.

"The blood of dreams," he had written.

Madgrin's blood was blue, Lucena remembered vividly. Her stomach clenched.

She went and sat in the shadow of the desk, clutching the letter and the vial to her chest, straining with her mind and her cold, dead heart to find her maker. How long she stayed like that, tired, hungry and miserable she didn't know. A few hours, perhaps? A day? A week?

Once, Willic poked his head in, saw her, and tactfully withdrew.

Lucena wished he hadn't; she wanted desperately to have someone to talk to, someone to tell her what to do. But she knew at heart that neither Willic nor any of her other friends would be able to advise her. This was her choice, the choice Madgrin had warned her of, and now it was upon her. And she was as terrified of it as she had been a hundred years before.

If there was anyone in the world who could advise her, it was probably Amstrass.

At the thought of her name the old vampire's voice sounded fiercely in her head.

"You've been too long on the edge of his world, it'll only take a step—or two—and *whoof!*"

Whoof. That was what Lucena was afraid of. *Whoof* . . . to where? To Dream? She turned the vial over slowly in her hand. It was warm to the touch, and as long as she held it the light grew brighter. She thought of the moon, the ferryman, the Garden at the Top of the World. She thought of Grimbald and Tobius and the demon . . . they were all in Dream too. It wasn't so bad. But something else Amstrass had said came back to her then:

"There is a magic in being human that they don't have."

She still did not know exactly what this magic was, and she realized she had imagined she would, before she let it go.

But this was it. She sat in the growing dark and pondered and wondered. Then she took out the letter again and reread the last few lines.

So fly free, free as a young dream,
and I shall remain

Madgrin.

She folded the letter again and slipped it into her pocket. Then she took the vial, uncorked it, and tipped the contents down her throat.

It was like drinking fire. It was like drinking moonlight. It burned and cooled her, and it set every nerve in her body tingling and raised the hairs on the back of her neck. She felt dizzy, and then she felt the floor beneath her hands. She must have fallen. When she rolled onto her back she saw above her not the wondrous ceiling of Madgrin's study, but a vast night sky filled with stars. Slowly, one by one, the stars turned to look at her, and they greeted her in their own language. They twinkled their delight at meeting her, just the way Madgrin's eyes did when he was pleased.

Visions flashed across the night sky. An empty schoolroom filled with weak sunlight; the charred remains of a building; a shadow dancing madly on a pale wall; a smile flashing in the dark. A galloping horse on an empty moor; a stone knife, stuck into a wooden table.

The little light at the bottom of the vial had spilled across her front when she had drained it, but now it had gathered together again into a soft ball of white light, floating expectantly above her head.

It pleased her for some reason, so she reached up her hands and drew it down to her face. She put her nose to its milky surface and breathed it in.

Warmth spread throughout her body, but from within, not from without. And she felt something hit her in the chest.

She coughed. She was hit again. Then she finally recognized the feeling; something she hadn't felt in a hundred and fifty years: it was her heart, and it was beating.

Pa-pound.

Pa-pound.

Pa-*pound*.

Slowly, with each beat, she felt the world melt back into place. The ceiling swam into focus above her, and she became aware of the hard, cool wood under her back. She also became aware of a strange itching that spread up her arms from her fingertips. It was followed by a tingling, like a thousand pins and needles slowly creeping up her arms and filling her body.

In time the tingling faded and a sort of numbness settled upon her. It was as though she felt everything distantly, and the real her was somehow separate from her body.

She wanted to see those stars again. They knew things, and they would help her. Perhaps they could help her find Madgrin.

But she couldn't move, couldn't leave the cold, numb body that was still chained to her.

So she got up. She made it move, first one arm and then the other, until finally she was standing on her feet. She went to the door and opened it, pushed her way through the empty room which had once been full of doors and into the rest of the house.

It was silent and still, but with her new, distant mind Lucena could tell exactly where everyone was: Willic had gone to sleep in his room, Beruse was drinking wine with Harga in the kitchen. The hoblins were cowering in the basement for some reason, and Soloma had gone to be a snake in the forest. Halfain was out hunting, and Rusion had finally gone up to roost.

CHAPTER 20: *Dawn*

To her surprise she also found her familiars, neither in the House nor out of it, but down and a little to the left and following close behind her. It was a comforting feeling, though like all others Lucena felt it faintly.

She came to the stairs that led to the Watch's terrace, and began to climb. There were small, high windows along one side of the wall, and through these she saw the pale grey light that heralded the dawn. She climbed faster. The air inside the house was stuffy and dusty, and she disliked breathing it. It was then she noticed that she was breathing at all. Indeed, now it was hard to make her body stop breathing; her lungs protested and her chest burned, just like it had when she was alive.

She reached the little door at the top of the stairs and went through it.

The sky was growing lighter by the minute, the greyness fleeing before a bright blue wave crested with pink clouds and, at the horizon, a thin strip of gold.

Lucena had seen sunrises long ago, in her youth, and even a few when she was traveling with Amstrass. But she had long forgotten the sunrises of her living days, and the ones she had seen with Amstrass had only been caught in hurried glances over her shoulder as she fled from them.

Now she stood at the eastern edge of the terrace, just as she had seen Madgrin do in her dream, and watched with wide eyes as the gold band brightened, intensified, and finally exploded, shooting bright yellow beams of light across the distant grounds as the sun began to wrestle itself free of the horizon.

Her heart was pounding in her chest like a hammer, beating at the walls like a trapped bird. She took a last, wheezing breath and raised heavy, numb arms to embrace the morning.

Her dead, vampire body evaporated in the sunlight. She felt it catch fire—one blazing moment when all the pins and needles turned to knives—and then it was falling in a cloud of dust to the ground, and she was shooting off into the sky, as light and as free as a thought on the wind.

For a while she became just that: a thought, an idea, blown hither and thither by the rising morning. She forgot her body, she forgot her own thoughts, and she forgot her name. Instead she became the thoughts and ideas of everything she found: she was the nervous, twitchy thoughts of a squirrel; she was the long, slow, deliberate thoughts of the tree it sat on; then she became the feather-light thoughts of a butterfly. The butterfly flapped over a hedge and alighted on a red poppy, only to fly off again immediately because of a cat that pounced on it. She was caught by the thoughts of the cat, which were more focused and complex than the thoughts of the squirrel or the tree or the butterfly. She began to remember a little of what she had been—and what she should be—and decided it was silly to be flitting about the world in thoughts.

So she extracted herself from the cat's mind and solidified herself into its shadow. From there she watched as the cat slinked through the field and hopped up onto a stone wall.

They were by a country lane in summer, and someone was walking down it. He wore clothes cut in a curious new fashion, and this oddness was compounded by the fact that every article was made of purple. As he passed he saluted the cat, and then shot a surprised glance at its shadow.

She felt a memory prick her with that glance. The same face, also surprised, but lit by candlelight and in a strange, dark place.

But then he was past, and the cat continued on down the wall beside the lane. There was a bright, morning-blue sky above her, with clouds piling up on the horizon like scoops of whipped cream. Now and then they passed through dappled spots of green shade cast by trees, and all around them the sounds and smells of the day hung heavy in the air.

Birdsong floated down from the trees and lit in her a wild, fierce joy. Breaking free of the cat's shadow she fashioned herself wings and fluttered into the sky. She had in her vague, airy mind some vague, airy thoughts of flying off to play in the buttery clouds, but soon she became tired and spread out to float on the air. Like that she was able to feel the pulsing and sparkling field of ideas, thoughts and dreams that rose up from the countryside. They came from houses, where children sat playing games and housemaids dreamed of perfect lovers while they washed the laundry and pressed the linen; they also came from the yards and fields, where dogs dreamed of chasing rabbits and pigs pondered possibilities for the future.

She laughed for joy at the sight of so many ideas and darted in among them, setting them spinning and whirling off in new directions, fanning the little ones until they worked their way free from their mind's subconscious and went galloping out into waking thought. She played with the ideas, watched them grow and unfold, and if they wilted to the back of their owner's mind she moved on.

So passed the day, but when evening came and the stars came peeping out from behind the sky she began to remember a little more of who she was. She knew, definitely, that she was searching for something. She hadn't the faintest notion what, but she was also certain that the stars could tell her. The stars saw everything, even during the day when they could not themselves be seen. So she went bobbing up into the night sky, hoping the stars would notice her and help her.

But she got lost among their bright, burning faces, and blown before the force of their own dreams and ideas (which burned like ice), she tumbled across the sky.

A bright milkiness rose up to one side, and she found herself looking into the wider, softer face of the moon. The moon looked back. And she saw that the moon did not have a face at all; there was a dragon curled around it, its wings spread to grip the moon on all sides. She could see the ridge of its back and neck going slantwise across the moon's surface, with a little ridge at the bottom where its tail had wrapped all the way around. Its head rested on its forepaws, and one dark eye was looking back at her.

A little embarrassed to have mistaken the moon for so long, she floated closer. The dragon lifted its head—the same, chalky white as the moon rock—and gave her a considering look.

"Well, aren't you a little lost?" it said in a musical, female voice.

"I'm afraid so," she replied, her voice a faint whisper by comparison.

"Come closer," said the moon. "Let me have a look at you."

CHAPTER 20: *Dawn*

Though for all she knew she was still invisible, she drifted closer. She saw old pockmarks on the dragon's scaly back, and the way little gusts of moondust drifted off into space whenever it moved. Still the dragon looked at her with the same kind, contemplative attitude.

"Oh, but you're only a child," the dragon in the moon said, sounding surprised and worried. "Where have you come from?"

"I was hoping you could tell me that," she said. "I seem to have forgotten."

"I'm afraid that's not my place," the moon said, kindly. "But here comes Old Grimby. You have the look of her kin. She will have your answers."

As the moon-dragon spoke she had floated closer, and turning around she saw the earth, a beautiful blue-and-green gem streaked with white, and from the earth there rose a giant stone stairway marching through the clouds until it came to a stop not far from the dragon's nose. She was about even with the highest step, and as she watched, a familiar figure climbed into view—a short, stout figure in a black velvet dress with blue skin and wild, twisting brown hair.

"What are you doing just floating there?" Grimbald demanded, for indeed it was Grimbald. "Come over here immediately, and go corporeal for goodness sakes, that should be easy for you now you're in the shadow of Reanen."

Chagrined, she drifted down and pulled herself into a physical form. Without thinking, she returned to the one she had originally held, but since it felt odd to be looking down at Grimbald she pulled her height in so that they were even. Grimbald seemed to approve; she smiled.

"Better," Grimbald said. "Now, we have several things to talk about. Firstly, are you ready to be Badgrave yet?"

She thought about this. Badgrave seemed to be a much grander, important person than she was used to being, and the name sounded somehow wrong.

"I'm not sure," she admitted. "It doesn't describe me very well."

"It doesn't describe you *at all*, that's the point," Grimbald said. "Like my name. That's how it started: you're so many things you can't possibly be called after them all, so you pick the things you're not: like Fearbright. And Madgrin."

The name Madgrin landed like an anchor in her mind. It brought with it the sensation of cool air against her skin, and her heart, which had been light and feathery until that moment, suddenly solidified and began to beat steadily.

The person that had until recently been Lucena Clarian Ashmoor, the vampire, regarded Grimbald thoughtfully. "I suppose Badgrave will do," she said. "Very well, and thank you."

"Good," Grimbald said, clasping her hands together and looking pleased. "Now I suggest you bring your familiars out and make sure they understand too."

Badgrave was a little confused at that, but she obligingly brought them out. One at a time, so they could get their bearings. First Keelback, who stared up at her in awe and said, "Cena?"

Badgrave blustered. "No, no," she said. "I'm Badgrave now."

Keelback shook his head. "Cena," he said firmly.

Badgrave sighed. "Well, I suppose I'll always be 'Cena' to you," she said. "But you understand, Urgolant?"

She asked this as Urgolant came tumbling out of the shadows behind her.

"Badgrave," Urgolant replied, clicking her mouthparts. "It fits you well."

Finally there was Intok, and whether or not she noticed the change from Lucena to Badgrave was uncertain; she stood beside them at the top of the stairway to the moon and regarded them with a pleased, alert expression, but not at all surprised. Instead it was Badgrave who was startled, as it appeared to her that Intok was the one that had changed: she was larger somehow, and more solid. It was as though before she had always been a little blurry and out of focus, but now she was sharp and clear: her dark glossy coat reflected the moonlight, and her eyes were like glass marbles with flames inside. Her mane and tail had become billowing clouds of smoke, and this smoke swirled and twisted about her, forming the vague shape of wings above her back.

"Have you always been this way?" Badgrave asked, and this time—for the first time—she heard the nightmare's answer.

"Of course," Intok said. She had a clear, high voice. A child's voice. "But most people can't see all of me."

No wonder I never heard a word she said before, Badgrave thought to herself. I never thought she would sound like that.

Beside them, Grimbald coughed impatiently. "This is all quite *grand*. Lovely. One big happy monster family. Badgrave, Mistress of Monsters, it's all very charming," she said. "Now, have you decided what your wish is to be?"

"My, my wish?" Badgrave stammered.

"Yes, yes, yes, your wish! I'm obliged to grant the wish of every lamphra that's born, so hurry up and make one!"

Badgrave stared at her. She had not the faintest clue what she wanted to wish for. However, while she had been greeting her old familiars, the rest of her memories had begun trickling back, and now that she had a chance to examine them she knew exactly what she wanted to do.

"I want to find Madgrin," she said. "I'm worried about him."

Grimbald went very quiet. "*That's* your wish?"

"No, no," Badgrave said. "Not at all . . . well, maybe. But I haven't decided yet. Could, could you find Madgrin for me?"

Grimbald shrugged. "I could. Though not much good that would do you. Madgrin is . . . unavailable, right now. It happens sometimes; he'll work his way out in a couple of centuries or so."

"Centuries?" Badgrave cried, dismayed.

Grimbald crossed her arms and looked at her critically. "And asking *me* to find him is an utter waste. You can find him very well on your own. Getting him . . . hmm . . . *extracted* might be a little difficult, but you have friends for that."

"Friends?"

Grimbald looked pointedly at Badgrave's familiars, clustered protectively around their mistress. "And there is also the Purple Magician. You don't know him, but he's been searching for you for years. He likes helping people, and he likes Madgrin. And that cocky vampire . . . the one from Svenia, she'll probably help you, too. She loves getting into trouble."

With a sigh Grimbald turned away and plodded off down the giant stone stairs. Badgrave had a moment to wonder if they were somehow a continua-

CHAPTER 20: *Dawn*

tion of the stairs through the ruined city beneath the Sea of Stories, but then she hurried after.

"But I don't even know *where* Madgrin is," she pleaded.

"Don't ask me, ask the Purple Magician," Grimbald said over her shoulder. "He'll know how to find out, and it won't cost you a boon from me. Your nightmare can find him for you. Oh," and here she paused and turned around. "If Madgrin's gone to pieces when you find him, don't waste time trying to get them all—just bring the biggest one up here. I'll fix him. Free of charge, too. In the meantime," she turned back again, descending the steps in twos and threes, "keep thinking of that wish—I won't wait forever!"

Badgrave watched her from the top step, a tiny blue-and-black figure crawling down an immense staircase, which itself withered away into a thin strip of pale grey against the vast blue-and-white-and-green orb that was the earth.

She decided she would go to Amstrass first. It felt strange, but she thought of Amstrass as an old friend now. Besides, it didn't feel nearly so awkward asking her for help since Badgrave knew she now had something to bargain with.

"I told her next time I might have secrets," she said to herself and her familiars. "Well, now I suppose I do."

She looked around. It would be very easy to call Amstrass to her, she discovered. For with her transformation had come a host of new ways of looking at the universe, and through one of them she saw exactly how she should say Amstrass's name in such a way that, not only would she appear, but she would have no choice but to do so.

But this struck Badgrave as rude, and not the thing to do when she would be asking for help. So she went to her, instead.

It was easy, she discovered, to feel out a person's location just by thinking of them very hard. Amstrass turned out to be far away, and since Badgrave was in a hurry she grabbed at the bit of space where Amstrass was and pulled it across to her bit of space, creating a huge wrinkle in the process.

This could cause problems for some people if I leave it this way, she thought to herself as she stepped across. So, when she arrived at her destination she took a moment to carefully unfold the wrinkle of space and smooth it out. In doing so she discovered many other wrinkles, some of them quite old and stiff, popping up all over the place. She didn't bother undoing those; for all she knew they were important. But it amazed her: the world truly was a much larger place than she had ever before imagined.

She stood up from smoothing out her wrinkle and turned around, still marveling at this discovery, to find Amstrass staring at her as though she had seen a ghost.

Badgrave had imagined a formal speech for greeting Amstrass, one she hoped the vampire would like, but the sight of Amstrass staring with her mouth slightly open was so comical and embarrassing that Badgrave only managed a mangled "H-hello."

Amstrass still stared. They were standing in a lonely grove of pine trees which grew among ragged slabs of granite. From the smell, Badgrave judged them to be very high up in the mountains, yet it was still strangely warm. Above them the stars twinkled merrily, and the moon, a fat crescent in the east, watched them with interest.

Eventually Amstrass shook herself. She eyed Badgrave, her soul working furiously across her face, and pulled at a strand of hair.

"I know you," she said in a quiet, uncertain voice. "Or at least I knew you, before you are as you are now."

"I was once a vampire," Badgrave said. "By the name of Lucena."

Recognition flashed across Amstrass's face, then she frowned. "And *now*?"

"I am Badgrave, Mistress of Monsters."

Amstrass kicked at a bit of stone. "Oh? And what would a grand old lamphra like yourself be wanting with me?"

Badgrave lost her patience. She stamped her foot angrily. "For heaven's sake Amstrass, it's me. Lucena. Little Lucena? You promised me secrets in return for mine, but I didn't have any so you let me go. Well, *now* I've got secrets, and I need some help."

Amstrass was beginning to look at her with a bit of the old steely glint in her eye, which Badgrave found strangely comforting.

"What sort of help?"

"My old maker, er, Madgrin, is in trouble. Someone took his heart and then he had to go away. I'm worried. I can't find him, and I'm afraid something bad has happened. I want to bring him back."

Amstrass put her head on one side. She seemed to be amused, even if she wasn't smiling.

"What sort of secrets?" she asked.

Badgrave went and sat down on one of the smaller boulders. "There was a war," she began. "A long time ago . . ."

She told Amstrass about the war between the lamphra and the demons and the sarlef. At first she had been afraid that she would forget what Madgrin had told her, or that she wouldn't be able to answer Amstrass's questions, but the memories came back to her as she spoke them, and she got the oddest sensation that the trees and the rocks and the grass and even the distant stars were paying her close attention. And Amstrass asked no questions. She stood, straight and mute, staring at Badgrave with an intensity that would have been disconcerting if Badgrave hadn't been used to it.

When she had finished, the stones shifted, the trees sighed in the gentle wind, and the stars turned away. Amstrass came to sit opposite Badgrave on another rock, resting her chin on her hand.

"Well," she said at length. "Those are secrets indeed." She turned her head this way and that so she could look at Badgrave from one side and then the other, like a hawk.

"Will you help me?" Badgrave asked.

Amstrass shrugged. "I suppose," she said. "Yes. Why not? It should be interesting."

Badgrave was so relieved she sprang to her feet. For one mad instant she entertained the idea of embracing Amstrass but quickly discarded it. For her part, Amstrass got up too, albeit with a little more dignity.

CHAPTER 20: *Dawn*

"Well, what are we going to do now?" she asked.

"I'm not sure," Badgrave said. "I don't know where Madgrin is, but Grimbald told me I should ask the Purple Magician for help. She told me he's been looking for me anyway. And I think I've seen him—twice, actually. She said Intok could find him . . . " but she trailed off. Amstrass was staring at her as though she had suggested summoning the Prince of Hell himself.

"The *Purple Magician?*" she said. "Do you have any idea who that *is?*"

When Badgrave shook her head Amstrass groaned.

"That's *Bouragner d'Felpass,*" she said, putting great emphasis on each syllable. "He's the greatest magician of this age . . . perhaps any age. He's *dangerous.*"

Where have I heard that name before? Badgrave thought to herself. Because she knew she had, but could not place it. But Amstrass was looking almost alarmed, so she pointed out: "*You* are dangerous."

Amstrass glared at her. Then she smiled ruefully. "Yes, and you are too, come to think of it. A dangerous fool." She chuckled to herself, shaking her head. "Well, if you're certain . . . "

"Grimbald said I should get his help, though I do not know why he should help me. That is why I came to you."

"And you trust *me* over *Grimbald?*" Amstrass looked incredulous.

"I trust you both to be true to yourselves," Badgrave said, without thinking. Then she did think, and explained: "Grimbald is my queen, but you are my friend."

Amstrass still stared at her, incredulous. Badgrave gazed back, mild and serene. She was not afraid of Amstrass anymore.

Then the vampire said, in a small voice quite unlike herself:

"If you say so."

Badgrave realized that she was smiling. A silent affirmation.

Amstrass gave an exasperated sigh and rolled her eyes dramatically. In her usual, harsh voice she said, "Very well, Lucena, Badgrave, Mistress of Monsters, whatever you are. Let's go find Felpass."

Badgrave stood up. She called out Intok and explained the situation. Intok nodded, ruffled her smokey wings, and stalked off into the night. Amstrass and Badgrave followed. And as they went she remembered where she had heard the Purple Magician's name before: Felpass had been the wizard who wrote the book about Amstrass. The book bound in pale purple cloth. And he had also been the wizard who the laboratory had belonged to. He had been the one to leave them Urgolant's shadowy egg!

As she put this together, Badgrave felt excitement rise in her chest. She had begun to feel like she had left the House of Madgrin behind her forever, but now she was going to meet someone who had known it as she had. Her step quickening, she marched behind Intok, while Amstrass stalked moodily in the rear.

The path Intok led them on soon left the forest behind. They walked through a sea of night sky, leaving trails of stardust in their wake. Badgrave recognized it as being part of Dream, and as she did so she saw that there were many places where it intermingled with the waking world. The two wove together, sometimes so subtly it was hard to tell where one ended and the other began.

"Oh," she exclaimed. "That is brilliant."

Her companions both snorted; Intok in gratitude, and Amstrass in annoyance.

After a short while Intok dove off to one side, and Badgrave followed. Together with Amstrass they tumbled into an attic room—she could tell it was an attic, because of the steeply slanted ceiling on one side—that was in a spectacular state of disarray. Papers, jars, bottles, pens, articles of clothing and dirty dishes were scattered everywhere, along with several artifacts Badgrave did not recognize. As they landed she barely avoided stepping on a delicate golden mechanism that looked like a globe inside a coil with a handle.

The proprietor of this mess was sitting in an armchair in the corner, writing in a large book with a quill pen, and seemed wholly unperturbed by the sudden appearance in his study of a large shadowy horse and two strange-looking women. But he did look up with some annoyance when Intok's hoof destroyed a china plate.

He was the same man Badgrave had seen in the country lane earlier, when she had been a cat's shadow. He looked at them with the same sharp, thin face, and wrinkled his strong, aquiline nose at the broken plate. His dark hair was disordered, and he was wearing a light lavender dressing gown instead of his usual purple suit, but he was unmistakable. He was also the very same same man that she had seen with Urgolant when they had taken the mirror path back to the House.

"Oh, no," he said, his voice deep with displeasure. He raised a long finger and pointed it at Intok. "*You* had better go."

Intok disappeared with a surprised pop, and Badgrave gasped. But when she examined herself she found Intok had just gone back to where she usually resided; in her mistress's shadow.

"It is nothing on my account," the magician explained apologetically. "But my landlady is rather fond of that china set." He closed the book, leaving his quill pen as a marker, and stood up. Standing, he was almost as tall as Amstrass, and Badgrave began to feel a bit like Grimbald, what with having to crane her neck to look up at them.

"Now," he said, looking piercingly from one to the other. "It's interesting that you two should come together, and I'm certain you"—he jabbed the finger at Badgrave, and she felt a wave of pure magic come off it that staggered her—"have something urgent to talk about, but before we get on with that I think we should have some tea."

Amstrass snorted. Bouragner d'Felpass gave her a vague, half-interested look, then smiled pleasantly and announced loudly that he would appreciate tea for three.

The tea set dropped unceremoniously out of the air and landed with a dangerous clatter upon a table already crowded with dirty cups and saucers, but the porcelain pot and clean cups held together, and Bouragner d'Felpass poured out three steaming servings and handed two of them to his guests as they sat down.

Amstrass looked at hers skeptically before taking a cautious sip. Her eyes went wide and she stared at the magician in surprise.

CHAPTER 20: *Dawn*

"Lamb's blood?" she asked.

"As I recall it was your favorite," Bouragner d'Felpass said. He motioned to Badgrave, who was still holding her cup and looking at it dubiously; it was filled with a steaming amber liquid that smelled faintly of beeswax and flowers. But when she took a sip she found it was the perfect temperature and tasted sweet and fresh, like nectar.

"It's wonderful," she exclaimed, and was rewarded by a brief, dazzling smile. For a moment his thin, raptor's face was welcoming and handsome as the day. Then the expression faded, and he sat back in his chair and placed his fingertips together, looking at them with sharp interest. Like that he more than a little resembled Madgrin, and Badgrave felt a wave of nerves as she remembered why she was there.

"Master Magician, Bouragner d'Felpass," she began.

"Just Felpass, if you please," the magician interrupted.

"Pardon?"

"I'm going by Felpass alone these days," he explained. "Reasons of my own. Can't blame you."

"I'm sorry, Master Felpass—"

"Please, I'm not a master of anything."

"Sir Felpass?" Badgrave tried hesitantly.

The magician gave her an exasperated look, and Badgrave began to wonder if she was being made fun of. Amstrass seemed to think so; she snorted, drained her cup, and shook a boney finger at him.

"Don't you worry, he likes making people feel *awkward*," she said. "Listen Felpass, this little lamphra's lost her maker and she's in a pickle over it so she wants you to help her find him."

Both of Felpass's eyebrows went up at that. He looked at Badgrave with great interest, and then sharply at Amstrass.

"And you give her your aid because . . . ?"

Amstrass glared at him stonily. "You never told me about the war."

Felpass shrugged. "You never asked." He sighed. Then he looked at Badgrave again, intensely, as though he were trying to look at something through her body. He blinked. Then he shot up, marched across the room and knelt before her. "But, my dear," he said, one hand fluttering across her face, making her jerk back. "What a dunce I am not to have seen it before—you're *her!*"

"Who?" Badgrave asked.

"The little vampire I saw on the mirror paths; I've been trying to find you for ages. Well, I shall be happy to help you in any way I can. Now pray tell, who is, or was, your maker?"

"Madgrin of Dream," Badgrave said, and Felpass nearly fell over in surprise. It would have been funny, had the situation not been so grim.

"I am getting old," he said, rising slowly and passing a hand over his face. "To think I did not notice."

"I've known of you for many years," Badgrave continued. "They still have your laboratory, but Orrus has cleaned it up rather. I read your book on Amstrass there, and it was very informative. I also helped hatch the darkness you left in the laboratory."

"It hatched?" Felpass said, momentarily brightening.

Badgrave nodded. "Urgolant, would you come out please? And do be careful of the mess."

With a bulge and a shove and a sound like distant rain Urgolant scrambled out of Lucena's shadow, daintily placing her many feet around the cluttered floor. She made a sort of bow to Felpass and clicked her mouthparts respectfully. Felpass was enchanted. He bowed back and reverently stroked her black, hairy head.

"If you don't mind, sir," Urgolant said politely. "I think it would be better to find Madgrin quickly: my feeling is that he is in a bad situation."

Regretfully Felpass stood up. He looked around at the peculiarities assembled in his attic room, and shrugged. "What is the situation?" he asked.

With great relief Badgrave explained the incident with the slime, the hole in Madgrin's chest, and his subsequent disappearance. She tried to describe the dead feeling within the House after he had left, but found it difficult. Felpass seemed to understand anyway.

"That is unfortunate," he said when she had finished. "It sounds as though he has been bound to a wizard; it has happened before. I expect he will return when the terms of his contract are fulfilled, or sooner if the wizard is defeated."

Two things immediately scrambled to the front of Badgrave's mind. First: incredulity that someone as powerful as Madgrin could be bound by a mere wizard. Second: that this had happened before. How blind I have been! she thought angrily. Everyone in the house must have seen what was coming except for *me*.

"How—how could he be bound . . . by a *wizard?*" she asked, her voice hoarse.

"Wizards can be quite powerful people in their own way," Felpass said modestly. "But I take your meaning. Briefly, it is this: Madgrin belongs to a caste of beings that, when proper form and regulations are fulfilled, can be summoned to serve the whims of mortal humans. It comes with the territory of being in exile."

"I get a bit of that, too," Amstrass put in. "Not nearly as strong, mind you. I can usually kill anyone who summons *me*."

"You said he will be freed when the terms of his contract are fulfilled, or the wizard is defeated," Badgrave said, ignoring Amstrass. "When will that be?"

"Maybe a year, maybe two," said Felpass. "Maybe one hundred. It depends on the contract. Some lamphra have been bound for many hundreds of years."

"Yes," sighed Amstrass, a sneer audible in her voice. "And the problem with challenging the wizard in the meantime is that whoever is fool enough to do so will have to prevail over whatever powers they've gained from Madgrin."

Badgrave felt her heart sink, but Felpass seemed not in the least discouraged.

"I have faced more dire odds than that," he said. He shrugged again, and this time his dressing gown wrinkled and jerked and then turned dark. It became the deep purple suit Badgrave had seen him in before, and several of the lines disappeared from his face. Suddenly a much younger man stood before them, yet there was no doubt that it was still Felpass. He leapt across the room and dashed off through a door to what must have been his dressing room, for he came back with a hat and cane in hand and his shoes on. He then went to one of the long windows and threw it open.

"Off we go to fight a wizard," he declared grandly. He gestured to Badgrave. "After you," he said.

"But I don't know where he is," she protested.

Behind her, Amstrass snorted. Felpass raised an eyebrow.

"That hardly matters," he said. "The line between your hearts is so strong I could swing from it. Now step up, my dear, and lead the way."

"What are you doing just floating there?" Grimbald demanded, for indeed it was
Grimbald.

CHAPTER 21:

Badgrave

It was a warm night, and the town below them was picked out in golden windows of light scattered down to the rolling, glinting darkness of the sea, veiled by a thin fog. Above it, clouds ringed the moon in milky ripples, and in its misty light Badgrave fancied she saw a myriad of half-visible creatures swirling around it.

She didn't look too closely at them—some didn't look at all nice—but instead tried to concentrate on finding Madgrin. No matter what Felpass had said she couldn't feel anything in her heart that resembled a line, only a hard tightness that reminded her of worry.

Felpass put a hand on her shoulder, and she suppressed a jump. "Try looking the other way," he said, and when she swiveled around in confusion he turned her back saying, "No, no, the *other way.*"

So Badgrave squinted into the darkness, trying to look with the other part of her mind. The part that saw ideas and could become a cat's shadow. And suddenly it appeared that there were two worlds overlaid on each other. In one they stood above the town and the sea with the foggy, pale moon; in the other there were no clouds or fog or town or sea, and above them the moon was whole and much closer. Badgrave could see the dragon in it clearly, curled around the globe so that its tail nearly touched its nose.

The moon-dragon winked at her.

In the distance something twinkled in the dark. A tiny glitter, like a distant star. Or an eye. Badgrave reached out for it experimentally, and discovered a hard, burning line of magic that ran from her chest to the distant star.

"Strong enough to swing on," she murmured to herself. She took the line in both hands and pulled herself along it.

Surprised shouts followed her, and a moment later two pairs of hands clapped onto her shoulders.

"Warn me before you do that next time," Amstrass hissed. "You nearly left us behind!"

Badgrave nodded, but she couldn't manage anything more; the tiny star was so distant and weak she feared it would go out, or the line would break, if she did not concentrate on both. So she pulled herself along it carefully, hauling Felpass and Amstrass in her wake. After a while it got easier, and she was able to hand herself along the line at a sort of lunging walk, at which point Felpass and Amstrass could keep up on their own.

"It's so tiny," she said at last. "Will he go out?"

"The magician has woven his net well," Felpass conceded. "It could be difficult to break."

"Pah," said Amstrass. "There's nothing he can do, now that we are coming. Step forward, Badgrave, I smell a traitor behind your maker's back."

"He's not my maker any more," Badgrave said sadly, realizing the full implications of this for the first time.

Madgrin was no longer her maker. What she had become now—what she was still in the process of becoming—was of her own doing. And what she did, she did of her own volition, and at her own risk.

It grew dark along the way, and cold. But before Badgrave noticed, she felt Intok's warm breath on her shoulder and Keelback's frill brush her leg. Urgolant clicked behind her, and when she looked she saw that Amstrass was now flanked by her giant dog and the blood-red stag. Felpass too had something that walked beside him, but it was too dark to see properly. Badgrave only got the impression of soft paws and a rolling gait, like large cat.

They had long since passed beyond the town and left the sea behind; all she could see around them was the black void and, in the distance, the tiny weak twinkle of light. No matter how long they walked it never seemed to get any closer, and in the dark everything grew cold around her except for the burning line of magic.

Then, without warning, the light flickered and went out. Badgrave was left in darkness with the line between her hands, while around her she heard the rushing of wings. In the distance she thought she heard Amstrass cry out—whether in pain or anger she could not tell—and Felpass shouted something.

Claws scraped at her face out of the darkness, but she couldn't raise a hand to deflect them for fear she would lose hold of the line, which was growing fainter and cooler. Desperately she pulled herself along it, hand over hand, until with a hard lurch she felt herself plunged into thick, cold slime.

She recognized this slime; it was the same stuff that had surrounded Madgrin. The stuff that had made him unrecognizable to even his staff. The work of the other wizard. Then it had hurt her physically, but now it hurt emotionally as well. The slime hated her—*really* hated her—and wanted to destroy her. It felt like being dragged through a tunnel lined with sharp teeth or broken glass and she would have screamed except she did not, on any account, want the stuff inside her.

She was losing her grip on the line, slowly but steadily it was being eaten away by the slime. Gritting her teeth to keep from gasping at the pain, she gave a desperate pull.

For a moment she thought the line had snapped. Then, with a feeling like her very skin peeling away, she shot forward and burst out of the slime. She fell to the ground with a hard thump and lay, twitching slightly, while the world solidified around her.

As the pain receded her vision cleared, and rolling onto her back she saw she was in a high, domed room with a stone floor and tall, narrow windows. It was bare and illuminated only by the faint streaks of starlight drifting in through the windows. At the far end a staircase led up and was lost in the shadows, and beside her was a door that stood open to a narrow garden path between rosemary hedges.

CHAPTER 21: *Badgrave*

There was someone standing in the shadows by the door. He must have been shocked at Badgrave's arrival, for he did not move until she had sat herself up and taken some gasping, shuddering breaths. Then he came forward and said in a chillingly familiar voice:

"What are you doing here, Munsmire?"

Badgrave looked up in disbelief to find Undergate leaning over her.

He was somewhat leaner than the last time she had seen him, somewhat bonier, and there was a hunted look in his eyes. Nevertheless, his bearing was confident, and he was dressed richly in fine clothes. Out of curiosity she peered inside his mind, looking for his real name, and was surprised when she did not find one.

"I won't bother correcting you anymore," she sighed, "when you cannot even remember your own name."

The statement displeased him. He scowled and stalked away across the hall, but a moment later he returned, now carrying a strange device that looked rather like a sword with a silver globe attached to the hilt. On the globe was carved a Holy Arrow, and at the sight Badgrave felt her skin prickle. She stood up.

"What are you doing here?" she asked.

Undergate pointed the strange sword at her, his expression blank. "I am his doorkeeper."

"Whose?"

"The magician's."

Badgrave felt her heart turn over. "He bound you?"

Undergate snorted. "Of course not; I'm serving him as repayment. He was the one who gave me all those rare books on Amstrass back when I was searching for her, but in return I had to be his servant after I had found her..." he trailed off, his blank look breaking into an anguished glower. "And a very fine deal it was, until you spoiled it!"

"Me?" Badgrave exclaimed in surprise.

"She was there. We *had* her," Undergate cried. The hand that held the sword was shaking. "I almost had the binding spell working, but then you took off with her!"

"Took off?" Badgrave echoed, confused.

"With Amstrass!" Undergate cried. "That night at La Daria Rouge! I was going to bind her and question her—*properly*. He gave me a binding spell, and after I had done with her I was to bring her to him! If I *had* I would have only had to serve him for a hundred years, but you ran off with her so now I'm stuck here *forever!*"

Badgrave was speechless. Though she was horrified to discover how devious his intentions had been, she found she had no anger for him: only pity.

He had not been sheltered. No house or home and no one to guide him through the strange, mysterious world he had suddenly become a part of. He had been stranded on the edge of Dream, where all the greatest wonders of the universe were only whispers in the shadows, and promises of things he could never have.

"I am sorry," she said, and meant it. "She told me her secrets, but they are not mine to tell you. I have others, though." And she gathered up her own secrets: her journey through the Teeth of Dream; dancing with Grimbald at the Garden at the Top of the World; the dragon in the moon. She put them all together in her hands and offered them to him.

Undergate's eyes went wide with fear and amazement. Perhaps he saw the secrets. Perhaps he saw Badgrave for what she was. But before he could reach out and take her secrets his body jerked and went rigid. Then, as though he were a puppet on a string, he lunged forward and impaled her with his sword.

Badgrave nearly toppled over backwards from sheer surprise. The sword had lodged under her breastbone, and she couldn't pull herself off it. Undergate's face had gone blank again, and he took her by the arm unfeelingly and marched her across the room.

Badgrave was horrified. Her limbs had begun to go numb, and it was as though a black cloth had been drawn over her mind. She saw nothing beyond the cold, stone flags and the dusty, stone stairs. There was nothing in the air but staleness and mildew, and she could no longer feel the comforting presence of her familiars in the back of her head. The sword was hard and cold inside her, and it hurt like a toothache. She wanted to pull it out, but her arms wouldn't move.

Something like this had happened to Madgrin, she realized.

The idea should have frightened her, but fear was too exciting an emotion for her numb body to maintain. So she walked, stumbling now as they reached the stairs, in a state of muted horror.

Undergate led her up to a low wooden door and pushed her through it, whence she tripped into a foul-smelling room filled with books and broken chairs and some ragged tables. The air was thick with the smell of dead animal from a disemboweled carcass strung across the wall, and on the nearest table was an array of unpleasant objects ranging from dead insects to a jar full of eyeballs. Next to the jar was a shallow dish, and in the dish were two eyes that were particularly black and glittering. Badgrave knew those eyes—had seen them twinkling at her in fondness and amusement countless times—and the sight of them sitting on a table so filled her with despair that she nearly collapsed. But Undergate still held the sword, and she was forced to stand. She was so distracted that she hardly noticed the magician until he straightened up from behind the table.

He was a small, brown, ordinary man. He wore a ridiculous white wig, but aside from that there was nothing remarkable about him at all. He was soft and round all over, inoffensive in a casual brown suit, with a round, pinkish face and light, inquisitive eyes. He had a lock of Madgrin's hair wound around his right hand.

Badgrave wanted to scream. She wanted to kick and bite and tear him into as many pieces as he had torn Madgrin. Or more. She wanted to shred him and feed him to Keelback. But the sword in her chest kept her firmly anchored in the filthy workroom, and she couldn't even turn herself into a shadow or a thought to escape.

CHAPTER 21: *Badgrave*

"Oh, what a splendid specimen," the magician was saying, rubbing his hands together eagerly. "A young one too, very rare. I shall have to keep you intact, my dear, to show at the next Conclave. Why I don't believe anyone has ever captured one so young—not even Forgin and Fiddle!" He squealed with delight and danced around the table. He seemed not to notice Undergate at all, who stood mute and blank, holding the sword in Badgrave's chest, and if he saw the look of pure hatred she was sending his way he took no notice.

For Badgrave found she hated this man very much. The fact that such a small, ordinary, and self-centered person had captured, bound, and apparently dismembered Madgrin—*her* Madgrin—made her skin boil with rage.

But as long as the sword was in her chest she could do nothing. That was how he worked. That was how he caught Madgrin. And if he had caught Madgrin, what could *she* do?

If only she had not lost Felpz and Amstrass. If only she could reach her familiars. But all she could do was stand transfixed as the wizard came around the table holding a sharp steel knife.

"I shall have to take the heart out," he was muttering, as if to himself. "Otherwise it might get away. Move," he said to Undergate, cold and unfeeling.

Undergate stepped aside, still keeping a hand on the sword.

Badgrave clenched her teeth. She gathered up all the strength she had ever possessed. She reached deep inside herself to a place that had been untouched by the sword and found the strength that had clawed her out from under a mountain of rubble and plaster and rock, the strength that had dragged Keelback's egg out of the depths of the lake. The strength that, so long ago, had fought the vampires in the school at Munsmire—and with it she choked out:

"*Amstrass!*"

In her lamphra voice it was quiet, yet reverberated throughout the room so that the wizard paused to stare at her.

Then Amstrass arrived.

She came in a rush of cold wind and jagged leaves, smashing a hole in the wall and riding through it on her blood-red stag. She saw Badgrave, saw Undergate, and recognition flashed across her face. The magician had dropped the knife and was muttering spells, but she took no notice. She reached around with one arm, which cracked loudly as it elongated, and gripping the silver ball of the sword where the Arrow was carved, she pulled.

"*There is a magic in being human that they don't have,*" she had said.

The sword slid out easily, like a greased pin, and with a wave of relief all of Badgrave's feelings came rushing back. Amstrass threw Undergate to the floor, where he stared, bewildered and terrified, as Amstrass towered above him, his sword in her hand. Before Badgrave could say or do a thing Amstrass swung the blade, and with an almighty crack she lopped off his head.

The magician was screaming a spell, and Badgrave felt herself being forced away. It was old magic that he knew well, and it tossed her about like a leaf caught in a river. So she called up Urgolant. She called Keelback and Intok. She called the Purple Magician.

"*Felpass!*"

Again the room was filled with wind; it whipped across the shelves, scattering papers and overturning chairs and tables, swirling around the magician and threatening to lift him off the ground.

Then it was gone, and in its place was the overwhelming presence of Felpass's magic. It fizzed in the air and made Badgrave's hair go on end.

For one moment the room was still. Like the dead calm before a thunderstorm. Or the eye of a hurricane.

The two magicians regarded one another, each recognizing in the other a worthy opponent. Then they clashed.

It was as though a star had burst within the room. Badgrave was thrown backwards and she felt herself crash clean through the wall behind her. She had the presence of mind to go insubstantial before she hit something more solid, and then her mind went blank as the tearing light coursed through her.

Dust motes drifted through the air before her. They glowed in the pale light of the early morning, and the smoke billowed lazily around them. The place was quiet and cool, and from the many holes blasted in the building's side there came wafts of fresh country air to relieve the stinking, stuffy room.

Badgrave came back to herself standing in the same entrance hall where she had been stabbed by Undergate. Urgolant, Keelback and Intok clustered around her, but Felpass and Amstrass were nowhere to be found.

Finding herself whole and uninjured she trotted up the stairs and stepped through the gaping hole in the wall that Amstrass had made with her entrance and into the magician's workroom.

It was a disaster of dust and fallen plaster; books, jars, boxes and bottles were strewn about the floor, most of them broken. The chairs and tables had been smashed to kindling, and the bookcases overturned. Felpass stood near the center of the mess, wiping his hands on a dirty silk kerchief. Next to him on the cracked and blackened floor was all that remained of the magician: a dirty boot and shreds of the white wig, now much torn and frazzled.

"He brought it on himself." Felpass sighed regretfully when he saw Badgrave. "This can happen when wizards meddle in magic too strong for them to handle."

With a rustling and a heaving Amstrass pushed a bookcase off of herself and stood up. He hair looked like a bird had tried to make a nest out of it, but aside from that she appeared unharmed. She kicked at a nearby box filled with dried lizard corpses and began to rummage through it.

Badgrave surveyed the scene with growing despair. The wizard had been defeated, but there was no sign of Madgrin's eyes (the table they had been on was now a jumble of splintered wood) nor the lock of his hair the magician had been holding. Amstrass stood up from her rummaging and said, "I think finding your old maker might be a little harder than we thought," and she held up what she had found: an elegant, long-fingered, white hand.

Badgrave stared at it. She wanted to weep.

CHAPTER 21: *Badgrave*

"Better start searching for his heart, then," said Felpass matter-of-factly. "The magician will have kept that intact, but hidden. I'm working on dismantling his warding spells, but they are proving rather complicated."

Torn between hope and despair Badgrave began to poke around in corners of the ruined room. She found several boxes of dead animals, a few more swords with arrows on them (which she had Intok crush), a lumpy pile of ashes and dirt which was all that was left of Undergate, but no heart. She felt weak and tired and useless, and was about to go sit in the middle of the room and have a good cry when she felt something tug at her own heart.

It was the cold, aching feeling she knew so well, only this time it seemed to be tugging her in a definite direction.

Down, it tugged.

Badgrave turned and hurried out of the room and down the stairs. The tugging was stronger here, and she followed it across the room and out the front door. The first rays of morning light were streaking across the sky, and the air was thick with the scent of rosemary and wet grass.

Beside the front door stood a barrel half-filled with black water. From within its depths Badgrave thought she saw something twinkle and glitter. Plunging her hands into the cold water she groped around until she felt something soft and knobbly the size of a tea kettle. Clutching it firmly she raised it out of the water and held it up before her.

It appeared to be a shapeless blob of dark blue glup, with skin like a toad and small warts all over. It had four very short, weak legs, which flapped uselessly below it, and towards the front it had a small red mouth. It had no eyes, but still seemed to stare at her apologetically.

"Oh don't be sorry," Badgrave said, feeling the tears welling up in her eyes despite herself. "I was so worried about you, I *had* to come."

The little glob that was Madgrin's heart opened its mouth and sighed. It reached one of its tiny legs forward and wrapped a small webbed hand over one of Badgrave's fingers. She gathered it up in her arms and hugged it to her chest, ignoring the sloppy wet spot it made.

Felpass and Amstrass came out of the building then, blinking in the morning light.

"Oh good, you found him," Amstrass said, eyeing the blob. "Who knew he was such an ugly little bugger on the inside."

"You should take him to Grimbald," Felpass advised. "The sun will do him no good in that state, and she is the only one who can restore him."

"I will," said Badgrave, turning to face them. "And *thank* you, both of you, very much."

"I was pleased to help," Felpass said, bowing low. "If you wish to repay me, you need only keep in contact."

Badgrave nodded. "I will do my very best," she said.

"When he gets himself reconstructed," Amstrass said, "tell him I took his left hand. Tell him I'm *not* sorry, and to stop being so nice."

Madgrin's heart squirmed out of her arms a bit and opened its wide red mouth in Amstrass's direction. It laughed.

"I think he can hear you fine right now," Badgrave said.

Amstrass snorted and stalked off down the path between the rosemary bushes. The farther she went the fainter she became, until by the time she reached the lane at the far end she was only a reddish smudge in the air, and then she was gone.

"Well, that's trouble for me to worry about later," Felpass said, once Amstrass had vanished. He turned to go back inside. "Good day to you, mistress."

"You are staying?" Badgrave asked.

Felpass nodded. "Our late friend, the magician, has left behind an improbable tangle of magical experiments; if left unattended I shudder to think the mischief they might cause. I will probably be days at sorting them out. Oh," he added: "If Madgrin still has that old druid hanging about his house, tell him what I am doing. He was always pestering me to be more tidy with my own magic."

Badgrave promised she would, and Felpass went away inside the building. After he had gone she stood where she was, gathering together her magic, which had gotten rather frayed, and Urgolant, Keelback and Intok, who had wandered off poking around at the interesting magical experiments. Then she stepped carefully out of the world and into Dream, walking along the stars until she came to the moon, who was waiting for her expectantly.

The moon was not the only one who was waiting: Grimbald was standing at the top of the stairs, her arms folded and one foot tapping, the picture of strained patience.

"Well?" she asked.

For answer Badgrave held up Madgrin's heart, which squirmed a little in her hands as if embarrassed. Grimbald reached up and took him, shaking her head.

"You always were far too nice," she told him sternly.

Madgrin's heart sighed, apparently tired of hearing this.

"Far too nice," Grimbald repeated. "Sometimes I think I named you too well."

She gave Madgrin's heart a good shake and dropped it at her feet. As his heart fell it became enveloped in twisting black smoke which shot up into a pillar, bulging in its center as though there were an animal inside trying to get out. In quick succession the smoke took on the shape of a dragon, then a giant bird, then a strange snake, and finally it condensed into a sort of catlike person who crouched at Grimbald's feet, until it shuddered, and the human-shaped Madgrin stood up, pushing the hair out of his eyes and smiling at them both.

For a long while no one spoke. Madgrin looked at Badgrave piercingly with his bright black eyes, obviously taking in her new appearance, while Badgrave stared right back. He looked as he always had before, save that perhaps his eyes were a little brighter now, or that his left hand was maybe a little smaller than his right. It didn't matter. He was Madgrin, safe and whole once again; she ran to him and he opened his arms and embraced her.

Grimbald cleared her throat, loudly.

"My, my," Madgrin said, smoothing her hair down. "You have grown some very fine wings. I'm afraid I cannot call you *La Flein* any more."

Beside them, Grimbald coughed again.

"I don't mind," Badgrave said. "It is strange enough to call *you* Madgrin now."

CHAPTER 21: *Badgrave*

He laughed, a deep, reverberating laugh that rumbled in her ears. "Come now, what is your name?"

"Can't you tell?"

"Of course. I would only like to hear you say it."

She smiled. "I'm Badgrave."

"Badgrave," he said. "A good name. Yes, what is it, my queen?" This last was directed at Grimbald, who was now in the throes of an outrageous coughing fit and going dark blue in the face. At Madgrin's words she recovered instantly and pointed at Badgrave.

"I *still* owe her a boon," she said. "So hurry up and make a wish before I decide to bestow on you a thousand gold cranes or some other such nonsense."

Reluctantly the two released each other, and Badgrave fidgeted with the sleeve of her robe. She glanced uncertainly at Madgrin, who only smiled and shrugged. Then she turned back to Grimbald.

"Before, you mentioned I could wish something for someone else," she said.

Grimbald raised an eyebrow, extending the dark shadow above her eye halfway up her forehead. "Maybe," she said. "It depends on what you're wishing for."

Badgrave glanced back at Madgrin, who cocked his head, curious.

"I have a question," she said to him.

"Ask it," he said.

"What happened just then, with the magician summoning you and then binding you and then taking you to pieces, has that happened before?"

Madgrin sighed, and he nodded.

"Does it happen often?"

"Thankfully, no."

"But it could happen again?"

"Yes." He wasn't smiling any more, in fact he was looking very, very sad.

"Why?" Badgrave asked.

"Why?" he echoed.

"Why do they get to *do* that to you? The magician.... He was so small, so ordinary—he shouldn't have been able to... to take you apart..." she trailed off.

Madgrin, deeply unhappy, looked helplessly at Grimbald.

"It's part of his reparation, innit? As an exile," she said bluntly. "All the exiled lamphra are of the summonable caste, along with third-order demons and some of those religious nutjobs. Didn't he explain to you about that?" She jabbed her head in Madgrin's direction. "I thought he loved telling that sob story."

Madgrin shot Grimbald a long-suffering look. He was still looking very sad. It was such a familiar expression that Badgrave realized he must have been feeling terrible about this for quite a long time. She made up her mind.

"That makes it easy then," she said. "I wish that Madgrin and his House and all his staff be returned from exile."

Madgrin stared at her, shocked, and Grimbald gave her a penetrating look. "Really? Is that *really* what you're wishing for? You were born in exile, remember? You might want to wish the same for yourself."

LUCENA IN THE HOUSE OF MADGRIN

Badgrave laughed. "But I don't need to, do I?" she said. "Born *in* exile isn't the same as *being* exiled. There's nothing binding me to either world, or to anyone—except maybe you."

She knew this even though no one had told her. After a hundred and fifty years bound to Madgrin, she knew what freedom felt like. And from the way Grimbald was looking at her, she knew the queen knew it too.

She thought of Madgrin and the way he had talked about Dream and the terrible longing sadness that had come over him. She thought of him looking up at the wall of his inner garden, and Harga saying, "It smells of home." And she thought of Madgrin reduced to a leathery blob in her hands.

She smiled and repeated her wish.

Grimbald shrugged. "So be it then," she said.

Nothing happened except that suddenly every single member of the House of Madgrin was there with them, and Badgrave found herself in the center of a massive group hug comprised of Beruse, Harga, Willic and Gydda, and all the rest.

"Oh you, you *did* it!" Beruse exclaimed, picking her up bodily and swinging her around.

When she was set down, Badgrave discovered that a celebration had broken out around them. Willic was jumping about and throwing handfuls of glittering confetti into the air. Above them Halfain and Rusion swooped and cooed and cried for joy, swirling the confetti into a small storm. Grimmach and Cobbin were dancing with each other, and even Rhyse and Soloma had cast off their usual sour attitudes to go hang lovingly off the ends of Madgrin's robe. Madgrin himself was staring at her with a stunned, blank expression, as though he could not believe what had just happened.

Grimbald laughed, but the smile was quickly wiped from her face as she was buried under a pile of jubilant habitants. Badgrave saw her out of the corner of her eye desperately trying to free herself from Willic, who was wound lovingly around her neck and purring. But most of Badgrave's attention was focused in front of her, where Madgrin had come forward and taken her hands.

"You really meant that," he said.

"Yes, obviously!" she replied, beaming at him.

Slowly the stunned blankness faded, and a little of his old glint came back. He smiled down at her. But it was still a sad smile, and Badgrave realized they both knew she would not be coming back to his House.

Lamphra, though they surrounded themselves with friends and familiars, did not live with other lamphra. The House of Madgrin was no longer her home, just as she was no longer Lucena.

"You are welcome to stay a little longer. With us, I mean. In Dream," he said anyway. And meant it.

"I will visit, of course," she said. "But I'm not done with the waking world. I like humans, you see, and I understand why you were exiled. To fix the balance, and all that. So I'm going to take over from you. Unofficially, of course."

Madgrin nodded. They embraced deeply and when they parted at last the festivities had more or less calmed down, with the habitants in a disorderly row behind Madgrin.

CHAPTER 21: *Badgrave*

"You will come for visits," he agreed. "Frequently." It was not a question.

"As often as I can," she replied, grinning.

Behind them and a little below someone cleared their throat, and the crowd turned to find a tattered figure with thick glasses had just clambered up onto the stone platform that was the peak of the stairway to the moon. As he approached, Badgrave recognized him as Orrus, albeit a disheveled and tired Orrus.

He came up, bowing low to Grimbald, before presenting himself to Madgrin.

"Forgive my absence," he said. "But I have just finished overseeing the relocation of the House of Madgrin, and now everything is in readiness for your return, which"—he peered over the rim of his glasses at them—"I hope will be soon. Kerebryt and Frayne are eagerly awaiting you."

As one, the whole crowd surged eagerly towards him, and together they began the long trek down the stair. Badgrave was embraced in quick succession by Willic and Beruse and Gydda and Cobbin, and Harga shook her hand.

Madgrin lingered. He seemed to have grown a little, for he had to stoop almost double to kiss Badgrave's forehead, and when he stood up she saw that the darkness in his eyes had increased, but for that the sparkle in them shone all the brighter.

"Speak with me whenever you wish," he said in his quiet lamphra voice. The voice of dreams.

I will hear you.

Then in a sweep of midnight robes he was gone, walking briskly after his retinue. For a moment he was outlined before the first step, a tall dark figure agains the luminous, glowing world, and then he passed over the edge and vanished from her sight.

"Well," said Grimbald, brushing herself off. "What are you going to do now?"

Badgrave didn't answer. She went over to where Intok was waiting and clambered onto her back. Settling herself between the shadowy wings she looked down at Grimbald and smiled. Behind her, in the special sideways space they always occupied, were Keelback and Urgolant, eagerly anticipating their next adventure. There were worlds out there she had only glimpsed, and more beyond she had not yet imagined, and they were all at her fingertips: no longer a tantalizing dream, but an imminently achievable reality. The lands beyond the cliff of knowledge were laid clear before her, and she was flying.

"I think," Badgrave said, "we shall go *exploring*."

Grimbald chuckled. She took out her fiddle and began to play, a deep, sweeping tune that boiled in the air around them. Intok lunged forward, and carried on the waves of music, they galloped off into the starry sky.

But most of Badgrave's attention was focused in front of her, where Madgrin had come forward and taken her hands.

Afterword.

There is the end of this story—the story of Lucena—but it is also where the myths of Badgrave begin. You may have heard some of these already: how she was eaten by a dragon to find a little girl's lost ring; how she talked the sun into hiding for an entire week; how she built a castle out of spring leaves; how she made all the statues in the world get up and turn around. These have been told, in one form or another, over the course of the centuries, and Orrus has all the copies filed away in my library. Badgrave, for all she loves hearing stories, has been singularly uninterested in her own, until recently when she came to visit, and Willic talked her into helping them expand the library. Then she discovered how wildly inaccurate the myths surrounding her had become, and when she acquired a librarian of her own, who has a natural inclination for telling stories, they determined to write hers before anyone else could get it wrong. Together they have spent the last year split between the Libraries of Badgrave and Madgrin, or—when they drove Orrus to distraction pestering him with questions about events that happened several hundred years ago—in my own study. Soloma has not been happy about this, though all the habitants are excited to be in a story.

Last night Badgrave came in to tell me that they had finished, and asked if I would put in a note at the end of it, which is what I am doing now. To be honest I am amazed at how accurate it is, though I understand she asked everyone for their own versions during the writing of it.

Except me. My side of this story has not been told, nor will it ever be told. It is my secret, and as I am the Master of Mysteries, I have every intention of keeping it. So I release you, reader, from this little dream. I hope you have enjoyed your visit, and remember that though the waking world can seem like a desolate, depressing place, filled with unkept promises and false hopes, we will always be here, waiting.

> Beyond the stony wall
> on the other side of the shadows.

—*Madgrin*

Grimbald chuckled. She took out her fiddle and began to play, a deep, sweeping tune that boiled in the air around them.

Intok lunged forward, and carried on the waves of music, they galloped off into the starry sky.

About the Author

Goldeen Ogawa is a self-taught author, illustrator, painter and cartoonist. She works primarily in fantasy and science fiction, watercolor and colored pencils, subverted tropes and underrepresented narrative voices. She began writing stories before she learned to read, which she didn't do until she was eleven. She has been drawing pictures all her life. She is left handed, and has never gone to school.

Born and raised in California, she currently lives in Bend, Oregon. Her official website is **goldeenogawa.com**.

Text and Design

The body of this book was typeset using LaTeX in Geller Text Light with titles in Neato Serif Rough.

Cover art, interior illustrations and book design by the author.

Made in the USA
Columbia, SC
13 March 2023